Bullets and Sunshine

The Striker's Series, Book One

By Cory Gaffner

Editing Team: Brittany Gaffner, Cory Gaffner, Joshua Holes, Jerome Koger

Alpha Readers: Brittany Gaffner, Collin Haworth

I0598251

Other Books By Cory Gaffner

Oliver's Universe

Oliver's Wishes
Oliver's Wishes Book 2 (Writing now!)

Striker's Universe

Bullets and Sunshine
I'll Be Back: Griffin's Tale
(Will write book three when B&S has 50 positive reviews.)

Arbiter's Universe

Killdozer
KillCycle (forthcoming)

Short Stories

Matchstick Mechanical (forthcoming)

Chapter 1

I chugged half of the coffee out of my thermos, even though it was way too hot. I needed the caffeine. Time for another day of work. I was way too tired from playing video games with some friends until one in the morning, which was my normal routine. I always tell myself I should stop and go to bed earlier, but video games are one of the best parts of my now boring life. I am a normal dude, a working class Joe. Well, with the exception of my extreme love of firearms and violence of course, but my coworkers didn't know about that. It's best to keep that kind of thing to yourself or you risk scaring the sheeple. I didn't know it yet but this day was going to be very different. My name is Bearengar Christensen. I know, I know, my name sounds ridiculous. My mom and dad both have Scandinavian heritage and mom's parents are first generation Scandinavian immigrants, so they pushed her to go with something more traditional for their first grandchild's name. My dad was only too happy to oblige because he knew it meant I would get stuck with the nickname Bear for life, and what father doesn't want to refer to their son as Bear. My parents are shitheads, but I like my name. It's the one good thing they gave to me.

I walked into the office of the pest control company I work at and was greeted by the homely secretary who liked cats just a little bit too much. It was too early for small talk, but that didn't seem to matter to her, especially small talk about cats. I stayed cordial, but I am a dog guy at heart. Once I was able to sneak away from Catwoman I headed into the back where the pest control men get their routes for the day. I grabbed my route paperwork and headed out to my company issued truck. Pest control is boring and gross in Arizona with 100+ degree temperatures and working with noxious chemicals all day. Long story short, it sucks.

✱✱✱

I was almost done with my day and was down to the last house on my route. Sometimes the paperwork for the routes they give me has special directions near the bottom in a special box. Some people want a certain out of the way spot checked in their yard, or they want blue dye in the chemical spray so they can see we were there and actually did something. Either way, the box is either empty or it's not, so it is very obvious if there are special directions. There were special directions for this house. It said that the owners were out of town for an extended amount of time and that their front door key was under a blue pot that held a leafy plant on the side of the house. I was to let myself in, spray around for bugs, bring in any mail or flyers from outside the house, lock the house up, and put the key back before I left.

When I walked inside I swear I had heard something...weird. It sounded like some kind of mix of a growl and a scuffle, maybe an animal had gotten inside? There were no lights on and I had just come in from a scorching Arizona day, so my eyes hadn't adjusted to the low light quite yet, but I could swear I saw someone run right by me, just ahead of the light of the door as I had opened it into the dark house.

The person looked like they had run from the living room into the back of the house.

I called out, "Hello! Hi, I'm from the pest control company. I am just here to spray for bugs!"

No one replied, though. I waited patiently for a response or a sound... any indication really, because in Arizona we had a little thing called The Castle Doctrine. Basically if a stranger enters your house without your permission, you can legally shoot them in the face, and I really like not having a shot face.

I waited for a minute just standing in the threshold of the doorway with the cool air from the house blowing over me and escaping out into the desert. If I didn't finish this soon, my boss was going to call me and start bitching, but I wasn't too keen on taking the ole lead injection either and something about this house just felt wrong. At the same time, if there was a squatter in this house I really did have to scare him or her out, and/or at a minimum alert the authorities. My boss was old school though. He might just tell me to quit being a little bitch and check the house out. Either way, I had to finish this job and get home before 5pm traffic or I would be stewing in my car like a piece of meat in a crock pot. I wanted to get home and relax. I was tired, sweaty, and hot, which basically made the decision for me that I was just going to have to check the house out myself. I walked a few steps further inside and listened for anything but the house was silent.

I called out one more time just in case "I'm coming in! I'm from the pest control company, HELLO!" still no response.

One final idea popped in my head and I shouted, "If you are a squatter, why don't you run out now and I won't have to call the cops!"

Still no response and no noise. I must have imagined whatever I saw. Maybe I was dehydrated or something. Or maybe I had a sunspot in my eye. My brain came up with a few more excuses, but surely I would have heard someone by now.

Just in case...and I was really hoping the customer didn't have cameras in their house at this point, watching me make a fool of myself. I decided to check out the back bedroom where I thought I had seen the person head toward. I walked down the hall and tried to look into the room that I suspected a runner might naturally gravitate towards. The dark room had heavy curtains drawn and I could just see the tiniest sliver of light coming out below them. I flipped the light switch...nothing. The light was out in the room. I walked a little further into the dark room, pulled out my phone and switched on the flashlight feature casting a little circle of light ahead of me and a ghostly dim glow to the rest of the room. I started scanning the room, and in the corner about 10 feet away from me on the side of a queen-size bed was what looked like an 18 year old girl in dirty clothes with a weird shine to her eyes. It almost reminded me of a wildlife picture of a coyote at night, when their eyes seem to almost glow. When my overworked brain, tired from a long day of dragging pesticide hoses, digging trenches, and sweating my ass off finally realized what the hell I was actually looking at I about jumped out of my shoes. I finally got my shit together, in what seemed like an eternity to me but was probably only a few seconds and I said: "Ma'am, do you need some help?"

She just smiled and said, "Nope, you are exactly what I need..." and then I shit you not, she jumped the 10 feet separating us, straight at me.

It was a surreal moment in my life and while I watched her sail across the room towards me, for whatever reason my brain thought this woman, who was obviously on steroids might be trying to rape me. Hell I was a handsome enough dude to get raped, wasn't I? Then she hit me like a bag of rebar, knees first right in the chest. She was dense as hell and sent my ass to the floor with her knees landing partially on my stomach and chest and knocking some of the air out of me. The pain hit me a second later spiraling outwards from the two impact points of her knees. Luckily the floor was carpeted so my back and head didn't take that much of a beating. After I got over the shock of the moment, I reached up and tried to push her off of me. She didn't budge. I tried one more time with a big shove, but she was ready this time and had leaned into it or something. If the last push did next to nothing this time, it was like I was pushing on a stone wall. She must have tightened her abs and core up. She tilted her head sideways and just smiled at me, like she was enjoying my frustration. Then she slapped me harder then I have ever been slapped in my life. My head rocked sideways and the noise reverberated in the room. No one hits me and gets away with it. "It's on now, bitch!" I shouted.

I'm not the biggest guy in the world but I'm bigger than average. I'm 6' 2" and about 265 pounds when I am in decent shape. I have a small beer belly forming as I get closer to 28 but who doesn't? I have sandy, mostly blonde hair with some dirty blonde mixed in. I would say I have a decently handsome face but my teeth are a little crooked in places. My asshole parents never got me braces as a kid, or anything else for that matter. I had just gotten out of the Army Reserves 5 years prior and I still worked out one or two times a week so I was in pretty good shape. I wasn't really what you would describe as muscular though, no matter how hard I worked out, my muscles didn't really seem to get bigger. They just stayed normal sized and barely defined even when I got stronger. Most people are surprised when they find out how heavy I am.

So let me tell you, I was surprised when I straight punched this lady in the nose as hard as I could and all she did was look at me and say "Ow."

Things weren't adding up or going my way, so I punched her again. She smiled as before. It was a strange smile though, like she was trying to figure out what to do with her face. My brain tried to rationalize what was happening and I figured maybe it was a bad angle or because she was on my chest, I just didn't have the leverage to really lay a clean hit on her; or maybe she was on PCP. Either way, I had to get this lady off of me before she gave me AIDS or something; or tried to grab Bear JR (yes, that is what I call him... it has a name). I think she must have read my body language or saw the intent in my eyes, maybe she just didn't want to get punched anymore. She reached down and pinned my biceps to the carpet faster than I thought possible.

I'm no slouch when it comes to ground and pound. I took a few months of MMA and Jiu Jitsu when I was younger with a bunch of guys from my Army Reserve unit and every soldier gets taught a few levels of Army Combatives, which is the Army's fancy term for the Jiu Jitsu moves they stole and rebranded. My point being, I had run this scenario a few hundred times with guys who were two or three times her weight and I had been able to get out of it. So when I started bucking and shrimping (yes that is what it's called, look it up you uneducated hillbilly fuck) and I didn't really move, I started getting really worried. She smirked at me and seemed to like that I had realized she had total control of this situation.

"Lady, I don't know what mixture of steroids and bath salts you are on but you have about two seconds to get off of me or you are going to have a very bad day." I said.

She lifted one hand off of me for a second and walloped me in the face hard, really hard, and I had been hit by amateur UFC fighters when I was training MMA so I knew what hard felt like.

My fight or flight instinct took over. She was still pinning both my biceps to the ground but I had use of my elbows on down. My company would have fired me if they knew this but I always carried a gun, ALWAYS. I had been in a few hairy situations growing up and seen too many dark parts of the world as a kid in a bad neighborhood and in the military to not be prepared. I had a small Ruger LCP in my front right hand pocket. I reached in, grabbed it and then pushed it into the outside of her thigh and fired twice. She screamed and grabbed the wound on her leg. As soon as she freed my arms I aimed center mass just like I had trained for thousands of times and pulled the trigger. Blood spattered my face. I stiff armed her wounded chest, and she rolled off of me.

I jumped up and trained my gun on her again. The little magazine in my gun only held seven rounds plus one in the chamber for a total of eight, so I had better make these count. I always stacked the first round as a hollow point and the rest as FMJ's (full metal jacket) because I wanted to be able to shoot through drywall if I had to, which hollow points can't really do since they split once they hit something. Her leg was fucked from the hollow point I had in the chamber and her chest looked pretty bad as well, but it wasn't bleeding much, just a small trickle. At the same time, it was hard to really tell since her clothes were still so dirty and the room was dark with the only light coming from my cell phone which had fallen on the floor, luckily aimed upwards so I still had the light from it to see by.

She slowly stood up and said, "I'm done playing with my food."

Almost quicker then I could see, she coiled herself flat to the floor and then pounced straight up at me like a frog using her hands to gain more momentum. I fired a round as she flew at me, she extended her arms out and transferred all of her momentum onto me. I was standing with my back to the door frame and I flew out into the tile hallway right through it. I landed butt first and slid a bit, both of my hands clenched onto the tiny pistol trying not to lose it. This bitch was invincible! She had landed on her hands and feet positioned like a frog again and gave me that stupid little smirk with her head tilted sideways as before. I had to take the initiative here before she rushed me again so I raised my tiny pocket pistol, centered it on her chest and fired.

As I was centering my pistol she had begun running at me. My shot hit her a second before she got to me, her eyes went wide and I could tell she was in a lot of pain. Her brain finished what it was doing before she got shot which was throwing a punch at the wrist of the hand I was holding the pistol in. All of my pain nerves in that hand fired and I involuntarily dropped my gun. I had been shot at before while I was doing convoy security in the military so I was used to keeping my cool in tense situations and I was fucking pissed! Without really thinking about it I sent a flying uppercut at her with my off hand that wasn't in pain, It landed hard! Her teeth snapped together so loud it sounded like my little gun had fired again, I think I even saw her toes lift off the floor. As she came back down I unleashed a savage headbutt but she was shorter than me or I must have done it wrong because it hurt like hell. As she was dazed from my gunshot plus beating combo, I sent a side kick at her thigh right where I had shot her twice, and she fell to the floor when it connected.

Once she was down, I threw another kick at her stomach, but she grabbed my foot and pulled hard and then threw my leg straight up. This crazy fuck must be on some amazing pharmaceuticals because I went flying and landed hard on my back. Unfortunately, the hallway was tiled and my head hit the ground...that hurt. I looked over at her without getting up. She wasn't looking good, but I wasn't feeling good either. I was dazed, I didn't know where my gun was and the crazy steroid-monkey started getting back up. Without getting up myself, I spun my body towards her and once more sent a kick her direction. She had both of her hands on the ground attempting to do a push up to get off the ground so she couldn't catch it this time and it hit her in the face. To my surprise, she still did not pass out or go down but I could tell it had hurt her badly.

I jumped up fast and started backing up, my body still in the fight or flight mode could tell that fight wasn't exactly working. I looked around for my gun but it was behind her current position. I started backing up, not paying attention to where in the house I was headed while walking backward. I was too busy watching her slowly rise to her feet with murder in her eyes. She started walking towards me slowly but with purpose. I kept backing up until I was finally in the kitchen of my customers home, then my back hit the kitchen island. I slowly started circling around it, leaving her on the other side. I began frantically looking for a weapon while I had her on the other side of my impromptu barricade, my eyes landed on a knife block. I grabbed the first knife I found and chucked it at her. It was weighted all wrong and it hit her handle first in the shoulder, she was not amused. She started slowly coming around the kitchen island enjoying my panic. Then she gave me that stupid smirk and head tilt thing again. It finally hit me that it reminded me of a wolf looking at a lamb before a slaughter, shit...

Something snapped in me, I'm not a victim, I'm a goddamn human chainsaw and I have the awards from the DOD to prove it! Who the hell did this lady think she was? I grabbed two of the largest knives and ran at her. She was going to pay. I lunged with both at once, she caught one of my wrists but the second knife sank into her right shoulder, deep. She squeezed my left wrist fucking hard and whatever drugs she was on won out over my brute adrenaline-filled strength. I dropped the knife from my left hand, right into my now open right hand. BOOM, I shoved it into her stomach.

"You didn't see that coming, did you crackhead?" I yelled in triumph.

At this point, she had a knife in her right shoulder, a knife in her stomach, two gunshots in her chest (I must have missed once?) and two gunshots in her right leg, one of which was from a hollow point. She had to have been ready to go down soon, right? She wasn't. She threw a hook which I was barely able to dodge, but what I didn't see was her knee coming up to meet my ball sack....OW. Pain flew up into my stomach and I'm pretty sure my penis inverted Looney Toons style but I'm not a penis doctor, and I didn't exactly have time to check so I don't really know. Either way, I could barely breathe and I was seeing red! My balls didn't want any more punishment. I threw a couple quick jabs at her face, the first of which she dodged but the second one hit. I backed up just enough to throw a straight kick at her stomach which hit the knife handle and pushed it further into her body and out of her back a smidge. It was time to run while she was fucked up. I turned around and started to sprint but I felt her land on my back and start to hook her arm around my throat. If she started to choke me and I went out this bitch was going to kill me. I did the first thing I could think of which was to spin around and let physics do its job. I fell backward

15

with her on my back and my full 270 some odd pound frame landed on her and crushed her beneath me. Her elbow loosened around my neck so I rolled over and grabbed her head and started bouncing it off the ground.

Chapter 2

I was in a haze of anger, adrenaline, pain, and fear. I have no idea how many times I had bounced her head off the ground but it was a lot. When I was finally able to calm down and take my hands off of her battered skull and notice the spreading pool of blood beneath her head, I jumped off of her and just stood there.

I don't know why, I must have been In shock, but the first thing I did was say "Well that isn't going to buff out," to the empty house.

My mind started reeling and I started heading towards the back bedroom to get my phone so I could call the police. Halfway there I looked down at the tile and the bloody boot prints I was leaving.

That sparked the thought in my head of "I am a murderer and I am going to jail."

I'm not sure why I thought that, it was so clearly a case of self defense. I had been taking criminal justice classes at the local community college off and on since I had gotten out of the Army. In that time I had learned of more than one case where innocent people had gone to prison over self defense situations. Also, as a gun owner, I've read many books, blogs, and articles about what to do after you shoot someone in self defense, the do's and don'ts, and the many things that could happen to you.

The story of Harold Fish came to mind. A true story of self defense that happened in my state in a city to the north called Prescott. A college professor in his 40's with no criminal record was hiking some of the back wood trails near his family home. He had recently bought a gun due to increased bear activity in the area and had been carrying it with him on his walks. On one of his long nature hikes, he came across a vagrant in a van with two Rottweilers. The vagrant had stolen the dogs from a shelter earlier that week under the guise of being a volunteer dog walker. He was out of his mind and had a long history of mental illness. He sicked the dogs on Harold Fish and Harold shot the ground near the dogs to scare them away. When the vagrant saw what Harold had done he rushed Harold and tried to attack him but Harold shot him once in the chest after repeated warnings and the vagrant went down. Harold stayed and rendered first aid to the man until the police arrived. He answered all of the police officer's questions and was honestly upset that he had to hurt someone. A few months later a prosecutor picked up his case and took him to trial. The prosecutor stacked his jury with anti-gun leftists and somehow was able to suppress the evidence that the vagrant had a long history of mental illness and violence in his past. The jury elected to send Harold Fish to prison. If a simple, nice, quiet, aging college professor could go to prison for defending himself then I definitely could!

Paranoia struck me like lightning. I ran back to the body of the woman and checked her for a pulse, there was nothing. Fuck, fuck, fuck, I am so fucked! I am a large brute of a man, a combat veteran, and the Veteran's Hospital has a record of me having PTSD induced insomnia. All of that can be used against me in court to paint me as some kind of unstable murderer. I am so fucked... She was just a little thing, maybe a one hundred pound lady... I had to bury her and hide this evidence NOW. The owners are out of town, and they will be for awhile. This lady is clearly a vagrant squatter of some type. No one will come looking for her. Almost all of the blood is on the tile, I can do this. I took off my boots and ran them under the sink to clean off any residual blood I had on the bottom. I took off my long sleeve work shirt that all the pest control men in my company have to wear. I stepped on it and scooted along the tile to the front door careful to make sure I didn't get any blood anywhere, but strangely enough, there wasn't that much. I got outside and ran to my work truck to grab towels, rags, tape, and the extra shirt I keep there in case of a chemical spill and then sprinted back to the house. I had to hurry, I'm not sure what time it is but this was only supposed to be a 20 minute job and I had been at this house for at least 10 minutes already.

Once I got back inside, I looked under the customers sink. Yes, garbage bags! I used my now dirty work shirt on the tile to soak up the blood around the woman's head and then I put a garbage bag over her head and shoulders before any more blood could leak out. These were the large industrial garbage bags meant to pick up yard trimmings and they were about 3 feet long. This woman was probably only 5' 5". I put another garbage bag over her feet and pulled it up to meet the one on her head. I started to tape the middle together before I remembered all of the documentaries I had watched about forensics. She could have my hair or clothing fibers on her or even pest control chemical particulate that could all link her to me, SHIT! I checked back underneath the sink for a chemical that could erase it all and sure enough, it was there: household bleach. I carefully lifted the garbage bag covering her head and doused her in bleach, I did the same with her lower half as well. I then taped the two bags together and dragged her near the back sliding glass door. I had to calm down and think things through. I had to use all of my knowledge I had learned at criminal justice school to make sure this wasn't connected to me. I walked back to my truck SLOWLY this time to grab my shovel and hoe that I used to dig up the dirt around peoples home foundations for termite treatments and walked through the back gate of the home.

Luckily, Arizona yards don't generally have any grass. Most yards have a thin layer of pebbles over black plastic to prevent weeds. Even more backyards just have dirt. I was in luck, this yard was soft Arizona moon dust style dirt. I'm glad it wasn't that mud crack clay packed shit that can withstand nuclear bombs. Either way, I got my hoe out and made a shallow trench VERY quickly. This was part of my job, after all, I did this around 20 times a day, so it was done quickly. I had it down about a foot in all directions at roughly the shape of the woman. It needed to be deep enough that if the homeowner decided to put sprinklers in at a later date they weren't going to get a cadaver surprise. I took the shovel and dug down another foot and a half. That should be deep enough, the sprinklers and drip systems here normally are only six inches to one foot deep, and I was running out of time. In Arizona, all the backyards have brick fences that run about five to six feet high all the way around the yards. I walked over to the brick fence and peeked over each side checking to see if any neighbors were out. They weren't, they were probably still on their way home from work. I went back inside and grabbed her, dragged her over to the hole and unceremoniously threw her ass in.

"May you rot in hell, you crazy bitch." I said to no one in particular.

I pushed the dirt back over her with the hoe quickly. Shit, I didn't even have to try hard to make it look normal. *Arizona is AWESOME for murderers*, wait what the hell am I thinking...

I went back inside and looked at the residual blood all over the tile. I needed a chemical to destroy this but I remember particularly from my criminal justice classes that forensics experts can tell if someone has hastily cleaned a house with bleach after a crime with a special light and a spray chemical they use. Think, damn it, THINK! I got it! I was supposed to spray this place for bugs anyway, right?! I went back out to my truck and started the engine that powers the pump for my pesticide sprayer. I then started unreeling the hose that connected back to the small pony engine and ultimately the 5,000-gallon tank that held a few hundred gallons of all-purpose pesticide in it. I dragged my chemical sprayer up to the doorway and sat it down in the threshold. I grabbed some of the rags from my truck and put on my thick black rubber chemical proof gloves and then hastily mopped up the blood all over the tile. Then, I took my chemical sprayer and tuned it to the lightest spray possible and put a light mist of it all over the tile. I even sprayed it in the kitchen which is a big no no in the pest control world, but I am not going to prison, no way no how. Finally, I mopped up all the mist with the same rags I used before and spread it around. The tile was a dark brown Spanish tile that is common in southwestern homes and the pesticide combined with the impromptu hand mopping diluted the blood down to invisibility. I stepped back and looked at my handy work, double checking that I had gotten it all. There were a few spots here and there on cabinets and whatnot that I wiped off with a pesticide soaked rag. There, perfect!

Last but not least I headed back to the bedroom. The light still didn't work in there. I reached up and checked the bulb. Sure enough, I just turned it a few times to the right and it lit the room. That tricky bitch had unscrewed it a little when she knew I was coming down the hallway. With the light on in the room, it didn't look that bad. The carpet was thick and brown, the kind you can squish between your toes on a cold winter day. If there was blood on it I couldn't tell. I took one last look around to see if I had missed anything. There, in the drywall was a small .380 sized hole. This must have been my one missed shot. There were no other holes in the drywall in the bedroom or in the hallway. The rounds must not have exited her body. That crazy crackhead Terminator 5,000 lady must have been dense. I put my eye close to the hole in the drywall and I could see the bullet wedged in a stud. I grabbed the multi-tool off my belt and worked the bullet out of the stud. It plopped out and promptly fell into the wall. I didn't have time to grab it, I had to fix this hole and get out of here. I had some plaster repair in my cargo pocket for when I have to poke holes in drywall and foam for termites. I quickly plastered the hole. It looked good as new. I checked the room one more time but it looked fine, all the other interior doors in the house were closed so I closed this one as well. The crazy lady must have opened it when she hid here from me. This house looked uniform, clean, and best of all not like anyone had been murdered here. I put everything back where I found it and locked the house up.

When I jumped back in my truck and looked in the mirror, I had several large red spots on my face. Those would be nasty bruises later. I put on my extra long sleeve work shirt over the undershirt I was wearing. I had the other work shirt I had worn earlier with me along with the rags I used to clean up in a grocery bag. I would throw those away later, far away from here. Before I put the soiled linens in the bag I had squirted them all with pesticide and wrung them out under a bush in the front yard of the customers home. I spent my drive home in a haze of worry and paranoia, but before I knew it I was back at my office. I quickly dropped off my paperwork for the day and my work truck, then headed home in my own vehicle. I didn't want to talk to anyone, I just wanted to get home.

I had an average 3 bedroom house in an average part of Phoenix that I had picked up after my tour in Afghanistan. When I was overseas I had made good friends with a Staff Sergeant who was a smart dude.

He was on his second deployment and was full of good life advice. He seemed like the kind of guy who had his shit together which was a nice contrast compared to most of the soldiers in my unit. I stuck to him like glue and learned everything I could. One of the best pieces of advice he had given me was to buy a house and not to rent. I took it to heart. When I came home from Afghanistan, I had a mild case of PTSD. It didn't affect my days or social interactions with friends and family but nights were hell, I couldn't even rationalize it. The sun would go down and my heart would just start pounding and sleep was almost out of the question. So I met a nice realtor, bought a fucked up foreclosure for pennies on the dollar and dumped all of my pent up feelings and anger into it in the form of renovations and repairs. It's not all that expensive to renovate a home if you are doing 95% of the work yourself.

This house, in particular, was great. It was built in the 70's during one of the first serious residential booms in Arizona. Wooden houses with siding don't work here, the sun tears them apart. Making a wooden house here is a money trap and all around a bad idea. Construction companies in that time frame learned that and started building homes out of something they just called "Block" which is a 16x8x4 solid block of concrete that has been mixed with Arizona stone and tan dye. Don't confuse this stuff with hollow cinder block. Cinder blocks are pussy willows compared to this stuff.

That "block" lines the front and most of the sides of my house that face the street, and it is functionally bullet proof. Don't ask me how I know... Fine, ask me! Shortly after I moved in, I picked up a few similar blocks at Home Depot and took them out to the desert and shot them with a few assorted calibers. It's bulletproof. Unfortunately, the back of my house is standard cinder block, but as a PTSD addled combat veteran returning home from war, I couldn't argue with having about 65% of my house bulletproof. My house was everything to me, I had dumped my heart and soul into it. I had done some serious introspection in there during the 15-16 hour days I was putting into painting, cutting out moldy drywall, and putting in new sinks and toilets. It was the first place I really had where I was calm after my deployment. It was my sanctum, my fortress of solitude, my everything. This house helped me build my inner peace and helped me feel secure again after feeling the exact opposite for over a year in Afghanistan.

When I pulled into my driveway, I felt immediately better. I felt like I could think again. I realized then I was a stupid asshole and I should have just called the police. I was an upstanding member of society, a veteran, no criminal history, hell I didn't even have a speeding ticket on my record. I had even spent more than a few weekends each year that I didn't have anything planned with the city's volunteer graffiti clean up detail... Well, the calling the police ship had sailed, it was too late now to call them and say that I had made an honest mistake and beaten a woman to death before burying her in hefty bags. That probably wouldn't fly... I'm never going to prison, never...

I jumped out of my personal truck, an old Dodge Ram and headed up to my front door. I unlocked the two deadbolts that I had bought that were lock-pick proof. Most front doors can be lock picked open in seconds, scary. I had taken up lockpicking when I was younger, it was stupidly easy to learn. I made sure the locks on my house couldn't be picked, at least not with any ease. Either way, I opened my specialty locks and headed inside where I was met by the most beautiful girl in the world. I ran at her, she ran at me, we met in the middle and my arms went around her. Then her giant rough tongue went up the side of my face and her tail started smacking my leg as she tried to get closer to me. The number one girl in my life Is Mia, my German Shepherd/Husky mix. I found Mia after I had gotten home from Afghanistan. She was part of my three step plan to kick PTSD's ass. I did a lot of independent research into PTSD after I was diagnosed. I skipped all the bullshit, the Kumbaya circles, and other new age politically correct crap and I broke it down into a plan I could understand. To beat PTSD I needed 3 things:

1. Security
2. Love
3. Confidence.

I had security in my home and on my person. I was a heavily armed combat veteran, covered in concealed weapons who now lived in a partially bulletproof house, I was secure. Next step, LOVE: my mom and dad were both kind of shit heads in their own light. They got divorced when I was really young and they had me way too early. Back in the day, judges always sided with the woman in a divorce when it came to custody hearings even if she was a piece of shit who couldn't hold a job or stop drinking and partying.

My mom got custody of me but she wasn't ready to be a mom. She was a young woman in her 20's and frankly a slut who liked to party. I didn't realize that when I was a kid trying to sleep on a school night, but couldn't due to my mom hosting a loud party in our living room and banging random dudes in our house, which I could hear through the thin drywall. My mom skipped work a lot when she was hung over and inevitably got fired over and over again. This led to our lights being turned off when we couldn't pay the power bill and me skipping a lot of meals or eating bologna and ramen. Believe it or not my white privilege didn't put food in my belly when I was a child. I don't know where this white privilege is that I keep hearing about in the media, but I could have used some of that when I was locked away in my room starving as a kid.

Every once in awhile, my mom would remember she loved me or that she was supposed to at least pretend to love me. Only then would she show me some small semblance of emotion but for the most part, I was on my own and locked in my room. I would say she was emotionally abusive but that is an understatement. Emotional abuse was my bread and butter as a kid. Being a single mom was tough for my mom, mostly because she didn't want to be a mom, but also because being a single mom is extremely hard for anyone. She always needed someone to babysit me so she could go to work or go out drinking, but we never had the money. This meant I got left with a lot of sub-par babysitters or someone from my moms crappy family. I had two different babysitters who decided to lay their hands on me. I was too young and naive to realize that being woken up from naps with a kick to the stomach wasn't normal. When I told my second grade teacher at school, she called the police and that particular babysitter was arrested. Some teachers are awesome.

In between babysitters, my mom would leave me with her family that emotionally and physically abused her as a child. I don't really know why she did that since she knew they had a history of abuse. Needless to say, I was physically and emotionally abused there as well. Mental illness and I went way back, we were old friends. I like to think you can't make a diamond without pressure and I wouldn't be the man I am today without the trials and adversity I went through as a kid. I could go on and on about what a crap mom I had, but I don't really like complaining and that's not what this book is about.

My dad was an alright sort. He was an enlisted soldier and had been awarded partial custody of me. This meant I got sent out to whatever state or country he was stationed at each summer. This was a good and bad thing because it meant I got to get away from my mom. The bad part was it took me away from my school friends who were the only constant in my life. My dad seemed like an okay guy, but I honestly don't know much about him. I saw him every other summer or so and he treated me well. Some summers he was deployed or at a duty station that wasn't safe for kids, so he would pay for me to fly to his parent's house in Nevada.

That was where some of my most cherished childhood memories came from and where I learned what real love for another human being was. My grandparents in Nevada are wonderful people who truly have always loved me no matter what I was doing in life. They treated me well and without the kindness and love that they showed me, I wouldn't be who I am today. I would be a much darker person and I am already a pretty dark person, so that is saying something. My only real complaint about my father is that as soon as I was out of his sight he would forget that I existed. Even as a young kid I knew he was someone I couldn't count on or confide in. I'm not sure when this happened but at some point, I promised myself that if I ever had kids I would be there for them and put them first unlike my unstable and unreliable parents.

Anyway, back to the present, boo hoo hoo for me, I had a crappy childhood, so fucking what. A lot of people do. I put my big boy undies on and cowboyed the fuck up. Crying about spilled emotional milk wasn't going to get me anywhere. I had to be strong because the world was a fucked up place and no one was going to help me, except me. I needed to get over my PTSD quickly and like I said before, the second thing in my self-prescribed get well quick medicine was: Love. I wasn't going to my nonexistent parents for love and I wasn't going to call my aging grandparents in Nevada just to scare them with details of dead

31

bodies, bloated and stinky in the Afghan sun. I didn't want to worry them telling them that I thought my interpreter might slit my throat in my sleep.

I didn't exactly have a booming love life either. Being in the Army Reserves and a gun nut scared a lot of women off, so did my lack of emotional investment in the relationships. Of course, there was also the part where I am always putting my dog, Mia, first. I know when to man up and say when something is my fault. Besides, I didn't want to need someone. I wanted someone to need me. Which led me to my best friend Mia. I was in Petsmart one day looking at the dogs for sale when a man came in the front door. He was telling the cashier that he had found a cardboard box out back in the alley near the dumpsters with two puppies in it. Who knows if his story was the truth or not, I don't really care. All I know is that I looked up and saw Mia in the box he was holding. She was the most beautiful dog in the world, she looked at me and our eyes locked. I knew that it was love at first sight, so I asked the man what he was going to do with the dogs and he told me he didn't know. That was why he had brought them inside from the Arizona heat. I asked if I could have one and he said yes, so I picked up my Mia and left the store before the man could change his mind. The rest is history, we have loved each other ever since. I now had security and love, I just needed the last part of my three part plan: Confidence.

In all of my reading and lectures from the doctors at the VA, a common consensus of sources say that the best way to gain confidence is to get better at something. A lot of folks recommended bowling and golf... GROSS. I was flipping channels one day thinking about what hobby to pick up and came across this t.v. show called "3-Gun Nation." Apparently, there was an entire sport dedicated to shooting things. The sport is called 3-Gun, and how it works is that there are four or five shooting courses set up with steel targets inside of dirt berms. Each course requires the contestant, or shooter, to use multiple guns to complete them. An example course might be 10 steel plates at varying ranges to the left of the shooter, and 10 steel plates to the right of the shooter out at varying ranges. The shooter would generally have a plywood table in front of him or her where they would set down their rifle and shotgun when not in use. A range officer will start a timer and the shooter can start gunning down steel targets. For example, you might have to use a pistol to shoot all of the steel targets on the left and then transition into the shotgun and shoot all of the steel targets on the right. When you are finished shooting all of the targets the range officer will write down your time. You would repeat that until you had finished all of the courses offered that day and at the end of the day, whichever shooter had the lowest overall time won the competition. I was baffled, amazed, and excited... There was a sport that involved guns and shooting things, now this I could do.

I surfed the web and found a weekly outlaw shooting match in my area. Outlaw meaning the match didn't follow the standard rules of IDPA or USPSA which were the major competitive shooting organizations. You just followed the house rules, which basically were modeled after the national rules with just a little bit of leeway. Every Thursday night they had a pistol competition and every other Sunday they ran a 3-Gun match. It was only 15 dollars to enter either. I went the next Thursday not really knowing what I was doing, but I met nice people and had a good time. I came in first place among the new guys and won the coveted "Tyro Pin" the word Tyro comes from the Latin word tiro, which means "young soldier" or "new recruit," or more generally, novice. I was filled with confidence and more importantly, I was hooked into competitive shooting. It was my version of cocaine.

That first night I found my unofficial mentor as well. He was a badass Vietnam veteran named Brian who gave startling great shooting advice to me, and he shot the different lanes with me. We didn't even talk that much besides basic introductions, and I told him how I had just returned home from Afghanistan. He told me he was a Vietnam veteran. We saw the pain in each other's eyes and just understood each other. I had unintentionally made a friend for life. In the coming months, Brian would motivate and guide me to becoming one of the best shooters at that little shooting club. Shit, according to my scores compared to the national average probably one of the best shooters in the country. Whether Brian knows it or not he was a major part of my life and he really helped me get over my PTSD and be mentally healthy. If I could have any dad in the world he would be a serious contender after Chuck Norris and Chris Kyle, may god rest his soul.

My three part plan of gaining security, love, and confidence was completed and within a few months I started sleeping better and I had gained the confidence to get my pest control job, but that is all ancient history. I don't need to worry about any of that now, I had my hands full with the current shit storm I had put myself in. I had a dead woman buried across town in one of my customer's backyards. I was worn out, beat up, scared, nervous, and paranoid. At least it was Friday, TGIF and all that. I sat down and for whatever reason, I grabbed a beer. It felt like the right thing to do. I wasn't the drinking type and the beers in my fridge were mostly for guests but I really needed one. I needed to think and relax, I was too mixed up in this. I needed help. It was time to call someone.

Chapter 3

I called my buddy Rook Moore. If you've ever seen those memes or surveys online with stupid headings like "tag one friend you would bury a body with" well yeah, Rook was that guy for me. I had a few others I trusted as much as him but he was the one who would need the least explained and might take it the best, or so I hoped. I told him over the phone that it was an emergency and to bring a gun and a bug out bag if he had it. I had a second thought and sent a quick text, "*Bring some ice as well, its part of the emergency*," I didn't have any ice at my house. I had cheaped out on my fridge and gotten one without the ice-maker, so I just used those little plastic ice trays, but currently, all of mine were empty. My whole body was starting to throb, I needed ice. I had known Rook 16 or 17 years now, and we had done a lot of crazy shit together. When we were kids we had broken a LOT of laws.

I basically had zero parental supervision and zero adult role models (besides Arnold Schwarzenegger in T2) and I was a young kid with too much testosterone and free time. I was the perfect recipe for disaster and mayhem. Rook had a cool dad but he was out of town a lot for work and Rook's mom didn't give a shit what we were doing. Which meant we started a lot of fires, made a lot of bombs, did a lot of "boys will be boys" kind of stuff and constantly pushed the envelope towards disaster. Our extreme behavior only impressed other kids when we were younger and some of them even joined our group of mayhem. As we progressed into our teens our shenanigans only increased further. We regularly blew up mail boxes with chlorine bombs and ran stuff over in our cars. That kind of stuff was just the tip of the iceberg. We eventually out grew all of that as we got older and more mature but we were BAD as kids and we were smart as hell which was not a good combination for property values in our area. Breaking the law was nothing new to me or to Rook, so I hoped he didn't immediately call the police when I told him what had happened to me.

Rook showed up about 20 minutes later. I had unlocked the door while we were on the phone, he knocked and I yelled: "YOU MAY ENTER PEASANT!"

Even in morbid and stressful situations I still had my humor, I picked that up in the Army. My buddy walked in wearing an AR-15 pistol on a one point sling that we had built together a few years back for him. His bug out bag in the form of an ACU backpack casually clung to his opposing shoulder hanging by one strap. If you aren't familiar with that weapon platform, it's basically a VERY VERY short and proficient rifle. It generally holds 30 rounds in the magazine but can be equipped to hold more or less. They are actually illegal to have buttstocks on the pistol variant according to federal law but smart people don't let politicians decide albatross things for them that might mean the difference between living and dying. Worst case scenario it only takes a second to pop off any part of an AR-15. They are fully modular for the most part.

Rook looked at me for a bit and said: "Damn dude is the ice for your face? You look like you went 10 rounds with Tyson."

I replied, "Nope, it's for my dick, not joking..." he chucked the ice bag my way and I immediately applied it to Bear Jr., the Mighty Dragon of Trouser Land.

I had taken a peek at the ole meat log earlier and it didn't look as bad as I thought it would, slight bruising but that was it. If I could kill that lady again I would, no one hurts Bear Jr. and lives.

Rook must have gotten tired of watching me ice my junk because he finally said, "You going to tell me what's going on?"

"Would you believe me if I told you that a psychopathic 100 pound 18 year oldish female on steroids kicked my ass for invading the house she was squatting in, and then I shot and beat her to death in self defense?" I stared deadpan at him hoping the levity of my situation would sink in.

"So why aren't you at the police station right now answering questions?" he retorted.

"Well, I may have gotten paranoid and been afraid of prison and accidentally doused her corpse in bleach, and then buried her body in one of my customer's backyards..." I said.

Rook let that sink in for a bit I could tell he believed me, he turned to me, "Tell me everything, start from the beginning."

I told him my story the best I could, hoping that if I had made a mistake he would catch it. Or maybe he would know what to do to get me out of this mess.

He turned towards me "Damn Bear, you really screwed the pooch here."

"You ain't kidding bud" I replied.

He seemed to be in deep thought,then his face lit up.

"So you already cleaned the scene and the only real piece of evidence there is the body, so let's go dig that bitch up and dump her in the desert. Remember in school, no body equals no crime."

I thought about it, he was right. There were thousands of miles of open desert just north of Phoenix and all of it was public land. There was no plan to ever develop any of it and the terrain was too rough and remote for anything to be built on it within the next 50 years anyway, by then I would be close to 80. Rook and I had taken a few classes together at school, we were on different paths educationally but he needed a few electives and humanity credits. So to fulfill those oddball credits he needed we had taken some of the same criminal justices classes for a while. One day in one of our shared classes, we talked about a case where someone had come forward and admitted to committing a murder but had destroyed and hidden the body so remotely that he couldn't find it again to show the police, so he couldn't be charged. If there is no body there is no crime!

"You would do that for me, you would go back there with me and help me move the corpse?" I asked him.

"Brothers for life man, let's fucking do this."

We loaded up my truck with digging tools from my backyard shed, and we loaded Rook's bug out bag and his rifle in the front passenger side near where his feet would be. Rook was also concealed carrying a Glock 19 and had packed an extra extended mag in his bug out bag for it. It was one of those 30 round Korean jobs that were surprisingly dependable, I owned a few myself. I went back inside and grabbed my own Glock 19, and hybrid concealed carry holster. They call it a hybrid holster because it was part leather and part Kydex. Kydex is like plastic on steroids, it is ultra durable, and can withstand temperatures over 1500 degrees. It's the most common material used to make modern holsters. Old style holsters were all leather, but leather wears out, bends, warps, etc. All things you really don't want to happen to a holster which is why the gun industry so happily switched to Kydex. Kydex has one major drawback though, it's really uncomfortable when it rubs against your skin. So someone came up with the bright idea of hybrid holsters, the best of both worlds. The part of the holster that rests against your skin is leather, then a Kydex frame is mounted over that and it holds your weapon. Your weapons rest against the leather inside of the Kydex frame. You get the comfortability level of leather with the reliability of Kydex, fucking awesome.

This was the gun I conceal carried outside of work and the gun I wish I could conceal carry all of the time, but I couldn't take the risk of printing. "Printing" is gun nut lingo for the rough shape of a gun seen through the clothing. 99% of people don't notice a concealed weapon, even a full size pistol like a Glock 19 can really disappear if you aren't wearing tight clothes. This still leaves one major problem for me: all it takes is one hoplophobe to call my boss and get me fired for trying to protect myself. The sudden realization came to me that if I hadn't been concealed carrying today I would probably be dead now... Spooky.

If I counted the number of times in Afghanistan that I had returned fire on Islamic terrorists that were trying to kill me, this was probably the 20th time or so that I had used a gun to save my life. This was still the first time ever that I had seen my rounds land on my attacker.

Almost all of my firefights in Afghanistan had been from a moving vehicle at 0300 in the morning, with us shooting at muzzle flashes 600 meters out. This time had been different, admittedly it had rattled me. Before this, I had always had some level of deniability and I was so morally in the right. Terrorists would try to kill me and my friends, we would shoot back and hope that they died so they couldn't hurt any more innocent people, black and white. This time though... There was no way to deny anything, I had killed that lady. Sure if I hadn't shot her I would most likely be dead now but I still felt sick about it. GAH, I can't think like that, this wasn't my fault. I didn't go out looking for trouble, this was her fault.

Before leaving my house, I grabbed my personal favorite rifle, my baby, a skeletonized WASR-10 with a side folding buttstock that I had paid the tax stamp for and gotten silenced a few years back. I had a one point sling on it so I threw it across my chest. I grabbed a lightweight tan windbreaker and threw it over it. The rifle stuck out the bottom a bit even with the buttstock collapsed but I felt better this way in case any of my neighbors were watching. I don't even know why I brought a rifle, Rook had one so symmetry I guess, MILD OCD FOR THE WIN!!! Also, something just felt right about at least one of us having a silenced weapon, god forbid one of us would have to use our weapons but I'm going to assume its best not to alert a neighborhood with loud noises whilst illegally transporting a corpse. Besides, a little paranoia is healthy, if I hadn't been prepared today that woman would be the one dealing with my corpse instead of the other way around.

We jumped in my truck and Rook looked over at me and said "Dude, we can't have the corpse rolling around in the bed of the truck on the highway and I'm not riding with it in the cab."

"See this is why I pay you the big bucks, let's take my car, oh and I just had a great idea" I replied.

I asked Rook to start transferring the gear to my car while I ran into the garage for something: painters tape. I came back out and applied painters tape fully over my license plate. My car was a small little Mitsubishi Mirage which I kept for the great gas mileage. My Old Dodge Ram was great, but it was hell on the wallet when it was time to fill the tank. So I drove the Mitsubishi every other day to save some money. The engine and air conditioner were in perfect condition but the body had seen too much Arizona sun and the silver paint was peeling on the roof and a few other places. When the paint originally had started to peel, I looked into how much a new paint job would cost me and the prices were astronomical.

So I googled up a few ways to paint your car yourself to save money and a common answer I got was: Plasti-Dip. Plasti-Dip is sprayable plastic paint that is pretty cheap and can be applied with a 100 dollar paint sprayer. You paint your car yourself any color you want and if you make a mistake you can literally just take a razor blade and cut off the mistake and peel it up. It only lasts one or two years but when it fails you can literally just peel it off in layers and reapply. It's pretty cool stuff, my car was currently painted a flat black because I loved the way the cop cars looked in the movie RoboCop where they were also a flat black.

Rook finished loading the car and came around the back to see what I was up to. "Decent idea dude but we can't roll on the highway like that, someone will call it in."

I replied to him "Yeah I know, we will take surface streets there, pick up the body, drive a few miles away and take the tape off, and then jump on the highway. If we get pulled over on the way there I will just say I was Plasti-Dipping the car and I forgot to take it off."

He seemed to be thinking about it. "That should work, better to be safe than sorry in case any of the neighbors in that area are the nosy type" said Rook.

We jumped in the car and were underway. Rook yelled, "LET'S GET SOME FUCKIN JAMS GOING!"

"You are acting like you aren't nervous about this at all?" I replied.

"No, I'm ready to shit my pants in fear but I am not exactly going to sit back and let one of my best friends go to prison for making a stupid mistake now am I?"

Damn, Rook is a good friend. I can honestly say though that I would have done the same thing for him or any of my close friends.

"Well, what music for driving a car somewhere, picking up a corpse, and then burying it in the desert?"

"Hmmm, something upbeat please" Rook replied.

I opened the music app on my phone and clicked on the playlists provided by the app. I scrolled down to the "U" section and sure enough there was a section literally labeled "UpBeat," I hit the play button. I had Bluetooth tech on my stereo so the music would come through my car's speakers. A second after the song started I paused it because I had a thought.

"SHIT, we need alibis!"

Rook looked at me for a second and said: "Call Griff man".

Griffin Mueller was a good buddy of ours, we had known him since 7th grade when his family moved into our area and he started attending middle school with us. He ended up joining the Army Reserves as well and becoming a combat medic. He was a good dude and one of our oldest friends. I dialed his number and set the call up on speaker phone, but since it was Bluetooth connected to my stereo his voice would come through my car speakers.

Griffin answered the phone and yelled "WAAAAZZZZZSUUUUUUPPPPP" like those old Bud Light commercials.

Considering the levity and somberness of the situation Rook and I couldn't hold in our laughter and we also couldn't stop from replying the same way.

We both yelled "WAAAZZZZZZZUPPPPEEEEHHHHHH!" Ha ha, god I love my friends.

Griffin heard the both of us and said: "Wait, is that Rook with you?"

I replied "Yeah man we got a serious favor to ask you. I'm just going to spit it out and not beat around the bush here because we have a lot of... uh, work to do tonight. We need you to be our alibi and this will probably never ever happen, but should you be questioned by a police officer or police detective about where Rook and I were tonight, you have to say we were at your house playing video games or something."

The line was silent for a few seconds and then Griffin said: "Shut the fuck up dude, what do you want. I'm trying to get my dick wet."

I heard Griffin's wife yell something angrily in the background, he was going to pay for that comment.

Rook broke into the conversation "We aren't joking this is a life and death situation... or it was or something, I don't know. We really are in a rush and we do really need this, will you please help us?"

Griffin replied quickly "Fuck guys, you can't just drop some heavy shit on me and not explain yourselves."

He was right we owed him that much, but telling him what we were doing would at least make him an accomplice, so would having him provide the alibi though... I hated this situation, I hated putting my friends in danger. If I ever won the lottery these two were getting their own mansions.

"Alright man, if you really want to know what is going on we can all do beers at my place tomorrow, but we really are running out of time here and this is an emergency. Will you please do it, will you be our alibi?"

Everyone was quiet for a minute, then Griffin finally responded "Yeah guys, I'll do it but you owe me. I'll be over tomorrow for the beers and we will get our story straight just in case anyone comes asking around. We should all be on the same page."

Griffin was the son of a cop, he knew the score. I was also hoping he was giving Rook and I the benefit of the doubt about whatever crime he was covering for us about. Legitimately Rook and I would NEVER hurt an innocent person, hell, I probably wouldn't hurt someone who wasn't innocent if they didn't instigate a problem first. We were good people, NO, we ARE good people.

"SWEET, THANK YOU THANK YOU THANK YOU. You are right I will owe you. I'll schedule a blowie for you ASAP. My gardener Juan gives great ones, he will be over Thursday to take care of you. He swallows the baby gravy and everything. Seriously though we have to go, thanks again bud."

"See you guys later, good luck with whatever the hell you are doing, be safe" Griffin said.

Rook looked at me after the call was over "Dude we have some good friends."

I replied, "That's what I was thinking."

We both sat in silence for a few minutes just staring out the windows as we drove to commit our dark deed.

I reflected on my life and the friends I had, I was a lucky man. I don't know what Rook was thinking about but I would assume something similar. Narrowly avoiding prison can really put your life into perspective. We hit the next traffic light, it was red, we stopped. We were almost at my customer's house and we were both still quietly reflecting on our own thoughts when all of a sudden a car started honking its horn, BEEP BEEP BEEP. Holy shit that scared the hell out of me. My hand went to my rifle and I looked out the car window towards the noise. The car to the left of us that was also stopped at the light was giving me the "roll down the window" hand motion, circling his fist in the air rolling down an imaginary window.

I rolled down my window with my adrenaline and heart both pounding and said, "Yeah?"

The stranger pointed at the rear of my car and said "Bro, you got tape or something on your license plate, just letting you know I didn't want you to get pulled over."

"Oh shit, thanks man, I forgot all about that, I'll pull over up here and take care of it!" I replied to him.

The light turned green and he yelled, "No problem, see ya."

We both drove forward, and I pulled into the first gas station we saw, giving the other driver the illusion that we were going to pull the painter's tape off of the plate.

Once the stranger's car was out of sight, we pulled back onto the road and kept heading towards our dark destination. We were both nervous as hell but we could do this! This time tomorrow I would be home free and sippin' brews with my buds, and then it started raining. Shit, that can't be a good sign.

"This is a bad omen" Rook said,

"That's what I was thinking" I replied.

Then we saw lightning on the horizon and a few seconds later we heard the thunder. Damn, that is depressing. I remembered the upbeat music we had paused so I hit play. The crooney voice of BJ Thomas singing "Raindrops are fallin' on my head" blared over my humble car's speakers. Rook and I exchanged incredulous looks with each other. What a coincidence, this night just keeps getting weirder.

Chapter 4

We pulled into the subdivision that my customer's home was located in. The closer we got the more anxiety I started having about this situation.

"Do a loop down the street and back, don't stop. Look for security cameras or anything else suspicious" Rook said.

I was glad he was here, I was having a problem thinking straight. I slapped each side of my face once and opened the window on my side to let some of the cool air and rain in. I needed to get in the moment here and quit worrying so much. We drove down the street and everything looked quiet. The rain was making it a little hard to see but there were no visible security cameras on any of the neighbor's homes. My customer's home looked completely vacant and quiet as well. Everything looked good, so we did a U-turn and came back down the street doing a final scan but seeing nothing out of the ordinary. There was a nice 50's or 60's style muscle car parked between my customer's home and the neighbor's house along the sidewalk. I couldn't tell what era the car was from. I wasn't really one of those "car guys." I didn't remember seeing it before. The neighbors must have guests over, or maybe that car was there earlier and I just didn't notice. All I cared about was that it wasn't a police car with officers inside waiting to arrest me. I backed the car into the driveway in case we had to get out in a hurry. Rook wasn't the only one with tactical tricks.

Rook and I both quietly got out of the car and started getting wet from the rain. I led the way since he wasn't familiar with the home. I thought about going in through the front door but there would be no point, the body was in the back. I continued leading us around the side of the house to the back gate. I suddenly stopped when I heard a very distinctive noise over the sound of the storm. The sound of a shovel scraping rocky Arizona soil. It was barely audible over the rain but I knew what I had heard... What the fuck is going on? I held up my fist over my shoulder, the universal sign for stop, so Rook would see. I put my hands along the top of the cinder block fence, pulled myself up just a bit and looked over the top.

There was someone digging her up! He looked like a Caucasian, about 30 years old, of average height with very wide shoulders. He was maybe Italian, it was hard to tell at night in the rain. He had on one of those 50's style leather greaser jackets where the zipper isn't quite in the middle. I looked down and sure enough, he even had some little cuffs rolled on the bottom of his jeans, and he was wearing some Oxford Black and Whites which were some of the more popular shoes from that era. I would bet dollars to donuts that under that jacket he would have a tight white t-shirt with the sleeves rolled up and a pack of cigarettes or a deck of cards rolled into one of the sleeves. Was this guy some kind of reenactor? Or maybe he just got off his shift at one of those themed restaurants? Well, I guess it didn't matter, he wasn't the homeowner. I had met them and he was fucking with evidence that could put me in prison for a long time.

I beckoned Rook forward and leaned really close to him. I cupped my hands fully over his ear and spoke into them. I was hoping that would stop any sound from leaking out but we probably wouldn't be heard over the storm anyway. I told him what I had seen and asked him what he thought we should do, but we were interrupted.

"HEY MORONS, I CAN HEAR YOU OVER THERE. WHY DON'T YOU COME BACK HERE AND JOIN THE PARTY," the dude in the leather jacket said.

Holy shit, my heart was really pounding now. We had to think quick. I reached for the gate handle and looked at Rook, he got a better grip on his rifle, then gave me a nod. I followed suit and got a better grip on the WASR below my jacket with my right hand, and opened the gate with my left hand. I walked in and tried to act casual with my rifle at the low ready. I quickly glanced at Rook, he had followed suit right behind me.

I didn't know what we were about to get into but I knew Rook had my back. We had been through a lot together as kids. Mostly running from cops and angry homeowners but we had basically been running our own operations with military precision since we were fourteen anyway. We didn't know that at the time, of course, we just thought we were really sneaky mailbox blower-uppers. When all the other kids were smoking pot, Griffin, Rook, and I, along with a few other kid's drug of choice was adrenaline. Joining the military for me had only strengthened the skills that I had already been building on my own inadvertently. Rook had also spent time in the military but he had gone active duty where I had gone Reserves.

Basically, all of my friends from my inner circle in high school had joined the military, the Army specifically because they gave the best deals and bonuses at the time and we wanted to get our hands dirty. But we were all good at different things, we all had different ASVAB scores, and even though we didn't want to, we knew it was time to grow up and go our separate ways. That was especially tough for me since I had spent almost every waking second with my buds since I had first stopped visiting my dad around age sixteen due to not wanting to lose whatever crappy summer job I had at the time. From age 16 to 18 my home life was so beyond shit it wasn't even funny. I was at the point where I would almost rather be homeless than head back home. This led to me crashing at Rook's house more often than not, I basically lived there.

Anyway, we all got older and separated. That hurt. Everyone else had parents and other family. My friends were my family and with them gone, I had nothing. I had to make my mark on the world, gain honor, and become financially independent. My friends needed to as well. So we all enlisted, Rook ended up going straight infantry. I don't know why he picked that. He had a great ASVAB score and his choice of infantry didn't make sense to me but it was his life, and his choice. We exchanged letters for as long as we could but we both got too busy to keep it up and we wouldn't truly re-unite until later when we both got honorably discharged.

Rook almost immediately got pulled for The Old Guard after joining the Army. The Old Guard pulls any infantry soldiers over 6 feet and 1 inches tall who have a halfway clean and handsome face. Rook was 6' 5" with spiky brown hair, he had that naturally tan skin that he didn't have to work at (asshole), and he was always 20-30 pounds underweight due to his insane metabolism which left him looking like a beanpole when we were growing up. When we were both joining the military he almost didn't make weight even though he was eating 3 cakes a day on top of his regular meals. For a while, he even considered the idea of eating marbles right before weigh in to increase his weight.

The Old Guard is a special military unit that conducts our nation's most important ceremonies. They mostly work out of the Washington D.C. area but they do travel sometimes. The Old Guard must maintain a perfect uniform and a rigid and unwavering sense of discipline because the whole world is watching them. You have probably heard of The Old Guard without really understanding that it was them. They handle duties like The Tomb of the Unknown Soldier, the nation's foremost color guard, the U.S. Drill Team, and the Presidential Salute Gun Battery. There are many more obligations and jobs they do but basically if you have seen a precision soldier in a nice blue dress uniform on the news or in a movie or one of those soldiers who can throw a rifle up in the air and it spins a million times before he catches it out of the air magically, yeah that was an Old Guard soldier.

The Old Guard was a non-deployable unit though and Rook had always wanted to deploy and serve his country, but due to his unit placement, he never got to. I could tell that irked him but I didn't care. I was proud of my friend for everything he had accomplished and I knew what kind of man he was. He was brave and courageous and his actions so far tonight only nailed those thoughts home further for me. Hell, somehow in the middle of all of his other Old Guard duties he had somehow managed to be awarded the EIB (Expert Infantryman Badge). I didn't know the exact nature of the beast that was the EIB since I had specialized in convoy security. All of my knowledge was in vehicle on vehicle combat or vehicle on soft target/hard target combat. Either way, if you weren't shooting it from the top of a speeding vehicle I didn't have much military knowledge on the subject. Of course I took my mandatory MOUT (military operations in urban terrain) training seriously but that was maybe once a year for a unit like the one I was in, and then I would promptly forgot 90% of it a month after the course since I knew for a fact I wouldn't be using it.

After Rook had gotten his EIB, I asked one of my senior NCO's who had been a former infantryman what it was all about. He basically told me to get an EIB you would have to perfectly perform every single task an infantryman would ever have to know, even obscure ones. A surprising amount of math was involved and knowledge of battlefield medicine. The testing varied but you would generally have to be able to perform between 37 and 40 infantryman tasks PERFECTLY and only after a grueling 12 mile speed march while heavily weighed down with packs and armor. One mistake and you were failed out. The NCO went on further to tell me that back when he had tried to take it there was a less than 10% pass rate and that he had personally studied a year straight for it before failing it twice back to back. Rook is a badass, an untested badass but a badass nonetheless.

I had to take charge of this current situation, I had to think of something fast. I spit out the first thing that came to mind "Good evening sir, we are detectives with Phoenix PD and we got a call that someone was trespassing on this property. What exactly are you doing here?"

He bent over and started reaching into the hole as he spoke, "I can hear from your increased heartbeat that you are lying. Which one of you buried my girl Lydia here? You know what, don't answer that, we will ask her in a minute." He continued reaching into the hole, he pulled a clump of the black plastic up and he ripped it in half before pushing it back down exposing the woman's face and upper torso.

The man's voice changed to an almost rigid and commanding shriek and yelled "LYDIA WAKE UP AND GET OUT OF THAT HOLE!"

The woman's eyes shot open and she casually leaned forward. Clumps of mud fell off of her. She reached around herself and pulled most of the black plastic off, then climbed out of the hole that was slowly filling with muddy rainwater to stand beside the man in the leather jacket. She looked disoriented for a second, then she looked over at me and her face radiated anger.

"You dick, you poured bleach on me and buried me!" she screamed.

Rook looked between the two of us and said, "I thought you killed her?"

"I did," I replied.

We sat there for a few seconds just staring at each other with the small ditch between us that once held Lydia's corpse. I was standing across from her, and Rook was standing across from the man in the leather jacket.

Leather jacket guy broke the silence first "Well cool cats, it's been a blast but it's time for you two to meet your untimely demise and ultimately end up in my belly."

This whole situation was so surreal, I don't know why but I spoke up, "Wait a minute you guys are vampires or zombies or something, and now you are going to kill us?"

Leather Jacket opened his mouth to say something but I was already raising my WASR. I opened fire on Lydia because she was straight across from me, pulling the trigger as fast as I could. I was mentally planning to shoot Leather Jacket next. I couldn't even properly shoulder the weapon because the buttstock was collapsed but at this range, I couldn't really miss. To my right Rook must have taken my cue because he was already firing as well, but Leather Jacket was gone. Then I heard a loud noise that sounded like slabs of meat hitting each other. I stopped shooting Lydia and turned my rifle just a second too late to see Rook spinning through the air. Leather Jacket was a blur chasing after him and before Rook could even hit the ground, Leather jacket hammer fisted his flying body straight down into the mud. Before I could even rationally think about it, I lined up the iron sights on Leather Jackets neck and snapped off a quick round. He clamped his hand over the hole and spun around to look at me, the exit wound was grisly. It looked like he had half a bowl of spaghetti for a neck and he was trying to hold it all together and failing. Oh, we got a tough guy here, I Mozambiqued him. A very common shooting drill for competition shooters. I had done this a thousand times and my muscle memory locked me precisely on target, two in the chest and one in the head. BAM BAM BAM. Leather Jacket spun around from the hits and landed face down in the mud.

SHIT, ROOK! I sprinted over to Rook and bent down over him, his eyes were closed. I gently cradled his head and back and started lifting him towards my chest, "ROOK, ROOK, ARE YOU OKAY!"

Why does everyone always ask if someone is alright when they clearly are not?

Rook's eyes opened and he said, "Stop bending my torso, you dick. I think I have some broken ribs." I slowly lowered Rook down to the ground.

"Did you kill that cum bucket that hit me?" Rook asked.

"Yeah I got him bud, you rest I'm going to make sure this clown stays down... in the brown..."

Rook tried to laugh but he just ended up saying ow. I got up and walked back over to Leather Jacket, then I kicked him In the head as hard I could with my size 12 steel toed work boot. I looked over at Rook, he had seen me do it and he threw the devil horns symbol with his hand my way. The one where you put your hand into a fist then point out your pinky, your pointer finger, and your thumb. With one arm outstretched I sighted my WASR on Leather Jackets back and ripped off the rest of my magazine.

I started walking towards Lydia, she was trying to crawl away but it didn't look like her legs were working too well. I calmly ejected my spent magazine into my off hand and put it into one of the pockets of my windbreaker. Throwing magazines on the ground is cool in movies and all but those things cost money. I drew my Glock 19 with my right hand and continued walking until I was in front of Lydia. She was laying flat, belly down in the mud propped up on her elbows trying to pull herself forward with her legs uselessly dragging behind her. I crouched down next to her balancing on the balls of my feet and I put the muzzle of my gun on her forehead.

"Give me one reason why I shouldn't kill you... uhhh, again." I said. She gave up on trying to crawl her way to freedom and rolled over. She let her head flap down into the mud and let out a big breath.

"You shot me in the spine asshole. That jerk Dante killed my roommate and turned me into a vampire last week, and believe it or not I'm one of the victims of this shitty set of circumstances."

Hmm... "Well my bruised testicles say otherwise, so goodbye" I replied.

"WAIT!" she shouted, "I can save your life and maybe make you rich."

"Okay I'm listening, you have 10 seconds to prove your worth or I'm popping a few rounds into your dome piece and putting you back into that mud hole over yonder."

"No you aren't mister, and before I talk, I want assurances that you are going to let me live," said Lydia.

"Listen, Lydia, I'm going to level with you. You aren't exactly in the position to be making demands right now. You kicked me in the dick earlier today after attacking me, and one of my best friends is laying in the mud injured thanks to one of your friends. If his injuries aren't temporary or superficial and if you don't start talking I'll let you live, alright? I'll let you live just long enough to go grab some pliers out of my car and then start ripping your fucking toes off with them. So unless you want to play *Little Piggy* then start talking. How good your information is and what you say next depends on if you live or die."

I stared at her without blinking. After saying that I could feel the anger radiating off me in waves, I wasn't bluffing. I knew she believed me, she looked absolutely terrified after I had said that.

"Alright alright, first of all, that guy over there, Dante, he isn't my friend. He is going to wake up in a few minutes or less if you don't cut off his head or stab him through the heart with a stake, and if he wakes up he is going to kill you. You got lucky knocking him down and only because he was distracted by your friend. Also, Dante is rich and I know where his house is. If you let me live I can take you there."

Hmmm, I grabbed her by the hair and started dragging her over to where Rook lay. I unceremoniously threw her ass down a few feet away from Rook.

"You fucking asshole!" she yelled at me.

"Listen, Rook... this lady says Leather Jacket over there has to have his head cut off or he is going to get back up in a few minutes."

Rook contemplated the problem. "I've got a small hatchet in my backpack" Rook labored through the words, I could tell he was hurting.

He started trying to shrug off the backpack straps, and I rushed over to help him before pulling the backpack out from under him. I found the small hatchet quickly. I walked over to Leather Jacket's body and started to lean over to try to cut his head off but I backed off. I had seen scary movies, homie don't play that shit. One more giant kick to the temple for good measure, WHAM. Damn, the vibrations shook my leg, if he was awake before he wasn't now. I bent over and started laying a few practice whacks on Leather Jackets neck. Blood was squirting everywhere in rivulets and his neck was still pretty spaghettied from when I had shot him. It was a big, giant disgusting mess. I scooted back a bit to avoid any splatter as I whacked more of his neck away. Finally, after I don't know how many whacks I saw the bone of his neck. I lifted my arm all the way back and brought it down with all of my strength. POP GOES THE WEASEL, his head popped off and his whole body got all bubbly looking and then melted, yes that's right it melted. It was disgusting, I was standing in Dante soup... I picked up his leather jacket out of the goop and held it up in the rain and let it wash off some of the blood, goop, and mud. I walked over to Rook and pulled his Glock off of his hip and put it in his hand

"If she moves kill her," I told Rook.

I went out to my car and threw the artist, formerly known as Dante's leather jacket, up on top of the fence on the way. Once at my car, I grabbed one of the shovels, then came back. Rook and Lydia were still where I had left them, good. I stabbed the shovel into the mud so I wouldn't have to carry it and then started policing up all of the brass from the mud using my cell phone light and stuffing the muddy shells into my pockets. Once I had policed all the brass I could see, I went over to the Dante soup. I reached into the soup and pulled his jeans out with two fingers and searched the pockets. I found a cell phone and a wallet so I stashed them in one of my pockets after turning the cell phone off. I dropped the jeans and then wiped my hand in the mud and tried to let the rain wash it clean. I took my shovel and scooped up Dante's jeans and shirt and threw them into the hole that Lydia was once buried in. I threw a bunch of mud on top of it until it looked relatively flat and the clothes couldn't be seen. Then I went back to the Dante soup and flipped the dirt over a few times until the bulk of it was just mud and less corpse soup. The rain should take care of the rest, hopefully.

I walked back over to Lydia and Rook. "Lydia, is there any more visible brass laying about?"

She looked at me like I was crazy "How the fuck should I know?" said Lydia.

"Don't you have like cool vampire senses?" I asked her.

"I don't know I have been a vampire for like a week," said Lydia. Stinky ball punching vampire lady is useless.

"Rook can you walk?"

He appeared to think about it and then slowly sat up, "Ow," he groaned. He climbed to his feet but didn't look happy about it.

"Lets get the fuck out of here," he said.

I grabbed Lydia's left leg and started dragging her behind us. I looked over my shoulder at her and said, "If you see someone and scream I'm going to step on your head. Stay quiet, got it?"

She just nodded. Once we got to the gate I grabbed Dante's jacket off the top of the fence. The bulk of the goop had been cleaned off by the continued rain it had received. Sweet, SPOILS OF WAR, I threw on the jacket of top of my windbreaker.

"This is my jacket now, totally my jacket," I looked at Rook and Lydia.

Rook just looked tired but Lydia lifted one eye like I was crazy. People don't respect casual "Hot Rod," movie quotes like they should, and where the fuck did Lydia get off looking self-righteous while being dragged through the mud. Women, can't live with them, can't bury them in a hole and have them stay dead and non-vampiric.

I had them wait at the threshold of the front yard and I walked into the carport. They had a light under the eve of the roof illuminating the driveway. I stole Lydia's trick from earlier and unscrewed it slightly until it turned off, then I went back to Rook and Lydia. I unconsciously put my hands into the pockets of the leather jacket and my hand hit keys. Do vampires drive?

"Lydia, what do these keys go to?" I barked a little meaner than I had to be.

"They go to Dante's car and house, he drives a 68 Dodge Charger in black," Lydia said.

"It's on the curb, we can't leave an abandoned car here. We can't do anything else that will draw attention to us. I'm not really in the mood to explain how I liquefied someone to the police right now. I'm going to go out on a limb here, Rook, and assume you can't drive a manual transmission 1960's muscle car?" Rook shook his head in the negative.

"Okay, Rook you are going to drive my car to my house or to the hospital, your choice. I'm going to take little miss sunshine here in the vamp-mobile over there, we still have to meet Griffin tomorrow for beers, don't forget."

Rook thought about it for a minute, "I'll head back to your place, as long as my ribs didn't puncture a lung I should be fine. You got any painkillers?" said Rook. Wow, that was tough even by my standards.

"Uhhhh yeah, I've got some Tramadol from my dog Mia's surgery she had last year. I'll see you at the house bud, godspeed. Oh also if you can, you might want to stop a few miles away from here and pull the painter's tape off the plates," I said.

"Shit, I forgot about that. I've got some ibuprofen in my bug out bag here. I'll pop some now before I take off and pull over a few miles out until they kick in. After that, I'll pull the tape and Charlie Mike to your house. Are you sure you can watch her and drive?" asked Rook.

"Yeah I got it man, she still looks pretty busted up too so it shouldn't be an issue. Hey Lydia, what's the deal with that? Aren't you supposed to have vamp healing, is that a thing?" I said. I was still pulling Lydia by one leg and she was laying down on her back in the carport at this point.

She replied to me with "I'm a newbie to all of this but I'm pretty sure I won't heal much until I get some blood in my system, want to volunteer?"

Ha, good joke dumb vampire.

"Hard pass, alright everyone let's move out. Well, Lydia, you just keep laying there like the useless scum you are, I'll drag your ass to the car." Yes I was being a dick but my friend was hurt and my balls were bruised along with the rest of my body.

Chapter 5

I dragged Lydia's useless ass over to the car like I said I would and opened her door, there are no powered locks on cars from the 60's. I propped her up on the seat even though I was sorely tempted to throw her on the passenger floor in a giant pile. I got in on the driver side and closed the door. Before starting the engine, I drew my Glock and put it in my left hand. I gently rested it on my stomach but had it pointed in Lydia's direction.

"Lydia, if you try anything, and I think this should probably go without saying, but I'm going to say it anyway. I'm going to shoot the shit out of you and then cut your head off if it's the last thing I do," I said.

She just nodded again. I wasn't bluffing and she knew it. It was going to be kind of awkward holding the gun and running a manual transmission at the same time but I had gotten really good at driving with my knees in high school. I used to text and eat behind the wheel constantly. Yeah I know it's a shitty thing to do, I was a bad kid with virtually no parents. I don't do stupid shit like that anymore but it doesn't change the fact that the skill was paying off in dividends right now.

I had a lot of questions running through my head about everything; vampires, zombies, who the hell owned this car legally since Dante was a vampire, and many more. Time to get some answers.

"Whose car is this, like who is it registered to?" I asked Lydia.

"The car is legally registered to one of Dante's identities and it is all legal with up to date tags. Being a vampire is all about not drawing attention to yourself or your coven. Sure Dante could just eat a cop if he was pulled over but then there could be witnesses, dash cam footage, etc. It's easier just to do things the legal way".

So that had actually answered a lot of my questions, but I had more.

"So how did you get mixed up in all of this?" I asked her.

"Believe it or not I went looking for this, I..." Lydia said, but I interrupted her.

"WHAT, you wanted to be an undead, ball sack kicking, bloodsucker?!!??!!" I said.

"Wow you aren't going to let me live that ball kick down, are you?" said Lydia.

"Nope not until my balls aren't some hue of blue and you buy me a gold plated Ferrari, finish your story vamp tits," I said.

"Ok, uhh, where to start... Well, I had or have, I don't really know now anymore... I guess I had a type of Muscular Dystrophy and was soon to be wheelchair bound and destined to generally have a crappy life. Some people with MD really rock it and make it work, they stay upbeat, their treatments work well, and they live life to the fullest. I wasn't that type of person, I had a particularly shitty kind. The treatments weren't working as well as I wanted them to, and I had no family left and little to no friends. People don't want to be friends with the sick girl and the ones that do just felt sorry for me and it came across in every conversation, it drove me crazy. Science failed me so I turned to the occult, you wouldn't believe how much bullshit is out there. I kept running into a recurring problem though, either the magic didn't work or it required too much. A human heart from a virgin, or giving my eternal soul to some dark god or some such. I didn't want to become a monster, I just didn't want to die in a wheelchair alone and weak," said Lydia.

She was openly crying blood now, it was disgusting but I still felt bad for her. I was a sucker for sad stories, "Continue," I said.

"I'm sorry about these tears, I've never told anyone all of this, and none of this is going according to plan. It's been so hard and I've felt so much pain, and my poor roommate..." sobbed Lydia.

She stayed quiet for a minute and I was about to ask her to continue but she did on her own. "I had found the answer, becoming a

Vampire would cure almost any illness I had, and it would lock my body in a healthy state, but with a hitch; everyone who becomes a vampire always transitions into a terrible monster. A shadow of themselves with all of their worst personality traits amplified. As I said before I didn't want to hurt people and I didn't want to lose myself. I had to find a way to turn into a vampire without losing myself and killing the people who had been nice to me in life. No one had ever done it before, or at least there was no record of it no matter how deep I searched.

I had to invent what I thought would be the process I needed to continue being myself after becoming a monster. I found directions for a potion to lock your mental state in place for 48 hours. People like professional athletes and scientists would use it, or people trying to pass a test. They would learn everything they needed to know, get super motivated and then lock themselves into that mental state, super pumped up, motivated and happy, until their test or match was over. I was never what you would consider pumped up and motivated but I didn't want to turn into a bloodthirsty lunatic right after becoming a vampire.

I also found spells for keeping optimism and innocence and dispelling violent thoughts. I don't even know if they worked but I cast a dozen of them on myself.

Then I found directions on how to make basic charms, small things like rings for luck, rings of positivity, rings to bring you closer to nature, etc. I cast every enchantment I could find that had anything to do with sunshine and butterflies and put them on this ring I'm wearing here. Anything that even remotely sounded like it would help me maintain myself after the transition, I tried it, and did it 10 fold," Lydia said. She then she showed me the ring. It was a simple silver band but it had a dozen different colored stones socketed all over it.

"So what happens if you take the ring off?" I asked.

"I don't know, I'm too afraid to try, but it didn't stop me from almost eating you today when I was half starved, but that is a different story. I need to finish telling you the rest first. Once I had prepared accordingly, I started looking for a vampire which was harder to do then you would think. Vampires are elusive and do their best to stay off the radar, and they only eat homeless people or people with no connections left to the world. They don't want any missing persons reports filed, you see that could attract attention they don't want. Not every vampire is content with eating stinky homeless dudes, and there were patterns I could look for. Rich or at a minimum wealthy would be a dead give away for any halfway smart vampire. Dressed nicely of course, what's the point of living forever if you don't even take pride in your appearance, right?

They would only come out at night, obviously. They might be out of touch with modern times, living forever and being driven insane with bloodlust would probably put a real damper on trying to follow modern fashion trends I assumed. Basically, I had some baselines and ways to rule people out and to seek out people I suspected of being a vampire. There was a lot more to it than that but I'm just trying to give you some examples. I developed a serious algorithm for finding vamps. I was a student at ASU and we had some homeless in the area. We also had students dropout of school all the time and just never come back. I had no idea if that was vampire attacks or just lazy people, but this was as good as place as any to start."

I butted into her spiel "Wait, you were a student at ASU, what did you study?" I asked.

"I was a Women's and Genders Studies major," Lydia said.

"Oh, so you wanted to eventually be a sandwich artist at Subway?" I replied.

"You dick there are some decent jobs you can get with a Gender Studies Degree!" yelled Lydia.

"Yeah I think McDonald's is hiring those as well, I heard if you have one you can skip mopping and go right to flipping the burgers, anyway continue your story," I said.

"Well I started asking all the girls in my classes that bar hopped if they had seen any guys that fit my criteria, I explained to them what I was looking for. I guess I could have easily looked for a female vampire as well but I thought I would have better luck flirting with a male over a female. I got a lot of false positives at first, people I was sure were a vampire and they just ended up being horny businessmen trying to find a college chick to relive the glory days or something. I knew though when I saw Dante, something was up. First of all, he was dressed like an extra from Grease. While he was still dashing in his own light despite his antiquated fashion style, that wasn't what made my vamp alarm go off. He walked with this unnatural grace, the kind of grace only seen in dancers." said Lydia.

I butted in again, "So he was either a strangely dressed gay dancer, or he was a vampire?" I asked.

"I want to berate your closed-mindedness but you are probably right and I had the same thoughts. I approached Dante and purposefully let him know that I was alone in town and subtly dropped hints that I had no family. I also lied to him and told him that I was independently wealthy. As the night progressed he kept buying me drinks trying to get me to lose my wits and kept asking me more prying questions. Like where did I work, would my boss care if I quit, etc. I was positive he was one of them, I changed the subject to my illness and kept telling him how rich I was and how I would do anything to be cured. That morning I had taken the potion to lock my mental state, in case he was the real deal since the potion only lasts 48 hours. I was right about him, he took me back to his place that night and changed me into a vampire. It was terrifying and when I woke up the next day I knew I was changed. I had less emotion overall and a lot of inner turmoil. I was trying to figure out if my plan had worked, if I was still myself. I wouldn't really know until the potion wore off. I didn't even know if the potion was still working on me at all now that I was a vampire.

She continued, "Dante interrogated me thoroughly throughout that first day, of course, I had planned for everything. I had taken all of the money out of my bank and left it clearly visible in my purse to give the illusion that I was so ridiculously rich and that I wasn't concerned with carrying around large amounts of disposable cash. I had on clothes and accessories from the nicest stores that I had to max my credit cards out on to afford. I had to get away from him before he saw through my lies and found out that I wasn't going to be his new cash cow. I was afraid that if he found out I had deceived him he might just rip my head off and chalk up his loss. The way he asked me some questions I was almost forced to answer, he had some kind of influence over me. I don't really understand it and I didn't run into it in my vampire studies.

One piece of truth he was able to get out of me was that my roommate might alert people if I didn't show up back at the apartment soon..." Lydia couldn't continue and she started crying again.

I knew what had happened, "Dante came and killed your roommate didn't he? Your roommate was a loner too?" I asked.

She sniffed back her tears and continued her story.

"She was, we were both on the same college grant. A special fund for people who were formerly foster children, we met each other in the Bursar's Office. She didn't have any living family, and I am the one who told Dante all of this... I killed her by not being able to keep my mouth shut. The next few days after that when the potion finally wore off I was starving for blood, I was still myself but my body needed blood. I had planned for this contingency and bought large amounts of animal blood in cash from a butcher that was down the street from my apartment. I had told him it was for a college project and he was only too happy to make some money off useless blood anyway. I had frozen some and refrigerated some because I didn't know what was edible to vamps and if freezing it would ruin it for vampire consumption. Also, I had to spread it out and disguise it, I didn't want my roommate asking me why I had gallons of blood in the fridge. Dante wouldn't let me go home though, he made me do...horrible things to feed that week. I had

78

to get away from him. I planned day and night how to escape but Dante had me watched twenty-four hours a day either by himself or one of his lackey vampires, but I did finally escape and went on the run. That's when you found me today..." Lydia put on her best puppy dog eyes and stared at me waiting for a response.

"I don't trust you and I don't even know if I believe you if that is what you are wondering," I told her.

"So are you going to kill me tonight?" Lydia asked.

"No, I'm not a cold-blooded murderer. I'm not sure if it's even considered murder for a person who is already dead. If you don't attack me or Rook you will stay breathing or whatever it is you do, animated I guess. I have a friend who is a P.I., I'll have him look into your story or the parts of it I can tell him without saying the word vampire. If I find out you are lying or that you hurt an innocent person of your own volition then I will cut your head off."

Yeah, so I had a pretty unwavering moral code, fuck bullies. If it turned out that this young woman was just another victim of Dante's, then I truly didn't know what I was going to do with her, even if she got herself into this mess. What the hell do you do with a half-good recovering newly turned vampire anyway?

By the time she finished telling me her story we were pulling into my cul-de-sac. I backed the Dodge Charger into my garage where my car normally went. I didn't want my neighbors asking questions about a new car that I couldn't explain. The storm looked like it was finally dying off, Arizona is notorious for monsoons. In retrospect, that surprise monsoon probably saved us by covering the sounds of the ruckus we made in my customer's backyard. Rook hadn't arrived yet but that wasn't too surprising since he said he was going to rest in the car for a bit until his ibuprofen kicked in. I still wanted to make sure he wasn't dying of internal bleeding or something, so I shot him a text "Rook, how you doing bud, status?" he texted me back "Doing good, just finished resting, gonna pull the tape, be at your house soon." It was a huge relief to hear Rook was okay.

I jumped out of the Charger and told Lydia to get out, she looked at me like I was crazy.

"Spine is still fucked up from when you shot me, retard," said Lydia.

My garage door closed and I walked over to her side of the car, opened her door, then roughly grabbed her arm and threw her on the floor of my garage. She landed in a pile and said, "ow."

"Who's the retard now?" so I can be petty from time to time...

"Don't move," I told Lydia.

I unlocked my door and greeted my true best friend, Ms. Mia, she was happy to see me and made those doggy whining noises when she saw Lydia and then she started barking like crazy.

I yelled at her, "Mia, BE QUIET! Guard this door and don't go into the garage! Sit here in this door frame!"

I pointed at the open door that led into my garage. I swear Mia speaks English sometimes, because she padded over to the door and sat right down and continued growling at Lydia.

"Hey Lydia this is my dog Mia, be good or you will be her dinner."

I looked over Lydia for the first time really while not being attacked or on the run of some sort. She was fucked up, covered in dirt, mud, blood, other fluids. She had bullet wounds almost all over her body, and she stunk, hmmm what to do with stinky vamp lady?

"Change of plans Mia, wait here for a second."

I went inside my house and grabbed my oldest towels and laid them out on my living room floor, a few layers thick. Then I went back to my garage and told Mia to scoot over on the way, she moved then started following me. I grabbed one of the blankets Mia uses for a bed sometime and I threw the whole thing over Lydia.

"What are you doing!" Lydia yelled.

"You'll see," I said.

I loosely wrapped it all the way around her careful to leave it on the top of her head but I exposed her face so she could breathe. I wasn't even sure if she needed to breathe.

Then I lifted her up and told her, "If you try to bite me I'm going to headbutt you into oblivion."

I said it with more confidence than I really had because my head was still pretty swollen and bruised from the headbutt I gave her earlier today.

I carried her through my house to my hallway bathroom and slowly lowered her in. Not because I particularly cared about her well being but mostly because I didn't want to fuck up my bathtub.

"Are you trying to watch me take a shower, is this some kind of sex thing? Lydia asked me.

"Nope, I like my women like I like my coffee: creamy, sweet and above room temperature; besides ain't nobody trying to catch vampire herpes up in here. Oh and you smell like shit," I replied.

Then I cranked on the cold shower water, she wasn't happy, and I think she used every curse word in the book on me. I didn't really feel like trying to take her soiled clothes off and I didn't have any to replace them with so I just kept hosing her down. The water eventually warmed up and she complained less. I turned the shower off for a second and squirted a whole bottle of shampoo on her, then I squirted a whole bottle of conditioner on her, for good measure I squirted some hand soap on her too, then I had a "fuck it" moment and poured half my bottle of mouthwash on her too. I was laughing so hard at this point I didn't even hear what names she was calling me. I didn't really feel like rubbing it in so I just let her sauté in her soap bukake for a few minutes, then I cranked on the shower again and hosed her off until all of the soap was gone. She was still pretty gross but it was a huge improvement from before. I picked her up this time with more confidence, laughing always made me feel better. Then, I carried her into my living room and put her on the pile of towels I had made. This was the first time I had actually looked at her without her being covered in blood and dirt. She was mildly pretty, her mouth was just a tad bit too wide for her face but it fit her. Her features were soft, she was pale and she had light brown hair framing dark brown eyes.

I had no idea if anything she was telling me was the truth and she did look pretty chewed up, but I didn't really feel like being murdered in my sleep and I did need to sleep at some point in time. So I went to my garage and grabbed some 550 cord. I tied her legs together around her ankles just tightly enough that it wouldn't cut her circulation off if she had that. Then I tied her hands together and ran a few lines from her hands to my coffee table and a line to my tv stand. I didn't have any illusion that it would hold her but if she was trying to escape or off me, at least I would hear it this way when she would have to inevitably start dragging my furniture across my house. I also left a loose line between her hands and her feet. Then I took some duct tape and ran a few layers over all of my knots so she couldn't pick at them. She asked me for a pillow so I got her one and put it below her head.

"I'm starving and I am going to be in pain all night if I don't eat and heal," Lydia told me.

Hmmmm... "So Vampires can drink animal blood right?" I asked.

"In my studies, I had found historical documents from vampire hunters stating that the vampires they were chasing had often stopped to drink the blood of small animals in times of need, that's why I bought the blood from my butcher. My plan was to survive off of animal blood, but I'm not drinking your dog if that is what you are thinking" said Lydia.

"Ew, WHAT, NO, Ms. Mia is my world, you aren't touching her. I have some bloody steaks in the fridge, and a couple other meat products, I'll figure something out," I replied.

I went into my kitchen and grabbed my blender. I had no idea what I was doing, I opened my fridge and grabbed the steak I had bought earlier that week and opened the plastic. I tilted the packaging and got as much of the residual blood as I could out of it and into the blender.

Then I squeezed each piece of steak above the blender, I got a few drops of blood out of each. I had some ground beef in my freezer. I pulled that out and put it in a bowl with some water and put it in the microwave for 5 minutes. While that was cooking I poured some vodka in the blender with the steak blood-juice to add some volume. Then I threw in some Melatonin and some over the counter sleep pills into the mixture. I wanted this chick to sleep tonight and to not be thinking about eating me. I also threw in some Tylenol since she said she was in pain and I threw in a Tramadol as well and left the bottle out for Rook. You aren't supposed to mix booze with that stuff but she is a vampire she doesn't need her kidneys, I think. My microwave was beeping, the ground beef was defrosted. Underneath the meat, there was a mixture of water and blood.

I yelled into my living room, "Hey vampires can drink water right?"

"Yes, but we gain no sustenance from it, but it is nice to have a wet mouth," she replied.

Hmmm... I poured the blood and water mixture that had come out of the defrosted beef into the blender. Raw meat has blood in it too, right? I threw a few spoonfuls of the ground beef in the blender as well. I pulled out my pocket knife since at this point there was very little actual blood in the blender and I made a small cut on the inside of my arm and hovered my arm over the blender. Only a little bit of blood

85

came out, but too bad I wasn't bleeding myself out for this lady. I cleaned up my arm with a paper towel and then wet the paper towel down a bit and squeezed the pink blood-tinted water into the blender. Lastly, I topped it off with some orange juice for flavor. So we had ourselves a Roofied Screwdriver with a mix of animal and human blood in it, and a little bit of raw meat. I blended it up into a truly disgusting mixture, *wait a minute*.

"Hey do you like your blood warm or cold?"

She replied, "Warm, but I'm new to this."

I poured the mixture into the biggest plastic cup I had and microwaved the whole thing until it was warm. Then I grabbed a funnel from my garage and cleaned it out so it was free of oil and gasoline. I came back into the living room holding the cup and funnel, Lydia took one look at it and yelled "No way!"

"Sorry, chicky, but I'm not untying you, and you need blood. This is what I've got, take it or leave it, and be glad that I am trying to feed you at all."

She looked dejected and upset, and she refused to meet my eyes. "Fine" she finally said.

It was awkward but I got the whole cup funneled into her mouth and she greedily drank it.

"I hate to admit this but that was pretty good, it needed more blood though," Lydia said.

"Well that was all I had, we can go raid your blood supply tomorrow," I replied.

"My mouth tastes like orange juice and blood," said Lydia.

"Well I don't have an extra toothbrush, nor do I feel like brushing your teeth right now, but do you want to rinse with some mouthwash?" I asked.

"Sure," she replied.

I went and grabbed my mouthwash and a cup from the cabinet and came back. I lifted her torso up with one hand then tilted the mouthwash into her mouth with my opposing hand, this put me close to her. I set the mouthwash down while she gargled and I put the empty cup in front of her mouth so she could spit into it. She spit the mouthwash into the cup and then quicker then I thought she could, she darted closer and kissed me on the cheek. I instinctively let her go in case she was trying to attack me. She plopped back down on the floor, her head landing on the pillow.

"Sorry for scaring you, and I'm sorry about everything today. I know I'm tied up right now, you don't trust me, and this is awkward but I feel safer here than I have in a long time."

I didn't know how to reply to that. Then I heard my garage door opening. Rook dragged himself through my door, saw the Tramadol I had left out for him, and made a beeline towards it.

"How you doing bud?" I asked.

Rook grabbed a cup from my cabinet and slammed a few Tramadol down with some water.

After he swallowed, he told me "A little better now, really tired. I have some serious whiplash in my neck and my ribs are killing me, I really think they are broken."

"Hmm well you can crash in my bed if you want. I need to stay out here and guard Lydia," I said.

"Okay see you in the morning," said Rook.

He headed back down the hall to my room. I went into my man cave, an extra room I had in my house where I kept my reloading benches, knife collection, ammo stores, etc. and grabbed a loaded WASR magazine off of the desk in there. Then I came back out to the living room and realized how tired I really was. I rocked the fresh magazine into my WASR, and then took off my muddy, wet pants and both of my jackets. I laid on my couch in the living room with my WASR across my chest, the muzzle oriented mostly in Lydia's direction. Mia jumped up and crawled between my legs and then laid down with her head resting on my knee closest to Lydia.

She stared at Lydia so I said "Mia if she moves you need to bark and growl okay?" Mia barked when she heard her name, Mia is awesome.

"You have a smart dog but I'm going to bed, hey what's your name?" Lydia asked.

I was so tired at this point I just said, "My friends call me Bear," then I fell asleep.

Chapter 6

So Saturday morning was pretty awkward, I didn't think I would ever be sitting in my living room eating cereal with a girl tied up next to me, but here I was. When I woke up Lydia was fast asleep so I made myself some breakfast. I almost did the same for her, then I remembered she probably wouldn't like it unless it was coated in A Negative (the blood type she had drank the night before, mine...) I was quietly munching and thinking about what to do with her but I didn't have a lot of ideas. Rook staggered out of my room and went to the kitchen right for the Tramadol bottle. After he had medicated the shit out of himself with Tylenol and Tramadol, he headed my way. I gave him the finger over the mouth, the quiet symbol, and pointed to Lydia's sleeping form.

I whispered to him "Can you sit here with her for 20 minutes I need to run to the hardware store and grab some essentials."

He gave me a thumbs up instead of nodding, I'm going to guess his neck was still hurting him. I set the WASR right next to him and half mouthed, half whispered LOADED, SAFETY OFF.

I went to my room, took a shower and grabbed a fresh set of clothes. I grabbed an extra magazine holder for my Glock which I normally never wear outside of competitive shooting, but my life had changed dramatically in the last 24 hours. With the magazine holder on and the 17+1 rounds in my weapon, that gave me a total of 52 rounds. Seems like a lot for a trip to the hardware store but yesterday I had cut a vampire's head off. I went to the hardware store and picked up a few different lengths of chain and the most hardcore I-bolts they had. I thought about grabbing some padlocks, but I had plenty of different locks at home since a lot of gun purchases came with a free one. I also grabbed a bunch of different sized duct clamps, those are pretty much thin steel circles that can be adjusted larger or smaller with a screw on the side of them.

I had driven Dante's car to the hardware store. The car was legally registered and I knew it wasn't reported stolen because I had murdered the fuck out of the owner just last night. I also wasn't too worried about any of his vampire buddies seeing me since the sun was up and shining. On the way out of my house, I had also swiped Dante's wallet and threw it in one of my back pockets. When I was checking out at the hardware store I pulled Dante's wallet instead of mine intending to use his money, but when I opened it I saw over a dozen hundred dollar bills. I had to work hard to keep my face neutral so the clerk wouldn't see my surprise and excitement. A few thousand dollars may not have been a lot to an asshole like Dante who could just take cash from his victims or just sell a baseball card from 1920 or whatever the hell it was vampires did for money, but to me it was a small fortune. Don't get me wrong I lived VERY comfortably for a single man in his 20's, but that was only because I worked my ass off, owned an old house, and I had a small veterans pension for injuries received in Afghanistan. Even though I lived nicely, I was still basically living paycheck to paycheck, finding this money was amazing.

That asshole Dante may have been comfortable carrying around thousands of dollars but I wasn't. So on the way home I stopped at the bank and dropped off a cool $1000.00. I wanted to deposit more but I wasn't really sure on the protocols the IRS used to check into people so I didn't want to deposit too much. Maybe I was just being paranoid but it doesn't hurt to play it safe. I counted the rest of the money and I still had a little over a grand left, SWEET! When I got home Rook looked like he was ready to pass out but he was still performing guard duty admirably.

"Rook do you want me to drive you to the VA hospital or something?" I asked.

"Hell no brother, I'm not waiting in a Saturday line at the Phoenix VA, I'll die of old age before I am seen."

He wasn't wrong, the Phoenix VA was the place where dreams went to die. We had a few satellite VA clinics in the area that weren't too bad but they were closed on the weekends.

"Okay well, are you going to make it until then, what's going on with you?" I asked.

"Like I said before I think I have a few broken ribs, really bad whiplash, bruises, and soreness all over. My airway is clear though so I should be fine. I googled it on my phone and it said I can expect 4-6 weeks of pain for a broken rib..." said Rook.

Wow that was going to suck.

"Alright it's your call but please don't die in my living room, I like that couch."

Lydia was sitting up at this point listening to us talk but she didn't have enough slack to stand since she was still tied off to my TV stand and my coffee table.

"Good morning, Lydia," I said.

"Uhh... Hi. I slept really good last night, what did you put in that shake thing you made me anyway?" she asked.

I didn't want to tell her I had impromptu roofied her so I just said: "Sugar and spice, everything nice and a little bit of Chemical X!" I shouted.

"Is that the theme song to the Power Puff Girls?" she asked.

I had her off the subject of my roofie-colada so I kept her talking, "I've devised a more mobile set up for you Lydia and we need to get you some real clothes today. We, or really I, need to swing by your apartment and grab your blood supply. You wouldn't happen to have your house keys would you?" I asked.

She shook her head in the negative and her eyes looked haunted. She had probably lost them while she was in Dante's captivity.

"Well, don't worry about it I'll pick the locks. Write down your address and anything you want from your apartment and I'll grab it for you."

I threw her a pen and paper while we were talking. Her hands were still tied but she managed to get them and start writing.

"You are going to pick the locks? Who the hell are you James Bond?" she asked.

"Nope, just a Combat Veteran who spent too much time reading zombie and science fiction books as a kid and wanted to emulate the hero type characters," I said.

I got to work on drilling some holes into the foundation of my house right through the tile and carpet. I threw an I-bolt into the ground near Lydia, and then I threw in one in my hallway. Then I padlocked some chains to each one. The one connected to the I-bolt in the hallway was about 30 feet long, the one next to Lydia was only about 15 feet long. Then I had Rook cover me with the WASR as I put three different duct clamps around Lydia's neck. I had lined each duct clamp with a piece of duct tape so she wouldn't have to have sharp metal rubbing against her neck. I tightened each duct clamp down to the point that she wouldn't be able to pull it off her head, but I made sure she had more than enough room to bend her head and breath. Then I padlocked the shorter length of chain through the duct clamps so she was chained to the floor with about 15 feet of slack in all directions. I slowly cut her out of the 550 cords and duct tape from the night before with my Kershaw Blur pocket knife then backed up out of the range of her chain length.

"Well, what do you think?" I asked her, as she slowly stood up and stretched.

She looked to be in pain and I could see a couple of scabbed over bullet holes on her forearms and a few through the many holes she had in the once white t-shirt she was wearing. It looked like her bottoms were once some capri style jeans but they were so stained and torn they weren't really anything now.

"It's got a real Princess Leia vibe, I like it!" she put on a big goofy smile.

"I don't like that analogy. Jabba the Hutt wasn't a dashingly handsome blonde veteran and at the moment you are too stinky to be Leia, but we'll get you some clean clothes today," I said.

"What's the chain in the hallway for?" she asked.

"In case you have to make a... if you have to use the bathroom... for girl stuff? Basically, we just unlock your current chain from the I-bolt and then lock the new longer length of chain on and you can go to the bathroom with the door closed. Wait do vampires uhh, you know?" I asked, but she interrupted me.

"You can just say poop, Bear... I was a human last week, humans take dumps," Lydia said.

"OHHH WHAT!!! GROSS, YOU SHUT YOUR MOUTH, GIRLS DON'T TAKE POOPS! Everyone knows girls just go in the bathroom and a fairy flies around in a circle and sprinkles glitter everywhere," I said.

"Are you sure you're an adult? And yes, if a Vampire eats solid foods we have to expel it after our bodies pull what we can from it. Same with liquids but 100% of the blood we consume is used to fuel our bodies" said Lydia.

"Ok whatever, I need to go get your blood supplies before you try to eat Rook. Rook you good for one more watch on Lydia?"

Rook told me he was good to go but before I left I made him a steaming hot pot of coffee. I was starting to trust Lydia *but not taking precautions is stupid.*

I headed out again in Dante's car and headed towards Lydia's apartment. Before I had left, I had thrown one of my old olive drab military duffel bags in the passenger seat. You know the kind Sylvester Stallone had in the beginning of *Rambo*; yes the Army still issues those. I really wanted to bring my WASR but a rifle was going to be a no-go since Lydia's apartment was just down the street from ASU. Open carrying a long rifle near a state college is a bad idea. I really didn't feel comfortable going out with only a pistol though with everything going on so I had also grabbed a collapsible baton, my U.S. Palm vest, and a Kimber Pepper Blaster. If you haven't heard of the Kimber Pepper Blaster, it's a 2 shot pocket pistol that is powered by gunpowder based charges. It fires a clump of pepper spray accurately up to 15 feet and it's basically completely silent. If you shoot someone with it and it lands anywhere on their body, they are going to have a really bad couple of hours. If you hit someone in the face with it, their whole day is basically over.

I was worried about breaking into an apartment in the middle of the day or just being seen anywhere near the apartment of two young women who had recently gone missing. I needed a disguise of some sort. I googled where to buy a high end wig in my area and there was a wig store on the way. I stopped in and got fitted for a VERY nice wig, it was medium length brown hair with a little bit of a curl to it that came down to my shoulders. The best part about it was that it looked NOTHING like my hair which is dirty blonde. Once a month, sometimes once every other month depending on my schedule, I just shave my hair down to a close-cropped high and tight, then I let it slowly grow out until it starts getting bushy and repeat the process. My point being is that never in my life have I, or will I ever have shoulder length brown hair so the wig was perfect, I didn't look anything like myself. Before I left the wig store, I pulled around back and took my shirt off, then threw on my vest over my bare skin. It was Level III Soft Armor, which meant it could basically stop any pistol round and some rifle rounds even though it's not really rated for a rifle. It's pretty thick and made of tough material so it would offer some protection against knives as well. I threw my shirt back on over the vest and then my tan windbreaker over that. I would look a little puffy but for the most part, it was invisible.

I pulled in to Lydia's apartment complex and there were students everywhere coming and going. This must be near one of the times when people came home from or left to go to classes, it was close to noon. I waited in Dante's car, well my car now, YOU KEEP WHAT YOU KILL as the Necromongers say. I listened to music until the crowd thinned out a little bit but I didn't want to be stuck out here all day so I didn't wait too long. Once I got out and looked at the door of Lydia's apartment I just really had a bad feeling about this whole situation. I took inventory of my arsenal, I had the extendable baton in the collapsed position and in a nylon holster on my belt, and the Kimber Pepper Blaster in my right front pocket. I was also concealed carrying a Glock 19 but I didn't want to use that since it wasn't silenced. I had a little pocket knife as well but if I had to use that before all my other weapons it would be too late anyway. Once my life settled down a bit I really needed to look into getting a silenced pistol, it would be great to have one for stuff like this.

I walked around near Lydia's front door and pretended to be studying the landscaping and texting, but really I was just looking around seeing if anyone was looking this way. Once I was content that I wasn't being watched, I bent down in front of the door and pulled out my lock pick kit. It was just a small leather case with a zipper on it, full of different sized picks and tension bars. I scraped my favorite pick over the tumblers in her door a few times and kept up tension on the lock, POP. I was in, the cheaper the lock the easier it is to pick. Places like apartments with high attrition rates where things are constantly changing and being repaired are extremely easy to pick. I put my set of picks away and prepared to enter, again I looked around first. Then I pulled out my baton and put it in my left hand. I loaded my right hand with my Kimber Pepper Blaster. Using the last two fingers of the hand my baton was in, I slowly opened the door to the dark apartment.

"Hi there," I heard from a voice inside.

I looked in and it took my eyes a second to adjust. There was a man inside sitting on a beat-up recliner, dressed in 90's grunge. You know that whole slightly too baggy jeans with the flannel shirt thrown over a t-shirt deal. He had shoulder length blonde hair, a five o'clock shadow and he was aiming a silenced pistol at my stomach... Damn, I need to get one of those! Eh, what do I do... Lie lie lie.

"Does Dante know you are here?" I took a gamble, I hope this guy knows Dante but I prepared to jump out of the threshold of the door and away from his shot.

"Of course he does, who are you?" the man said.

"I'm Dante's friend. I take care of things for him during the day when he is indisposed," I lied.

"I've known Dante for 30 years and I've never seen you before, what's your name?" he asked.

"I'm Bear and of course you haven't heard of me, I'm Dante's ace in the hole. Did you think he told you all of his secrets? Listen he has been trying to get a hold of you but your phone is off or something so he sent me over to see what is going on here. Check your phone," I said.

The man switched his gun to his left hand and reached into his right pocket with his right hand to get his phone out. The second he looked down at his phone I shot a pepper ball right at his face and jumped further into the apartment before I could even see where it would hit. He must have reflex fired as well, either when my pepper ball hit him or when I moved because I heard a suppressed shot fly through the open doorway where I had been standing. When I landed I took another shot at his face with the pepper blaster while laying on the floor. I immediately started scrambling forward towards Lydia's tiny kitchenette. I careened around her little kitchen table as I heard suppressed shots smacking the drywall where I had just crawled from. I flipped the kitchen table over and hid behind it but a chunk of plywood smacked me in the face as he shot through the table at me, shit this thing isn't bulletproof! I jumped again, away from the kitchen table this time and took a peek at the Grunge Man. His face was covered in red angry capsaicin and his eyes were pinched closed. He had shot at the table when he heard me flip it over, HE WAS SHOOTING AT THE SOUND! I threw the now empty Kimber Pepper Blaster at the drywall closer to where I had come in. As soon as it hit the man fired the rest of the rounds in his magazine at the noise. He was using a 1911 in what looked to be .38. Super, those only have a 9 round magazine. If the stupid asshole would have had a Glock with my magazine capacity, I would have been in real trouble. He dropped his spent magazine to reload...

My time was now, I jumped up and sprinted at him with my baton overhead. He slapped his new magazine in, but I was already on him. I brought down the baton with all of my might directly onto his wrist, *CRACK.* The noise of the metal hitting his wrist bone was sickening and he cried out. Then he threw his hand straight out, he was still sitting in the chair so his push landed right on my stomach and I went flying. I flew all the way across the apartment and landed in the drywall leaving a rough Bear shaped imprint, I think my head had hit a stud. Ow. I slid down to the floor with the sunlight from the open door shining on me and tried to regain my senses. I still had the baton clutched in my hand.

Then I heard hissing right in front of me... the asshole had tried to rush me. He must have been burned when he hit the sun shaft that was on me, *okay so he is a vampire*. I probably should have figured that out from when he super threw me across the apartment... Now he was bent over in pain, burning from the sunlight and pepper ball treatment. He was trying in vain to rub the pepper spray out of his face and eyes and choking. I stood up and brought my baton down on his shoulder hard, he lashed out but his hand hit the sun and he retracted it back to the shadow of the apartment and held it in pain. I spun the baton hard and smacked him in the temple and he fell down.

Everyone is a tough guy until they get hit in the head with a baton. I grabbed one of his feet and dragged him into the light. His skin slowly started to burn and then bubble, then he just kind of popped like a giant zit. Luckily his internal fluid stuff only convulsed about an inch or two outwards from where his body was before gravity pulled it back down. It started congealing into the carpet around his charred clothes.

I slammed the front door closed and locked it, then I went through Lydia's kitchen drawers until I found some salad tongs. I also stole the rubber gloves off of her sink that she used for doing the dishes. The gloves were too small for me but I was able to get two fingers wiggled into them. I lifted the Grunge Guy's pants with the salad tongs and reached in with my partially gloved hand and flipped his wallet and phone out of the pockets and onto a dry part of the carpet. We had just made a lot of noise in our little tussle, I had to get out of here in case someone had heard. Even if they had, I figured I still had at least 10 minutes or so before trouble arrived, I think... I hope all the kids in the surrounding apartments were at class and whatever slugs that had punched through the walls hadn't hit anyone. Thinking about it, this was the third vampire I had killed or disabled... Vampires: 0, Bear: 3. I was getting good at this, but I had to admit if I hadn't blinded him with the pepper balls he probably would have handed my ass to me. It seems the trick to fighting vampires is to cheat, I can do that. Bear Christensen, the monster hunter, it had a nice ring to it.

I grabbed some paper towels and wet them down in the sink and then cleaned off his wallet and phone the best I could. After I was finished with them I threw both into my Army duffel bag. I also picked up his super sweet, but super illegal silenced 1911 and threw it into the bag as well. I used the salad tongs and threw the rest of his clothes into Lydia's garbage can. I pulled the milk out of her fridge and dumped it on all of the vampire goo. Then I filled the milk jug up again with tap water from her sink and poured it on the goo again, diluting it into the carpet. It wasn't perfect but it would have to do. I ran into the room that Lydia had told me was hers and I grabbed a bunch of clothes from her drawers and closet as fast as I could and shoved them into the bag. Then I went to her fridge and freezer and loaded all of her blood containers into the bag. She had told me that her roommate hated prune juice so everything in the fridge and freezer labeled prune juice was animal blood. I flipped the kitchen table back over and then looked around the apartment to see what was out of place. The holes in the drywall... How the hell could I fix those? I GOT IT! I ran into Lydia's room looking for posters or pictures on her wall. Lydia had a nice giant hand painted flower thing, I wonder if she painted that. What am I thinking, it doesn't matter, I've got to go! I carried the painting back into her living room and set it near the holes in the wall. I went back to Lydia's room one more time and I grabbed the nail from the wall and hammered it in near the bulk of the holes in the plaster using the mag plate of my Glock, then hung the painting up.

There were still a couple of holes that the painting didn't cover, hmmm... I ran to Lydia's bathroom with my duffel bag and grabbed the bulk of her girly bathroom shit. I was throwing in hair dryers, makeup, toothpaste, etc. Wait a minute... toothpaste. I had used toothpaste as a kid to hastily patch some drywall that my friend had made a hole in during a sleepover. I used my old childhood trick and filled the holes with white toothpaste and smoothed it out with my fingers. It wouldn't hold up to a close inspection but at a cursory glance, someone might not notice. I grabbed some more paper towels and wet them down and tried to wipe down everything I had touched. I didn't want to leave fingerprints anywhere in this place, but at this point, I wasn't even sure where all I had been, my body had been pounding with adrenaline since the fight with the Kurt Cobain look alike. I still did my best to wipe down everything I had touched. I really needed to wear gloves in the future.

I looked under her sink and found some bleach, I needed to kill any forensic evidence that I had left. I wasn't even sure if this would work if I just splashed the bleach around or what. I needed a delivery system that was better than just sloshing bleach all over the place. I looked back under her sink and found a bottle of Windex that was about half full, and popped the top off. I filled up the empty space in the bottle with bleach, mixing Windex and bleach is a big no-no, but I was in a rush. I don't know why I didn't just empty the Windex into the sink first before filling the remainder of the bottle with bleach, but I wasn't thinking straight and I was in a rush to get out of there in case someone had called the cops. I ran through the apartment spraying the shit out of anything I thought I had touched or anywhere I had been, even misting the air behind me as I backed out, better to be safe than sorry. I didn't want to inhale the noxious mixture I had made so I pulled my shirt up over my nose and mouth and made sure to check that no overspray was getting near my eyes. I had worked with chemicals too long in pest control to make that mistake. Once I had misted everything, I collected all of my weapons and tools, threw the duffel bag over my shoulder and backed out of her apartment, locking the door on the way out.

Chapter 7

When I got in the car and started heading back towards my side of town, I felt something wet run down the back of my neck. I reached back to check the dampness and my hands came back red, SHIT! My head was the only thing not clothed or armored during the fight. I must have hit something too hard when Grunge Man vampire guy threw me against the wall. I need to super glue this wound closed or go to the hospital... Or, maybe I have another idea. I had dated a girl the year prior who was just starting med school. She should be around this area and in her second year of med school now. I sent her a text asking her if we could meet for a quick lunch, my treat. I also told her that I had a cut that wouldn't stop bleeding that I had picked up gardening and asked her if she could bring some stuff to sew it closed. She sent me a reply text back pretty quickly telling me that she was very interested in meeting up. I had netted her in, I wasn't sure if she was happy to see me, happy to get some free lunch, or happy to sew closed an open wound, but if I could skip a long emergency room wait I didn't really care.

We agreed on a little Italian restaurant that I like in downtown Phoenix and met in the parking lot. I had parked my car around the side of the building out of view from the main road, I didn't want some random person to see my bloody head and call 911. She embraced me with a hug which was a surprise to me since we hadn't last seen each other on the best of terms. Her name was Emily and she was around 5' 4", maybe around 25 years old (I never ask a woman her age,) she had blonde hair that went slightly past her shoulders. She was very classically pretty, but not overly so that she would be a distraction in a social setting. She had blue-gray eyes and a cute little pert nose that matched her face perfectly.

"Well, do you want to show me this cut before we eat?" She asked.

"Yeah sure," I showed her the back of my head.

"You said you got that gardening! Let's head to your car and I'll see what I can do," said Emily.

We headed over to Dante's car and she was very surprised, "Whoa you got a new car, this is nice!" she said.

"Yeah I got a part-time job on top of my other, it's been pretty lucrative so far... but a little dangerous" I replied. She decided she would sit on the trunk of the car and I would stand between her legs with my back to her so she could work on my head. I was much taller than her, and I didn't really feel like kneeling down in a parking lot, so this was the best way she could get the height she needed to put my stitches in.

While she was fixing me up she said, "I can see you have a bulletproof vest on under this shirt, you have some brand new historical sports car thing, bruises everywhere, and a mysterious new job. Tell me Bear, is what you're doing illegal?" she asked me.

"You don't miss much, though I suppose most of this is obvious. I need to be more discreet and to answer your question, I am one hundred percent positive that there is no law on the books for my second job," I replied.

"Bear you didn't say you weren't breaking the law..." she said.

"There is no law to break, so yes my new job is completely in the realm of legality. I would like to tell you more but you know client privacy privilege."

I had lied a little, but most of what I was saying was true. I had scathed the Arizona self defense laws when I first got red-pilled on self defense trials, and to the best of my knowledge it was legal to kill vampires. While she was working I kept feeling wetness leak down my back and then feeling a burn, I think it smelled like rubbing alcohol.

"Alright Bear I'm all done here," she patted my shoulder hard.

I don't know why I did it but I spun around, looked into her eyes and just kissed her. She reciprocated but before we were done she pushed me away.

"Bear we are friends, but we aren't that kind of friends. You don't get to just call me out of the blue and have me answer your beck and call," she told me.

She was right, I was being way too forward. The year before we had gotten really close but, she was in med school and I was working full time and finishing up the renovations on my house among other things. We both sort of realized that we weren't going to sacrifice our professional lives for each other and had slowly drifted apart.

"You are right, Emily. I'm sorry, I've just had a rough couple of days and you were being so nice to me and you are so pretty in this afternoon light. I don't know what came over me, are we still on for lunch?"

Yep, I could be smooth when I wanted to be. She blushed and smiled, then hopped off of the trunk of my car and collected her things with her back to me.

Without turning around she said, "Yes Bear we can still do lunch, but not like that, your jacket and shirt both have blood around the collar."

Hmm... I can fix that. I took off the tan windbreaker, t-shirt and U.S. Palm vest before throwing them into my passenger seat. I turned and looked at Emily and caught her looking my way, she was trying in vain to pretend to be looking elsewhere. I wasn't in the best shape in the world, but I had a physical type job and I worked out once or twice a week. I pulled my t-shirt back on and then pulled out Dante's black leather jacket and threw it on over my t-shirt. It was full of holes but it wasn't bloodstained, the rain the night before had taken care of that.

"Bear that is full of holes..." she said.

"Yeah, but I am hungry and there is no blood on it!" I replied.

"Fine you caveman, let's go, and if your head gets infected and you have to go to a hospital, don't mention my name. The back of a parking lot isn't the most sterile location," she said.

We had an amazing lunch, she had some kind of special spaghetti and a Bellini. I had fettuccine alfredo with broccoli and chicken and a Hefeweizen. We caught up on everything we had been doing over the last year. We didn't bring it up but I could tell we both regretted drifting apart. Emily was nice and down to earth. I could tell she actually wanted to hear what I was saying versus just waiting for her turn to talk. I never really did get her opinion on guns; it was hard to talk about life without bringing them up for me since I had been in the military, nine out of ten of my hobbies involved them and I carried one on a daily basis. But from other dates I had been on, I knew some women went ballistic when they were brought up. I had been called everything from baby killer to insane asshole by leftist women for carrying a gun in self defense. So I tried to avoid the topic when I could in social settings. I had breezed over a few topics involving guns with Emily but her smile never faltered so maybe she was cool with them? If we ever got more serious, I would have to discuss it with her further. More serious? What was I thinking here... Did I really like this woman? My thoughts drifted some during the lunch, back to Rook in pain on my couch, Lydia chained to the floor and everything that had happened to me. I think Emily noticed because she recommended that I pay the bill and we leave.

I walked her out to her car and on the way there she looked at me and said "Listen Bear, I can tell you have a lot going on in your life right now and you were a little distracted at lunch. I had a lot of fun today, why don't you take care of whatever you have going on right now and call me for another date?"

Emily was great and that sounded fun but you never give away the upper hand in the world of 20's dating.

"Desperation isn't very becoming Emily..." I said sarcastically.

She laughed and punched me in the stomach surprisingly hard.

"Ow, okay yes another date sounds great, just don't beat me anymore."

We finished walking to her car and before she could say anything else I kissed her cheek, she smiled at me and threw her arms around me in a big hug. Her elbow was resting slightly on my concealed carry since she was shorter than me. When we parted she gave me a look that she knew what it was.

I started to stammer something out but she said, "Don't worry about it, I like manly men."

Wow, that was unexpected, she was definitely comfortable around guns. I could fall in love with this girl if she kept up this behavior.

"Hey, before you go... if my friends or I have any more of this kind of injury, would it be ok to call you? We could pay for your services of course, but we all lead busy lives and five hour emergency room waits aren't how we like to spend our time," I said.

"I guess that would be ok, it's super illegal but I have college loans to pay for... just keep in mind I'm not a hospital, just a med student and I don't really want to go to jail for practicing without a license so only bring people who can keep their mouths shut," Emily said.

WOW! Cupid's arrow straight to my heart... she was cool with me concealed carrying and she didn't give a crap about pointless overreaching government regulations. I needed to get away from this woman before I proposed. We had been getting close last year when we were dating, but I felt like I had learned more about her today than

114

during all of our other previous interactions. Today had been different for some reason and we had just clicked.

I headed home after lunch with Emily feeling a million times better. I didn't realize how much stress and anger I had been carrying around. Most of it had been wiped away at the flirty, relaxing lunch. My new leather jacket felt great, but as Emily had said, it didn't look that great with all of the bullet holes in it. That gave me an idea. When I got home, Rook looked worse for wear, like he needed to sleep. Lydia looked bored as hell and was sitting on my ottoman since it was the only furniture she could reach within the length of her chain.

"Did you get my blood I'm so hungry!" Lydia inquired.

I wasn't surprised, there had barely been any blood in the roofie-colada, cow juice, blood thing I had made her the night before.

"And you left me here with nothing to do except stare at your sick, butt picking friend over there," Lydia added.

"Bro! You been picking your butt on my couch?" I said to Rook with mock anger in my voice.

"Fuck you guys, I'm going back to sleep," Rook said as he got up and started heading to one of the back bedrooms.

I yelled after him, "Seriously if you need anything man let me know, otherwise I'll come get you when Griffin gets here."

I got started on making another vamp-shake for Lydia. I poured blood into my blender until it was about 70% full of the unknown animal blood from Lydia's apartment. I also popped in a few Tylenol in case her bullet wounds were hurting her. Then I put in a spoonful of raw beef, and topped it off with orange juice, a shot of vodka and some ice, and then hit the blend button. Again, it made a pretty disgusting mixture but I'm not a vampire so what do I know about blood smoothies. Since this one was frozen and not warm like the last one, I poured it into a giant margarita glass. There was still more in the blender so I put the rest in my fridge with the rest of the blood from Lydia's apartment. I brought it out to her and explained to her that I had made a blood-margarita of sorts and that she should try it. She was really happy about it and said it was tasty. I let her relax and enjoy her drink for a few minutes while I sat on the couch with my WASR that Rook had left behind.

I was about to speak with her but she spoke first.

"I smell a woman on you... I've been trying to figure it out this whole time but I'm new to this whole vampire thing. I smell you have been around a woman, she is young and pretty... I think. When did you have time to do that?" Lydia asked.

"How about I ask the questions? Did you know about the little surprise waiting for me in your apartment?" I asked.

Lydia looked really confused. "When I got to your apartment there was a Kurt Cobain look alike who tried to shoot me to death" I told her.

"That's Robert, he is one of Dante's top lieutenants. I didn't really get to know him, but I did speak with him a few times because he was one of my guards most of the time that I was at Dante's house. That creep tried to sleep with me a few times shortly after I was turned, and to answer your question, no, I didn't know he was at my apartment, and how did you get the blood out if he was there?" asked Lydia.

"Easily enough. I kicked his ass and then fed him to the sun."

I exaggerated a little bit, but I did win and it would be good to have Lydia afraid of me if she was going to be sticking around. She is a blood sucking monster after all. Besides, all semantics and self doubt aside, I'm a goddamn human fucking chainsaw. I've purposely thrown myself into an environment dominated by alpha males and I always manage to come out on top, Robert is a pile of goo and I'm the victor. Two men went in and one man came out, *THUNDERDOME BITCH!*

"Wow, the first time I tried to escape from Dante's house Robert picked me up and threw me across the room no problem. I can't believe anyone was tough enough to beat him," said Lydia. I knew that pain, he had used that same throw move on me.

"Well if you know what you are doing it's not that difficult to get the upper hand in a fight," again I lied. I had no idea what I was doing when I fought Robert and I was lucky to be alive.

"You are an interesting person Bear, now tell me about this woman you were with today."

Whoa, did she sound jealous? This is the same lady that had just tried to kill me and eat me the day before, right?

"I don't want to talk about that, but while I have you here I need to ask you a favor. Do you know anything about sewing?" I asked.

"Strange question, but yes. When I was younger, my grandmother and I would sew and make small things like pillows and blankets, that kind of thing... Why?" she asked.

I took off Dante's jacket and handed it to her.

"Can you patch up these holes, I've got some kevlar sheets I ordered online a while back that I haven't used yet. I'll get you them, some various black fabrics, and sewing supplies. You will be stuck here all day anyway just watching TV until I figure out what to do with you. Do you feel like having a project that will help me trust you?" I asked.

She took the jacket and agreed.

118

"Alright, well, my buddy Griffin is coming over in a couple of hours. If I am going to have a chained up woman in my house she should be presentable," I said.

I went and grabbed the duffel bag and dumped it out, out of her reach of course. I took Robert's wallet and 1911 out of the pile of Lydia's clothes and toiletries and put them in my man cave for now, far away from Lydia. Then I lifted the WASR to the low ready and told Lydia to back up. With one arm outstretched I removed the padlock from the I-bolt in the floor near her and oriented the gun in her general direction. Then I took the longer length of chain that was connected to the hallway I-bolt and padlocked it to the shorter length of chain around Lydia's neck. I never once took my eyes off of Lydia and I never let the gun waiver. If she had moved an inch, I would have taken her face off but she was good and didn't try anything.

She went to the pile of clothes I had made, which she could now reach with the longer length of chain attached. She picked through her things and grabbed all of her makeup and toiletries and a few different articles of clothes, and then dipped off into my bathroom and locked the door behind her. This was a very stressful situation. I hadn't been this stressed out since Afghanistan. Memories flooded into my mind of some of the shitty prisoner guarding details I had been on. One night in the sandbox, I had just fallen asleep but was shaken awake out of all people by the Captain of my company.

"I have a detail for you," he said.

"YES SIR" I robotically replied.

The staff sergeant I spoke about earlier in this story overheard what was going on and hopped out of his bunk and came over.

"Sir, what is going on? Why are you pulling one of my soldiers out of bed in the middle of the night?" the Staff Sergeant asked.

"He is going on a guard detail; we have some local truck drivers we have been using who were too afraid to sleep outside of the wire and be recognized by insurgents. They are sleeping inside the wire tonight but I need a guard detail on them," the Captain said.

With no hesitation, the Staff Sergeant looked at me and said "I'm coming with."

The Captain knew not to argue with this NCO, he just threw that kind of vibe around. The rest of that night we sat just outside a small circle of concertina wire laughing and talking as we guarded the sleeping locals. There were about 20 of them and only two of us, if the Staff Sergeant hadn't agreed to come on this detail with me I would have had to sit out there alone, all night by myself with twenty locals who may or may not have been terrorists. That situation taught me a lot about the military and men in general.

Good times and bad times... The military was never really for me. I didn't really like following orders and my favorite things to do in real life was to play war games and go shooting. Something that surprisingly the military does little of. There were units that specialized in that kind of stuff, but as a kid who grew up with asthma, a heart murmur and casual malnourishment, I would never be able to make it into one of those. It turns out you can't eat bologna and Ramen for 18 years and turn into a healthy Tier 1 warrior, *thanks mom and dad*. My heart and soul would be in it for one of those kinds of jobs, but my physical body wouldn't be. The doctors at MEPS ignore a lot, but if my paperwork had some kind of extreme combat arms job on it I would bet they would have been a lot less inclined to ignore my health complications.

I had joined the military to gain a sense of honor. I was a kid with nothing before I joined, I didn't want to be just another person. I wanted to be a noble warrior, I had high ideals. Once in the military though, it was nothing like that. The actual military is a strange mix of sexual harassment powerpoints, old men on power trips, and a lot of sitting around and getting yelled at for things you didn't do. I did well though, I tried my hardest and kept my head down. I earned a lot of accolades and was honorably discharged. I didn't know or care why everyone else was in the military but I had been in to earn my place in the world and I felt that I had done that. That was enough for me.

Chapter 8

I don't know how long I had been sitting there reminiscing on the couch, but at some point, Mia must have noticed my somber mood and crawled up into my lap. I heard my bathroom door crack open and saw some steam slip out. Lydia came out very self consciously staring at her feet. She was wearing a black loose fitting halter top that exposed a little bit of cleavage and some very tight blue jeans. Her light brown hair hung wet around her face. I could smell her girly shampoo and perfume from where I was. She was absolutely beautiful... She approached me, but had to stop when the slack in her chain ran out.

"I had to use your towel. I'm sorry, it uhh, smelled nice like you," she said.

"If this is some kind of vampire seduction magic I'm going to shoot you in the mouth," I calmly said.

"And there you go ruining a perfectly civil moment. I know you don't trust me and I know I have done some bad things, but I am going to earn your trust if it's the last thing I do. In a roundabout way, you probably saved me from a life of servitude in Dante's crew or maybe death depending on his mood. Dante was trying to groom me into a monster, you stopped that and then you probably should have killed me but instead, you gave me a chance. You are a good man Bear, and I am going to pay you back for all of your help and kindness," Lydia said.

"That's great and I am glad you feel that way but you are right, I don't trust you. You tried to kill me yesterday, you see these bruises on my face? They are from you. Who knows what would have happened yesterday during the fight with Dante if I hadn't had shot you first. Maybe you were going to go for my throat, I DON'T KNOW. It will take time for me to trust you and more than just words and your exposed cleavage," I said.

She didn't say anything else after that to me, she just turned her back away from me and sat down as far away as she could.

I chucked Lydia the remotes to my T.V. and said "Mia if she moves, start barking!" Mia barked in acknowledgment; I have no idea if Mia really understood me but she tended to bark after I gave her an order. Besides, it's not like Lydia knew if Mia understood me.

I went to my man cave and grabbed a beer and a cigar out of my mini fridge and then headed to the little set of table and chairs I had out back. I only smoke cigars on special occasions and that is if I can remember them so I end up only smoking one once every two years or so but it felt right to have one now. I could just barely see Lydia's location through my sliding glass door from the back porch. I lit the cigar and drank my beer and just reflected on everything that had happened to me in the last 24 hours or so. Dinner was coming up and I bet Rook was starving. I texted Griffin to bring 3 large pizzas on his way over and that I had the cash to pay for all of them and that dinner was on me. He sent me back an acknowledgment and said he would grab some "Pizza By Napoli," which is the best pizza in Phoenix. I poured some beer on my back porch.

"Thanks for dinner Dante, may you rest in hell."

I went back inside and collected all of my sewing supplies, various fabrics that I had used repairing clothes and furniture over the years (Mia was a hellhound as a puppy,) and I grabbed the extra Kevlar material I had ordered. I threw them in Lydia's general direction, picked up one of my favorite books and sat on the couch to read until Griffin arrived.

Griffin got there a few hours later. Rook was up then, refreshing his Tramadol which we were about to run out of. He had stopped taking Tylenol so he could drink some beers with us this evening. I opened the door a crack as Griffin's old Bronco pulled along the sidewalk in front of my house. I only opened it a few inches so Mia wouldn't run out and pounce on him. Mia was remarkably well trained but she still loved guests that she had deemed "good," especially my friends. I had my WASR shouldered with the buttstock snapped into place aimed at Lydia's back. She was still turned away from me ignoring me, but she was sitting down cross legged sewing on Dante's leather jacket. When I was out back she had put on that goofy MTV show "Teen Mom" and was listening to it but not looking at the screen. The front door came straight into my living room where Lydia was currently bolted to the floor, the length of her chain didn't enable her to actually reach the door but I wasn't taking any chances with my friend's life.

Rook took his pill and meandered over to the couch and gently sat down near me but as far away from Lydia as he could. Mia went and sat next to him and laid her head gently on his knee, her tail was wagging wildly knowing we had more guests arriving soon. Rook smiled down at her before letting his head flop back to rest. Mia can make anyone feel better. Griffin must have seen my door was cracked because he pushed it open with one of his feet and struggled his way inside carrying three pizza's, some wings and some two liters of soda. He came in and closed the door behind him before throwing the lock, veterans are paranoid and we like locked doors. He turned around and took in the scene before him.

Rook was on the couch looking like death warmed over in obvious pain and a little zoned out on painkillers. I was still standing and aiming my rifle at Lydia but I was covered in bruises and scrapes. Lydia was chained to the floor still sitting cross-legged but she had stopped working on the jacket to look up at Griffin.

"Hi, I'm Lydia!" she cheerfully said to Griffin.

"What kind of kinky shit is this? You guys know I'm married, right? This is a line I'm not willing to cross," said Griffin.

"Well I'm flattered that you would think of me that way Griff, but I'm also not interested in any ménage à trois with you and Rook, and don't act all conservative with me, I know how you and your wife pay the rent. Come inside and step away from that woman, get out of the radius of her chain please, and then we will tell you what is going on," I said.

Griffin was one of the funnier members of our group, he was somewhere between 5' 6" and 5' 8" but I had never asked him. He was a currently serving combat medic in the Army Reserves. He and his wife made a lot of money uploading videos of her vacuuming. Yes you read that right, he would upload videos of her vacuuming in different clothes, sometimes in skimpy stuff or lingerie, but mostly just regular old clothes. It seems strange but it's something single men don't see and it is a sought after thing for those chronically single guys who daydream while humping their 'waifus' (Japanese pillow wife, google it).

There are a lot of creeps out there and Griffin and his wife were raking in the cash as her popularity grew. Griffin ran the website and finances and she "performed," which basically boiled down to her vacuuming their apartment a lot. They had really clean floors and they made great money. Griffin had even once told me that they had sold a pair of her old stinky tennis shoes for $1,000.00 to one of her fans. Griffin had light brown hair just a few shades darker than my own dirty blonde hair. He kept his hair more close-cropped then I kept mine since he was still in the military and had to adhere to their grooming standards. I would say he had the build of a welterweight boxer, kind of short but you could tell he worked out and was in great shape. I would like to think I am the funniest member of the group but if I was honest Griffin probably had me beat in that department.

Once Griffin was safely on my side of the room I had him set the food and drink on my kitchen counter and we grabbed some beers. I gave him a quick rundown of everything that had transpired in the last 40 hours or so.

"So what's the punchline?" Griffin asked.

"No punchline amigo, I'm telling you the truth. I've been too busy to really interrogate Lydia, and Rook thinks he has some broken ribs so he has been resting mostly." I said.

When Rook heard his name he held up the beer in a salute towards Griffin and I, and just kind of smiled stupidly. Mixing painkillers and alcohol, ALRIGHT! I don't advocate abusing drugs like that but the dude did have broken ribs, he might as well have a reprieve. Griffin just stared at me as if waiting for me to tell him the jig was up and that this was some giant joke. I told Griffin to stay where he was and I set my WASR down on the kitchen counter next to him.

I headed back to my man cave and grabbed my most balanced throwing knife. Throwing knives isn't exactly a skill I had kept up on. When I was younger and full of piss and vinegar I had tried to master every martial art including throwing knives. I had basically gotten proficient enough where I could sink a knife somewhere near the target about half the time and called it good. Realistically, if I ever got into an altercation with a crazy, I was going to shoot them, not try to fumble around for some throwing knife. I came back to my kitchen carrying my throwing knife and without warning, I threw it as hard as I could at Lydia's arm. I missed the mark and it lodged squarely in the back of her shoulder.

"WHAT THE FUCK!" both Lydia and Griffin yelled, though Lydia followed hers up with a quick scream and an OW.

Rook just started laughing and then stopped when he realized the action was hurting his ribs. Griffin was just staring as Lydia reached behind her and ripped the throwing knife out. I went into my fridge and grabbed the blender full of Lydia's gross blood power drink and poured her a cup. I lifted the WASR with my right hand and put the drink in my left hand and approached Lydia.

"Let's trade, throw the knife somewhere near my kitchen and I'll give you this drink," I said.

She complied and chucked the knife as hard as she could at the drywall near my kitchen, it hit back end first and plopped onto the carpet, *it's not as easy as it looks*. She took the drink and then continued giving me the cold shoulder. If she wasn't pissed before, she really was now.

"I'm sorry Lydia, I just had to prove to Griffin over there that I was telling the truth," I said.

I returned to Griffin and snapped up the throwing knife on the way.

"So do you believe me now?" I asked.

"I really don't want to, but I think I do," said Griffin.

"Lydia will you please show Griffin your shoulder, it would mean a lot to me," I asked Lydia.

Without answering me she lowered her shirt a bit and showed Griffin her shoulder, in front of our eyes the wound was slowly closing.

"Why don't we all sit down here close to Rook and Lydia, within reason, of course and I'll bring some beers," I said to the room.

Lydia got as close as she could to us which was about 4 feet away from Rook's position on the couch. Griffin and I sat cross-legged about the same distance away from Lydia on my living room floor. I carried over all the food, drink, pizza, and a six pack of one of my favorite beers. We were kind of in a loose circle now, as close as we could be but still out of Lydia's reach and if she decided to lunge the slack in her chain would run out.

Lydia stretched her arm out and grabbed a beer, "Can you drink that?" I asked.

"I don't really know, to be honest. Dante had me on an all blood diet at his house but you have been putting orange juice in my drinks right?" she asked.

"Yeah, but just a little" I said.

She popped the top and chugged a huge part of the beer, then she waited a minute and we all watched her waiting to see what would happen, nothing did.

"Damn this beer is pretty good, what is it?" Lydia asked.

"It's a canned hefeweizen with honey flavor added," I replied.

"I feel like it might be better with a little bit of blood in it, but it's hard to tell," said Lydia.

She then took her cup of blood shake I had handed her after the throwing knife incident and poured the rest of her beer into it. Then she took another big gulp and burped while giving me a thumbs up. Griffin just stared at me.

"She was an ASU student." That was all I needed to say. ASU had been rated top party school in the nation for more than a decade and had alcohol related injuries every weekend.

"You guys are so cordial around each other. Why do you even have her chained up?" Griffin asked.

"Remember the part of the story I just told you where she tried to murder me?" I asked.

"Uhh yeah, I can see where that would put a damper on a budding friendship," Griff said.

"In my defense, I was starving and acting on pure instinct, but I am sorry..." Lydia said and then she looked down at the ground.

"What's the deal with that anyway, how long can you go in between meals?" I asked.

"Dante's crew was hesitant to answer my questions, or maybe they just didn't care enough since I was the low woman on the totem pole in his crew, or really the beginning of my stint in indentured servitude. From what I gleaned in my research before changing, newer vampires have to eat every day to control themselves. Older vampires are more in control of their faculties and can eat once a week if they don't expend too much energy. I have no idea how long it takes each vampire to settle down or gain control, whatever they call it," Lydia explained.

"So at a minimum, you are going to need some animal blood every day. Does it taste good?" I asked.

"The stuff you made tastes good but you have it all doctored up with extra ingredients. I have no idea if just straight animal blood tastes good but I don't think I'm going to try it," Lydia said.

Then she reached out and grabbed a paper plate and a piece of pizza. She drizzled some of her blood shake all over the pizza and took a big bite. Griffin and I sat there shocked.

"That's pretty good!" Lydia said.

"This is too weird," Griffin said.

Rook just sat behind us grinning and sipping his beer. How much Tramadol did he take?

Griffin's combat medic side must have kicked in because he jumped up all of a sudden and headed over to Rook and then put his hands down Rook's shirt without even asking him first. Then he felt all around Rook's ears, head and neck, he even squeezed down Rook's legs. He went back to his torso and began touching things and asking Rook about when he felt pain and what it felt like.

Griffin stood up and announced "He probably has some broken ribs and maybe a mildly cracked sternum. Technically they are mild injuries but he really needs to rest. The only way to check for sure would be to get him some x-rays."

"I think he plans on hitting the VA Thunderbird Satellite Clinic on Monday for that. They will give him pain meds too," I said. Rook overheard me and gave us all the thumbs up.

"So Lydia, while we are all here chillin' like villains, why did you tell us yesterday that we had to chop off Dante's head right away or he could get back up, but it took you all night to barely heal enough to stand. Wait, let me guess I've read a lot of Science Fiction and Fantasy books, the older the vampire the more powerful they are?" I asked.

"Bingo, sort of. Dante was the oldest one in the local crew, coven, whatever they call it and I think he was only around 120. If you couldn't tell he really liked the 50's and 60's and never got over it.

Robert, the guy you killed today I think was around 50, vampire years that is. I don't know how old he was before he died, the first time. Yes, if you couldn't tell, again he had a major hardon for the 90's, specifically for Nirvana and Kurt Cobain. I'm not so sure it's the age that makes them powerful, as much as the blood. Blood straight from something living gives us the most sustenance, human blood especially so. We do get sustenance from blood bags, or stored animal blood like this but not as much. Keep in mind most of my information is from books, not actual vampires, but I think the more blood they, or rather we, drink, the more powerful we become," Lydia finished.

"Let's back up to the part where you were telling us about Dante's house being full of treasures and lackey vamps," I said.

"Yes, Dante's house... Well, he always had four or five vampires there counting Robert, but you took care of him. He also had two 'daytime' guys, humans. One guy gets there really early, a few minutes after sunrise. The other one comes around noon, and then the first guy leaves shortly after. On top of the vampires that live in his home, something else comes around every few days in the evening. It looks like a man but it feels dark... I'm not sure what he was but he gave me the creeps. I could tell he wasn't a vampire because he had a heartbeat but he just put off this aura of evil. I think Dante called him 'The Broker'. Sometimes he would try to buy Dante's treasures or sell him more. You know, I'm calling them treasures but more likely they would be considered valuables or antiques. I didn't get to see them all because I was confined to my room most days but there was so much to look at, I was a little overwhelmed. Dante also had a few rare magical and cursed items. A lot of magical artifacts don't actually work for you unless you have a heartbeat though, so most of them were useless to Dante but I think he liked feeling powerful by being surrounded by so much wealth" said Lydia.

"So why doesn't one of his lackeys just steal some valuables, run off, and get rich? Why live under Dante?" I asked.

"For one they are terrified of Dante, he is young for having accrued so much clout and power. He wasn't necessarily the strongest, but being cunning helped him succeed where others had failed. Those who swore fealty to him knew him to be amazingly smart and vicious. The only reason you were able to best him is because he was beating Rook to death and he underestimated you. He had been the King of Arizona for so long he had grown arrogant," said Lydia.

"What do you mean King?" I asked.

"Well every state has a 'vampire king', I think Dante was really only the king here because no one else wanted it. All this open desert and sun with no cover is bad for vampires in more ways than one. He wouldn't be able to be a king in a different state, the vampires there would be too powerful. Vampires like a place where they can blend into a crowd, places with lots of shade and hidey holes. Places where people go missing already, so a few more missing won't draw attention. Places like Chicago and New York City are meccas for vampires for all of those reasons. Back to Dante, one of his crew who was trying to scare me into submission told me that a few years ago one of Dante's crew tried to take the crown and shot him with a magical handgun. The bullet bounced right off his leather jacket. Then Dante snapped the attacker's neck before anyone had even seen him move. I don't know how your shots went through his jacket." Lydia finished.

"Throw me his jacket," I said.

She chucked it over and I caught it out of the air, I could see she had started work on it in multiple places. I picked one of the bullet holes that she hadn't started on yet and pried back some of the leather a little bit, sure enough, there was a very slim layer of kevlar that had been coated in some kind of green stuff.

"It's a got a kevlar lining, a pistol bullet wouldn't be able to pierce this, but I was firing 7.62 by 39 through an AK variant. 7.62 don't give a shit about soft armor," I said and threw her back the jacket.

She pried the jacket apart a little where I had. "Oh see this dark green stuff on it, this is a very basic curse shield it can block some kinds of magic," Lydia said.

"Wait, magic is real too?" Griff asked.

Lydia and Griffin started a side conversation about some of the in's and out's of basic magic. Lydia was basically saying how it was more trouble than it was worth nine out of ten times, and how most magicians had to give some piece of them self away or were destroyed by their own magics in the process, which is why magic isn't common, it's not worth the price. I zoned out though, thinking about Dante's house.

Hmmm... the opportunity to secure countless artifacts, treasures and valuables. It wouldn't even be stealing since the owners are already dead, or undead really. There was more to it than that though. The vampires in that house had been hurting innocent people for a long time and would continue to do so unless we stopped them. It's not like I could just call the police and tell them there were some vampires that needed slaying. They would throw my ass in the loony bin. I also didn't want to send some unsuspecting police officers to their deaths either. No, this was my problem. I had a chance to be an honorable warrior, and make some money in the process... I needed to run some things by my friends.

Chapter 9

I told my friends my proposal and the decision I had come to. I was going to kill the vampires in that house, and get rich doing it. I could never forgive myself If I let murderers roam free in my city. I also couldn't exactly leave possibly millions of dollars in valuables lay unclaimed either, I mean come on, who would?

"Welp, you are nuts but you are right," Griffin said.

"I'll do what I can to help," said Lydia.

Rook just held his beer in the air and said: "IN."

Like I said before, my friends are awesome.

"Dude, Rook is all jacked up, we can't trust this she-vamp, no offense lady. I'm also not too excited about just you and I as the only able bodies here against a nest of vampires, we need more help," said Griff.

"Let's call Zach," I said.

Zach Siler was the last of our childhood crew that was always hanging around when we were growing up. He had about Griffin's proportions body wise but he had very dark hair, paler skin and sharper facial features. He kind of looked like a less handsome Zac Efron with a longer chin. I always thought it was funny that he shared a name with that actor because they did look a little similar. He always had some fancy undercut style hairdo much like the actor. Maybe it wasn't as fancy as I was making it out to be but I cut my own fade into my hair in my bathroom mirror myself so any haircut is fancier than mine.

Zach had joined the Army leaving high school like me and the rest of my friends. He had become a military mechanic and was promptly deployed to Afghanistan. I never really talked to him about his deployment but whatever happened to him there probably wasn't good, that was just the vibe I got from him at least. I knew he went out with patrolling convoys in a wrecker which is a very dangerous job. "Wrecker" is military slang for a long truck full of mechanic tools, spare parts, winches and a giant tow hook. I had a lot of respect for those guys that went out in the wreckers. Imagine having to try and fix an 18-ton vehicle in a combat zone while radical Muslims are trying to kill you, no thanks. That took a major set of cojones, Zach is a badass.

Griffin stepped out of the room to call Zach and invite him over. I'm not sure what he was going to say to him but he was trying to soften the eventual blow of finding out that I had a vampire woman chained up in my living room. Zach had two kids so I wasn't sure if he was going to be able to make it over, even for something exciting. We had been extremely close before we both left to join the military but I barely saw Zach these days, maybe once a year or so. We were both busy and had our own lives. Adulthood does that to you, you just drift away from people you were once deemed inseparable with.

"So you are really going to do this, raid a vampire den?" Lydia asked.

"Yes, I wasn't cut out for this life," I swung my finger in a circle above my head.

"For living in a mid-size suburban house?" asked Lydia.

"No, for being normal... Working a 9 to 5 bullshit job that I don't give a shit about until I get old and die. That's not for me, part of me feels like I should have died in Afghanistan. The other part of me knows there is more out there. I've always dreamed of being an honorable warrior and the military couldn't provide that for me. I've never been afraid of death in combat but dying old in a nursing home, that fucking terrifies me. This is my chance to do something honorable, something meaningful," I said.

"Bear... I just don't want to see you get hurt. I just met you... and..." she stopped talking for a moment and stared at the floor, before resuming. "I just don't want to see you get hurt, you are acting like some kind of samurai and talking about honor. You don't have to do this," said Lydia.

"Wait a minute, how do you know what a samurai is Ms. Gender Studies?" I asked her.

"That stupid Tom Cruise movie '*The Last Samurai*,' it's one of my guilty pleasures," said Lydia. *Lydia just went up a notch in my book.*

Rook was the only other one in the room with us. He turned to us in his drunken haze and made some smooching noises with his mouth. I chucked an empty beer can in his general direction.

Griffin came back into the room, "Alright, Zach is on his way over. I basically told him to expect some weirdness and to keep an open mind. I filled him in on some other parts but left everything very vague, and I didn't mention the '*V*' word," said Griffin.

I popped open my third beer and sat back down in our impromptu talking circle. That dumb show "Teen Mom," was still on, Griffin sat next to me. Every once in a while I sing goofy little tunes to make people laugh or to break the ice. So I jokingly made an 80's rock ballad up and sang it.

"WATCHING TEEN MOM IN MY LIVING ROOOM! WITH A VAMPIRE I HAVE CHAINED UP!" I finished my song and everyone giggled. I'm a terrible singer but that only makes my singing funnier, ha.

We sat there sipping beers and nibbling on pizza until Zach arrived. We let him in through the garage so he wouldn't have to go in the door near Lydia.

Griffin walked him into my living room and he stopped and stared for a bit and then said, "Not what I was expecting..."

I got up and grabbed a bunch of my cheap silverware and started walking back towards the group.

Lydia shouted, "BEAR YOU BETTER NOT THROW THOSE AT ME!" I laughed and then I chucked the pile of them at her feet. It was just spoons, forks, and butter knives.

"Will you bend those into the word Zach, do a good job please, make it artsy."

I saw the relief on Lydia's face when she realized that I wasn't going to throw silverware at her again. She picked up a bunch of them and then amazingly fast started bending them and intertwining them until she had them bent into the word "Zach" in a very stylish font. She had even used a few to make a base to hold all the letters into place and then she stood the whole thing upright.

"Wow that is amazing!" said Zach, he then started walking forwards towards Lydia to grab his cool new nameplate. I jumped up and put my hand on his chest.

"Don't go near her, she is a vampire," I said, Zach just stared at me incredulously. "Lydia, show him something else please," I asked her.

She put her tongue in her cheek like she was thinking, and then she looked up at us. The room felt like it got a little colder. Lydia's face almost looked like it had lengthened and then her mouth cracked open and gruesomely long fangs extended out of her maw. She snapped her teeth together loudly and hissed, then before I could even tell the difference all of the changes receded and it was just Lydia again smiling at us.

Zach looked baffled, "Cool special effects guys, but what is this all for?" He didn't look so sure of himself when he said that.

"You know that wasn't special effects Zach, this is real. She is a vampire. Rook is lying over there in a pile of sorriness because a different vampire broke his ribs before we killed it. You know what I'm telling you is the truth, I know this is hard to accept man but this is all real and we need your helpm" I told him.

"Give me one of those beers, please," Zach said.

Griffin threw him a beer, he opened it up and drank half of it.

"This is just a lot to take in..." Zach said, and then he fell back onto my couch. We spent the next 30 minutes or so filling him in on the last 48 hours assuming he believed us since he didn't confirm. We were trying to catch him up the best we could. Then we told him our plan to raid Dante's house soon.

"We need another set of eyes and another trigger puller. Griffin and I would be point, we just need you to cover our six. We know you have kids to care for, we would do our best to keep you out of danger, but if everything goes right there should be enough loot in that house to put both of your kids through college," I told him.

"I do love loot..." Zach said.

"Can we count on you, will you help us?" Griffin asked.

"Just quit being a pussy and say yes," said Rook.

Zach looked around the room one final time and seemed to think about it. "I'm in."

The Semen Demons were back together, okay that name probably wouldn't fly now that we aren't all 14. We need a new crew name, I'll put that problem on the back burner for now.

That night, we started planning our raid. We all decided we would at a minimum, need a week to get all of the gear, equipment and full plan together. We didn't want to wait longer than that since Dante was "missing" and end up having one of his lackeys decide that now was the best time to steal some of the best valuables and run off with Dante gone, but we had a plan to even cover that. I had Robert's cell phone. I asked Lydia if she had any idea if Dante ever took off for

vacation. She mentioned that she thinks she heard that he goes to

Mexico every once in a while to eat some senoritas. Later that night I

would drive far away from my house, turn Robert's cell phone on and

text one of the lackeys pretending to be Robert. I would tell them that

we had caught Lydia and were going to take a vacation to Mexico and

that they should hold down the fort. Then I would turn the cell phone

off, I didn't know what kind of capabilities these vampires had and

didn't want them tracking the phone back to my house, better to be

safe.

I wanted all of the boys to have soft armor and maybe hard armor.

As I had learned from that assclown Robert, vampires weren't afraid to

use firearms. I didn't want any of my best friends to get shot, so we

would need to armor up this week. I had plenty of money left over

from Dante's wallet to get a few more vests. I hadn't even checked

how much money was in Robert's wallet or tried either of their bank

cards. I would be more hesitant to use the bank cards if the owners

were alive, but since Robert and Dante were both smelly piles of

vampire soup they wouldn't be reporting the cards stolen anytime

soon. Bottom line was: we had the funds to get basically any

equipment we would need, now we needed the plan.

We weren't really sure if we should go during the day or at night. The day seems like the obvious answer against vampires but it isn't. We didn't want to kill humans, and Dante had daytime human guards. Lydia had told us she didn't even think the guards knew Dante was a vampire. They thought he was just a paranoid rich guy, either way, they weren't exactly going to let me walk up to Dante's front door, kill everyone inside and then load up his shit and drive off. Also during the day, the neighbors would be awake which would mean possible witnesses. Lydia had told me the nearest neighbors were at least three quarters of a mile away, but it wouldn't be worth the risk. We discovered something else when we were bouncing ideas off of each other: if we went at night we might have fewer vampires to face. Some of the lackeys went out at night, not necessarily to feed since that draws a lot of attention but just to explore the city and not go stir crazy. If we commenced the raid at night there might only be one or two inside that we would have to deal with. Then we could set up some kind of fatal funnel near the front door and wait for the rest of the vampires to dribble in from their nightly activities and just shoot the unsuspecting bastards to death.

We had the beginnings of a plan but it was getting late. The guys helped me clean up. Even Lydia had tried to help but couldn't do much from her chained position. Zach had to take off first to get home to his kids. Griffin stayed long enough to help me cover Lydia with the WASR as I switched her to the longer chain so she could use the restroom and get in pajamas. I could have done it myself but I had been drinking and Griffin just wanted to make sure no one made a dumb mistake that would end in blood. Once she was done in the bathroom and back on the shorter chain, Griffin took off for the night. Rook had fallen asleep on the couch and looked comfortable so I didn't wake him. It was Saturday night, a lot of people I knew were probably out drinking and partying. I was at home planning a raid on a monster den with a chained up vampress.

I gave Lydia some proper linens and threw her one of my old military sleeping bags as a base so she wouldn't have to sleep on old towels like the night before. I threw a quilt over Rook, I wanted to go sleep in my bed but I couldn't leave Lydia out here unattended with Rook, even if he was out of reach. Hell, I probably couldn't or shouldn't leave her unattended at all. I pulled out another one of my sleeping bags and put it on the carpet at the edge of my living room before it turned into the kitchen, about 20 feet away from Lydia. I didn't want to fall asleep before Lydia did, or let her wake up before me so I set my alarm for 5 a.m. and turned the volume way down. I wish I would have thought of putting sleeping pills in her blood like last time. I threw on that movie *The Last Samurai* since I had to stay awake anyway and I knew Lydia liked it. I curled up in my sleeping bag and threw the WASR over the top of me with the safety on. Lydia gave me the thumbs up and a cute little smile when she saw what movie I had put on. She made it through about half the movie before passing out, I went to bed shortly after her.

I was the first to wake up the next morning which is a good thing. I wanted to trust Lydia but I haven't gotten this far in my life making stupid mistakes. I made some bacon and pancakes for everyone, the perfect Sunday morning breakfast. I also blended up some blood with fresh strawberries and orange juice for Lydia, I put my signature spoonful of raw meat in there as well. When she took her first sip she was pleasantly surprised.

"Bear you are going to have to write all these blood recipes down for me, these are great," she said.

I carried some plates of food over to Rook and Lydia. I set Rook up with a little wooden tray so he could eat on the couch.

"I was surprised to see you slept out here last night, were you afraid Lydia was going to suck my blood?" Rook asked.

"No, I didn't want Lydia to take advantage of you and steal your virginity, someone has to protect your maidenhead," I replied.

Lydia snorted hard and had to swallow the blood covered pancakes she was eating so she could laugh properly.

"I'm going to head over to Scottsdale Gun Club at some point today and buy some soft armor for everyone. Would you mind being Lydia's prison guard while I am gone?" I asked Rook.

Lydia looked a little dejected at my question, but I didn't care. You can't guilt trip me into doing stupid stuff, like leaving blood-sucking monsters unguarded.

"Dude if you are buying me a vest I'll do whatever you want, I'll give you a Z.J. right now bro. I've wanted my own soft armor for a while. Don't ask too much of me though. I'm in a lot of pain and I plan on lying on your couch most of the day today," Rook replied.

"That's fine, take the WASR, I just need you to shoot her if she gets squirrely," I said.

"Can do, but I don't need the WASR," said Rook, and then he tapped his waist where his Glock was concealed.

"No way dude, if you are going to shoot her it has to be with a silenced weapon," I said.

Rook begrudgingly took the WASR and leaned back further into the couch.

"Can we stop talking about shooting me please?" said Lydia.

151

Rook and I both looked at each other and then at Lydia, "NO," we both said in unison.

"Wait what's a ZJ?" asked Lydia.

Rook and I both simultaneously said, "If you don't know, you can't afford it."

The trip to Scottsdale Gun Club was uneventful. Except for the pretty saleswoman who slipped me her number when I casually dropped almost 2,000 dollars in cash on the counter for 3 bulletproof soft vests and some assorted ammo. I don't think she liked me as much as my ability to throw cash around like a Rockefeller. Little did she know the cash was just stuff I had plundered from Dante and Robert's wallets.

Unfortunately, a lot of attractive women like a man with money in his wallet over a man with morals and brains. Don't get me wrong, I'm not some he-man-woman-hater. I had met a lot of amazingly beautiful women who I respected dearly, but ignoring the reality of a situation to be politically correct is for chumps.

The reality was for every down to earth good looking woman out there, there were five other vapid ones who just wanted to land a rich dude. While I was still at SGC I grabbed a few more mags for the 1911 I had plundered from Robert, and a butt load of .38 Super to feed it. She looked like a hungry girl and we needed as many silenced weapons as possible ready to rock.

When I was driving back home, I realized we only had two silenced weapons among the four of us. My WASR and the plundered 1911. Getting more silenced weapons would take months waiting on the paperwork for the tax stamps and approvals, we needed silenced weapons NOW. So I stopped at a sporting goods store on the way home and bought two extremely high-end crossbows, I used the rest of the petty cash from the wallets on them, and I put the remainder of the bill on my personal credit card since the cash didn't cover 100% of it. I thought about using Dante's or Robert's credit cards but I didn't want to do that without putting my fancy schmancy wig on first in case the store cameras were ever reviewed at a later date. I didn't think they would be but better to play it safe. Better to play it safe seemed to be my new motto.

Chapter 10

That next week was one of the more interesting weeks of my life. Helping my best friend recover and bonding with a she-vamp. I called my work and told them that my father had died and that I needed a few weeks to go and arrange his out of state funeral. I wasn't worried about them calling my bluff since they didn't know my dad. I'm pretty sure my dad didn't even know where I worked, and they would have no way to check anyway since they don't know my father's name. I had bigger fish to fry so I didn't really care if they found out anyway, well bigger vamps to fry at least. Our plan was going from a rough idea to a tactical masterpiece.

We were trying to meet up every night and refine it as we went. We had an impromptu "sand table" set up in my living room just out of Lydia's reach which we had set up on my coffee table. A "sand table" is something the military uses to plan and explain military movements to the guys on the ground to make sure everyone is on the same page. I had given and listened to at least a hundred of them when I was doing CLP's (combat logistical patrols). You basically set up little figurines to represent your unit or "element" and run different scenarios on it, and make contingency plans and SOP's (standard operating procedures) ahead of any operation. We had bought some matchbox cars and built a few little houses out of popsicle sticks and had them arranged in the same fashion as Dante's neighborhood. We had gone through a lot of different scenarios on here for the raid and had back up plans for almost every contingency. Most actual military sand tables literally had sand on them, but I wasn't doing that shit in my house.

Dante's neighborhood was an affluent area at the base of South Mountain. It's one of the bigger mountains that wall off Phoenix. They don't call us "The Valley of the Sun" for nothing, Phoenix is literally a valley. Bordering the valley on almost all sides are mountains. It's wonderful getting up in the morning and looking in any direction and seeing mountains over the top of saguaros. It's not for everyone but I always thought Phoenix had a certain majesty to it. We were the ultimate example of the hubris of man.

Living in a completely inhospitable desert surrounded by man made cool air and green landscaping. Never before had a civilization been able to tame this wild and scorched land. Only one before had ever really tried though, The Hohokam. They were an ancient civilization that had built great canals all over the ancient Phoenix area to move water around among their tribes but they all mysteriously disappeared or died off right around 1400 AD, I tried not to think about that too much. The reason the city is now called Phoenix is because a lot of the early settlers built new canals right on top of the old Hohokam ones. A lot of guys I deployed with just could not understand how I lived in a place so hot. Which is funny because I couldn't understand how they lived in a place so cold. Guess who has never had to scrape ice off a windshield, and gets to wear shorts all winter? THIS GUY!

Dante's house was at the back end of his subdivision right at the base of the mountain. They actually don't allow people to build so close to the mountain anymore and that area has been zoned off as national park or recreational land but a few people had ancient land rights from before those zoning laws and never sold them back to the state. Somehow, Dante had come by some of that land. Thanks to his house being so close to the mountain he didn't have any neighbors close by which is I'm sure something he enjoyed. I didn't even want to think of how many bodies were buried on that property. Do vampires even bother burying them? That's something to ask Lydia about.

Lydia didn't know the exact address, but we had found the house easily on google maps. It didn't even have an asphalt road leading up to it, which I'm sure was due to the zoning laws. An asphalt road started in the subdivision and headed towards Dante's house before abruptly stopping. Where the asphalt stopped and the dirt road began was positively covered in "NO TRESPASSING" signs. If you went a quarter mile down that dirt road, after that you would hit Dante's property which was bordered by a chain link fence that had tan privacy slats ran through the link. You could barely even see the fence because the tan blended in so well with the desert. There was a tiny wooden guard booth that had also been painted tan where the dirt road intersected with the fence with just a simple guard pole coming out of it that ran across the road. Lydia said it wasn't even locked, you could hand lift the pole after pressing a release or use a garage door opener on it, a copy of which we had in Dante's car.

We had bought massive amounts of UV lights and UV light bulbs. We had a lot of different versions of the plan based on what circumstances would be waiting for us upon arrival, but a few of them involved roasting or catching the vampires off guard with UV light. Before we got to that point we weren't exactly sure which mechanism of the sun actually burnt vampires since the sun was constantly spitting off all kinds of radiation and light types, but we did have an unwilling test subject only a few feet away at all times.

You could buy high-end UV lights everywhere. People use UV for tanning, teeth whitening, keeping aquariums cleaned, growing vegetables, all kinds of stuff. I had to do some research into different light types before purchasing, I was no scientist. I figured or hoped that the same mechanism that worked on humans who went into tanning beds would be what hurt vampires. I tried a little full spectrum light that I had bought to jump start some vegetable seeds into gestation a few years back on Lydia's arm but it had no effect on her. Through my amateur google research, I found out it was because most cheap grow lights were just a mixture of the blue and red light spectrums which plants liked and had very little actual UV light. The first time I tried an actual UV bulb on a small patch of her arm through, it immediately caught fire and she began to scream. Sorry, Lydia, it was in the name of science. Lydia was pretty pissed at me after that, but hey, I had a new weapon now to use on the vamps.

In one of our many sand table centered meetings where we were throwing worst case scenario ideas back and forth and then trying to make contingency plans to cover those scenarios, Griffin had brought up a scary proposition.

"What if one of these vampires throws something at us? You said they were so strong that they threw you across the room and you weigh what, 240 pounds Bear?" asked Griffin.

"I weigh 260, maybe 270 right now, I've been skipping cardio day. You make a scary and great point though, we need hard armor. The soft armor is great and all but it won't mean much if one of these assholes hits us in the stomach with a baseball and liquefies our organs," I replied.

The group really didn't like that proposition and I saw Lydia out of the corner of my eye staring at me, she looked sad.

We all decided as a group that our new soft armor vests would have to be upgraded to hard armor. Luckily the vests we had bought had slots for plates to be added. Normally you would slip in ceramic based plates but we needed something stronger. I went to a specialty shop in my area which sold and created AR500 steel plate targets and had them cut me some plates the size of the armor for each vest. While I was there, they warned me of "spalling" which is when a bullet hits a metal plate and microscopic pieces of the plate break off in every direction. Meaning it would be great when the plates stopped a bullet from hitting us but not so great when hot shards of metal flew into our dicks and necks, a perfect example of spalling. We needed to add anti-spalling to the plates.

So we went to the center of all intelligence for the answer on how to do that, Google. Google told us that the best way to stop spalling was some standard truck bed liner that you could buy basically anywhere. We took it a step further and had Lydia cut some one-inch kevlar squares which we would later embed in the wet truck bed liner as it was drying at spaced intervals. Anti-spalling is tough because you wanted a material spongy enough to absorb the shrapnel yet durable enough that it wouldn't all fall off after the first bullet impact. The first thing we did was sand and clean the plates, then we wrapped them in duct tape. We added a thin layer of truck bed liner on after the duct tape and set the one inch kevlar squares into it about one inch apart from each other. After that, we did another very thin layer of truck bed liner and then made a grid of duct tape into the thin layer of truck bed liner while it was still wet. We let the whole thing dry and laid another thin layer of truck bed liner on it and another grid of duct tape into the wet layer overlapping the last grid but slightly off. We basically repeated that process over and over again until the plate was so thick we were afraid it might not fit in the vests. Before we were done, we covered the last layer of duct tape in a final layer of truck bed liner so there was no tape exposed, anti-spalling complete or so we hoped, none of us were experts.

After our planning and study of the previous plans we had created each night, Griffin, Zach and I had started a pretty serious workout and sparring routine. We only had a week, so we didn't expect to get much out of it but staying loose and ready was never a bad thing. Rook would sit in a chair next to us as we sparred, and point out inefficiencies when he could spot them. Being veterans we all had personal firearms that we were all comfortable and proficient with so I wasn't too worried about anything on that front. However none of us knew shit about crossbows so we practiced a lot with them, we broke a lot of bolts... I would be using my silenced WASR on the night of the raid but it didn't hurt to be cross trained on all mission equipment, military habits die hard. I also had the boys help me peel all of the black plasti-dip off of my car. If the original fight with Dante at my customers home had been reported to the police, I didn't want a description of my car floating around. They could look for the flat black Mitsubishi all they wanted, it didn't exist anymore. It's now a beat to shit silver Mitsubishi. Going to prison is for retards.

I had been buying all the extra equipment like the crossbow bolts, UV lights, steel plates, high-end radios, etc. with Dante's credit card. I would have Griffin drop me off about a block away from whatever store we were buying from that day and I would walk it in, that way no security cameras in the area would see Dante's plates. I would wear my wig and some zero prescription glasses while making the purchases so I looked nothing like myself. I'm not sure what his credit limit was but we hadn't hit it yet, so let the good times roll. I'm not ashamed to admit that I had bought me and all of the boys brand new, top of the line video cards and processors for our gaming desktops. We might die this weekend so we might as well game in style in the meantime. We also bought a 75-inch flat screen and a video game console for my living room. I would have bought one for all of the guys but I didn't want to throw any red flags with the credit card company, and it's not like I wasn't going to share. Besides, we were using my house as the staging area, and I was the main one doing prisoner duty.

Rook had made it to the VA clinic on Monday and had been given some real painkillers that were for human consumption, not like the dog Tramadol he had been taking at my house. He had some x-rays done and they did confirm that he had some cracked ribs and a bruised sternum. He faxed all of the medical paperwork and some copies of his x-rays over to the bank he worked at and made a lie about falling down during hiking on Camelback Mountain. He told them he needed some time off to heal from his injuries which they were only too happy to give him after seeing his disturbing x-rays and hearing his pained voiced over the phone. Rook was in the clear on convalescent leave until further notice and now had a solid alibi for his injuries. He also has a bunch of sick time saved up so the lucky bastard was getting paid.

The rest of the week in between training, planning, purchasing and equipment prepping, I played waiter to Lydia and Rook. Rook was still on the mend and it hurt him to move too much and Lydia was chained to the floor so I was making every meal for them. The three of us binge watched a lot of science fiction stuff that week, and we even took turns playing co-op on some video games on my new console. I was a

"PC Master Race" type guy myself, but Lydia was trapped in the living room so console gaming was our best option. I also loaned Lydia a few of my favorite books, stuff like *MHI* by Correia, *Confessions of a D-List Supervillain* by Jim Bernheimer, The *'WE ARE BOB'* series by Dennis E. Taylor and *Delvers LLC* by Blaise Corvin. Which she burned through pretty quickly. She did have a lot of time on her hands though. Every second she wasn't hanging with us she was working on the torn up leather jacket. She had confided in me that normally she used a sewing machine for that kind of work which of course I didn't have so she was worried about the overall quality the finished product might have. She finished my new jacket by Wednesday that week.

The jacket was AMAZING, Lydia's work was impeccable. She showed me how she had sewn layers and layers of kevlar over each of the bullet holes in different patterns using Kevlar thread, but kevlar was naturally a shade of beige which didn't exactly fit in with a black leather jacket. She had fixed that problem by sewing some faux black gator skin in the shape of diamonds over the kevlar patches. I had bought the faux gator skin a few years back and done some shitty reupholstering on some of my backyard furniture. The diamonds of faux black gator skin added a whole new design and feel to the jacket. The overall product was beautiful. She had even added a few kevlar panels on the interior of the jacket as well for extra protection and covered them with some standard black cotton material. Between the Kevlar that the jacket already had in it and the kevlar that Lydia had added to it, this jacket could take an insane beating. So cool, if she wasn't a blood-sucking monster, I would have picked her up and hugged her.

"Lydia, this is one of the nicest things that anyone has ever done for me... ever," I told her. She blushed deeply.

We had decided the raid would be Saturday night and Sunday morning. Mainly because Zach's wife had work Saturday morning and didn't want to stay up late Friday night with the kids all by herself. I was nervous as hell even though I wouldn't show my friends that, and I appreciated the extra day to mentally prepare myself if nothing else. I don't know how, but I had become the impromptu leader of this crew of bandits and badasses. The Friday night before the raid Rook asked me to head out back and smoke a cigar with him. Two cigars in one week... I would have to lock the cigars in the safe for awhile after this one, I didn't have an addictive personality but tempting fate is stupid. Besides my morning cup of coffee and drinking three to four beers at a restaurant with some friends or on a date once a month, I led a really chemical free life. Not because I have some moral qualms or I'm particularly straight edge or anything like that, it's just that vices are expensive and I prefer to put my money into my house, my gun collection, or my bank.

Once out back Rook carefully sat down. He told me he was feeling better but everything still really hurt. We closed the sliding glass door but had left my curtains wide open so we could still see Lydia. Rook pulled out his cell phone and turned on some 80's punk which sounded surprisingly good over the tiny cell phone speakers, but I was a sucker for punk.

Rook stared at me for a second and then said "I don't want Lydia to hear our conversation."

Ok that's weird, what could he have to say to me that she couldn't hear, she had been a part of all of our planning sessions so far, why was this conversation different?

"You know that girl... vampire... that woman in there is in love with you right?" Rook said.

"What, you are being ridiculous!" I said.

"Oh really mister oblivious, you think she laughs at all your goofy ass jokes and reads all your nerdy ass books because she is getting something out of them?" Rook asked.

"Hey, those books are awesome, asshole!" I said.

"You get my point, yes those books are great but they aren't exactly aimed at a female audience. She is reading them to impress you, she is laughing at your jokes to impress you, she is flirting with you to try to get you interested. At first, I thought this was some kind of Stockholm syndrome shit, or she was sucking up to you to try to goad you into doing something dumb like unchaining her, but she hasn't asked or even hinted at that once. She is either the best actor on earth or she is in love with you," Rook finished.

When Rook put it in that context it all snapped together. All the times she had given me sideways looks. All the times she had seemed sad at the prospect of me going into danger. I had just never seen her in that light before. I have always thought of her as a vampire asshole who kicked the shit out of me, now recently I had started thinking of her as a bro with unsteady loyalty. Lydia was beautiful but she was also a monster and an attempted murderer, with me as the potential murder victim. I like not being murdered. For some reason the last few days, Emily had been bouncing around in my head, never Lydia. At the same time now I just felt bad for Lydia. I wasn't the kind of person who toyed with people's emotions. I had had women do that to me when I was younger and dumber and it never felt good. This was a lot to process and deal with and I had never lead Lydia on.

"We will worry about that later Rook, we have too many other problems to tackle right now. If you are wondering if I'm also falling in love with her, the answer is a hard no," I told him.

"I wasn't wondering that I was just tired of you being oblivious to the situation. Want to go play some co-op?" Rook asked.

"Does the Tin Man have a sheet metal cock?" I replied.

Saturday morning came quick, I was still nervous but we had all of our cards in order. We had a plan, we had equipment and I had a tier one team of qualified professionals that I loved and trusted like family. Griffin and I went out that morning and rented a large moving truck. If Dante really had as many valuables as Lydia said he did, we wouldn't want to be making trips back and forth to get them, it's better to not return to the scene of a crime if this was even a crime. I had bought an extra paint sprayer from the local hardware store, again using Dante's credit card and Griffin and I got busy plasti-dipping black squares over all of the moving truck companies logos. Once we were done we had cut some stencil design fake logos that simply said "Exotic Transportation" and we were spraying those on white inside of the black squares.

Since Dante collected antiquities we figured it wasn't an unimaginable scenario that a truck might drop one off from time to time, but not a rented truck so we were trying to make this thing look like we owned it. We would use our painters tape over the license plate trick as well tonight on the moving truck just in case. We threw a few blankets down in the back of the truck and loaded in all of the assorted UV lights we had bought, along with extension cords, surge protectors, brackets, work lights that we had switched UV bulbs into and some tools and straps we might need. We were ready, tonight was the night.

Chapter 11

The rest of the day went by quick. We ate some good lunch when we were done masking and packing the moving truck and then watched a few comedies on the giant t.v. we had bought. Griffin went out in the Dodge Charger around five p.m. to get us some more Pizza By Napoli, the pizza from there was amazing like always. I even broke my 'no human food' rule and gave Mia a piece. Zach came over around seven p.m. and joined our pizza party. He had told his wife he was going to my house tonight to catch up with Rook, Griffin and I, and that we would all be drinking so he might stay the night instead of driving home drunk. Zach said she was pretty pissed about that but she understood, it's hard to argue that your husband should drive home drunk. I have no idea what Griffin had told his wife, he was pretty vague on that front and just said that she was cool with it. Rook and I were single so we didn't have to worry about that kind of stuff.

At midnight we put a pot of coffee on and went over the sand table one more time. We also went over all of our attack and contingency plans. We couldn't leave Lydia alone at my house so we loaded her into the back of the moving truck but not before handcuffing both of her ankles to a folding chair. We handcuffed her arms together as well and then Griffin and I carried the chair she was chained to into the back of the truck while Zach stood by with my WASR and covered us. I had backed the truck right up to the lip of my garage so none of my neighbors saw what we were loading. Once we had her in the back of the van, we ratchet strapped her chair into place so she wouldn't slide around and then took the handcuffs off of her arms. I handed her a thermos of half blood and half coffee with some sugar and cream added. She eye-balled it suspiciously and then took a tentative sip, "Damn that is good Bear, you are an artist," Lydia said.

"You're welcome, maybe when all of this is over, you and I can open up a coffee bar for the undead," I told her.

"I would like that!" she squealed.

"Let's live through tonight first," I said. Before we left I ran back inside to have a word with Mia. I hugged her for a long time and made sure she knew that I loved her.

All of us had a thermos full of coffee because we needed to be alert for this evening's pending raid. Griffin, Zach and I were fully kitted out wearing our U.S. Palm bulletproof vests with added homemade hard plates. The vest I was wearing was multicam so I had matched theirs to mine in color when I bought them. Rook had his vest with him as well but he had it sitting next to him rather than wearing it since his chest and ribs would be sore for weeks to come and putting weight on them wasn't an option.

I had also thrown on my new kevlar reinforced leather jacket over my vest. I'm not afraid to admit it, but I had worn some olive drab cargo shorts instead of pants like the rest of the crew. It was hot as hell near the end of the summer in Phoenix. Even at midnight we had temperatures up in the 90's. Sure, I could have worn pants with this get up and looked super badass but then I would have had sweaty legs all night. If I'm even more honest, I even debated with myself about wearing sandals or not. I was decent at running in sandals but then I remembered all the cactus and sagebrush I saw around Dante's house on the satellite images and decided if I had to run through that I didn't want to be in sandals. So I begrudgingly threw on some black tennis shoes.

I had also thrown on an impulse buy from a few years back, a 1917 Cold Steel Cutlass. The name is somewhat of a misnomer since the sword was probably made within the last 5 years. The date in the title is the style of the make and Cold Steel is the company. If you haven't heard of Cold Steel, then look them up as soon as possible. They specialize in making all kinds of nasty melee weapons. Their main selling point: all of their stuff works, it's sharp as hell and it doesn't break.

Sure you can buy a sword basically anywhere in this day and age. Hell, if you aren't in a commie state, you could probably buy a cheap one at a gas station. With swords though, the old idiom of "you get what you pay for" is especially true. Nine out of ten swords on the market will break after the first impact with anything. They are meant to sit on the shelf at a level 87 virgin's house, not to actually be used. Cold Steel's products are meant to be used, so much so that they literally cut dead cows in half with them, film it and then use the video to sell more product. I'm honestly surprised that PETA hasn't bombed Cold Steel yet. I had read way too many zombie books to not own a sword and that night I was glad about my impulse buy. If we had to chop a vampire's head off, I was going to do it in style.

Griffin and Zach had on black t-shirts under their multicam bulletproof vests, and long blue jeans, with black tennis shoes. They both were open carrying their personal Glock 19's in BlackHawk retention holsters. I had strongly urged them both to go get night sights installed during our week of prepping, and they had. They would both be carrying crossbows and they had basically all of the MOLLE hoops on their vests stuffed full of crossbow bolts, even on their backs so they could draw from each other's armor if they needed to reload. Hopefully, they didn't have to use their Glocks since they weren't silenced. Before the mission I had picked up collapsible batons for everyone during our week of prep, which they were wearing now. My first instinct was to get more Cold Steel weapons for everyone, but then I realized a bunch of people who know nothing about edged weapons swinging around edged weapons in confined quarters under duress was probably a bad idea. We were more likely to chop each other to pieces than hit a vampire. If we survived tonight we would need to do some training on that front.

Since Rook would be staying in the truck and providing overwatch, he was dressed in a black polo shirt and black dress slacks. He was supposed to look like the truck driver in case he was seen or questioned, but we didn't know what a high end antiquities delivery truck driver looked like, hence Rook's current clothing. He would be keeping the silenced 1911 I had plundered from Robert with him in case he ran into any trouble, he also had his AR pistol with him but we were all trying to use a silenced weapon as our primary. During the ride over, Zach would ride in the back with Lydia to make sure she didn't get squirrely. We all liked Lydia as a person but for all we knew, she may have been waiting for an opportunity like this all week. Time would tell, but if she betrayed us now I would personally put a few well placed shots between her eyes. My friends didn't know it yet but I was willing to do anything to protect them from harm, and I literally meant anything. If there was something so dangerous that it was going to kill one of us, I was going to be the one to die, I would make sure of it. I'm not letting them get hurt, every danger we faced tonight I would be sure to jump in front first. This is my idea, my plan, I am leading from the front and no one is going to pay for a decision that I have made!

We got on the road and started driving towards Dante's house. I threw on that song by The Doors "When You're Strange." Which is also the theme song to a vampire movie from the 80's called *The Lost Boys*, my friends caught the reference and hard eye rolls were had all around. We stopped a few miles out to put painters tape over the license plate. We were all checking and rechecking our weapons, taking the safeties off and making sure we had rounds in the chambers. Except for me, I was driving and I had done all of that stuff before I had left the house. It didn't hurt to be thorough though. We drove through the quiet neighborhood that was in front of Dante's house.

It was about one in the morning now so most people were asleep and the sun had been down for hours. We hit the dirt road that went up to Dante's house and slowed the truck down considerably, we passed a lot of "NO TRESPASSING" signs. We stopped in front of the little guard booth with a security pole that was lowered above the road that went through the privacy fence. I hit the button on the garage door opener that I had taken out of Dante's car and the pole lifted. I drove through and parked the truck in front of the front door of the house, sideways. That way, Rook would have a view of the front door and a view of the entrance we had just come in at.

I put in a Bluetooth headset that was wirelessly connected to my phone and called Rook. He put in his own headset in and accepted the call, "Mic check."

This way Rook could warn us if someone was coming or if he needed back up at the truck. I had bought some high end radios before the mission but I was hesitant to use them with a human guard force possibly showing up before we left. They might also be on similar radios and possibly even the same frequencies, and it wouldn't do to have them hear our plans. Before getting out of the truck and on our drive up I had been surveying the property the best I could. There was only one car in the driveway. Logically to me, that meant there were only one or two inside. I would bet any amount of money that Dante had some kind of rule that there always had to be someone home to guard the property and his precious collection, let's hope my logic is sound.

"Plan 'A' guys. It looks like the vampires are out to play," I said.

Griffin and I hopped out of the truck, Rook scooted over to the driver seat. We went to the back of the truck and threw the sliding truck door up. Zach was standing there crossbow in hand. Lydia was still sipping her coffee in the back.

"Zach was telling me the funniest stories about you guys as kids," said Lydia.

"Plan 'A' guys and gals let's get this show on the road. Put your gloves on now if you haven't done so."

Zach and Griffin set their crossbows just inside the storage space of the moving truck so they could easily be grabbed. "Plan A" required us to look like private security or mercenaries which is hard to do while carrying fifth century weapons, even if we had modern editions as well. I remembered how worried I was about fingerprints when I was in Lydia's apartment so I had made all of the guys wear gloves tonight, that would have to be SOP for now if we were going to be doing this kind of thing.

Zach went to the back of the truck and handcuffed Lydia's hands together while Griffin and I covered him, me with my WASR and Griffin had temporarily drawn his Glock. Griffin was a lefty which is why he loved fourth generation Glocks, you could switch them over to left-handed mode by just moving a few parts around, they are pretty awesome. Zach uncuffed Lydia's ankles from the chair and then chained them back together, she should have enough room to shuffle but not to get up to a run. I didn't particularly want to restrain her arms and legs like this, but the alternative of her possibly being team vamp and trying to kill one of my friends tonight wasn't worth the risk. Zach helped Lydia stand up from the chair and I grabbed the back of her shirt roughly and hoisted her down the extendable ramp that came out of the back of the moving truck. Zach And Griffin slung out their extendable police batons *SHING*, *SHING*, the noise from their batons rang out.

I roughly continued shoving Lydia towards the front door. One of my hands was on her shoulder and the other had the muzzle of my WASR dug into her lower back.

"MOVE BITCH" I yelled, before looking over at Lydia and winking, she winked back.

I can sound very demanding when I want to. I had been in one too many MOUT training scenarios stacked with real actors from the middle east courtesy of the U.S. Army, and the only way to get some of those jaded individuals to listen to you is to yell like a demon. One time after returning home from an AT (annual training) where we had a lot of that type of thing, a homeless man had approached me at a gas station to ask me for some money. I was tired and my training kicked in and I yelled at him with the full force of my military bearing. The poor guy was so scared he fell backward trying to get away from me. I felt bad about it afterwards but I had also learned something about myself, my command voice was terrifying to regular people. Let's see how it works on vampires.

We got to the front door and I roughly pounded, "OPEN THE FUCK UP, THE PACKAGE IS HERE!" I yelled.

A very confused looking 20 something year old with black hair, mascara, and a black trench coat on opened the door. "Who the hell are you?" he asked.

"We are VST, Veteran Security Tactical. Dante hired us to retrieve this woman. Let us in before the neighbors see!" I said, but before he could respond I started roughly shoving Lydia through the door and he had to back up to get out of our way. Once we were through the doorway Griffin closed it behind us and locked it. I looked over at Lydia and she gave me a positive nod and then said, "Cake Farts."

Griffin and Zach heard the code word that they were the most excited for.

Part of "plan A" was that if we successfully gained entrance into the house and there was only one vampire on guard duty, then Lydia would verify if the guard on duty could be physically overpowered, or if he was too old or powerful for that to work. If the vampire was too powerful she would either shake her head from the left to the right,

178

back and forth in the negative or just stay quiet if she was being watched. If it was a low man on the totem pole, she would use our predetermined attack code phrase 'Cake Farts.' Yes, it seems very silly but you couldn't just yell "ATTACK!" while attacking superpowered immortals on their home turf. We needed something innocuous and confusing, hence "Cake Farts." I had voted "Red Eye" for the attack phrase but Griffin had started the "Cake Farts" counter-campaign and won the popular vote among the crew, even that traitor Lydia had voted "Cake Farts."

She wasn't so happy about her vote though once I showed her the video associated with that term, she had voted for it because she thought it had sounded silly. Revenge is a dish best served cold, or with a disgusting video from the internet. If the hypothetical vampire guard we ran into in "Plan A" was too powerful, my plan was to just dump a magazine of silenced 7.62 by 39 into him from my WASR, but that would fuck up a lot of our other plans and surely wreck the entrance way into Dante's house and maybe even destroy some valuables. However, since she had nodded her head in the positive and used our god awful attack phrase identifying that this vampire was a noobie, Griffin and Zach had the green light to beat the ever living piss out of this guy at the first opportune moment.

"Did you just say 'Cake Farts,' what the hell is going on?" the noobling goth vampire asked.

"You must have misheard her, take us to a place where we can lock this lady down. We need to get out of here and onto our next job, LEAD THE WAY!" I tried to sound demanding.

The vampire turned around to lead us further into the house. As soon as his back was turned to us, we struck. *CLUNK* *CLUNK* the twin sounds of my teammate's batons hitting his skull reverberated into the room.

"ARGHHHHH!" the vampire shouted in pain and spun around with vampire speed, his fangs had extended. Whoa, this sucker must have been well fed to have not gone down, it didn't matter, by the time he had spun around Griffin and Zach were already mid-swing. Griffin had taken the left side since he was left handed and Zach had taken the right. Their twin batons hit his skull again each on a different side. Griffins bounced right off his temple, and Zach's landed on his chin. Everything was in slow motion and I watched the vampire's lights turn off as the two forces of overwhelming physics collided with his skull for a second time. It was a truly awesome sight. The vampire hit the floor and the boys continued to give him the beating of a lifetime, systematically hitting every part of him. From what I understood from Lydia's explanation, a beating from humans like this would only work on a low level vamp. I stepped ahead of them and aimed my WASR further into the house covering the crew in case we weren't alone.

I heard Lydia yell behind me, "Move out of the way!"

Everyone looked over, including me, which was probably dumb since I was supposed to be making sure no vampires could sneak up on us.

Lydia then yelled "FLYING ELBOW BITCH!" as she used vampire strength and jumped straight up into the air and let her body move to the horizontal position and then fell with all of her weight elbow down onto the unconscious vampire. Oh my god, that was hilarious. I lost my shit and started laughing like a madman. I was trying to cover the interior of the house but I was laughing so hard my muzzle was shaking all over the place and I had tears in my eyes.

Through my laughter, I finally sputtered out "Continue the plan, go retrieve the crossbows, let's go!" Rook must have heard the situation pretty clearly because I could hear him laughing as well over the headset.

"Did Lydia just WWE style attack someone?" Rook asked.

"Fuck yeah she did, I about shit my pants I laughed so hard," I replied.

"Damn it, I'm never getting injured again. I'm missing out on all of the cool stuff," said Rook.

Griffin and Zach came back a second later with loaded crossbows in hand.

"Lydia, control the door and watch our Marilyn Manson wanna be here!" I shouted.

We moved into the house with me on point since I was double armored thanks to my new leather and kevlar hybrid jacket and I had the silenced rifle, well that was the excuse I gave my friends for being upfront. Really I just wanted to make sure I was the only one in danger. We systematically cleared every room in the house looking for other vampires. We made sure to check closets, corners, ceilings, everywhere, we weren't sure what capabilities these vampires had. Once we were sure the house was clear, we went back to the entryway where Lydia was sitting on the downed vampire.

"Sorry about earlier guys, this asshole kicked me while I was down a few times after a few of my escape attempts. I owed him," said Lydia.

"That's fine, let's move him and finish the plan. We don't know what kind of time we have, we should hurry," I said.

We dragged trench coat vampire down the hall bumping him into corners and furniture, which was way too funny. One of Dante's back rooms had two very large lay-down refrigerator and freezer combos which were both half full of stolen hospital grade blood bags. I needed to find out where he was getting these. I kicked trench coat guy in the head really hard and the boys gave him a few more blows to the skull with their batons. Then, I dumped one of the freezers over on its side and let all the blood bags land on the carpet.

I opened the other freezer and said "Lydia start picking these blood bags up and put them into that one," I pointed at the one I had opened. "Griffin, Zach, pick that freezer up, and then throw shitbag in there."

Griffin and Zach complied. They picked up the now empty freezer I had knocked over and then dumped trench coat guy inside, face first, he hit the bottom hard.

"Shit I'm sorry guys, will you please check for a wallet or any weapons he has on him," I asked.

They went about their chore and grabbed his wallet but didn't find any weapons on him, except an off brand pocket knife. I guess some vampires were like some humans, they didn't carry a weapon and had no plan in case of a confrontation, *idiots*. There was an empty bracket meant for a lock on the side of the freezer connecting the body of it to the lid. I threw a couple zip ties through it from my vest and zipped them closed. I doubted he was going to be getting up anytime soon since he was in the vampire equivalent of a coma while slowly turning into a popsicle but it's better to play it safe. We could have just chopped his head off but we didn't know the range of smell these new vampires would have and we didn't want them to smell their dead comrades. Eventually, that would be inevitable but we were trying to set ourselves up for success.

"Lydia sit on this freezer please" I pointed to the one with the vampire in it.

"No problem Bear," Lydia cheerfully replied like I had just asked her to hand me the ketchup or something.

The levity of the situation made me chuckle, which in turn made Lydia chuckle. "When you go out to the truck, will you grab my coffee, that stuff was good?" Lydia asked.

"Yeah, no problem," I replied. "Friendlies coming out Rook, hold fire," I said into my headset.

We went out into the back of the truck and collected all the supplies including the extension cords and work lights with UV bulbs installed in them, and then started dragging it all into the house. We dragged the pile of it into the room they used to confine Lydia in. Then we started setting up; we plugged in a surge protector and started running extension cords every which way. We set up UV lights in every direction in this room. Once we had this room coated in UV lights, we started stealthily installing UV lights everywhere but trying to make it

184

less obvious outside of Lydia's room. We had them stashed liberally behind potted plants, under tables, on the sides of furniture, etc. The ones outside of Lydia's room didn't have a lot of coverage since we had to hide them but those were just back up lights anyway.

"BEAR, GET IN HERE!" I heard Griffin yell, and I took off at a jog towards his voice. He was in one of Dante's many living rooms, this was a big property. He was kneeling down next to what looked like a glass-topped wooden box that was being used as a coffee table, it even had a chessboard on top of it set up. It looked like he was in the middle of setting up a UV light behind it at an angle where you wouldn't see it from the main hallways that goes down the center of the house.

"What! What's the problem?" I shouted while aiming my WASR at every corner of the room and scanning for threats.

"Look under the glass man..." Griffin said.

I leaned over the little coffee table and looked into the glass, there was a man inside. This wasn't a coffee table at all, it was just a rectangular coffin of polished wood with a glass front on it. When I looked closer I noticed there were antique locks all over it holding the top in place. Zach came in a second later and I heard Lydia yell from the back "What's going on out there!"

I knelt down in front of the coffin, I knocked the chess board to the floor and peered through the glass at the man inside. He was wearing

185

an absolutely beautiful three-piece suit, I didn't really have an eye for fashion since nine out of ten of my outfits were blue jeans and a black t-shirt with cowboy boots but even I could tell this suit was nice.

The suit was a super dark navy blue with white pinstriping. The vest he had on underneath was the same color and pattern. Under that, he had a long sleeved collared shirt that was a lighter shade of blue with no pinstriping, topping it all off he had a beautiful tan colored satin tie in some intricate knot that I knew I could never pull off. I wore clip-ons for a reason. He had light green eyes which I could tell because his eyes were wide open. He had blonde hair that looked like it was just starting to recede, and he had the undercut from hell. His hair was extremely long on top and slicked back, the sides were completely shaved down to stubble. I could even see on one side of his head his hair had become disheveled and parts of the longer top had fallen over onto the shaved portion. His eyes looked too large for his face to me, and his chin almost had that 'butt chin' thing going on but just ever so slightly. I'm comfortable enough with my sexuality to admit that he was very classically handsome. I looked down at his right arm and noticed he was holding a Tommy Gun aimed straight down towards his feet, in his left hand he had some sort of antique sword. It also looked like someone had hastily thrown a fedora over his naval area. He looked maybe somewhere between the ages of 35 and 40, but it was hard to tell.

On top of his suit he was wearing a long dark grey overcoat, I could tell the style was very antiquated. He looked almost alive, like he was frozen. Was this guy a vampire? Or some disgusting taxidermied human? Before I could finish that line of thought, Lydia bunny hopped into the room. She still had her ankles chained so she probably figured that was the fastest way to get to us.

"Guys, what the fuck, no one answered me!" Lydia yelled.

"I don't know, we found this guy in the table, have you seen this before?" I asked her.

"Yes I saw it once, that thing creeps me out. I asked about it once but the other vampires just told me that Dante won it in a poker game in the 40's against some high level vampire in a different state." I noticed on the top of the coffin near where the gentleman's feet lay and where the glass met the wood there was a tiny bronze plaque. It was only about two inches across and it read *Otto Richter - A Cautionary Tale*, who the hell is Otto Richter?

Chapter 12

"Fuck it, we will deal with this later. Let's finish setting up the honey trap here," I said.

We all shook off our amazement and finished rigging the house with lights. We had split the lights onto two different surge protectors, one was plugged into an outlet in Lydia's room and the other was plugged into the bathroom across the hall from Lydia's room but we had run an extension cord from that one to a surge protector in Lydia's room, that way we could turn all the UV lights on or off by hitting both of the two master power switches on the surge protectors from this room. We didn't want to blow a fuse by putting too much of a load on just one which is why we had split them up. We test fired the lights on both cords once Lydia was in a safe spot to make sure the fuses wouldn't pop and everything had held. We had also either duct taped or stapled all of our cords into place, we didn't want someone accidentally tripping over one of the cords and ruining our master weapon.

Once we had finished rigging everything, we all sat down on Lydia's bed. It was about two a.m., now we just had to wait for our first customers. It didn't take long for us to start joking and laughing about the situation but we were a fun bunch. My friends knew how to have a good time, just being around them made me happy.

"You guys are kind of fuckers you know that," I said.

"What the hell are you talking about?" Griffin asked.

"I'm guilty too here, it took a vampire menace to get us all hanging out together regularly again, did you guys realize that?" I asked.

"Yeah it did, you're right," Zach said.

"Well let's try to see each other more, how about we try to do dinner Sunday nights from now on, all of us," I said.

"I could swing that" Griffin said.

"I'm in too" Rook said over the headset.

"Rook says he is in too," I said.

"Me too," said Zach and Lydia at the same time.

"You are still on friend probation Lydia but I appreciate the sentiment," I replied.

"Oh SHIT, you guys got company! Black sedan coming in!" Rook shouted into my headset.

"We're on," I said to the room.

Griffin and Zach both jumped behind the nightstands on either side of the bed, they were big gaudy stained wood things. Big enough to conceal them, but they had to push them a few feet off the wall to get behind them. Griffin had control of both of the surge protectors, it would be his job to flip them when either Lydia or I gave the signal. I moved just inside the closet on the side of the room, but the closet door opened up facing the threshold of the doorway that came into the room from the hallway, so all I would have to do is open the door and fire when it was time. I didn't even shut the door all the way because I didn't want to have to worry about turning the handle, I just left it about an inch open so I could see the doorway that led into this room but no one could see me in the closet. Lydia jumped in the bed and got under the covers. Her job was to pull the covers over her head before the UV lights came on, that way she wouldn't fry. Just to play it safe we had put a blue tarp in between the sheets and blankets that she was under to make sure that no UV light would seep in and burn her. We had clear lines of overlapping fire and we were all generally on the same side of the room which was good to avoid friendly fire.

"Two men are getting out of the car with a female," Rook said over the headset.

"Lydia, does Dante have any other female vampires?" I asked. She shook her head in the negative.

"The female is most likely human," I told Rook. "Don't shoot the female unless she attacks first," I said to the room, Rook heard me as well of course because we still had our Bluetooth call open.

190

"They have seen me, maintaining radio silence from here on out." Rook said.

I waited a minute, then Rook whispered onto the line "They ignored me and walked inside, you have incoming."

We heard boisterous laughter a second later, I leaned slightly out of the closet and pointed my finger at Lydia and then made the hand signal for a talking mouth.

Lydia yelled, "Hey guys, I'm back here!" We heard the laughing stop and then everything was quiet for a second. Then we heard footsteps on the tile outside of the room,

"Lydia?" a male vampire said from the hallway. He had a girl hoisted between him and his friend, he let her go for a second and stepped into the room leaving his friend and the girl in the hallway. His friend with the girl on his shoulder followed a second later. The girl looked drunk as hell.

"What's with the girl?" Lydia asked.

"Late night snack, did you come home with Dante?" the vampire asked her.

"Cake Farts these mother fuckers to hell!" Lydia yelled before throwing the blankets and tarp over her head.

Griffin threw both of the power buttons on the surge protectors. **CLICK CLICK**, the room flooded with brilliant UV light and both of the vampires started to scream as their skin sizzled like a steak on a grill. The one holding the girl immediately dropped her. We had agreed beforehand that Zach and Griff would work the room left to right and I would work it right to left since they had crossbows and I had the WASR. Two crossbows twanged and bolts flew across the room into the vampire on the left, one landed in his neck, one in his stomach. I opened fire on the one on the right that had been holding the girl. I stitched a perfect line from his crotch to his head, once I hit his head he slumped over. I jumped out of the closet (that's not a metaphor assholes.)

"Go, confirm status, and secure wallets and weapons!" I shouted.

Griffin flipped the UV lights off and then he and Zach jumped out of cover and sprinted at the downed vamps. They both kicked each vampire in the head several times. I don't know how well that tactic actually worked but it seemed like good practice while dealing with things that had regenerative abilities. Try regenerating quickly from a TBI, fuckers.

The one with the crossbow bolts in him was still twitching, "Bolt him," I said.

Griffin was the first to reload so he fired a point blank crossbow shot right into the vampires head. It went in one side and popped out the other, the carpet stopped it from coming out all of the way. I zipped tied the one with the bullet wounds, securing his hands and feet well. Then we carried them both to the freezer where we had left the other vampire. I cut the zip ties that were securing the freezer closed and helped dump the new guys in. We kind of had to "Tetris" them all in to place to make a more compact pile and for good measure. I got in the freezer and jumped on them a few times to make the pile a little more compact. I had a lot more vampires I wanted to put into this thing after all.

The door frame and hallway wall had caught some 7.62 x 39 rounds that had exited out of the vampire's back that I had shot, but we had thought ahead for this and I had brought a few tubes of caulk. We caulked all of the holes in the walls and over any other damage or splintering in the door frame. There was some blood splatter on the carpet and walls but we had brought white spray paint for this and just sprayed it over all of the blood, even the blood on the carpet since the carpet was white.

This area just needed to look okay at a cursory glance so we could spring our trap again and again. We didn't really know what to do with the drunk girl who must have passed out in either fear or drunkenness so we just threw her on the bed with Lydia, we didn't put her under the covers though. It wouldn't be good if she woke up and freaked out, and threw the covers off while we had the UV lights on, inadvertently killing Lydia. So on top of the covers was a good place for her. Plus

Lydia was afraid the drunk girl might start farting and give her a 'dutch oven.'

We all went back to Lydia's room, it was about 2:30 a.m. now. Half the vampires down already, good timing.

"They say dream jobs don't exist," I joked, and everyone laughed.

I thought tonight would be tense, terrifying and a general pain in the ass but so far everyone was having a great time. I took the three wallets and counted the cash that was in them, there was about 800 dollars. I divvied it up into five even piles on the bed while the rest of the crew joked and laughed. It was about 160 bucks each after splitting it and we had basically started the job at midnight, so I was making about 80 dollars an hour tax-free so far. *Vampire hunting is great money!* I put my portion in my personal wallet and I handed Griffin, Zach, and Lydia their piles. Griffin and Zach started crisping the bills and putting them away in their wallets, Lydia just looked confused.

"What's this for?" she asked.

"Your part of the loot, every adventuring party splits loot," I said matter of factly.

"Oh, thanks Bear... I'm just happy to be here with you guys, your friends are darling. I wish I would have met you guys before... you know, all of this shit..." she said.

"Don't have an existential crisis on me just yet, we've got work to do woman!" I told her.

That seemed to cheer her up because she looked up at me and said "YES SIR!" in her girly voice and threw me a mock salute.

"I need to go check on Rook, I'll be right back," I told everyone in the room.

I know Rook had heard me but just in case when I got to the front door I whispered "Friendlies coming out," into my headset. I really didn't want to get friendly fragged. It's one thing to die in glorious battle, but dying because I didn't communicate my movements effectively would be just downright embarrassing.

Rook was happily sipping on his thermos of coffee in the truck. I jumped in the passenger seat and handed him his pile of cash.

"Here is your part of the take so far," I told him.

"SWEET!" he said and pocketed it.

"I can't stay long, I need to be inside in case anyone shows up," I told him.

"I hate being stuck out here, I want to be inside helping you guys," Rook said.

"I know, everyone knows you would if you could," I said.

"You guys are awesome, I'm just tired of not being in the right place at the right time to take out the bad guys, to make a difference," Rook said.

So that's what this is about, I was 90% sure he is referencing the fact that he never got his chance to deploy when we were actively serving.

"I know your character, you are a warrior. Lydia was telling me she has an algorithm she used to find Dante the first time. We can use it again and find another vampire nest. Somewhere out there a bunch of vampires are killing innocent people right now. You heal up from your injury, we will use Lydia's help and together me and you will kill all those fuckers," I said. We bumped fists and he smiled but I could tell he was deep in thought. I had to get back inside.

We had two more vampires roll in that night, but one at a time this go around. It was like shooting fish in a barrel, especially with the drunk girl laying next to Lydia. Both of the assholes thought they were going to be able to share a snack with her and they had tunnel vision so hard they didn't even notice us. Apparently, all of those amazing vampire senses go out the window when they are hangry, (hungry + angry,) with a buffet in front of them. The last vampire must have had some natural resilience to UV because even though he started to sizzle, steam and scream, he took off running right at the only window in Lydia's room. He made a flying leap and smacked right into it, the noise it made was like a giant drum and he bounced back all the way into the room and landed on his back on the carpet.

I lit him up with a full mag from the WASR until parts of his torso were just bloody ribbons. We were all very confused. We all went to check out the window, it turns out it was a special custom job. It was extremely thick, it looked UV proof but I couldn't tell and it had a little 3M sticker on the bottom right. I had heard of this before, 3M makes this film that they can tie into your window frames at the time of installation, it stops the window from breaking. It's great for places with tropical storms so you don't have to replace your windows every six months from flying tree branches and what not. It made sense that a vampire would have this in his home. No one wants to burn to death because the neighbor kid hits a baseball in the wrong direction.

The last vampire, the squirrely one, had even stopped by Rook's fake antiquities transport truck on the way in and asked him to roll down his window and questioned him. Rook just told him they had a night time delivery for a "Mr. Dante" and that the movers were inside setting it up, the vampire found that answer good enough and wandered inside to his demise. Rook and I should have put some coal between our butt cheeks because it surely would have turned into diamonds after that encounter. The rest of the crew didn't know about that since I was the only one who had heard, due to the Bluetooth call. We had just kept putting the bodies in the freezer the whole night. I really wanted to use my cutlass and cut their heads off but the math wasn't there for it. Five vampires at about two hundred pounds a piece, that means there would be about one thousand pounds of loose vampire soup on the floor inside of Dante's house. The freezer was the best option for now if we didn't want to be ankle deep in gore while we worked.

The sun was just about to come up, we were all tired, still filled with nervous energy and excitement from doing so well. We were just about to start packing up, Griffin was in the kitchen making espresso with Dante's extremely overpriced coffee and I'm sure overpriced espresso machine. Then Rook called in, "TRIPLE SHIT! Someone is here, I was taking a piss I didn't notice them, I'm sorry!"

"GRIFFIN! RED ALERT, GET BACK HERE!" I shouted into the house.

Griffin came barreling through the door and jumped over his nightstand to get into position. A second after he had hidden, the front door opened. We heard dress shoes on the tile of the entryway.

Lydia shouted, "We're back here!"

The sound of dress shoes in the tile hallway continued this direction. The man stepped into the room, he was about average height, with curly brown hair, a small goatee, and wearing an all-black business suit, holding a briefcase.

"Where is Dante?" he asked Lydia.

"Guys this isn't a vampire but he isn't a good guy either," said Lydia.

Griffin, Zach and I all burst out of cover with our weapons trained on the newcomer.

"DROP THE BRIEFCASE AND PUT YOUR HANDS IN THE AIR RALPH LAUREN!" I yelled. Zach and Griffin laughed but kept their crossbows aimed at him.

"Uhh how about no," the man said, then he threw his briefcase at me. I saw it coming and jumped to the side while letting off a few snap shots in his direction. I hit the carpet and heard a bang. I looked up and the briefcase was embedded in the drywall behind me. I looked back to the doorway but he was gone.

"I think I got a bolt into him!" Griffin yelled, Zach's bolt was stuck in the door frame. If Zach missed that critter must have been fast.

"ROOK YOU HAVE INCOMING!" I yelled into the Bluetooth. "Let's get him!" I yelled to Zach and Griffin, they were already reloading their crossbows so I jumped up and started heading for the door.

"I turned him around when he came out front. He is in the house somewhere!" Rook yelled, he must have fired a bunch of rounds from the silenced 1911 at the guy because I hadn't heard anything.

I relayed Rook's message to the team as we jumped into the hallway and started searching the house. Once I turned the corner into the first living area, a hand landed on my vest and shoved. I flew back a few feet, it wasn't like being shoved by Robert, it was a lot weaker than that but it was a lot stronger than a normal man's shove. I skidded back and smashed through what I assumed to be a priceless vase on a pedestal. Dante's house was one part bachelor pad, one part priceless museum, there were valuables everywhere.

"Avoid collateral damage, don't break the valuables!" I shouted back at Griffin and Zach. The man casually walked around the corner that he had pushed me from.

"Now that we can agree on, why don't we have a little chat?" he said while straightening his suit jacket.

"Sorry, I don't negotiate with terrorists," I said from my crappy position on the floor. I was still trying to dig my way out of the pottery and pedestal I had landed in. I tried to turn the WASR in his direction but he was on me in an instant. He grabbed the barrel and receiver and was holding it away from himself, trying to pin it sideways to my chest.

Thwack *Thwack* Two crossbow bolts landed in his side, Zach and Griffin had just fired and were running down the hallway towards

200

us drawing their batons. The man pushed himself much closer to me pinning the AK variant to my chest and he grabbed the straps on my vest and stood me up with him. There wasn't enough space for me to turn my WASR barrel into his chest so I reached back for my Glock. He saw what I was doing so he shoved me with all of his strength towards Griffin and Zach.

Me being a bigger than average dude worked against us in this situation because I bowled them both over. We were trying to get untangled from each other when we heard fast footsteps, the man was running towards us with a K-BAR in his hand. This was going to hurt. All of a sudden almost faster then my eye could track, a length of silvery chain and pale arms popped out of the nearest doorway and wrapped around his neck. Two manacled feet hit the back of his knees and he fell down onto his knees on the tile. Lydia had somehow been able to sneak around us and was choking the ever living shit out of this guy. He flipped the K-bar around in his hand and drove it behind him, landing it deep in Lydia's stomach. Zach had made it up first between the three of us and he ran at the man and straight kicked his face. He bent backward on top of Lydia.

"How about a little stick time fucker!" Zach yelled. He then started beating the man with his baton. Griffin and I joined in, trying to not hit Lydia, the dude eventually passed out.

We pulled him off of Lydia, she was bleeding all over the place out of her stomach. Griffin stepped in, he looked confused. I'm sure military medic school didn't cover vampire physiology.

"You regenerate right?" he asked her. She nodded her head and spit up some blood. "Then I apologize in advance for this," he said.

Then he yanked the blade out and blood started coming out of the wound faster. He opened his IFAK and pulled out some clotting powder and sprinkled it over the wound. Then he put a quick bandage over it, wiped the excess blood away and taped it down. We all stood Lydia up at Griffin's insistence, and then Griffin pressure wrapped it with an ACE bandage all the way around her torso so it would stay in place. I reached into one of the ammo slots on my vest and pulled out a plastic vial of animal blood. A few days prior I had ordered a thousand plastic vials off of eBay and had them next day shipped to my house.

"Power up woman!" I handed her one of the vials. She looked really confused but drank it.

"You brought blood for me, that's so nice..." she said.

Zach was bent over searching the unconscious man for any more weapons.

"Lydia we are going to need those handcuffs and chains," I said pointing at her. I pulled the keys out of a different pouch I had on the front of my vest and unlatched her arms and legs. Then I handed them all to Zach and asked him to politely chain up the guy in the suit. Lydia was staring at me, she looked completely befuddled. She was rubbing her wrists and smiling at me.

"You trust me now?" she asked.

"You just saved our lives, welcome to The Strikers!"

Chapter 13

"Who the hell are The Strikers?" asked Griffin.

"We are, we can't exactly be the Semen Demons forever; we aren't 14 anymore and I'm pretty sure Lydia doesn't even make semen," I replied.

"Fair point, Strikers it is. I like it. Lydia stop being a fucking noob and make some semen," Griffin replied.

Lydia and I couldn't stop laughing after that one. The sun was fully over the horizon now so we weren't worried about any more vampires showing up. I guess it was possible with the right UV protective automobile glass and what not but the advantage was on our side with the sun up. Speaking of that we needed a safe way to get Lydia into the truck, but I'll worry about that later. Zach grabbed the metal folding chair and put the unconscious man in the black suit in it. He left his legs and arms cuffed and then put about a thousand layers of duct tape around him thoroughly securing him to the chair.

"Okay, so I guess let's load everything we can into the truck. Lydia, can you go around and try to find out which of these things is the most valuable, and just generally organize. We might not have room for it all," I said.

"Wait! Some of these are cursed items, especially the ones behind glass. Not all of the ones behind glass are, but a lot of them will be. Don't touch anything without gloves on, even the non-cursed things. The cursed items, if you want them, we will have to roll up in a blanket or something and even then you should use gloves. I learned a little bit about this stuff in my supernatural research before I became a vampire. Everything not in a display case can be carried out now though safely but it still might be safer to keep the gloves on," Lydia said.

"Okay guys, you heard her. Let's start carrying this stuff out to the truck" I said.

"WAIT WAIT WAIT," yelled Rook into our Bluetooth call. I held up my fist so everyone could see, the universal sign for stop.

"What's up Rook," I asked him.

"A car just arrived and parked just outside the gate... Hang on... It's the daytime guard, he went straight into the guard booth," Rook finished. Then we heard a staticy voice along the wall next to the door, there was an intercom.

"Mr. Dante, this is Sam checking in for the day," Oh shit.

"What does Dante normally say back, or does he say anything?" I asked Lydia.

"Just say 'Thanks, Sam' and then tell him something about the movers," replied Lydia.

I put my shirt over my mouth to distort my voice a little and repeated what Lydia told me to say. I also mentioned we had some movers on the property replacing old furniture and that the intercom was acting up so we might have a repairman by later to check on it.

"Sounds good boss," he said without hesitation. Either he was a great liar and he was calling 911, or he really believed me.

"Rook did you hear all of that? If you see him make a call, let us know," I said into my headset.

"Got it, also I'm going to back this truck up right to the front door so he won't see you guys loading it," said Rook.

We loaded the truck for a couple of hours making sure to stay out of the view of the guard, but he was mostly looking outwards towards the dirt road. We loaded everything from ancient tomes, paintings, jewelry, pottery, scrolls and carpet to random assorted weapons. Things like maces, swords, flails, a few pieces of what looked like ancient armor, but I didn't know I'm not an armor expert. Hell, Griffin even took the espresso machine, he told me he had wanted one for awhile but this model was upwards of 500 dollars. We noticed as we were carrying things out that almost everything had an eight digit number on it, or on the pedestal or shelf that it was located on so we tried to keep those together or label those things with a small piece of duct tape and a sharpie with the number from the pedestal if we weren't also loading that.

Zach took a garbage bag he had filled full of console games out of one of the bedrooms which didn't seem like Dante's style but they may have belonged to one of the younger vampires. When we finally started working our way towards the back of the house, I got to a door that was locked. I called Griffin and Zach back to help me open it. It wouldn't budge so I had them cover the door with crossbows while I kicked it. It was tougher than it looked for an interior door so it didn't open until the third kick. When the door finally swung up it looked just like a normal office. Griffin and Zach cleared the room with their crossbows and then backed up when they were sure it was empty. I told them that I would check this room out then they went back to loading the truck and helping Lydia sort.

The office looked really normal, really just like any other home office you had seen. Some photos on the wall, a fake potted plant in the corner, some books and technical manuals on a bookshelf. The only thing really strange about this place was how far back the photos on the wall went, time wise. There were pictures of Dante on the wall clear back to what looked like the 1920's. There was only one older but it was a painting of him. He must have been well off as a human to be able to afford a painting, or maybe this was done right after he was made a vampire and he had forced someone to do it, who knew? He had a photograph for basically every decade after the 20's on up, it was neat seeing the clothing styles change.

It looked like he always had a different crew of lackeys in each picture or maybe he was one of the lackeys then. I wonder what was happening to them that stopped them from being in all of the continued photos. The landscapes in the background changed a lot as well. Dante must have been moving, trying to find his place in the world. When it got to what I assumed to be the 60's I recognized a face, Robert. The Kurt Cobain loving vampire that had attacked me in Lydia's apartment. Him, Dante, and a few others were standing in front of the Phoenix Coliseum, well that's what the locals of Phoenix called it. It's a giant building in downtown Phoenix that has a strong resemblance to the ancient Roman Coliseum, only much bigger, it's often rented out for car shows, and concerts and whatnot. I remember specifically that Nirvana had played there during the height of their music career, I bet Robert went to that show. So this must have been around the time that he had become "King" of Arizona, or at least the Phoenix area. I don't know why but I took that 60's era picture down, intending to take it with me. I sat in the office chair behind the desk in the room and started searching through the drawers. It was mostly stationary and different kinds of pens.

I felt something strange with the edge of my foot, I could see some black metal on the floor. I pushed the desk a foot or so back so I could see what it was. It was a small 80's or 90's style safe sunk into the floor. It went out to the truck and grabbed a crowbar and a cheater bar. I jogged back to the office excited to see what was in the safe. I wedged the crowbar into the crease between the door on the safe and the safe wall. I stepped on it a bit to make sure it was seated then I slid the cheater bar over the crowbar and threw my full weight against it. I felt a lot of give which is good news. I moved the crowbar around to a different side of the safe and repeated the process. I just kept doing that for about 10 minutes when finally the door popped out of the frame and then fell back down due to gravity. I seated the crowbar one last time and slowly opened the safe door. I only opened it about a quarter inch, then I ran my pocket knife around all three sides of the interior door checking for traps. I didn't feel anything obvious or hear anything so I opened the door the rest of the way.

Inside the safe was a bunch of paperwork, a nondescript book, a 1911, one thousand dollars cash and a grenade. I had a feeling that grenade wasn't a paperweight so I didn't touch it for now. I opened the book, it was a ledger of some sort with numbers on a side column and then strange explanations to the right of the numbers... OH! These were the numbers that the items were labeled with and the writing on the right was what Dante knew about the items. This is perfect! Lydia would love this. I called Lydia back and showed her the book and the rest of the things in the safe. I took two hundred dollars out of the thousand dollars and told her to split the rest of the money between her and the crew, then I told her to make sure the entire contents of the safe got into the truck including the grenade. She told me she would see it done.

I remembered that briefcase the asshole had thrown at me. I went into Lydia's former confinement room and rocked the briefcase back and forth until it popped out of the drywall. It was locked with some little briefcase clasps and a combo. So I took the K-BAR that the suited man had once carried out of the drywall of the hallway where I had stabbed it earlier, and jammed it into one of the clasps. I set the whole briefcase on the ground and applied pressure with my foot on the grip of the K-Bar. The clasp snapped very easily. I did the same with the other side, then I bent down and opened the case.

HOLY SHIT! There was row after row of cash in different numerical amounts with different colored bands around them. I closed the whole thing up and texted Rook to come inside for a minute. We had closed our call earlier now that the daylight was up. Rook was coming in every once in a while to stretch his legs and look for loot but we needed someone on over watch and he couldn't do any heavy lifting yet so he had mostly been sitting in the moving truck outside keeping an eye out. When I got to the living room the guy taped in the chair had woken up. He was trying to shout something but someone had taped his mouth shut.

Rook came in the front door and closed it behind him so no sunlight would burn Lydia. Lydia and Zach stopped organizing random valuables and came over. Griffin was sitting in what looked like a reclinable chair massager and just said "I am not moving dude, this thing is awesome, show me from here."

I set the briefcase on the ground and opened it, everyone inhaled sharply.

"Whoa," said Rook. Griffin jumped out of the chair and ran over, he pulled a stack out and flipped through it, then put it back.

"Why do some of the same denominations have different colored bands?" Griffin asked.

"I don't know, ask him," I said and pointed at the guy taped to the chair. Zach walked over to him and roughly pulled the tape off of his mouth.

"Answer my friend, what's with the different colored bands?" Zach said.

The guy in the chair just yelled "Fuck you!" and then he spit on Zach, big mistake. Zach punched the dude right in the stomach with no hesitation. The guy let out a little bit of air and then let out a pained laugh in Zach's face.

"Scoot over novice, you can't just punch the target, you have to punch through the target," I said to Zach. I stepped in front of our captive and wound up with everything I had. I was aiming right at his chest, I wanted to hit his stomach but I was too tall to drop a power hit on something that low. Keep in mind I'm 6' 2", almost 300 pounds and I punch a heavy bag for fun. I hit this dude so hard I am positive his mother felt it, him and the chair both went backwards and he hit the ground hard.

"Okay, that hurt," his strained voice barely escaped his mouth.

Zach kicked him for good measure, then yelled, "ANSWER THE QUESTION!" Then Zach lifted the man back up so his chair was on the ground again.

"The red bands are counterfeit money, and the green bands are real stacks."

At least three quarters of the briefcase was in a green band. Even with 25% of it or so being fake, this was a lot of cash.

"You would give counterfeit cash to a vampire, do you have a death-wish?" I asked him.

"No, I am giving him over the asking amount for the item I sold for him. He knows it's partially counterfeit. He gets more money for the item, and I have to pay less, it's a win-win," the man in the chair said.

"Tape his mouth again please Zach," I said.

Lydia interrupted us, "The woman in the room is stirring a little bit, I think she will wake soon. I saw her purse discarded earlier and used her phone from inside of it to call for an Uber, you will need to tell Sam to let the Uber in," Lydia said.

"Damn, good thinking Lydia!" I said.

Lydia smiled at me and blushed profusely, I needed to be careful with compliments around her. I called Sam over the intercom using the shirt over the mouth trick and told him to let an Uber car in when it arrived. When it pulled up out front next to the moving truck I took all of my armor off and checked myself in one of Dante's many mirrors and made sure I looked normal. Then I gently woke the woman in the bedroom and wrapped one of my arms around her and hoisted her up without giving her a choice.

"Whoa, good morning strong man, you look more handsome than you did last night. Where is your friend?" she asked me as I carried her down the hallway. Everyone else was out of sight and they had taken

213

the man strapped to the chair with them, we thought it would be best if she just saw me and not a house full of armed strangers and a captive.

"Oh, he is sleeping off the alcohol still," I said as I carried her. We reached the front door and I handed her 300 dollars cash. "Here, this is to pay for your ride home, I have to go help my sick grandma so I can't drive you myself. Hop in that car right there, it's an UBER," I told her.

"Just call me okay? Last night was amazing," she said, then kissed me on the cheek. I was feeling squirrely so I slapped her ass and pushed her out the door and locked it.

We really wanted to just leave all the cursed items behind but we couldn't in good conscience. I didn't exactly know what a cursed item was, but in my head, I was just imagining some realtor trying to sell this place and then growing tentacles out of his face for picking up the wrong keychain. We are the good guys, we can't do stuff like that. So once we had picked out all of the stuff that looked valuable, and all of the stuff that Lydia had assured us was valuable even though it didn't look it, we had Lydia lay out a blanket and put on some oven mitts from Dante's kitchen and one by one put all of the cursed items inside the blanket. Then she bundled it all up and tied all four corners into a knot. We then duct taped the knot as extra insurance. For good measure we pulled the tarp off of Lydia's bed, the one we were using to protect her from the UV and wrapped all the cursed items in that AGAIN over the blanket, it was "double bagged" so to speak.

We didn't bring even remotely enough packing gear and we didn't want to lose priceless valuables doing something as stupid as making a sharp turn in the truck so we ended up having to steal all of the bed sheets in the house for buffer protection. I would have been more hesitant to touch the sheets but I had gloves on, the idea of accidentally touching dried vampire jizz really grossed me out. Griffin recognized the sheets and told me they were Egyptian cotton 1,000 thread count and that they went for 500 dollars a set! DANG! Going to have to see if I can resell these, for now though, they are going to be my version of packing peanuts.

Once we had everything packed including the cursed items and everything even remotely valuable in the house, we made sure to load the freezer that was Dante's blood supply as well. Lydia would have to eat forever and I am a cheapskate at heart so we might as well take what I assumed to be thousands of dollars worth of vampire food with us. Plus it would be nice to put all of Lydia's blood in my garage, and I could now with this lay down freezer. Having a bunch of animal blood in my fridge had been a real appetite killer of late. We wrapped Lydia in a bunch of different blankets and then put her in the back of the truck, the overhang of the house went almost all the way to the truck so she was only in the sun for a second.

Once we had her settled, we went back for the guy tied to the chair and moved him in. Lydia would watch him as we drove. The last thing we had to do was to find some way to dispose of the all of the vampire popsicles that we had on ice. We were running out of time and didn't want to deal with the midday guard switch and have to risk lying to a second guard so we just unplugged the freezer, locked it with zip-ties and duct tape, and then dollied it into the truck as well. We did one more walkthrough of the house trying to cover any weird evidence and making sure we didn't leave any valuables that we might want.

I passed Otto Richter in his coffee table slash coffin. I couldn't just leave him here, he deserved to be put to rest. If vampires hated him, then he was probably a good guy in life. If this house was ever discovered by the authorities they might be asking some serious questions about a taxidermied human. We couldn't leave him for a myriad of reasons so we loaded him into the truck as well. I really wanted to ride in front with Rook but I didn't have a disguise and we figured the fewer people the guard saw the better so I got in the back with everyone else and we closed the door, we had also locked Dante's front door on the way out. We left a note we had printed out at my house pretending to be Dante saying he was going out of town and that he was having some money problems and that he didn't know when he would be back. Later tonight I would buy some plane tickets with his credit card using a VPN and then I would burn the credit card.

Rook pulled us off of Dante's property and he told me over my headset that the guard was happily watching movies on a tablet and had willingly let us through. Rook drove us about 10 miles away from Dante's property and then pulled behind a little strip mall that we had verified earlier in the week had no cameras in the rear. Zach and I carefully got out of the back making sure we didn't burn Lydia with any sunlight. We put all of our armor and weapons up in the front of the cab with Rook. Then we went to work peeling off all of the Plasti-dip. We also pulled all of the painters tape off of the license plate. When we had applied it, we had made sure to pull it very taunt, that way the metal ridges that made up the plate numbers wouldn't be seen through the tape if we were caught on camera.

We drove back to my house after that with Zach and I up front, and Griffin, Lydia, and Taped-To-Chair-Guy in the back. We were all crashing now that we were coming down off of our adrenaline high so we were too tired to unload. We got Lydia and the guy taped to the chair inside of my garage and then locked the truck up tight. Zach and Griffin had to get home to their wives and we assured them that was fine. Lydia, Rook and I would hold down the fort, and watch the truck and our newest prisoner. We all hugged each other goodbye, Lydia was really surprised when all of my friends hugged her, I saw her trying to hide some tears.

Rook asked if he could go crash, he was the injured one so I was more than happy for him to go rest up. He wasn't leaving but I hugged him anyways and made sure he knew I was happy for all of his help scouting the night before. Life is short, hug your friends. I was crashing hard now myself I could barely keep my eyes open. Lydia must have noticed.

"Bear, you can barely keep your eyes open. Go rest, I'll watch this guy," she told me.

I really wasn't sure if I trusted her enough to leave her unattended in my house while I was asleep but I didn't see another option with how tired I was. I was mentally and physically exhausted. I told her thanks for all the help, hugged her and then went to my room, Rook was in my guest room. I locked my bedroom door behind me, threw my gear at the base of my bed except for my WASR which I threw in the bed next to me, then passed out.

I woke up to the most amazing smell, 'bacon!' Someone was cooking bacon, it must have been one of my neighbors. There was no light coming in from outside the curtains so it must have been night time, I was going to go back to sleep. Then I heard a soft knock at my door. All of the memories of the last week came flying back to me, there was some kind of dark superhuman chained to a chair in my house and a vampire unattended as well somewhere around here. I grabbed my WASR and shouldered it. I slowly crept to the door and unlocked it and backed up a few feet. Then I put on a fake overly tired voice.

"Uhh, hello I'm sleeping..." my door handle started to turn so I aimed the WASR at the door. Lydia came in the room, I considered it a while but lowered the WASR. "Ah, I'm sorry this has just been a crazy week and I didn't know who was at the door," I told her.

"That's okay Bear, I just wanted to tell you that I made some food for you and Rook if you are hungry, oh and... nice boxers Romeo," said Lydia, then she turned and walked out of the room. I looked down, sure enough, I was in my boxers. I must have taken my pants off before crawling in bed, DOH!

I threw on some gym shorts and washed my face in the bathroom that was connected to my bedroom. I threw the WASR over one shoulder via the single point sling and headed towards the delicious smell of bacon. I met Rook in the hallway as he was coming out of my guest room,

"Bacon bro, I smell bacon," he told me still rubbing sleep out of his eyes.

Once we entered the kitchen we were amazingly surprised. First of all, some of the nicest artifacts, swords, paintings, vases, and pieces of armor had been prestigiously arranged and placed strategically around my house. Some on their original pedestals and some Lydia had hung on my walls or placed on my existing shelves. The whole kitchen was organized and smelled vaguely of cleaning products. On the kitchen table were three plates sitting out with giant bacon cheeseburgers on them with steamed broccoli on the side that had been drenched in melted cheese. I peeked into my living room and the suited man was still tied to the chair, but it looked like he had a fresh set of duct tape on him. This room had some valuables in it as well, it looked like Lydia had put some on my entertainment center and she had reorganized my books and parts of my bookshelves were now holding them too. The whole living room had been dusted and organized as well.

I heard my oven beeping back in my kitchen, so I headed that way. Lydia was pulling some cookies out of the oven! "LYDIA!" I shouted.

"What?" she asked.

"DON'T ACT LIKE YOU DON'T KNOW, THIS IS AMAZING!" I shouted. Lydia blushed deeply and started piling the cookies onto one of my plates.

"Come sit down," she said as she walked towards my kitchen table.

I was a decently clean and organized guy but this week had been hectic and I had been busy all week playing waiter and leader of The Strikers, so my house had been in a disarray before I had gone to sleep. It was spotless now, organized better than ever before, covered in valuables and it smelled like bacon and cookies... WOW!

"Lydia if you keep this up you are getting a raise! Seriously though, thank you so much!" I said.

"Well I had a lot of time. I was tired but someone had to be awake to watch dipshit over there. By the way, I untied him and let him use the bathroom once, don't worry I watched him…. That part really wasn't cool, but I figured you didn't want him dropping deuces in your house though and we have had him tied up all day. Besides that, I had nothing else to do and I couldn't exactly enjoy "Teen Mom" reruns with this dude tied up in there, so I made myself useful. I unloaded about half of the truck, I didn't know where to put it all so I just kind of put it everywhere," said Lydia.

"Welp, you are officially employee of the month!" I told her.

"HERE, HERE!" Rook lifted his beer in the air, when did he grab that? That man is a beer Houdini.

Chapter 14

We sat there around my kitchen table eating bacon cheeseburgers and cookies. Lydia had drenched most of her burger in animal blood which I pretended wasn't happening. I was hoping to make her feel normal, more like part of the crew. I had thought a lot about Lydia's situation and I had a deep and profound respect for her which was slightly overshadowed by my pity for her. Lydia had been destined to spend her short life getting weaker and weaker until she would ultimately have ended up in a wheelchair due to her sickness. She had denied fate its chance to paralyze her and thrown herself into a perilous situation. She had done her research and preparation and against all odds had done something that no one else had ever done before: she had become a sane and rational vampire. She was definitely bloodthirsty, no question about that, since the first time I met her she was half starved and was willing to murder me but as long as we kept her fed she seemed to be almost normal.

I remembered her mentioning that she and her roommate had been on a special college grant for foster kids but she had also said her grandmother had taught her how to sew and bake...

"Lydia, I hope this isn't too personal, and if it is, don't feel like you have to answer but how did you end up in foster care?" I asked.

"My grandma died when I was 12, she was a good lady. I bounced around foster homes after that. I had a bad attitude and was mad at the world. My Muscular Dystrophy scared a lot of adoptive parents off, and the ones it didn't scare off, I did with my crap behavior. I didn't want to be adopted, I just wanted my grandma back. She was the one who had raised me since my parents died when I was too young to remember. She was my last living relative as far as I know. I didn't really have any serious friends growing up. I was a bookworm and changed schools a lot whenever I went from foster home to foster home. My sickness was a ticking time bomb that I was constantly worried about which scared off romantic suitors as well so I have really always been alone. My roommate was the first person I have really connected with, her story was similar to mine. Then Dante killed her..." Lydia finished.

I didn't know what to say... This strong independent woman didn't need my sympathy. I'm sure she had gotten that her whole life from the people that had passed her around. She needed a friend.

"Lydia, look at me," I said.

She stared downwards a lot when she was embarrassed or sad, she didn't have a lot of self-esteem. We would have to fix that. I knew how to kick self-inflicted mental illnesses ass, I would help Lydia.

Once she looked at me I stared at her back, locking my eyes to hers, "You're not alone anymore, you have friends now. You helped save the life of me and my friends today, you are ALWAYS welcome here. If you need anything, you ask me and we will see it done. Also, you have something else you've never had before, LOTS OF FUCKING MONEY! Don't forget about the briefcase, we are all rich!" I told her.

She started crying out of happiness and laughing at the same time.

"I'm serious Lydia... We are bonded now. You are part of our inner circle, a part of our team." I reached across the table and grabbed her arm just above her wrist. Rook reached across the table and gently held her other wrist and we smiled at her.

"Thank you," she choked out.

"Okay enough emotional hobnobbing, we need to decide what to do with the guy taped to the chair. My vote is to interrogate and murder him. He worked with Dante and never tried to stop him. Meaning he is an accomplice to every bad thing Dante has ever done, every life he destroyed. I would also like to know why he is so damn strong," I said.

We discussed the issue a bit at the table and Rook and Lydia generally agreed with my verdict. Rook was a little more hesitant to outright murder but once he got the general idea that it would probably be me who would be doing the actual choppy choppy, he was a little less hesitant to embrace the plan. Lydia was still harboring a lot of hatred for everything Dante had put her through. So she was on board from the beginning knowing that this guy was one of Dante's associates.

I checked my clock, it was just after nine p.m. Sunday night, meaning Lydia had been up for a long ass time. I assumed vampires had better than average stamina but it can't be this good.

"Lydia why don't you head to bed, I'll deal with this dude," I said while pointing at the man taped to the chair.

"No way Bear, you are strong but you aren't fledgling vampire strong. I'm staying to help, I'll sleep when we are done," she replied.

Well, I guess we are doing this as a team, I grabbed a tarp out of my garage and brought it back in. I had Lydia lift the man's whole chair up with him in it and I spread the tarp out below him. I didn't want to fuck up my carpet with blood. Rook, Lydia and I were all standing in a semi-circle around him wondering how to start this, none of us had ever interrogated someone before. I broke the circle and went and got my cutlass. I'm the leader of this group and good leaders lead from the front. I'm not going to ask my people to do something that I am not willing to do. I would be the one to push the interrogation forward.

I walked up to the man and roughly ripped the duct tape off of his mouth, he started to scream the word "Help" but Lydia used her vampire speed and super open hand slapped him across the face which stopped his scream.

"That hurts, doesn't it? She did that to me last week, check it out." I turned the side of the face towards him where Lydia had slapped me and showed him my now yellowing bruise that was almost done healing. "Anyway, here is the deal pal. We are going to be asking you a lot of questions tonight. If you answer everything correctly we won't hurt you. If you answer correctly all night you have a strong chance of walking out of here alive if you promise to leave Arizona forever" I said. So what I lied, this asshole works with murderers.

"First of all, what is your place in Dante's crew, and what is your name?" I asked. At first, he didn't answer so I pulled my cutlass out of the scabbard. Before I could cut him he spoke up.

"For the purposes of this conversation you may call me The Broker, it is what most of my clients call me. Even though I am sure your bank accounts are missing a few zeros for me to ever seriously consider any of you as clients. I am not part of Dante's 'crew' as you so crudely put it. I don't work for Dante, I work with him occasionally. Through his long life, he has accrued many powerful and expensive items that I help him trade and sell for a price. I appraise said items, and sometimes I sell him more. Dante is, or I should say was, an interesting man and a man of wealth, but he was nothing more to me than a casual business associate. I know many like him. If you three are smart you will let me out of this chair and I will handsomely reward you. I'm not sure what you had against Dante, but I am not him." the Broker finished.

"Alright Mr. Brokeback Mountain fancy pants broker dude, so you sell and trade valuables and antiquities and you have a very screwy moral compass. So much so, that you are willing to ignore murder and kidnapping as long as you can make a buck, I get the gist of it. Why are you so strong?" I asked.

"I like to work out," he replied. I lifted my cutlass and rested it against his chest.

"Last chance before I go full slice and dice," I said.

"Alright, alright... I have very dangerous clientele, I have had to take certain precautions to protect myself. Having said that I consider myself a man of refinement and I avoid physical confrontation. My clients also have a vested interest in keeping me alive if they want to make money so this isn't exactly a problem I have run into before." said The Broker.

"Not good enough, you need to explain further. What do you mean by enhancements, you got a bionic penis or something? You were able to throw me around like I was your red headed step child, I need to know how" I said.

"I think our conversation ends here, this is one of the questions I am absolutely unwilling to answer. I'll warn you now one last time, my associates are very dangerous men. If they find out you have me here and you have hindered their business, they will come here and kill you. Then they will kill everyone you love" he said.

"So just to be clear you are refusing to answer even though you know I am going to cut you?" I asked.

He just stared straight ahead and pretended to not hear me. I really didn't want to torture this guy. What I wanted to do was to take him out to the desert and put a bullet in the back of his head and wrap this whole Dante saga up and move on with my life, but the key to winning any war is intel. I had to show him now that I wasn't playing around. I dragged a slow jagged line with my cutlass down his chest next to his right nipple cutting right through his suit, I could see the pain in his eyes but he didn't cry out. Blood welled up and soaked through that part of his suit.

"Ready to answer?" I asked.

228

"You don't have what it takes to truly torture me. I will heal from this petty wound in a matter of hours. I see how you preen over that lost little bird there, taking your pathetic revenge out on Dante over some sense of justice. You see yourself as some kind of a 'moral crusader,' give up this pointless pursuit now and I won't have my associates murder you..." The Broker finished.

"Pal, you don't know anything about me, you say you will heal from this. I'll give you something you can't heal from," I said.

I started cutting into his chest more where I had left off. I just kept cutting all around his right nipple. I pulled at his suit where I had been cutting, ripping off the pieces that were hanging by shreds now. I could see his bloody chest and the wound I was creating more clearly now. I cut a rough square around his nipple and then used the tip of my sword to rip the whole thing off of his chest. He was openly screaming now so Lydia put her hand over his mouth. I had his nipple and the skin around it on the tip of my cutlass and I made sure to hover it around his eyes so he could see it before I flipped it onto the tarp at my feet, and then the self-proclaimed big bad Broker passed out.

"Wait, am I the little helpless bird in this situation?" Lydia asked.

Rook looked a little green around the gills but he stuck with us, he had left the room when I had started cutting and he went and grabbed

229

an IFAK. I wiped the excess blood off of The Broker's chest and then sprinkled a lot of clotting powder in his wound. Then I folded up a bunch of gauze into a thick square and pushed it onto the wound and used some medical tape on all 4 sides to hold it in place. I was no slouch when it came to field medicine either. I'm no Griffin but I did go through the CLS (combat lifesaver) course a few times in the army.

"Lydia, when this guy wakes up can you go all scary vampire face on him?" I asked.

"No problem Bear," she replied.

Rook handed me some smelling salts and I cracked them right in The Broker's face. 'Smelling salts' is actually a misnomer since there is no actual salt in them. The Broker's eyes snapped open and his head shot off of his chest.

"That's right cum bucket, welcome back to reality!" I shouted.

I snapped my fingers in his face a few times "Are you with us? Fucking answer me!" I slapped each side of his face hard.

"STOP! I'm here, I'm awake," he said.

"Okay, old buddy old pal, let's try this again," I said, then I placed my cutlass on the left side of his chest that I hadn't cut yet. "Are you going to be a good boy and start answering my questions or do I need to make your chest a little more symmetrical and cut off your other nipple? You know if you make me go that far I'm just going to cut some

230

of your toes off too, and I bet your cool little powers don't regrow toes." I said.

"Don't hurt me... what do you want?" he asked. He seemed out of it, if he starts dozing off I'm going to have to hit him with the smelling salts again.

"You were just about to tell me how you are so strong" I reminded him.

"Right... right... human sacrifice..." He was really in a lot of pain.

"What? That can't be right... you just kill a bunch of people and you get stronger?" I asked.

"No... You have to call a dark deity first," he choked out.

I could tell his chest must have really been on fire. I went to my kitchen and grabbed an old bottle of vodka I had and filled up a shot glass. I came back into the room and put it The Broker's lips and yelled, "DRINK!" He drank it down, I filled it up again and repeated the process.

"Vodka makes all things better. Let's start with something easy, what is your real name?" I asked.

"My name... My real name is Percival," he said.

"Okay Percival, I'm Bear and I'll be your interrogator this evening. I think we are clear on what happens when you don't answer my questions quickly and honestly. I'm not opposed to cutting more of your various parts off, so if you want to be in one piece when you leave this house in the morning, I recommend you play ball. So let's try this again. Why are you so powerful? Who did you sacrifice? What dark god are you talking about? Tell me everything, GO!" I said.

"I've never spoken of this... and my chest really hurts. I became this way on accident but it has worked in my favor..." He looked deep in thought but still in pain, there was a lull in his explanation so I put my cutlass back on his chest and applied the slightest pressure.

"Alright, sorry, I'm thinking, please stop that. Where was I... Well, it all started because my neighbor was an uncultured swine of the highest order... Can I have some more of that vodka?" he asked. I poured a shot and put it to his lips and lifted, he greedily drank it down.

"Right, I have always been an antiquities dealer. I got into the business early, It was a family business that my father never got into so it was just my grandfather and I. I became his protege and he taught me everything. When I was in my late 20's, he died and passed the business and a considerable sum of money onto me. My father was always mad at me about that but I didn't care. I bought a nice condo in downtown Phoenix. It was the perfect spot. It had everything; a pool, a view, sophistication... it even came with free cable," Percival said.

"Free cable? What year was this?" I asked.

"This was in 1991," he replied.

"What the fuck, how old are you? You look like you are about 30," I said.

"I was 29 in 1991, today I am 55 years old. I made a deal with a... with a *divinity* for lack of a better word. I never found out its true nature, but I will get to that. I was in my amazing new condo with a thriving business and a booming bank account. Everything was perfect except for my neighbor... Larry. Every morning he would wake me up with his noxious workout racket. I was a gentleman... an aristocrat... I had moved into a high-end apartment so I wouldn't have to deal with things like that. I told management about it but it turns out Larry was related to someone in management and I couldn't force their hand. Every morning he would be playing loud music and banging weights around for his daily workout which he insisted he had to do promptly at five a.m., I didn't open my storefront until 10 a.m. so this was extremely early for me. I had asked politely over and over again for him to please be quiet in the morning or to move his workout to another time, he always refused and slammed his door in my face..." Percival finished.

"More alcohol please good sir, I am actually enjoying telling someone this story that I have had buried deep inside of myself for so long, but I am afraid this chest wound you have inflicted on me is much too painful," he said. I complied and gave him another shot, he was in deep thought for a minute but then he continued his story.

"One morning when I was at my wit's end, I was rudely awakened from my sleep. I was absolutely furious, I had had a stressful week at work. I had a few cranky clients who were berating me because I couldn't sell their exotic goods in record time. These wealthy troglodytes were relentlessly hounding me and on top of it all, my neighbor didn't have the common courtesy to let me sleep in the early morning. I marched over to his door and pounded on it until he shouted that it was open and to come in. He had a small home gym set up in one corner of his condo and he didn't even stop exercising when I entered. He was on one of those ridiculous weight bench thingies. I yelled at him that he needed to quiet down or he would be speaking to my lawyer, and he laughed! He then proceeded to call me a faggot and told me to leave his apartment. I couldn't control myself, I grabbed one of his smaller weights and hit him over the head with it. He couldn't even attempt to stop me because he was still lifting a heavy weight and laying down on his workout bench, it was easy... He dropped the heavy weight on himself that he was carrying which only exacerbated his already gruesome injuries... I was able to wiggle the weight off of him once I realized what I had done but it was too late, he was dying..." Percival finished.

Chapter 15

"So then what happened," I asked.

Percival... The Broker... Whatever you want to call him ignored me. I couldn't tell if he was drunk, in pain, or having some kind of psychological trauma induced psychosis. I used pain to snap him out of it. WHOP. I smacked him across the face open-handed.

"FINISH YOUR STORY!" I yelled in his face. He seemed to snap out of whatever he was doing and continued on.

"Oh yes, where was I? I had attacked Larry in a moment of anger, his blood was flowing quite freely and I am sure he was only minutes away from death... Something possessed me, not in the religious sense just a dark thought at first, a spark in the night but it triggered a memory. I had begun collecting occult tomes in my price range for one of my higher end clients who would buy them from me at quite a mark up. One of the tomes discussed an ancient ritual used by the Aztecs to summon what they assumed to be a Demigod named Mictlantecuhtli," said Percival.

"Micka who?" I asked.

"Mictlantecuhtli, you uneducated Luddite. That doesn't matter though, let us move on. I had only browsed some of the tomes but this one had called to me. I read it from beginning to end, well the translated version of it. Something kept urging me onward as I read it, some latent power whispered to me. I was a man possessed as I burned through it but then I was done and I never much thought of it again, until I almost killed Larry. As I said before it was clear to me that Larry only had minutes left in this world. His injuries were severe and he was bleeding profusely. The book that explained the ritual of Mictlantecuhtli promised unfounded power with limitless potential. I ran to my apartment and grabbed my translated version of the tome, then ran back. I opened it to the page that explained the ritual. The ritual was simple you just had to have a source of fire nearby, even a candle would work. Then you throw a handful of salt on your sacrifice, whisper an incantation and wait for Mictlantecuhtli to arrive. I repeated the words from the tome, they were rough on my tongue...

Seconds later a disgusting visage appeared. He looked like a blood-spattered skeleton with fully functioning eyeballs roaming around in his empty skull. His voice was that of the chitters of thousands of spiders. I still have nightmares about him. He told me to kill the sacrifice which I very happily did. That asshole Larry was already on the precipice of death so I just hit him with the weight one more time to extinguish his life, I felt no remorse for killing Larry. I got on my knees in front of Mictlantecuhtli, ready to receive his dark gift of power. I didn't even fully understand what it would be. Before he could bestow it upon me though, I heard a small voice come from behind me, 'Daddy?' it said. Children weren't allowed to be in these condos, it was one of the main reasons I had moved here. Later I would find out that Larry was divorced with split custody and it was his weekend to have his two girls. That imbecilic asshole was breaking the condo's rules. I couldn't have the children reporting me so... so they also became more sacrifices to Mictlantecuhtli..." Percival finished.

I had heard enough... I was floored with righteous fury, I could barely contain my voice but I tried anyway. "Where is the tome now?" I said through gritted teeth. He still seemed confused or something but at my question, his eyes became focused.

"The tome? Oh that item is much too dangerous, I destroyed it and the translated copy. I tattooed the incantation on my arm. I have heard that there are copies of it elsewhere in the world but I have never been able to acquire them. I couldn't have someone else using the ritual and becoming as powerful as me, but I didn't want to forget the incantation. What if I wanted to empower my offspring one day or renew my own dark abilities? Yes... this is why I had the incantation tattooed on my arm with a special symbol that I am told helps make you resistant to otherworldly nudges, as it were."

I stopped him there, I had the information I needed. I was seething with anger, I was seeing red.

"Just to be clear, you killed both of Larry's little girls didn't you?" I asked him.

"Well yes, I had to. What choice did I have, they had seen me and..." Percival didn't get to finish that sentence.

I had taken a mighty overhead swing with my cutlass and cleaved his head almost in two parts starting at his forehead and going all the way down to the middle of his neck. Blood sprayed all of us.

Rook gasped and Lydia just licked her lips and said "I was wondering when you were going to do that."

I used my cutlass again and cut off Percival's arm. I took out a piece of paper from a nearby drawer and copied the words and symbol that was tattooed on the arm onto the paper, then I roughly threw the arm back at Percival's body. The arm bounced off of his chest and landed on the tarp at Percival's feet. The vibration from the arm hitting his chest made the two halves of his head fall apart. I was shaking now, I had to sit down. The monster in front of me had killed children... Death was too good for him. I should have tortured him longer, I should have filleted all of the flesh from his body. I was stopped mid-thought by a strange noise emanating from Percival's corpse, it sounded like a deep growl and then a slow purple neon vapor with a slight glow to it started leaking from his neck, it was followed by a purple flash and then it was gone. Everything was still again.

239

"WHAT THE FUCK WAS THAT?" Rook asked.

"I bet it was his stolen life force... or whatever Michelob Ultra or whatever his name was, gave him," I said.

"Dude, next time you cut someone's head in half fucking warn me first, I liked this shirt!" Rook yelled.

"Yeah... Yeah, I'm sorry." I think I was going into shock.

Now I had truly killed a human with no remorse. He had been a disgusting human with no morals, but I had crossed a line that I wasn't ready to cross... Lydia saw my pained expression and disappeared into the kitchen. She came back with a wet washcloth and wiped my face, I barely even noticed her presence. Then she got Percival's restraints off and took him out of the chair and gently laid him on the tarp. She took the chair out of sight and came back, then started slowly rolling up the tarp around Percival. She easily picked the whole thing up and went to my backyard.

"Listen dude, I'm going to head home. I think I'm mobile enough to make my own meals and stuff now. Thank you for taking care of me when I was sick, but I'm tired, exhausted, covered in blood spatter and I need some time alone. I love you brother but I'm heading to my apartment for a few days," Rook told me. Then he patted my shoulder and grabbed a few of his things and left.

I'm not sure how long I sat on that couch but I couldn't help but think about those poor girls Percival had killed. I needed to be stronger, and I needed to be faster. I needed to be there when it mattered. I needed to stop terrible things from happening. I made a promise to myself that I would get better at being the hero. I'm not sure how long I sat there but Lydia came back at some point. She took my bloody shirt off and lead me to my room and told me to go to bed. I laid in my bed in a fitful state, trying my best to rest for awhile before finally falling asleep.

I woke up the next morning, Monday morning. I hadn't even opened my eyes fully yet but I could sense the muted sunlight coming in around the edges of my curtain. I rolled slightly over but couldn't move too much because there was an unfamiliar weight on my arm, did Mia crawl into bed with me last night? I cracked my sleepy eyes open and then was startled, there was a woman in my bed. She slowly roused and turned over to look at me.

"Lydia?" I asked.

"Oh yeah, hi!" she replied.

"Why are you in my bed?" I calmly asked her.

"Oh! Well, I didn't want to sleep on the floor again like I have been doing and you looked so upset last night, I didn't want to leave you alone. I didn't know where you wanted me to sleep, and when I checked on you last night you were having a nightmare so I sat down to check on you but I hadn't slept yet so I got tired and fell asleep. I am sorry Bear" she said.

"Listen Lydia... I like you, I really do and I appreciate everything you have been doing for me and my friends, but we just met and we are both in an emotional and stressful place. If I am completely honest with you, I just started something up again that I have had with someone else for awhile, a confusing off again and on again situation but I think she means something to me. It wouldn't be fair to you or to her if I was with you right now. I know you care for me and I am truly humbled by that. You are an amazing and beautiful woman but now is not the right time. In the future can you take the guest room until we figure stuff out? It's empty now that Rook has left," I said.

Lydia looked upset at first, and then resolute. "I'm sorry Bear. I overstepped my bounds, I understand. This won't happen again," she said and then she slowly stood up and got out of my bed. "You will tell me about this woman during breakfast, yes?" she asked.

"Sure Lydia," I said, then she left my room. Oh shit... my life had went from simple to uber complicated in a very short amount of time... I laid there in my bed and couldn't help but think about last night's events, especially the Michelin Man or Mickle Pickles or whatever that deities name was. A dark thought kept bouncing around in my brain, could I steal power from this deity and use it for good? Is there a shortcut to becoming a more efficient holy warrior? A common idiom that gets bounced around the military came to mind *"If you aren't cheating, you aren't trying."*

OH MY GOD! I JUST REMEMBERED THE FREEZER FULL OF VAMPIRES IN THE TRUCK! I jumped out of bed and grabbed my WASR and started sprinting down my hall towards the moving truck. Lydia heard the commotion and shouted from the kitchen "Bear, everything okay?"

"NO, I just remembered the vampires locked in the now unplugged freezer!" I shouted back.

"Bear, stop! I unloaded that last night and plugged it into your garage along with the freezer full of blood. Everything is good, those vampires are still in popsicle mode," said Lydia.

A huge weight was lifted off of my chest upon hearing that. I was at my front door about to open the locks when Lydia had yelled that so I gravitated towards where I had heard her voice, the kitchen.

When I got there I said, "Lydia, you know what you are? You are a god damn life saver, I don't know what I would do without you." Lydia blushed profusely. Well, I was already in the kitchen now so I might as well get some breakfast.

"I'm going to grab a bowl of cereal, can I make you one?" I asked Lydia.

"Sure, but I was going to make you breakfast," she replied.

"Oh don't worry about it, you are too kind. I'll make us some cereal. It's no fancy amazing Lydia breakfast, but you can't beat an early morning sugar overdose," I said.

She seemed to think about it, "Sounds good Bear, but don't add milk. I'm going to make blood cereal!" she said excitedly. I couldn't help but laugh out loud, then the mental picture of blood cereal hit me and I was grossed out.

Lydia and I had a great breakfast together, we talked about everything including Emily, which she was surprisingly cordial about. She even said Emily sounded like a nice person. Lydia was turning out to be an amazing friend. While we were talking I had a thought.

"Lydia I have been thinking about all of the human blood we now have in the garage. I was also thinking how well you seem to be doing with the animal blood. I grew up poor as hell so I can't go throwing away what is essentially high end food for you, but maybe we should mix that stuff 50/50 with animal blood so you don't... I don't know... get a taste for the good stuff," I said awkwardly, hoping I wasn't offending her.

"That's a good idea Bear!" she said cheerfully. Whew, that's another problem taken care of.

"We should probably contact the boys today and let them know we took care of Percival and that we aren't running off to Mexico with all of the money and loot, by the way, what did you end up doing with him?" I asked.

"Oh, I buried him VERY deeply in your backyard, no one will ever find him. Vampire strength is very useful while digging. I poured all of your bleach on him as well before I filled the hole up, just like you did to me, asshole," Lydia said. Okay, that made me laugh and Lydia joined me in laughter over that one.

We sent a group text message out to everyone with a rough summary of Percival's crimes and what we had ended up doing with him and told everyone they should come over Sunday night for dinner like we had talked about during the raid. We could split loot and cash then, and discuss future plans for The Strikers. I spent the rest of that day unloading the moving truck into my house, and Lydia was helping me organize it all. She didn't want to help me unload and accidentally get burned by the sun. I didn't know what to do with Otto Richter and his coffin so I just brought him inside for now. I really wanted to lay him to rest but that fully automatic pristine Tommy Gun that I could see with him in his coffin kept drawing my eye. Is it grave robbing if the person isn't in a grave? If Otto was the enemy of vampires, wouldn't he want me to use his weapon in a war against them? Or is that kind of logic just me trying to moralize grave robbing? I don't know. I will figure out all of that later, for now, he will be a cool decoration in my house. I made a promise to myself though that eventually he would get the funeral he deserves.

I returned the moving truck later that day after thoroughly cleaning it and double checking that no plasti-dip or blood was inside of it. When I got home, Lydia and I counted the money in the briefcase. There was 75,000 dollars in real cash, and 25,000 dollars in counterfeit. I thought there might be more but there was a lot of smaller denomination bundles in there. I had no idea what we were going to do with the fake money but for now, I would just lock it in my safe; I had a VERY LARGE safe. Lydia and I discussed what we would do with the cash, for now, we counted out five stacks of 4,000 dollars each. 4,000 dollars for each of the members of the party. We hoped this would be okay with them. We still had about 55,000 dollars left of real cash. Lydia and I discussed what we could or should do with the money for a very long time. We finally decided that The Strikers really needed a headquarters and we couldn't keep using my house for everything. $55,000 would make an amazing down payment, and we would have even more if we sold off a bunch of these valuables and antiques. I gave Lydia the job of using Dante's ledger and finding all of the items that actually had some kind of magical worth to them that might yield a real world utility for The Strikers, she happily accepted the task.

The rest of the week was uneventful except on Wednesday I had a really good date with Emily. We met at her house for obvious reasons while Lydia stayed at my house on guard duty. We basically always needed someone at my home now since I had over an estimated million dollars worth of valuables there. Emily and I stayed up late at her place watching goofy movies. I ended up staying the night, take that information for what you will, a gentleman doesn't kiss and tell. She was really interested in how my part-time private security job was going and that gave me a great idea. We couldn't just all become rich overnight, the IRS would be all over our asses. We needed a legitimate business to launder all this vampire money through. Why not open a security business? It would give us a good excuse to register a bunch of automatic weapons and to have armored vehicles and what not. If we were a registered security business, all kinds of doors would open for us and people would expect us to be carrying guns and armor... This could be a game changer for The Strikers. I kissed Emily hard and told her she was a genius after I had the thought which confused her, so I just told her I was thinking about opening my own security business and that I had just come into some money and the idea was thanks to her. Emily told me that she wanted to make me more of a priority in her life, I felt the same way about her so I told her I would do the same. When I had returned from Emily's the next day, Lydia gave me the cold shoulder for a few hours before she finally broke down and started talking to me again.

Lydia was an amazing roommate, she even insisted on paying part of the mortgage that month at my house since she was officially living with me until she got her own place. She was pretty sure she was legally dead or at least had a missing persons case put out on her so she didn't know how she would do that. Plus, if she came forward she might also be a person of interest in her roommate's disappearance case as well. Which would lead to all kinds of questions she couldn't answer and thanks to me and Robert's scuffle, her off campus apartment is full of bullet holes and vampire blood soup; so for now, she had to lay low. I felt really guilty about the whole dating Emily thing for some reason even though I had been very clear with Lydia about my feelings on the subject. Lydia had really had a short and rough life, and now she was eternally damned and the sad part was that that was the better alternative for her. I had also had a pretty shitty and rough life so I could really empathize with her. So it should go without saying but I really didn't want to hurt her. Thursday night I told Lydia we should go out for a night of goofing off, I called Griffin and asked if he could watch my place for awhile, he agreed once he heard my reasoning.

When Griffin arrived, I had two giant pizzas laid out with a side of garlic knots from Pizza By Napoli. He was super thankful for the amazing dinner I had bought for him. I also paid him with a one hundred dollar bill for watching the house which he tried to refuse but I wouldn't let him. I love my friends and when I was younger and had daydreamed about someday being rich, I had always told myself that I would make my friend's lives better too. Lydia and I went out as soon as the sun went down. We first went to the mall and I bought a ridiculously expensive dark grey two-piece suit with a cobalt blue satin tie. This was the kind of suit that I would have laughed at people for buying just a few weeks ago due to its price, I would have considered it a giant waste of money, but now I have money to waste! I took it to the tailor in the mall and paid him triple his asking price if he could have it fitted within the hour, he agreed. Lydia bought a strapless, knee length, emerald green party dress with black floral tulle overlay.

Lydia was looking amazing in her dress. The green in the dress really made her dark brown eyes pop. It blended well with her light brown hair as well. I was looking pretty snazzy myself in my suit. I had to buy some dress shoes to go with it before we left the mall but Lydia was more than happy to help me search for some. We didn't really know where to go from there, Lydia suggested dancing but I am an absolute terrible dancer so I suggested video games and alcohol. We have a large establishment here just off the highway called Dave and Busters. It's basically a two story bar covered in video games and those goofy games like skee ball and weasel pop that give you tickets when you win. Except the "Winners Circle" in this place where you exchange your tickets for prizes is meant for adults so you can win things like beer tumblers, beach towels, guitars, basketballs, etc. We played and drank for hours, Lydia's superior strength and reflexes netted us tons of tickets. They actually had a really good food menu there as well so we ordered some giant nachos and had them split it onto two different plates. I had loaded a bunch of the mini vials I had ordered offline with animal blood and stored them in my fridge so Lydia grabbed some before we had left that night. She used one of the mini vials on her own nachos now and drenched them in blood.

This establishment doesn't give you actual tickets, it gives you virtual tickets that it puts onto a Dave and Busters credit card. By the end of the night, we had thousands upon thousands of tickets to spend at the winner's shop but we didn't really see anything we wanted.

"Who do you think are the poorest people in here? Not the laziest, but you know, the down on their luck type of folks?" I asked.

"Hmm... Let's see," Lydia said. Then she pinched her eyes closed and stood very still, after about a minute she opened her eyes and said "Them over there," and she pointed at a young couple in average looking clothes who were sitting at a booth.

"How the hell do you know that?" I asked.

"Vampire hearing. They were talking about splitting a meal so they could afford to pay their rent, it wasn't a joke," she said.

"Follow me," I told Lydia and walked over to the couple. They were young, somewhere between maybe twenty and twenty three years of age. I put our Dave and Busters credit card on their table and a one hundred dollar bill.

"Hi! We would like to cover your dinner this evening, pay it forward someday! Also, there are some tickets on that card there. I hope you guys can get something good. Have a good night!" I said.

Before they could reply I took Lydia's hand and guided her away. The female of the couple stood up and yelled, "THANK YOU, SIR!" at us as we were walking away. I kept pulling Lydia towards the exit.

Once we got outside, Lydia threw her arms around me which surprised me. "You are a good man, Bear," she said. I gently patted her back before pulling away.

"Well, thank you, Lydia. I like to think so. Let's head home. Griffin is probably bored out of his mind and I don't want him to have to wait up on us all night," I said. Lydia agreed and we walked, talked, laughed, and joked all the way to the car. Once we got home we told Griffin about our night and Lydia proudly told him the story of how we had paid for the young couples dinner and given them enough tickets to get any prize in the shop. Griffin thought it was really cool. We all said our goodbyes and Lydia and I hugged Griffin. Once Griffin left, Lydia walked over to me and grabbed my hand. I tried to look into her eyes but she stared at the floor.

"Thank you for an amazing evening, Bear," she said. I gently took her chin and raised her head until we were eye to eye.

"You are supposed to look at people when you talk to them," I told her.

"Old habits die hard," Lydia replied.

"You don't need old habits, now you are a mildly wealthy woman who is a founding member of Arizona's premier up and coming security company. You have a circle of friends that love and trust you. You are a powerful vampire that will stay young and beautiful forever. Fuck old habits Lydia, realize who you are NOW," I told her. Then she hugged me for a long time, she cried a little bit but finally stopped.

"I'm going to sleep, thank you for everything," she said.

"Night Lydia," I told her, then went to bed myself.

Chapter 16

It was finally Sunday. The day of our 'friend dinner,' and the first official planning meeting of The Strikers. Lydia had completely remodeled my guest bedroom and bought some more clothes for herself during the week. Friday evening right after sunset, she had even taken my car and gone and bought herself some soft armor from Scottsdale Gun Club. She had wanted to buy a gun while she was there but I told her that she probably shouldn't use her driver's license for anything since she might be part of an active police investigation. I could have gone with her and used my license for the background check but I didn't want to crowd her and I wanted her to know that I trusted her to go out on her own. When she got back, I had pulled a Remington 870 out of my safe which is a really nice universal pump shotgun. A while back I had bought some subsonic rounds for it which basically meant they fired very quietly, it wasn't quite a silenced weapon but it was close. I handed her the shotgun and a bandolier full of shells.

"Every member of The Strikers needs a weapon Lydia, this is yours," I told her.

"YOU GOT THIS FOR MEEEEEEEEE?" she squealed excitedly, jumping up and down.

"Let's consider it a long term loan until you get your own. I'll teach you how to use it soon. These are special subsonic shells I've loaded into a bandolier for you and there are five in the weapon now. They're not as loud as normal shells, but still pretty loud," I told her.

Sunday had come very fast, but time flies when you are having fun. With me not being at work and catching up on reading and gaming while confidently sitting on thousands of dollars, which to me was a lot of money, had just melted all of my stress away. We were all a little burnt on pizza, so I had picked up a bunch of party platters of mini-chimis (chimichangas) from a local restaurant called Manuel's.

I thought about getting a keg for the boys, but we were all rowdy alpha male veterans and my house was now full of valuables, so drunken tomfoolery was probably the wrong answer for this meeting. Instead, I put out a pitcher of purified water, a pitcher of juice and put on a pot of coffee. We were having this meeting at four pm since Zach had work in the morning and his wife would murder him if he stayed out 'drinking' again, especially on a night that his kids had school the next morning.

Lydia and I had been doing a lot of research into magical items which is a lot harder than you would imagine. If you run a Google

255

search on them, you just get a bunch of information about video games which I do enjoy but that wouldn't help me in this current endeavor. We had to go old school and hit libraries and some of the books we had plundered from Dante's house. Most of what we read was theory and speculation, a lot of this Lydia had already gone over in her own independent research. Long story short, the strong ones were next to impossible to create without doing something disgusting and irredeemable, like murdering a bunch of puppies, or your first born kid, or eating another human, etc. The weaker charms were basically almost useless. Their effects were so minimal unless they were stacked with other charms, but that could have terrible side effects as well.

Lydia's ring was an example of this. Her ring basically helped to keep her staunch moral code and most of her sanity during her transition into vampire. She didn't want to become a monster so to speak, so she had stacked every weak charm and spell she possibly could onto the ring and combined it with other untested magical processes. This is normally something people aren't willing to do, but since she was planning on technically dying and becoming a blood sucking monster anyway, she didn't have much to lose. As a further example, imagine you stack a bunch of charms and enchantments that can make people happy all onto a hypothetical amulet. You plan on giving this amulet to a friend of yours that is having problems with depression. You give them the amulet and all of the charms and enchants combined make them so happy that they decide they are now ready for even more happiness which can only be attained in heaven, and then they kill themselves to get there. Or maybe this same hypothetical person is wearing this hypothetical amulet and they accidentally cut their hand while cooking. Well now that everything is fun and happy to them, they realize even cutting their hand is fun so they just keep cutting and cutting until they are dead. Boom... Not only has your original plan backfired, you have also accidentally made what scholars call a 'cursed object.'

There is a fine line you have to walk because combining magical enchantments is very dangerous and should only be done as a last resort, or preferably never. It's normally a situation where you have to fail twenty times to succeed once but the failures in this scenario are often represented by human lives. Every up and coming magical scholar throughout history thought they were going to be the one to find the solution and crack the code. That thinking almost always ended in bloodshed. Even Lydia's cure for keeping your morality and possibly your human soul after a transition to vampire, repeated exactly, might not work on someone else. It worked on Lydia due to her complete lack of drive for power or other standard human wants, she went into her vampire transition with no hubris. Her only want was to not be paralyzed, this created a unique set of circumstances. Which leads me to believe that she is a one of a kind.

However, after saying all of this there are those who have succeeded in making stable magical objects but that only happens once in a lifetime if you are lucky and normally at great cost. That asshole Dante had somehow collected two dozen or so of these items. We had no idea how they were created unless Dante had written that part down in his ledger which more often than not he hadn't. Most likely because he didn't know himself. Lydia and I had found four of the most stable defensive pieces, and four of the most stable offensive pieces. We had decided we didn't want to push our luck, so each of the boys and I would only carry two pieces each, one offensive and one defensive. The four offensive items we had picked were long daggers, almost short swords. Three of which were part of a set which Dante had notes on. They had actually all been created by the same man in the sixteenth century. I'm paraphrasing here but he was a 'nobody' who had been trying to make a name for himself. So he took his life savings and commissioned the building of three daggers meant for a king.

He needed a way to imbue these three daggers. A power source so to speak which he had been looking for, for years. He had married a woman with three sons from a former marriage and her sons were all dickheads in one way or another. Eventually one day in a fit of rage he decided to use them as the power source. He stole their life force and put the life force from each son into a dagger. No one quite knows how he pulled that off, some say he paid the court mage a great sum of money to learn the ritual. The pommel of each dagger was a pointed piece of quartz, the dagger's guard was two sturdy metal prongs that were curved towards the blade. The grip was a mix of rough metal bands that jutted out from the tang to help you maintain grip, and in between the rough metal sections someone had expertly wrapped black stained leather.

After the transfusion of life force into the three daggers, the quartz on the end of each one had picked up a colored hue which best represented each son's personal style of assholery. One had turned red for the fiery anger that son exhibited. One had turned blue for the ice like demeanor of the second son. The last one had turned black for the vile behavior of the third son. The man's wife, upon learning what he had done to her three crotch fruit, attacked him. He was a large man though and he easily subdued her. He bound her to a chair and tested his new super powered daggers on her. The one with the red crystal severely burned her, the one with the blue crystal froze her incisions. He never could figure out what the black crystal dagger did because his neighbor had alerted the constabulary when the three sons disappeared. They arrived and killed the man while trying to take him into custody. The daggers may have been powerful but they didn't make you a good fighter and he was no match for the constables.

Dante had tested the black quartz dagger on one of his lackey's arms. The lackey had reported feeling extremely sad for three days afterwards, and the wound took longer than average to heal. Vampire and human physiology are different though so this dagger was still somewhat of a mystery. The fourth dagger, the one that wasn't part of the set was extremely plain and well balanced. Dante didn't know its origins, but its purpose had been discovered. If you kept the dagger on your person for seven days, you would always instinctively know where it was. Basically making it impossible to lose. Seems like the worst dagger among the four, but I had already thought up some interesting uses for it and claimed it for myself. The main reason I had claimed it though was because of how balanced it was. I was the only one among my friends that knew anything about throwing edged weapons so it made sense that I should take the throwable one. Dante also indicated that he had come up with an interesting use for it, thief bait. It was one of the pieces he always kept the least guarded and near an exit. He would display it on a red velvet pillow with golden tassels on each corner on top of a marble pedestal to make it look like it must have extravagant worth. Then when someone inevitably stole the item every decade or so, he would use the latent power inside of it to track the person down, already having bound himself to the dagger he knew its location at all times. Good thing Dante was dead now.

On the defensive item front, we had something called 'The Greave of Achilles'. Dante had a lot of notes on this one, as the name denoted it was believed to belong to the great hero Achilles. Everyone knew at the time of his life that Achilles' sword and shield were enchanted items crafted by the divine blacksmith, Hephaestus. So upon his death those were claimed quickly, but his greaves were overlooked. A young shield bearer in the Greek Army quickly claimed one of them as a souvenir of the great hero and decided to wear it for luck. Upon wearing the item he found he was a much faster runner and more sure footed. He passed the greave down father to son style for generations, but soon its use became a myth and the item became a museum piece, something not to be worn. Well fuck that, one of us is going to wear it. It was also said Achilles was quick to anger, very vengeful, and just entirely emotionally unstable. Magical scholars would later hypothesize that was due to him using too many conflicting enchanted items. We wouldn't make that mistake either. All enchanted items have innately extreme high levels of durability so despite its age the greave looked great and felt sturdy in my hands.

I put the greave on and did a few laps around my backyard, it was hilarious how fast I was running and I was having trouble not laughing. It wasn't supernaturally fast but I did feel like I went from a couch potato to a professional linebacker simply by putting on the armor piece. The second piece of defensive gear was a steel pauldron meant to be worn on the left shoulder. It was made up of five interlocking angular and rounded plates. The biggest one rode on the left shoulder and had a wolf's head emblazoned on it. Leather straps mounted inside of it which went across the chest and then went into a Y-split around the right nipple. One strap from there would go under the right arm and one over the right shoulder which would help hold the pauldron firmly in place. Dante had written that the Pauldron was said to bring the wearer good fortune, and since it was an enchanted item it had higher than average durability. In the ledger, it was simply labeled 'Pauldron of the Wolf.' He had tried to wear it himself for a few days but it had no obvious effect so he speculated that it didn't work on the undead like most defensive enchanted items. I hoped my friends wouldn't mind, but I claimed this item for myself. I tried it on and it fit me perfectly. Something snapped inside of me and I knew this item was for me, it just felt right. To be honest, I had a hard time taking it off. I felt like I was cutting a pinky off when I laid it back down on my table. You know what? Fuck it! It's mine anyway, I might as well wear it; so I threw it back on. I also put my dagger in the sheath it came with and threw it on my belt.

The third piece of enchanted defensive armor was a left handed steel gauntlet. It had four raised spikes along each of the knuckles that weren't overly sharp. It looked like a very standard gauntlet you might see anywhere except someone had taken some kind of mix of gold and bronze and made magical symbols over the entire thing. This thing was covered In everything: crosses, pentagrams, strange Egyptian symbols, hell I even saw a swastika on there. This thing looked older than the World War Two era though so it was probably related to the old Egyptian swastika, not the Nazi one. Dante's notes just had this thing labeled as 'The Hand of God.' Like the other items, it had higher than average durability. Unlike the other items, this one actually worked for the undead so Dante had thoroughly tested it. In his notes he had said the hand he had put it on felt immediately stronger, but not the upper arm just the hand and the parts of his forearm that it covered. He had squeezed two identical bricks, one in each hand and the one in the gauntlet crumbled to dust instantly.

He had trouble determining if that was a placebo effect or not since he could have eventually accomplished this feat on his own with his vampire strength. He had tried to bend a tiny edge of the gauntlet but found it unyielding. He had accidentally discovered that the gauntlet could not be removed unless he wanted it to be. He had three of his lackeys try to pull it off of him at once and they were unable to even get it to budge. He had even referenced that he had once used it to defeat a much more powerful vampire that had tried to take his throne. He had choked the other vampire so violently that he snapped his spine, something that he wouldn't have been able to do to such a powerful vampire without the gauntlet, this was one of Dante's favorites.

The last piece was an absolutely beautiful leather lined steel bracer with a raised, red steel cross on it. Dante had this one labeled in his book as 'The Vitality Bracer.' It's exact origins were unknown, but this one was relatively new compared to the others. A story that had been passed around with it was that it had belonged to a Knight Templar blacksmith who had been trying to make these for his whole battalion but the cost was so high for one he could never recreate it, but that story was just rumor and Dante wasn't sure of its accuracy. The red cross on it did it make it look like Templar armor though. The piece was supposed to protect the user from basic sickness and infection and even granted slightly increased healing speed. In the years the main force of the Templar was active, a piece like this could have saved thousands. Tons of soldiers and Knights died from basic infections in battle, which would mean in the time frame that this was created, this piece would have been priceless. By today's standards, it wasn't that amazing... Well, who am I kidding? I didn't even know vampires, magic, enchantments, and what not existed last week... this thing was very amazing. Anyone who ended up with it would be lucky, getting sick sucks even if we have modern medicine to fix it.

To avoid potential arguments about who got what, we paired the remaining daggers with each piece of armor. We put the black quartz dagger with 'The Vitality Bracer,' sort of a yin and yang combo. Especially since if someone accidentally cut themselves with the black quartz dagger they would need 'The Vitality Bracer' to close the wound in a timely manner, theoretically. We put the fire dagger with 'The Greave of Achilles,' and lastly, we put the ice dagger with 'The Hand of God' gauntlet. We had three sets of enchanted items, one set for each of my friends. With each set, we added four thousand dollars cash next to it for their portion of money from The Broker's briefcase. We would have to vote on what to do with the rest of it. My vote would go towards opening a security company for the obvious benefits that would provide. When they arrived they would have quite a little prize package waiting for them. Plus get real, who isn't excited about chimichangas?

Four in the evening rolled around and my friends started showing up. Once they were all there and had happily stuffed their faces full of mini-chimies, I had them all follow me over to my kitchen counter where I had the three piles set up. Lydia and I carefully explained what each one did.

Zach looked at me and said, "You auditioning for Road Warrior?" while pointing at my pauldron and dagger.

"No, these are the magical items I chose before you guys got here. The pauldron grants me good fortune and the dagger can be tracked by its owner," I said.

"Oh I see, this is giving me serious Pokemon Red & Blue vibes bro. You are Gary and you snuck into Professor Oak's house before the other trainers and stole the best Pokemon first," said Griffin.

"What the fuck dude? I'm not Gary, if anything I'm Brock, okay? So back the fuck off. I don't know why I picked the pauldron but I felt bad about choosing first so I paired it with the weakest dagger offense wise. Besides, don't pretend these other items aren't awesome. Can you guys start picking now?" I said.

Griffin was the first one to speak up again "I can't take the gauntlet bundle, it's left-handed and I'm left-handed. I won't be able to manipulate a weapon trigger correctly while wearing a gauntlet literally over my trigger finger."

"So the gauntlet should go to Zach or Rook," I said.

"If it's cool with you Rook, I'll take the gauntlet, I work with my hands as a mechanic. I know very well how important hand strength is. Plus punching people with those spikes sounds pretty fucking cool too, even if I am not left handed..." Zach said.

"Cool with me broheimen, I'll take the greave. I'm the fastest runner anyway with my lanky ass legs. So this will take me to a whole new level," Rook said.

"For those of you who have done the quick math you have probably figured out by now that there is a lot more loose cash left. We need to vote on what to do with that. We can split it now and spend it VERY carefully. You can't go buy a brand new fancy car or anything like that with the money or the Internal Revenue Service will be all over your ass. You would have to use it on untraceable things or slowly over time. OR and this is a big OR... We can keep the money as a group and invest it into a storefront for V.S.T., the premier security company in Arizona. Our security company; if you were wondering VST would stand for Veteran Security Tactical. I'm not in love with that name it's just what I came up with on the fly. If we have a legit business we can launder any more money we make from plundering vampires through it and make it all completely legal, which will keep the IRS off of our ass and enable us to safely make a lot more money that we could spend on anything we wanted. Lydia and I are voting for investing the extra money in the business. Which means as a group you three would have to all vote against us to get the majority. What say you?" I asked the group.

"What do you know about laundering money," Zach asked.

"Not much, I understand the concept but honestly I'm terrible at math and if I was in charge of it I would probably quickly get us audited. We are going to need an accountant, and we are going to have to make a choice on whether we are going to let said accountant think we are criminals or tell them the truth that we are laundering the money so we don't have to explain vampires to the U.S. Government and then subsequently end up in the loony bin," I said.

"My uncle is an accountant but he won't work for criminals," said Griffin.

"Okay... well, would he work for vampire hunters?" I asked.

"Yeah, if you could convince him that vampires are real..." replied Griffin.

"Lydia can do that, we can let him throw knives at her," I said jokingly.

"I'm still pissed about that..." said Lydia.

"Well, IF we can get my uncle on board... I vote we open the security company," said Griffin.

"It would be nice to be my own boss," Zach said.

"Technically, I would be your boss, but you can make your own schedule and wear gym shorts to work," I said.

"I'm tired of working at the bank, let's open the company," said Rook.

Chapter 17

Everyone strapped on their new armor pieces and daggers which had all come with some sheaths and we headed out to my backyard. Rook immediately took off at a run that would have impressed a Kenyan. I live in the corner of a cul-de-sac so I have a BIG backyard. Griffin gave himself a small cut on his arm with his pocket knife (not the dagger) and nothing happened, well it did say the healing it provided was slow. Zach walked over to one of my free-standing wooden throwing knife targets and punched it... It exploded and wood chips went everywhere.

"Dude those take like twenty minutes to make!" I yelled.

"Sorry! That was awesome though!" Zach replied with a huge smile on his face.

Rook yelled, "WATCH THIS!" then he took off at a sprint and ran at my cinder block wall. He somehow ran along the side of it and then transitioned onto the skinny ledge at the top. He ran again at top speed along the top of my wall and then cleanly jumped back into my backyard all in a matter of seconds. He made a gymnast look clumsy. We were all yelling some variation of "Holy shit!" Then Rook grabbed his ribs and chest and bent over "Dammit..." he got back up and painfully walked over to one of my lawn chairs and sat down.

"My turn!" I yelled. I positioned myself straight in front of one of my throwing knife targets about 20 feet away and chucked my new dagger at the bullseye I had drawn on it. I can normally only hit the center of the bullseye maybe one out of every fifteen throws but this time I hit it dead center on my first try. I felt the pauldron on my shoulder tingle a little... good fortune indeed.

I had Griffin try on my pauldron and attempt the same throw. While he did hit the target close to the center, his knife bounced off since it landed mostly on its hilt. So the pauldron can't make you do something that you already couldn't do it just increases your odds a little more in your favor, interesting. Zach picked up a two by four that had been part of the throwing knife target he destroyed. He crushed the wood in his hand like it was made of nothing. He tried to do the same with a brick from my firepit but he couldn't crush it. He did eventually break it though. We all took turns trying on each others armor pieces, careful to not wear two at once at Lydia's request. Lydia was standing just inside the threshold of my back door since the sun was still setting.

We messed around out there for about an hour when Griffin yelled, "DUDES! LOOK!" We all jogged over to him, the cut on his arm was almost all the way healed! It looked like it had been healing for days but it had only been about an hour or so! Griffin and Rook switched magical armor after that, not permanently but just to help Rook heal up. That would probably be our new S.O.P. for now on, whoever was the most injured would switch armor pieces with Griffin until they were back at full health. We were a serious force to be reckoned with before, now we were mortal titans. We would still have to be careful since a vampire could probably rip our arms off if we weren't constantly vigilant but this day, the scales had been tipped a little farther in our favor.

Now that the general consensus was to open the security company as a front for our vampire killing business, we needed a realtor and a lawyer to handle all of the bullshit paperwork. I had a nice pro-veteran realtor who I had used to buy my own house. I'm sure she was only used to selling residential listings; but for a former customer, veteran, and an all around nice dude with oodles of money I'm sure she would make an exception and I trusted her. Her name was Marilyn Kershaw. Marilyn was a 40 something attractive older woman with shoulder length brown hair. She was very polite and professional at all times. She has a son in the military which is what I think makes her like veterans so much. I called her up and she answered happily once she saw my name on the caller ID. She asked me how my house was and I assured her that everything was great and that I couldn't be happier with the purchase. I told her that I was opening a business and needed a VERY large building to house it. The more private the better, but I wasn't going to be picky if she could get me a good deal. I also told her I would give her five thousand dollars extra on top of her standard commission since she was working outside of her normal comfort zone. She said she would start searching immediately.

Rook had a female cousin who he had grown up with and she had just married a lawyer. We figured he would have to do. It's not like we knew a better way to hire a lawyer who might bend normal rules and regulations for us. Nepotism at its finest, but honestly, it's not like there is a monster hunter forum I could go on and ask what lawyer they were all using. Rook got a hold of his cousin that first night and we discussed opening the business and told her he needed her husband's help in starting a business and that he had come into some money so we would be willing to keep him on retainer. He had just started at a new firm so he was happy for the business and happy to gain brownie points with his wife by helping out her 'darling' cousin. Rook met up with him, ate lunch and then handed him a briefcase with five thousand dollars in it and told him to get started in filing whatever paperwork we would need to open a security business in the state of Arizona.

A few weeks had gone by and we really had the ball rolling now on the business. It's amazing how fast you can get the bureaucrats and businessmen working when you start throwing handfuls of money around. We had a new problem though, we were running out of capital. We still had all of the counterfeit cash but we were saving that for when we had to bribe politicians... might as well pay that special brand of cocksucker in 90% monopoly money. It's not like they could report us if they were accepting a bribe anyway. Technically we were still rich but all of our money was tied up in valuables, we had to unload some of these fast and get more petty cash. You can't just run around selling valuables though, especially potentially ones that had been stolen. We had no idea how Dante had gotten his valuables, maybe they were all stolen who knows. Either way, whenever you make any sale to any type of dealer over a certain monetary amount they are supposed to make a copy of your driver's license and upload a picture of the item to a national database. This is how a lot of stupid jewelry thieves get caught.

We needed a high end antiquities dealer with shady morals and unfortunately, the main one that worked in this area that fit that criteria was now buried seven feet deep under the Arizona soil of my backyard. We needed a brainstorming session with The Strikers. We sent out a group text that Sunday night dinner had been moved to the open desert just north of the city right off of the I-17. A place where we regularly went to shoot targets for fun and blow up copious amounts of tannerite; it's cool, Google it. Lydia and I had been coming out here almost every night for the past two weeks and target shooting. She was quickly becoming a crack shot with the Remington 870.

Lydia wasn't the only one training, every Wednesday the boys and I had been working out and sparring in my backyard. I had even convinced them to do ten minutes of knife throwing at the end of every work out session. Rook had even started participating a little now that he was nearing the end of his convalescence thanks to the magical healing properties of the bracer. Him and Griffin had even traded their enchanted armor pieces back now that Rook was semi-comfortable with training again. I had been pushing myself hard on my own time when I wasn't working with Lydia or the crew. I had even toyed around with the idea of getting some steroids. Running doesn't really work against vampires, but brute strength can be useful. I had been learning a lot about steroids and doing a lot of research into the subject. They had a very negative connotation associated with them but that generally came from people who abused them. If you only did one cycle every six or seven months, they could be used semi-safely. The other problem was buying a clean product and making sure that you weren't accidentally using some pitbull steroids from Mexico or some other cancerous cocktail.

It would take a lot of time and effort to get legitimate steroids so I tabled that line of thought for now and hired a personal trainer who I was seeing a few times a week. Our Sunday desert dinner came up quickly, time also flies fast when you are busy and we had all been keeping very busy. Lydia and I left shortly before sunset in my Dodge Ram. She wore long sleeves, long pants, a shawl around her head and some sunglasses with that fancy woman's makeup that has a built in SPF (sun protection factor.) She used an umbrella to get into the truck, but once she was in she was relatively safe. I wouldn't be putting her in danger, I would drive like an angel until the sun went down. We went straight to Pizza by Napoli and picked up dinner for everyone. I had been giving these guys so much business lately they were always excited when I came in. They even loaded my truck for me and said hi to the reclusive Lydia that they had come to meet and know over the short phone conversations they were having when she ordered for me sometimes. I bet they had all kinds of theories about who she was to me.

The sun went down once we were almost at the highway exit for the empty piece of desert we went shooting at. The sunsets in Arizona are absolutely beautiful, no matter how long I live here I am always amazed by them. This far out of the city things actually cool off pretty quickly, the city maintains all of the day's heat in the asphalt and concrete but out here in the open desert it almost gets chilly so I had mirrored Lydia's long sleeve fashion statement to avoid the chill, while she had gone that route to avoid the light. We were the first to arrive so Lydia and I hopped out, and she ditched her shawl and sunglasses. She and I set up a long folding table and some folding chairs and laid out the pizzas with some paper plates, beers and sodas. We had to put a rock on each paper plate so they wouldn't fly away. I had brought a bag of logs with me and I put them about 15 feet away from the table and dumped an extremely unhealthy amount of gasoline on them. I went back to the table and lit a road flare and threw it at the logs, 'WHOOMPF!' Damn, that never gets old.

An old Ford pickup pulled up carrying Zach and Rook and following them was a beat up old Bronco carrying Griffin. We all sat down to some glorious pizza in the middle of the Arizona desert with a majestic roaring fire just far enough away from us to not feel the heat. The setting was beyond delightful, people in other states don't know what they are missing. Many jokes were told, many laughs were had; this Sunday dinner ritual was growing on everyone. Zach had been talking about bringing his wife and kids out to this once everything calmed down, Griffin wanted to bring his wife as well. It would be nice to bring Emily, but we weren't quite at that point yet. Once we are all done eating and laughing we started discussing business.

I told everyone how it was time to sell the antiques and valuables, but I also told them our dilemma about not knowing if they were stolen or not. Knowing Dante, some of those things could have been stolen from anywhere. For all I knew, I could sell one and then ping some obscure European database and end up having Interpol on my ass. We needed money as soon as possible to feed the beast that was our up and coming security company so we had to come up with something. We discussed the problem for a long time. We basically decided we didn't know shit about finding antiquity buyers or finding shadow brokers.

The only thing we could really come up with was waking up the most senior vampire out of the freezer and interrogating him. Lydia told us that she thought the one with the crossbow bolt in his head was the most senior after Robert. So if anyone knew anything it would be him. Now that we had a somewhat coherent plan on what we were going to do, we all pulled out firearms and did some night shooting. Lydia impressed everyone by shooting some clays out of the air at night which is pretty good for a beginner but I'm sure her vampire senses were helping her. We all had a good time...guns, beer, food and friends, the American dream.

Zach had to take off after that to get home to his kids but Griffin and Rook followed me back to my place, we had a plan formulated to wake up the dickhead. We pulled him to the top of the freezer and we planned to meet the next morning at 10 a.m. at my house. True to their word, after breakfast the next morning Rook and Griffin came to my house. We pulled out the vampire covered in crossbow bolts including the one comically sticking out of his head. We wrapped him up in a bunch of tarps and then ran a length of chain around him and padlocked it end to end once it had no slack left in it. We carried him out to the bed of my truck and threw him in. We weren't really worried about him escaping since he would instantly burn up in the sun if he got out of the tarps.

We headed to the hardware store and grabbed something they call a 'stock tank.' It was basically a giant metal tub, about six feet long and two feet wide. It was surprisingly cheap for what it was. Then we hit the grocery store and bought all of the packaged water in the place which was only about fifty gallons but that is all we would need. I had also brought three gallons of blood from my fridge; animal blood, this asshole was never drinking human again. Once we got back out to our desert spot we pulled the stock tub out and Rook started filling it with water. Griffin and I set up a portable camping sun shade that went completely over the tub. We pulled the tied up vampire that I am sure was mostly thawed out by now and threw him into the tub and started taking the chains and tarps off of him. The tub was in the shade, but in every direction besides the small camping shade there was miles of open sunny desert, except for my truck which we had pulled about 100 feet away and locked. Nowhere for him to run except straight into the sun.

We put all of the water into the tub which just barely covered the vampire's body. Then I dumped two of the three gallons of blood straight into the water, before I cranked the bolts out of his head and body. Vampires needed blood to regenerate right? So what better way to get it then to be submerged into it. The bloody water mixture was going into his nostrils, his wounds, his mouth, his ears, etc. Now it was a waiting game, we had no idea how long it would take a vampire to regenerate from being shot and frozen which is why we had started this so early in the day. We set up some steel targets while we waited and went target shooting with our pistols. We lost track of time we were training so hard and then we heard the water start sloshing around in the stock tank. I took an empty water bottle and filled it up a quarter of the way with animal blood. I carefully approached the water tank with it in my hands. Griffin and Rook each got on a different support strut of the sunshade. Our plan was if the vampire attacked me or any of us we would just move the shade and let him burn.

As I got closer, the vampire was still trying to sit up, he finally got one hand over the edge of the metal tub and pulled himself upright. He looked very confused and pained. I thrust the water bottle as far out away from myself as possible and touched the tip of his hand with it.

"Here drink this!" I yelled and he snatched the water bottle from me and greedily drank it down.

It looked like his head was clearing a little the more he drank and he finally shouted, "WHAT'S HAPPENING?"

"Well, I really hate to be the one to tell you this but it's the year two thousand three hundred and eleven. You have been cryogenically frozen for almost three hundred years. Civilization has been erased. Look around, see how all of the buildings are gone? The machines rule supreme now, you are humanity's last hope," I told him. Rook and Griffin looked at each other, I could tell they were trying hard to not laugh.

The vampire was looking around the desert really confused now "Oh man, this can't be right..." he said.

"I'm just kidding man, you have been frozen in a shitty used freezer in my garage for like four weeks. We brought you out here to interrogate you... You are welcome to run if you want, but as you can see there is nowhere to go. We are going to use a punishment and reward system. If you don't answer our questions correctly we are going to move the shade and burn you a little bit; if you answer them correctly, you get to live a little longer and I'll give you some blood. Also, don't get out of that tub or we will just back up into the sun and shoot that thing full of holes," I said. Griffin and Rook were fully laughing at the Terminator reference now.

"When Dante finds out about this, he is going to kill you!" the random vampire said.

"Dude, I killed Dante like forever ago. You are the last of your little club of rejects and if you want to remain on this mortal plane it's time to answer some questions. Tell me all of the places or people Dante buys and sells valuables and antiques at," I said.

The vampire looked really confused again and I couldn't tell if he was thinking about it or stalling.

"Burn him for a second," I said.

Griffin and Rook moved the sunshade until the sun covered the vampires exposed feet and arms, they stopped before the light touched his face and then started retracting the shade back until the vampire was fully shaded. The vampire had started screaming as soon as the sun had touched him, some of the blood water he was sitting in had started to steam.

"Answer the question!" I yelled.

"Dante uses some guy called The Broker, alright, stop fucking burning me!" the vampire yelled. I handed him another water bottle but this one was only about one-fifth full of blood.

"Yeah we know about him, we killed him too. Where else does he buy and sell them, and are any of them stolen? I asked.

"He gets them at a lot of places, he doesn't openly talk about it often and he doesn't like to answer questions. They shouldn't be stolen, he stopped taking stolen goods in the 70's when one of his dealers rolled over on him to the police. It created all kinds of problems for him so he only deals in legit valuables now, or he ensures that the owners are beyond dead and hidden so there will be no one left alive to report them," he said. Again, I handed him another water bottle with some blood in the bottom of it.

I walked over to Griffin and Rook and pulled them about twenty feet away from the sunshade out into the sunny desert. "Well, we got our answer guys, those items are not reported stolen which means we can sell them at a legitimate auction house or something now. What do we want to do with this guy?" I whispered.

"I say we question him a little bit longer then burn him. That night we captured him he had been about to murder that poor girl he had with him," Rook said.

"That's fine with me, Griff anything to add?" I asked.

"No dude. I just want to see what happens when we burn a vamp who is sitting in a shallow pool of water. I think this is going to be cool." We walked back over to the vamp in the tub.

"Are you one hundred percent positive that The Broker was the only way Dante sold and bought valuables that you can remember?" I asked him.

"He also used a storefront, the location moved every year or so. It's on the northeast corner of 28th Avenue and Weldon. There will be no sign on the front, they are open twelve to twelve, you just walk in," said the vampire.

"Thanks for your help, I believe our business has concluded," I said.

I looked back at Griffin and Rook who each had one hand on a support strut of the sunshade and their other hand casually resting on their pistols. They started slowly pulling the shade away from the vampire in the tub.

"WAIT, WAIT! I HELPED YOU! WHAT ARE YOU DOING?" the vampire started to scream.

"You are also a murderer who has killed innocent people. Meet your maker with some dignity!" I yelled back at him.

Griffin and Rook just kept pulling the shade and soon the vampire was fully exposed to the sun. He tried to get fully under the cloudy red water but there just wasn't enough room in the tub and different parts of him kept being exposed to the sun which would immediately catch fire after boiling the dampness off of him. He kept spinning in the water putting the fires out and screaming. Sometimes we could hear his screams clearly and sometimes we couldn't when he would go face down in the liquid.

The tub started rocking and I was afraid he was going to tip it over but he never got the chance. He ran out of energy or something. He stopped spinning in the juice and his scream died out as he burned. We all inched closer to the tub so we could see the show better. Parts of the bloody water mixture were boiling and the vampire's exposed face was burning profusely now, which we could see because he had stopped spinning face up. I could see parts of his exposed skull as the flesh of his face burned. The parts of him that were submerged were trying to burn as well but the water in the tub was trying to put out the fire and it just couldn't quite keep up. Steam was flying everywhere and the smell was horrendous. Finally, as he kept breaking down and his skull collapsed, he sunk beneath the water which became an even

285

darker red cloud which boiled and steamed for another minute before finally settling down. We dumped the metal tub over and let the gross mixture spill over into the Arizona soil.

We picked up the tub and put it into the truck bed along with all of our brass and assorted trash and then left the area. It looked bad now but the desert sun would bleach that blood into non-existence in a matter of days and we were in a remote area so I wasn't worried about someone finding it. That scenario had me thinking though, what would happen if someone found that and the police tried to pull DNA from it? Would they find the DNA of a human or no DNA? Maybe the DNA of a bat? Or maybe the DNA of all of the vampire's combined victims? That line of thought left me with a lot more questions than answers. I needed to get home and tie up some loose ends.

"Griffin do you have a copy of your notary stamp in your car?" I asked.

"Yep," Griffin replied.

"Cool, can you stick around for a bit when we get back to my place?" I asked.

Griffin grunted his agreement. I had been planning this for awhile. It's nice having a friend who is a notary, a small certification Griffin has picked up a few years back as another passive way to make income, but I don't think he had ever gotten serious about it.

Chapter 18

So one of the main documents of interest that we found in Dante's safe was none other than the title to the Dodge Charger. When we got back to my house, I had Griffin use his notary stamp on Dante's title 'proving' that I was legally buying the car. Lydia forged Dante's signature from the driver's license in his wallet which read 'Dante Smith' of course, that dude seriously lacked in the creative department. I was the proud new owner of a vintage Dodge Charger. I took it right over to the motor vehicle department and made it fully legal with some historical plates, very cool. I also called my boss and kind of told him a version of the truth. I just told him that my life had become ever more complicated and that I was resigning. I thanked him for the opportunity and told him that I hoped he had a good life.

Then I called my fancy new lawyer, Rook's cousin's husband, Randall. I told him we had come into the possession of a lot of rare and valuable items and that we wanted them sold at a reputable auction house using him as our legal cutout. He told me he didn't know much about that so he would have to bill us for any time he spent researching how to get that done and I told him that was fine. Once those items started selling we would have a really stable form of

288

income for a while. I sent Rook a quick text and told him I had quit my job and that he could do the same now if he wanted since we would have some income soon from the items we were auctioning off. He happily accepted my offer and quit his job as well. That meant that Zach was the only one of us left with a regular old nine to five job, but I could understand that. He had kids to feed so making risky decisions with his income probably wasn't a good idea.

I hadn't had a lot of time with Emily lately, so once I finished up all of my errands I went and got us some takeout from that small Italian restaurant that we had had lunch at awhile back and rekindled our relationship. I drove over to her house and met her as she was coming home from med school. We had a great evening and ate that delicious food. She was getting curious as to why we were never meeting at my place so I had to give her a blow off answer. Emily is cool but I don't think she would be okay with me having an attractive twenty something female roommate, and Lydia was absolutely jealous of Emily. I did not want Emily around a jealous and angry vampire. I really liked both women, Emily romantically and Lydia because of our amazing friendship that we just kept building. The more time I spent with Lydia the more I realized I needed her in my life. I needed to find a way to defuse that powder keg before it was too late.

I had been wearing my dagger everywhere trying to establish that seven day bond. I had even been wearing a belt over my boxers to bed at night and keeping the dagger in its sheath on the belt. I wasn't exactly sure how it worked, but Dante's ledger had clearly stipulated that you have to have it on your person for seven full days to establish the link. While I was eating dinner with Emily, I texted Lydia to let her know I would be home late. I still felt guilty every time I saw Emily for some reason and the last thing I needed was Lydia making me some kind of amazing food for us and then have me come home and have to explain to her that I had already eaten... with Emily... that would suck. Thanks to her vampire senses she could probably already tell exactly when I had been with Emily anyway, but I still avoided the subject with her simply because it felt rude to do otherwise.

The next day rolled around, Tuesday. Today was my 'rest' day... I had been working out, training, juggling errands and trying to get everything done that we needed to get done to get our company off of the ground. I had been running myself at such a hectic pace that I was just completely worn out. I spent that day in gym shorts and a loose t-shirt watching some of Lydia's favorite movies. I had made her watch all of my favorites when she was chained up so this was kind of karma paying me back I guess. We watched a few romances and a chick flick, but not as many as I thought she was going to make me sit through.

Lydia was also a mild fan of anime and she showed me a neat one called *Howl's Moving Castle*. It wasn't the best movie I have ever seen or anything but it was worth a watch. I wasn't really an 'anime guy' I just couldn't ever get into it, with the exception of *Fullmetal Alchemist: Brotherhood* of course, but every guy likes that. Overall though, I enjoy leaving my comfort zone every once in awhile so it was still a good day.

Just after sunset, we heard a pounding on my front door, the sun was down... VAMPIRE! I grabbed the WASR which I had been keeping close. I reached down and felt the dagger on my waist for reassurance and I screamed through the door "WHO IS IT?"

Lydia was behind me throwing her bandoleer over her shoulder with her Remington 870 in hand. Mia's hackles were raised and she was slowly growling.

"It's me, Emily, open up!" Whoops false alarm. I threw the WASR behind me onto my couch, and then patted Mia's head letting her know it was all alright. I stepped out onto my front porch and closed the door behind me.

"Hi, what are you doing here? Did we have something planned for tonight?" I asked innocently.

"I'm trying to figure out why you were dodging my questions last night about meeting at your place and now I am trying to figure out why we are on your front porch and I am not invited inside," Emily said.

Oh shit! My brain scrambled to try and think up some new line of bullshit. I hated Lying to Emily but I couldn't exactly tell her I was a vampire hunter now and I didn't want her inside because my friend the vampire might eat her. Emily could tell I was stalling and she opened her mouth to say something but the door behind me opened and Lydia came out. "That would be my fault. Hi, I am Lydia..." Lydia said with her hand outstretched towards Emily. Emily reached forward and shook her hand.

"And who exactly are you Lydia?" Emily asked.

"That's a long story, but I am Bear's friend. Bear recently helped me out of a VERY abusive relationship. I lost everything in the break and Bear is helping me get back on my feet. It was either here or the homeless shelter for me. I don't have any family. Bear has been so kind to me and he has told me so much about you. I'm sorry for the subterfuge Emily, but Bear didn't tell you about me because it wasn't his story to tell. He was being a gentleman, I hope you understand," Lydia finished.

"I don't really know what to think about this, it's a lot to take in. I'm really sorry that happened to you. Are you still in danger, from the man you were in the abusive relationship with?" Emily asked.

"From him, no. Bear beat his ass so badly he won't be hurting any women anymore. The lifestyle he dragged me into is still very dangerous though, and this is something I don't like to talk about but it added to my self-esteem problems. Bear has been helping me with all of this, helping me get on my feet, he might even have a job lined up for me. Bear is the best man I have ever met and you are an extremely lucky woman Emily." Wow, that was really nice of her to say.

"Okay, everyone stop please, this is getting heavy. Lydia, you don't have to say anymore, thank you. How about we all go get some pizza and beer, my treat?" I said.

You could probably guess where we went... That's right, Pizza by Napoli. The inside is a little lackluster but that just adds to the atmosphere. Their oven in the back must have terrible ventilation because the place smelled like decades of pizza odor stacked on top of itself. It's actually really hard to describe but if you were able to bottle this smell and spray it in a crowded room, everyone in there would have to run out and get pizza. There were a few decade old t.v.'s playing sports games that we weren't interested in and some arcade games that hadn't been serviced since the 90's. All of the booths were some form of the cheapest laminated particle board possible in an ultra light tan wood grain. There were neon beer signs from every cheap beer company in the window. Everyone that worked there had a

thick accent, some kind of mix of Italian and New Yorker. This was my
kind of place. As soon as we walked in the guys behind the counter
yelled "LYDIA, BEAR!" Okay, maybe we were eating here too much.

Lydia and Emily instantly hit it off once we had the beer flowing.
They talked a lot about Emily's med school and Lydia's experience at
college. Emily was polite enough to stay away from any subject that
she thought might offend Lydia. The best part of Lydia's story was that
it was almost true so we didn't really have to lie to Emily, all we had to
do was not say the word 'vampire.' Then something terrible happened,
they started talking about me.

"Have you ever noticed that when Bear is around pretty women he
tries to puff his chest out?" asked Emily.

"HE DOES DO THAT!" said Lydia excitedly.

"Hey, what the hell?" I asked.

"Shhh honey, let the girls talk, go get us another pitcher of beer,"
Emily said... Well damn, I think I just got officially bamboozled by these
women. The rest of the evening went like that, the three of us joking
and laughing over cheap beer and amazing pizza with the occasional
friendly jab thrown at me and laughing at my expense. Honestly, the
embarrassment was worth seeing Lydia and Emily bond.

We had all ridden in the same vehicle over to Pizza by Napoli so we had to go back to my house so Emily could get her car. It was a beautiful night, I suggested we sit on the front porch and sip on some coffee. Mostly, I just didn't want to have to explain all the rare and valuable crap in my house to Emily and I also didn't want to rush her into driving home and have her end up getting a D.U.I. After we were done with the coffees Lydia said she had to go inside and get some studying done. She hugged Emily and asked her if they could do a girls night soon, Emily agreed. Once Lydia was inside Emily hugged me hard, "I'm sorry for doubting you Bear," she told me.

"It's fine, it's not a normal situation and I had no idea how to tell you something like this," I told her.

"I can tell you are still keeping things from me, you don't have to do that you know," Emily said. I was done lying to her but I wasn't ready to tell her everything yet.

"It's not that simple, but I promise that I will tell you everything when I am ready," I told her. She kissed me and then headed home.

The next morning my lawyer called and told us he could start getting our items sold at a rate of six per week. Three in a Friday auction and three at a Saturday auction, at two separate auction houses. If they didn't sell, they might have to be put on loan to different auctions houses out of state. I told him to do what he thought was best and that I trusted him. To be honest, I didn't trust him that much, yes he was related to Rook but I hadn't even met the guy face to face yet, only Rook had. I just wasn't worried about, it's not like it was my capital on the line. I was making money from nothing by selling Dante's old shit that I didn't care about anyway. If you couldn't stab or shoot a vampire with it or play a video game on it, then I didn't really care about it... sell all of it.

The rest of that week was spent slowly shuttling the valuables with no enchantments on them or those that were of no use to us over to the Lawyer's firm building. We would be selling the items that had magical enchantments on them that were so weak they made no practical difference. Same with the cursed items where the curses were so weak they wouldn't matter. I made sure to get a signed inventory receipt every time we dropped stuff off. I picked up that habit in the military, you never hand over something valuable without a receipt. For some reason that I couldn't shake I was feeling a kind of nervous energy, I was at a nexus. Our team had been training hard, we had almost all of our loose ends tied off. We had new weapons and tools to fight evil with. It was time to kill some vampires.

Later that week, we had our new Sunday ritual dinner among friends. We were trying to do something different so Lydia and I had made dinner together for all of the guys. I had made a ton of steaks on the grill just out back and Lydia had made mashed potatoes from scratch, corn on the cob and steamed green beans all fresh. We kept the back door open so Lydia and I could talk to each other, me at the grill and her at the stove. We had bought a few cheap bottles of dessert wine as well since we were celebrating selling the antiques and valuables. The Lawyer said it would take the auction house a couple of days to process payments and then our Lawyer's firm would write us up an invoice and receipt after taking their cut and our first checks would be rolling in Thursday or Friday.

Once everyone had stuffed their face, I stood up to address the table.

"Alright everyone, we have money rolling in next week as you all know. The first 10,000 dollars that comes in will be split five ways among all of us. Rook and I have to pay some rent and buy groceries and it wouldn't be fair if we were the only ones taking money here. Let's not forget, last week before we burnt that vampire he told us about some kind of a shop that Dante visited to buy and sell valuables, we still need to look into that. Also, I have been thinking since the first raid about how we need more silenced weapons so I have begun the paperwork to get four more threaded WASR's in 7.62x39. It may not be everyone's favorite platform but we need to get universal so we know each others equipment and so we can all share magazines. Personally, I think it is high time we find some more monsters to kill. We know they are out there now, and we know we have the power to stop them. With the addition of our new enchanted items, we are stronger than ever. The last time we took out a den of vampires, we did it with half a clue while Rook was injured, which means next time will be a cakewalk if we plan accordingly. Does anyone have anything to add or any idea on how to find more vampires?" I finished.

"What about Lydia's algorithm?" Rook asked.

"Great question, Lydia has told me that as a last resort we can do that but she is afraid that older and more powerful vampires might have some way to influence younger vampires or to even spot if someone is a vampire so she won't be able to play the 'lost scared girl' a second time now that she is a creature of the night, also that was a time-consuming method," I said.

"Why don't we just wake up another freezer vampire the same way we did last time and ask them if they know where any more vampires are?" asked Griffin.

"We could do that," I said.

"I've got nothing, but I like Griffin's plan," said Zach.

"That settles it, sometime this week we can wake up another freezer vamp and question them. We can repeat that with all of the freezer vamps if one doesn't yield enough information, we kill them and wake another. If that fails we can try Lydia's algorithm. If that doesn't work we can study more of the tomes from Dante's house, we will find a way..." I said.

I had more on my mind but I didn't know how to tell my friends. The truth was I really wanted to go visit Mick, which was my new name for Mictlantecuhtli since I would never call IT that. It also took some of the edge off to humanize whatever IT was. I needed to become more powerful for myself and for the safety of my friends, but visiting Mick could be dangerous and I wouldn't lead my friends into danger unless I had some way to mitigate the risk. I also didn't know what they would think of me if I told them I was interested in pursuing that path since the main way we knew to get power out of Mick was to kill someone. I wasn't thinking about hurting some innocent person or anything like that but I had a few ideas on how and where to get sacrifices.

The sex offender registry list was public record in the state of Arizona, maybe the world could use a few less kiddie diddlers. A few years back I had even gotten a letter in the mail that one had moved into my neighborhood. I didn't know it at the time but every time a sex offender over a certain 'level,' which is deemed by the state based on the severity of their crimes, moves to a new area the state has to alert the homeowners in a few mile radius around the home the sex offender will be staying at. Hence the letter I had received. Does the world really need more child molesters floating around, personally I think not. My friends, however, might consider me a monster if I started advocating casual murder. Besides it's not like I hadn't murdered a human before, I had killed Percival with no regrets. In fact, after the shock of it, I had felt really good about the situation. I had even shot at terrorists in Afghanistan, admittedly they were really far away and I never got to see if I had hit them, but I had never been squeamish about removing evil things from this earth so maybe this was just the natural progression of things. Or maybe I was becoming a serial killer and trying to rationalize murdering people, I'm not really sure. It's not like crazy people know they are crazy... These are all things I can't tell my friends. This was something I was planning on doing alone, at least at first.

I remembered something I had been wanting to show my friends while I had them all here. "Hey guys I just remembered, here hide this dagger and don't tell me where it is," I said to the table.

I unsheathed my dagger and slid it on to the middle of the table within reach of everyone. Then I stood up from the table and walked a few feet away and put my hands over my ears and closed my eyes. After about ten seconds, I turned around and looked at all of my friends. I imagined the dagger and where it might be, I knew Zach was holding it. "Zach has it," I said and Zach brought his hands up and showed me he was holding the dagger, he slid it back to me.

"So how are you doing it?" asked Rook,

"That's a tough question, it's like I can remember where it is even though I didn't put it there. I just have a real short memory of where it is, and I feel a slight pull in the general direction. Honestly, it is really fucking cool," I said. My friends were very impressed with my useful new ability. We had a great rest of the night.

Later that evening after everyone had left, I brewed a pot of coffee and waited until midnight. Then I started armoring up, I threw on some blue jeans, a black t-shirt and my bulletproof vest loaded for bear (no pun intended) with WASR magazines. Then I threw on my reinforced leather jacket and put the pauldron on my left shoulder. It was a little awkward over the jacket, I would probably need to either ditch the jacket in the future or transition my magazines to a belt rig, but for tonight it was good enough. I threw on my Glock 19 set up for competition in an open carry holster. I didn't even bother bringing magazines for it. If I couldn't stop a problem with the WASR, than more Glock ammo wouldn't help me anyway. Lastly, I grabbed something that I had ordered a lot more of, a Kimber Pepper Blaster. The same type of weapon I had used to take out Robert.

I came out of my room and tried to sneak out to my garage, "So where are you going?" Lydia asked from the open doorway of my guest room which was now behind me.

"I'm going out, this is personal, only for me. Please stay here and don't argue with me about this, I'll be home in a few hours," I said with a stern voice and without turning around. I felt Lydia walk around me, once she was in front of me she embraced me in a tight hug, vampires can hug really hard.

"Please be safe Bear, I can't lose you," she said.

"I will, but I have to go now, see you in a few hours." I walked away from her. I was planning on sneaking out through the garage to not alert Lydia but it was too late for that now so I headed towards my front door, as soon as I opened the door Mia darted out. She ran over to my truck and sat down by the passenger side door.

"Mia, get your ass inside," I told her. She didn't move an inch, which was really out of character for her, she normally listens to everything I say. I was about to really yell at her when I swear I felt my pauldron tingle... hmmm. "Okay, but it's your funeral," I told Mia, I opened my truck door and she jumped right in.

Chapter 19

Before I left my cul-de-sac, I walked over to my neighbor's front yard across the way from my house, sure enough, their son had left his bike on their front door stoop. Their house was positioned in such a way that you couldn't see their door stoop from the main road and their son had a bad habit of never putting his bike away. If they had lived on my side of the cul-de-sac, the bike probably would have been stolen by now. It was after midnight on a Sunday so all of my neighbors were most likely sleeping. I picked up the bike and carried it over to my truck and threw it in the truck bed, I would just be borrowing it. I'm glad my neighbors weren't awake because randomly seeing their militant neighbor stealing their son's bike while carrying an AK-47 variant and wearing modern and archaic armor might be concerning to them.

We got on the road heading in the opposite direction of the open desert where I was planning on summoning Mick, we needed a human sacrifice still. I drove to the worst part of Phoenix, at least according to my google search, it's not like I hang out in bad neighborhoods for fun. Google told me that the I-17 and Camelback road was the highest crime per capita area in my city. I was afraid to go straight there because high crime means a high amount of police so I went one road to the north of Camelback which is Bethany Home Road. I didn't want to waste too much time on this part of the plan, I was antsy to get to the 'big show' so to speak, so I just pulled into the first establishment that wasn't a pawn shop or a cash for gold place because those would surely have cameras.

The first place I found was a Chinese food restaurant that had been closed for hours of course since it was Sunday night, or technically Monday morning by now since it was past midnight. As luck would have it, there was a bike rack outside. I told Mia to wait in the truck and I jumped out and carried the bike over to the rack. I put a few zip ties around some of the spokes and ran them through the rack. I would have felt really dumb if I went through all of this work just to have some crack head steal my neighbor's bike. At this point you are probably wondering what the fuck I am doing, let me explain. I had nothing as a kid, nothing. Every few years someone with a medium sized heart would hear my plight either from me directly or through the grapevine. Apparently, they didn't care enough to call child protective services but they did care enough to do something nice for me. A few of those people had bought me really high end bicycles and other gifts. I loved those bikes, I cherished them. For me a nice bike as a kid was the equivalent of a gold bar, or better yet a gold plated Hungarian AK-47, Hungarian AK's are pretty.

A bike to a poor kid is a gift from the gods, and inevitably every time I got a new bike it would eventually get stolen. When you live in a city of five million people, these things happen. Even if I had locked it up, some asshole would clip the lock or remove my front wheel and steal my bike anyway. Admittedly, I had lost one bike because I didn't lock it up but in my defense, I had basically raised myself. My parents were absent assholes, and I only got to learn some of life's greatest lessons by making mistakes. Since I had no one to teach me these things otherwise I had to learn from the school of hard knocks. Every time I lost a bike to some thief, something broke inside of my soul, I felt murder in my blood even if I couldn't explain it at the time because I was so young. What kind of fucking animal would steal a child's bike? So needless to say, when it came time to pick a sacrifice, the first thing I thought of was a bike thief and to make sure I was getting a really bad guy... a children's bike thief.

The trap was set, now it was a waiting game. I had to imagine that bike thieves were fucking stupid, otherwise, they wouldn't be out at one in the morning stealing kids bikes so I didn't even park my truck far away. I was only about 30 feet away from the bike rack, so I leaned back really far in my seat so people wouldn't see me. I made Mia get down on the floorboard of the truck so she wouldn't be seen either. We didn't have to wait long, there were vagrants and homeless all over this area. I wasn't even too worried about people seeing me, they would probably just think I was an undercover officer with a bait bike. I had killed my dome light so it wouldn't turn on when I opened my truck door. Our first customer had arrived to survey the goods. The man walking up to the bike looked like a standard drug addict, jerky movements, dark hoodie, etc. I had laid as low to my seat as I could and I could barely see over the ledge of my door. The thief looked over at my truck so I sunk even lower for a few seconds and didn't move, I whispered "STAY" at Mia and she complied.

When I looked back out of my trucks window the thief had turned back around and was jiggling the bike and trying to pull it out of the rack, I guess he hadn't seen the zip ties yet. I quietly opened my truck door, again I whispered to Mia that she should stay. I pulled my Kimber Pepper Blaster out and crept towards him. Once I was about twelve feet away he must have heard something because he turned to look at me and as soon as his face was oriented my way I fired. Red angry liquid engulfed his face, he didn't feel anything at first and then he looked confused. Then the pain hit him and he started making a whining noise while trying to clear the poison from his face with his hands, that wasn't going to work. He must have remembered there was a predator in the area, me. He tried to bolt obviously knowing he was in serious danger now. He started to run but without his vision, he ran face first into the side of the Chinese restaurant and went down like a bag of bricks.

I ran over to him and put a foot on his back before he could begin to rise. I roughly cranked his hands behind his back and zip tied them together. Then I started lifting him up and he tried to run again, but I had a good hold on him.

I kidney punched him once, hard, and yelled "You are under arrest shit bag!" and started pushing him towards my truck.

My truck had a very small backseat that could only be accessed by a mini-door that opened backward using an internal handle that you couldn't see until you opened up the driver's side door first. I quickly popped both doors and threw him into the back belly down. Then I roughly dragged a burlap sack over his head and cinched it tight. Not because I cared if he saw me or not, I just didn't want him rubbing pepper spray chemical all over my upholstery. Lastly, I put some zip ties around his feet and dragged them up to his arms, I zip tied his arms and feet together so he was hogtied, he wouldn't be moving around or trying to escape now.

I got us onto the highway quickly heading away from the area. Mia looked at the guy in the back and sniffed her nose hard and then closed her eyes for a second, she must have picked up the chemical from the pepper blaster.

"You wanted to come, fucking deal with it," I told her.

I kept it at the speed limit and focused on driving. Now would not be a good time to get pulled over. The thief in the back tried to move around a little but he still had a face full of capsaicin and he was tied up tight. It sounded like he was having trouble breathing but I was having a hard time feeling bad for him. Who walks around at one in the morning trying to steal from people anyway? Evil fucking shit heads, that is who. I was pretty calm, all things considered. I knew what I was doing, I had no regrets and honestly, this was a long time coming. I had joked with my friends about leaving a bait bike out before and paintballing the fuck out of the first thief that would inevitably come and try to steal it. Only I hadn't really been joking, I had really wanted to do that.

I drove about twenty miles north the of city limits and pulled off of the highway. There wasn't even a fence lining the desert since this was public land, just a cattle crossing so wild animals wouldn't haphazardly walk onto the highway. I started driving real slowly out into the desert, and I didn't stop until the lights of the highway were barely visible. I parked my truck and got out, and then I pulled the shit head out of the back, he wasn't even that heavy. I dragged him a few feet away from the truck and threw him into the dirt. I had been keeping a few bags of logs in the bed of my truck for when Lydia and I would go night shooting. So I threw one of the bags out and doused it in gasoline then lit it with a thrown road flare, that is always awesome, expensive but awesome. I also had a grocery bag in my truck with only two items inside of it, a canister of salt and a piece of paper with the incantation to summon Mick on it.

I had done some research and I couldn't figure out what language the words on the paper were. I speculated that the original tome was in a language called Classical Nahuatl which was what the Aztecs spoke but the translated incantation that Percival had was something else... It was hard to pronounce the words so I had practiced saying them a few times away from any sources of fire of course. I didn't want some Demigod showing up in my house looking for a human sacrifice. I was at the point now where I could read it with relative speed, and it wasn't that long. I poured a big hand full of salt into my palm and took it over to the thief and then threw it on him. Then I began reciting the incantation. The second I finished the incantation, a brilliant purple flame burst out of the ground only a few feet away from me, there was no heat. The flame grew and grew until it was about seven feet tall and four feet across, almost as soon as it had appeared it receded back into the earth. Where the flame once was, now stood a blood-soaked skeleton with two eyeballs roaming around inside of its skull somehow being magically held in place, they locked onto me. Mia jumped next to me and assumed a fight stance and the deepest most visceral growl she had ever made came out of her.

The skeleton pointed at me and yelled something incoherent, the noise grated against my mind. I didn't really know what to do, so I did what came natural when meeting someone new, I introduced myself.

"Hi, I'm Bear, this is my dog, Mia. It's nice to meet you. Would you mind terribly speaking English please? And since you are so obviously a god of true power can you change your appearance. You are scaring the shit out of my dog here," I said.

The skeleton Demigod thing stopped what he was doing, then took a step back and raised both of its hands in the air. Again the purple flame erupted and covered him wholly. A second later it died and in place of the flames stood a man wearing a purple business suit. He was meticulously groomed and strikingly handsome. He was maybe 50 years old with dark brown hair with just a touch of grey.

"Well met Bear, I hope you have a sacrifice for me," said the Demigod I referred to as Mick, this is too weird.

"That I do good sir, he is the person laying in the dirt here. Mick, may I ask you some questions please before we commence with the sacrificing of Dirtbag McGee here?" I asked.

"I am busy mortal known as Bear, and information is not free. My normal deal for sacrifices is a fifty and fifty split of the life force. If I give you information, the deal will be altered to a sixty and forty split in my favor, do you accept these terms Bear?" asked Mick.

"I do accept the terms. First I would like to know what exactly you would be giving me?" I asked.

"The regular deal, which can be altered if you wish it, is that myself and the mortal split the life force of the sacrifice. Your weak mortal body can not contain or utilize the extra life force yet so I must give you a very small piece of myself so that you can hold the life force in and convert it to a usable energy. The life force combined with my essence does unknown things to each specimen. Others of your species have become stronger and lived longer but the true potential is not yet known. It does different things to different species, I deal with many," said Mick.

"If you are constantly giving away pieces of yourself, pieces of your 'essence,' so that mortals can access the taken life force, then doesn't that weaken you?" I asked.

"Ah... you ask an interesting question mortal and the answer is simple, no. Yes, it lessens me but mortal lifespans are short in my perspective, when the mortal dies with my life force in them the force returns to me. I am still attaining what you would call a 'net gain' in all of this since mortals on many planes of existence are constantly feeding me life force through sacrifice," said Mick.

"Why do you do this, Mick, what are you getting out of it?" I asked.

"For power, to grow in strength... the same reason you are doing it. Do not worry mortal known as Bear, I currently pose no threat to your plane of existence and won't within your lifetime or the lifetime of your offspring or their offspring and so on," said Mick.

"Are there any negatives to this? This deal seems too good to be true," I said.

"In the context you are asking, no. The stolen life force will always be draining out of your container. If you don't actively use the life force then it will last a long time from your perspective in a passive capacity. If you were to actively use it then it would burn out shortly and you would need more life force, that aspect of it can be considered a negative. Also in some cultures, it is considered 'bad' to sacrifice others, this can also be considered a negative," said Mick.

"What did you mean earlier when you said the deal can be altered?" I asked.

"You may ask for anything you want as long as you are paying in sacrificed life force equal to the difficulty of the request. For example, your people have asked for me to make their crops prosperous and have paid me in life force for this task. I will not or can not do 'anything,' there are limits, but if you have life force to give I will try to accomplish the task requested," replied Mick.

"What are some of the things you won't do?" I asked.

"I won't do something that would slow down the amount of sacrifices I get from this plane of existence. There are other stipulations that I will not talk about," said Mick.

That answer made me want to ask more on that subject but I figured that I better not push my luck with a Demigod.

"Are you omnipotent, can you be in more than one place at once?" I asked.

"Somewhat, I am not fully omnipotent, which is why I said I was busy earlier. The closest analogy in your culture might be that of a supercomputer. I can do a lot of things at once but not everything. Earlier when I told you I was busy, I meant it. If a piece of me is here on this plane of existence, then I am neglecting a task elsewhere," Mick replied.

"Last question, what would happen if I shot you right now, with this gun?" I asked and held my WASR in the air.

"Nothing, I am not truly here. This is like what you might call a video chat. I can physically come to your plane of existence in some forms but I have no reason to and that takes power that I don't want to spend. Now commence the sacrifice," Mick said.

I walked over to the downed thief, I knew I should be more upset or anxious about this situation but I just wasn't. I pulled the thief's head back and roughly slit his throat using my dagger. Then I wiped the dagger off on the thief's clothing. He gurgled for a bit, choking on his own blood and then he lay still.

"Deal complete. I'll see you soon Bear, you must now prepare yourself and your party for the pain of receiving my gift. I am told the first time hurts the most due to my personal essence being in the mixture, goodbye!"

Wait, my party? What was he talking about...Oh my god, MIA! I opened my mouth to scream at him to stop but the purple flame erupted from the earth and covered him, and then he was gone. Immediately the pain hit me, every nerve in my body was on fire. My whole body went stiff as a board and I tried to scream out but I was in too much pain to even do that. I heard Mia yelping next to me and true regret washed over me. I didn't want my poor Mia to be hurt.

I came to later, it was still dark outside and I was laying on my back in the dirt, looking up at the stars. I pulled out my cell phone, it was 3:28 a.m. I think I had been passed out for about an hour and a half, maybe less. I had a bunch of text messages from Lydia, I sent her a quick reply and told her I was on the way home and everything was good. I looked around, shit the corpse is still here! I thought Mick might take the body with him. Then I noticed Mia laying next to the corpse of the thief, I ran over to her and fell to my knees beside her. I laid my head on her chest, she was breathing!

I slowly started petting her fur "Ms. Mia, time to wake up now sweety, we need to get home. Come on girl, wake up!" I anxiously told her. She opened her eyes and slowly climbed to her feet. Then she did that super cute dog stretch thing where she stretches first her back legs then her front legs. "Are you okay honey?" I asked her, she barked at me and wagged her tail, guess she is good.

I grabbed a shovel from my truck and started digging a rough hole, before I had begun I made sure that we weren't near a desert wash. It wouldn't be good if the first heavy rain we got dislodged this guy from the earth. I dug deep and fast... too fast. I could feel unnatural strength

315

flowing through me, but I also still had the pauldron on which seemed to make me more efficient at things I was already good at, I was mixing magic now... Fuck it. I wasn't hearing any voices or having any other indications of going nutso and I was digging a deep ass hole without even breaking a sweat, so far the pros were outweighing the cons because there are no cons. I chucked señor dipshit the third duke of dipshitville in the hole and doused him in bleach, then I pushed the dirt back over him.

Chapter 20

When I walked in Lydia was in my kitchen just starting to make some bacon and eggs. "I heard you pull up, so I started breakfast," she said.

Mia ran in ahead of me and sat politely at Lydia's feet, which meant she wanted some eggs.

"Sorry Mia, they aren't ready yet," Lydia told her. Mia walked away and jumped on the couch in her favorite spot. "She normally doesn't come up to me like that," said Lydia.

"Yeah she has been a little more confident lately, I think that trend will continue after tonight," I said.

"Okay," said Lydia and then she went back to cooking.

"Really? You aren't going to ask me where I was or what I was doing?" I asked.

"Well you killed someone, I can smell the blood residue on your dagger. You have fresh desert dirt on your shoes and jeans so you buried them I take it. Vampire senses remember? I may be new at this but some things are just easy, especially when you are this close and we are the only two in the room. You are a good man Bear, I'm sure you had a good reason for doing whatever it was you did tonight. You deserve your privacy, if you don't want me to know then I don't have to know..." she said.

Her words had cut me deep and made me feel terrible, I couldn't even really explain why.

"You do deserve to know, you are my friend, my REALLY good friend. I trust you and you trust me, if you want to know I will tell you. No, I'm going to tell you anyway because I want to tell someone and I trust you," I told her.

She stopped cooking and turned to look at me with a slight smile.

"I took some power from the Demigod, I call him Mick. I had to kill someone to do it so I killed a thief, he deserved it, trust me. I think I am stronger now but it is hard to tell. I only killed or sacrificed I guess you would call it, one person and the power was split between Mia and I. Percival killed three people and didn't split the power with anyone. Still, Mick said something about actively and passively spending the life force. Hmm..." I said.

I grabbed a knife from my knife block and made a small cut on the top of my forearm. I focused on it hard, small bits of purple light came out of the wound and then it closed. I could feel the power slipping away from me, I had used a portion of it. So that is what he meant by "actively" using it, I wonder what else I can do... Now I need more life force.

Lydia was staring at me "That was awesome, you are like a mutant now, that's a compliment by the way. Part of me wanted this to happen..." she said.

"What? You wanted me to sacrifice someone?" I asked.

"I saw your face that night when Percival told you his story. You were disgusted when you learned that he had hurt innocents but you were also intrigued when he described the power. I'm starting to understand you a little better Bear. You will do anything to protect your friends, but some selfish part of you also just wants more power. That's not a bad thing, you are a good man, you are someone that deserves more power. I am also getting something out of this, Percival had barely aged at all over a twenty six year span. He looked like he had only aged months. That means your aging is slowed now as well. I'm afraid to be alone Bear, I'm going to outlive everyone I come to love and have to watch them die. With this power in you though... That isn't the case anymore. I won't be alone," Lydia finished.

Whoa, I had no idea she felt that way. Lydia was scary perceptive, was she right about me being power hungry? Honestly, she probably was, but she was also right that I was a good dude. I LIKED doing good things, it makes me feel good when I do good. I don't know or care if

Mick is good or evil, I'm going to take this power and use it to rip apart those who would hurt others. I was tired from being awake all night but also invigorated at the possibilities of what I could accomplish now. The passive side of the stolen life force made sense to me. No one wants to get older, so you don't, your body puts the life force on low boil without even thinking about it and it somehow slows down your aging. Everyone wants to be strong, so the same thing happens again, you are stronger but just ever so slightly, just enough so only a tiny portion of the power is burning. Percival made the sacrifice of three people in the last twenty six years and I am betting he didn't even touch the surface of what you could do with Mick's gift.

This could also be a key tool in protecting my friends, with less than half of one sacrifice I had been able to completely close a small wound. I needed all of my friends to do this with me at least once so they would have an 'emergency reserve' of power in case of grave injury.

"Lydia, come with me tonight. I need to do it again. With your help, I can get more sacrifices. I'm not asking you to do something evil, I'm talking about bad guys, the worst of the worst. Not all monsters are monsters if you know what I mean, this is a city of five million people. There are murderers and rapists out there right now. We can catch them and protect the good people of this city, and I can get stronger in the process. Will you do it?" I asked.

"When do we start?" asked Lydia.

Lydia and I ate those bacon and eggs, I shared mine with Mia since she had accompanied me on a dangerous mission, she deserved it. On the other side of the table, Lydia had drenched her bacon and eggs in her human/animal blood mixture and she was drinking one of my patented blood smoothies, this one was mostly ice, strawberries and blood of course.

We were both excited about tonight, most likely for completely different reasons. We each had developed our own plans on what the best way to catch the worst shit bag possible was. Personally, I was fine with killing more thieves... Lydia however, wanted bigger fish to fry. She was looking to catch a potential rapist which was fine with me as well. Part of me wished Lydia was more hesitant to agree to outright murder, and I told her as much. She explained to me that her whole life she had been weak until now. She had been the one that needed help, now she was the one that was going to be helping people. The tables had turned and for the first time in her life, she had the power to make a positive change in this world. Her motivations didn't have anything to do with murder, they had everything to do with stopping evil. I felt guilty for not realizing that, I should have seen it. After we were done eating I crashed out hard, part of me wanted to see if I could push my new power into keeping myself awake but I needed to be alert for tonight so I didn't risk it.

We headed out together at one in the morning that night, just late enough to make sure we weren't going to accidentally pick up some drunks leaving a bar. It was technically Monday night so that shouldn't be an issue but it's better to have all bases covered. I had bought a cheap white panel van through an online ad I had found today at our local buy and sell vehicle market. It ran like shit but it was topped off with oil and gasoline and I had test drove it all around my neighborhood. I just needed it to hold together tonight, tomorrow I could take it to the shop and have them repair it. I didn't really have a vehicle big enough to hold more than one or two captives so this was my only real option. Besides, I could register it to the business we were opening later, businesses need fleet vehicles right?

Another reason I had bought this particular vehicle is because white panel vans aren't conspicuous in any way shape or form. They are everywhere, every business uses them, they are one of the most common vehicles on the road. We wanted to blend in, or be mistaken for law enforcement, either would work. We didn't want to establish a pattern so tonight we would be on Indian School road which is one road south of Camelback road. Indian School and the I-17 is a little different than other roads around this area. The north side of the road is mostly residential and the south side is a mix of business and residential. That was an absolute CRAP neighborhood. Criminals lived there, criminals hung out there and criminals committed crimes there, it was the perfect spot. Lydia wanted to try her game plan first, which was to just walk around in this neighborhood and see if any creeps tried to grab her.

She sat at a bus stop dressed very conservatively, she had a 'sexy' outfit in the van but we wanted to try this one first. Phoenix is a city of five million people so even at one in the morning there are people everywhere. Within twenty minutes she had two different guys hit on her. One pulled up in a car and asked if she needed a ride and the second one walked by her and told her she looked beautiful and asked her if she needed a place to stay for the night, she declined and he left. She had been sitting at the bus stop for about half an hour and I was just about to text her to let her know we should call it quits when three urban youths started heading her direction. I was nearby behind the wheel of the van. I had Mia in the passenger seat. Mia started to growl so I told her to be quiet and she complied.

The three men continued their beeline straight towards Lydia. She stood when they were about ten feet out from her location. There were dressed in the typical 'gang banger' fashion of this area.

"Yo girl, you ready for a good time?" one of them shouted. I had the window down and I could hear the conversation quite clearly.

"No thanks, just waiting for my bus," Lydia lied. I don't think the buses even ran this late.

"Fuck that shit lady, come have a good time with us," one of them said, and then he reached out and touched Lydia's shoulder, she jerked her body away.

"I SAID, NO THANKS!" she shouted back at him.

"Don't be like that girl," another one of them said. We had planned ahead for this, if it got this far Lydia was going to run around the back of the bus stop and into the landscaping behind it.

We don't have many storm drains here in Arizona, not in the traditional sense at least. We have a few on major roads but they are quickly overworked or almost never used because it never really rains here and when it does rain it flash floods so quickly that the drains fill up. To combat this problem, civil engineers had the bright idea to make large basins in our landscaping that catch the rain. There was one such basin behind the bus stop with bushes in it evenly spaced out every fifteen feet or so. There were street lights nearby but they were all aimed at the road and the sidewalk, the basin was dark and lower than the street level so no passing cars would be able to easily see into it.

Lydia ran into the basin and the three urban youths chased after her; bait taken, we have some fish on the line. I quietly exited the van and started heading towards them. The first urban youth tried to tackle Lydia and she used vampire speed and dodged it; before he made it past her she put her hand on his back and pushed downward and he hit the dirt. The second one jumped on her and gripped her in a bear hug, she head butted him hard but he held on. The third one saw what was happening to his friend so he punched Lydia in the side of the face, that fucking pissed me off. I was almost on them now and when I saw his punch land, my vision went red and a deep growl came out of my throat. I was on the one who punched her in an instant. I grabbed the front of his clothes and stared into his terrified eyes, then I threw him low and far. He bounced along the ground like a pebble skipping across a pond until finally his momentum was stopped by one of the bushes. Without his friend helping him, Lydia quickly overpowered the one holding her and head butting him one more time, he passed out.

The one she had thrown in the dirt originally was just getting up, she kicked him in the stomach before he could fully rise and he fell back down gripping his stomach. We zip tied the two closest to us, then I went and pulled the third one out of the bush and zip tied him too. We zip tied their arms and legs independently then hogtied them by running a few zip ties between the ones already on their arms and their legs. I reached inside of myself and felt for my power granted to me by the stolen life force, I seemed to have a little less in the tank. I had been practicing most of the day trying to sense it. I had a very rudimentary notion of where my power level was at now but I was improving quickly. I must have used some of the power on accident when I was angry, no wonder that I guy I threw had gone so far.

I was hesitant to burn more power but I also wanted to test my strengths, and knowing that I was getting a 'recharge' soon, I was less hesitant. I grabbed two of the downed thugs by the waistbands on the back of their pants and turned on the juice ever so slightly, picking them both up. Gross, one of these sick bastards wasn't wearing underwear, I was glad I had gloves on.

"Get the last one please," I told Lydia.

We carried them both over to the van, it was hard but I'm pretty sure it would have been impossible if I wasn't using power to help me lift them. Once they were all in the back of the van laying on their bellies on the floor, for good measure, I yelled "All of you fuckers are under arrest for attempted rape, if you try to get out of your bonds or cause any trouble I'll slap a resisting arrest charge on you as well!"

Then I threw burlap sacks over each of their heads and cinched them tight under their chins. I closed the van doors and looked at Lydia

"I admit it, your plan was awesome. Three would-be rapists off of the streets, high five!" We high fived each other and laughed a little.

"Catching rapists is surprisingly fun," said Lydia.

"Right.. Alright, are we doing my plan next or yours again?" I asked her.

"Sitting at the bus stop forever was boring, let's do yours," she said.

We went down the street a little to a hair salon. We had picked this place because there were no exterior cameras. There was a 'No Loitering' sign mounted on a metal pole that was sunk into the concrete close by so we zip tied a children's bike that I had bought earlier that day to it. I didn't want to have to keep stealing my neighbor's bike every time I wanted to pull this little trick so buying one of my own only made sense.

Lydia looked over at me and said, "Watch this!" She jumped straight up and her fingertips grabbed the edge of the roof of the salon, then she easily pulled herself up.

"HOLY SHIT! That was awesome! Fuck Team Edward, I'm Team Lydia!" I yelled.

"Was that a Twilight reference?" she asked.

"If you tell anyone I will kill you, but hey, how did you know you would be able to make that jump?" I asked.

"I didn't make the jump, not the one I was trying to make at least. I was trying to jump straight up here. I wasn't powerful enough which was why I had to pull myself up with my arms, I should practice this stuff," said Lydia.

"That is probably a good idea, hell, after tonight we might be closer to the same power level and I can probably practice with you," I said. We bullshitted back and forth like that for a while more but I went back to the van in case we were scaring off would be thieves.

We only had to wait about twenty minutes before two more urban youths rolled in. These ones had the baggy pants that were so low they had to waddle and you could see their boxers from the back, I really hated that. Wear whatever fashion statements you want, but if you make me look at your underwear your going to have a bad day unless you are an attractive female, then you are welcome to show me your underwear.

Yes, I understand that is a double standard and I don't care. Once the two were at the bike they noticed the zip ties, one pulled a knife to cut them. Oh shit, I hope Lydia saw the one with the weapon. A little pocket knife wouldn't kill her but I didn't want her to get hurt helping me. Lydia jumped down from the rooftop with her fangs fully extended and her face in the grimace of a monster. The two urban youths saw her and tried to run, only their pants were so baggy they both fell down on the asphalt. I was already heading towards them. They were both trying to get back up while holding their pants and it just wasn't working. I kicked one in the chin and Lydia punched the other one in the back of the head.

We loaded them up and were on our way with five shit heads zip tied in the back. They all had burlap sacks over their heads. One was crying and his friend was telling him to shut up. Mia was between Lydia and I, there is no center console in these panel vans so she had ample room. She was facing our captives and growling menacingly, Mia is awesome. Beside the mild whimpers from the shit heads in the back and the occasional insult from their friend who still thought they were in the back of a police paddy wagon, the rest of the ride was uneventful.

We unloaded the dipshit squad into the desert dirt and I summoned Mick.

"That was fucking awesome!" Lydia shouted after seeing the roaring purple flame with no heat.

"Hello Bear, Mia and company, I am ready to receive your sacrifice. Just know that I will not imbue your new companion with my life force. She carries the essence of Lilith, our gifts don't mix well, and loaning immortal people my essence is bad practice since I have no return time on my investment," said Mick. We hadn't discussed this scenario, I wasn't even sure if Lydia wanted a piece of the power, but Mick had now pulled that option anyway.

"Hello to you too Mick, it is good to see you. We have brought you five sacrifices this evening. My companion here is Lydia, she helped me procure them. Would it be possible if you were to give Mia the life force from one sacrifice and me the other four?" I asked.

"Easily done, friend Bear," said Mick,

"We are friends now?" I asked him.

"Anyone who helps me procure power and bears me no ill will is my friend. Now please commence with the sacrifice," said Mick.

I had already thrown the handfuls of salt on each of these guys so I went down the line slitting their throats. By the time I got to the last one, I could tell Mick was already feeding me my part of the life force, I could feel myself growing stronger. There was also a level of pain associated with it, kind of like sitting in hot water that was just a tad too hot. The first sacrifice didn't hurt that bad but the pain compounded. As I said earlier, my understanding of the power was growing and I could almost physically see in my mind's eye my power gauge filling, four times it went up, the fifth sacrifice went to Mia. By the fourth power charge, I was down on one knee trying to handle the pain. If Lydia wasn't here I might have cried out, but I had to stay strong as the leader of The Strikers with one of my team members present, I learned that in the military.

I shakily stood up and turned to Mick "Thank you again, Mick, it was good doing business with you," I said.

"And you as well, farewell for now," said Mick, and then the purple flame erupted and he disappeared behind it.

"So how do you feel?" asked Lydia.

I walked around the desert a bit thinking about it, trying to feel my power. My pauldron tingled and for some reason, my dagger came to mind. I pulled my dagger and threw it at the nearest saguaro and it sank in to the hilt. For the record, it's a felony to harm a saguaro so this is a 'do as I say and not as I do' type situation. I reached out to my power and I could almost see the dagger's link to my body. I pushed the smallest amount of life force at the link and the dagger ripped out of the cactus and came flying back at me, I caught it right out of the air.

"HOLY SHIT, THAT WAS AWESOME!" Lydia shouted.

"Yeah the best part about this, that's just the first thing I've tried and it didn't take much power at all, I bet I can do all kinds of awesome shit," I said.

Chapter 21

This is going to sound really serial killer-like, but burying bodies is way better with a friend... between Lydia's vampire strength and my new found well of power, we had the graves dug very quickly. With more of a power reserve, I had more power to practice with. When we were digging the graves I found out how to bring up my power draw just above the passive burn rate. It made everything a lot easier when I did that and life just felt really good; it felt good to breathe, to look at things, to move... even if it was still difficult to dig with this low amount of power being fed to my muscles it was still an awesome experience. I couldn't do that forever though, I didn't want to waste power I needed my reserves for emergencies.

We had taken the wallets from each of the sacrifices before burying them, we weren't trying to get rich off of the cash from hood rats but we didn't want to leave ways to easily identify them. Even though the chance of them being found buried that far out in the desert was slim to none, it's better to be safe than sorry. If any of the hood rats had jewelry on them we would have taken that too for the same reason. We also doused everyone in bleach before pushing the dirt over them.

On the drive back to my house Lydia asked me, "So when are you going to tell your friends?"

That's a good question, I've wanted to bring this subject up with them since I tortured Percival. I was mostly just worried about what they would think about me, but I had to tell them soon as this could be a serious weapon against evil vamps, and I wanted my friends to be safe.

"Soon. Sunday dinner at the latest. We need to wake up a freezer vamp soon and get the location of a new vamp nest, my trigger finger is itchy" I said.

"Yeah, I want to raid too, but killing vampires isn't my main motivation. I want to MAKE THAT MONEY!" she shouted in glee.

"Yeah, that part of it is really nice," I said.

It started to rain ever so slightly so I flipped on the wipers. Of course, since this was a used vehicle the wipers were dry rotted to all hell and they barely worked. I pushed the smallest amount of power I could at my eyes and my vision sharpened, I could see clearly now right through the rain. A huge smile formed on my face.

"What are you smiling about," Lydia asked.

"I have T-800 terminator vision when I push my power," I said.

"I forget how much of a nerd you are sometimes, and then you go out of your way to remind me," Lydia said.

"Hardy har har," I said sarcastically.

By the time we got home the rain was really coming down. We jumped out of the van and Mia ran ahead of me into my now open garage. Once we walked inside I noticed the coffin of Otto Richter, I really needed to get rid of him. For one, to lay him to rest and two, it's probably super illegal to have a taxidermied human in the house.

"It's about time we buried Otto," I said to Lydia.

"You bury him, I'll make us some food and drinks after I get out of my wet clothes," Lydia replied.

"FINE!" I said sarcastically. I pushed a little more stolen life force into my muscles and lifted the whole coffin, it was a pain in the ass. I dragged it out to my backyard, the rain was coming down hard now, good. Maybe it would soften the dirt up for me.

I was thinking about the power flowing through my body now and I came to the conclusion that I couldn't keep calling it stolen life force, especially if I was going to have to convince my friends and try to get them on board with also getting some of their own. I sat in one of my lawn chairs and pulled out my phone and ran an internet search for 'Aztec sacrificing ritual.' The Aztecs had a word for the stolen life force that they traded Mick for, they called it 'Tonalli.' I suppose that is as good as any other word. It makes it a little more user friendly as well when you don't have to constantly remind yourself that you are using someone else's soul to make yourself stronger. Tonalli... Tonalli.. the word felt right. I flared my tonalli hard for a second and flexed every muscle in my body, that felt awesome. Okay, time to bury my predecessor.

I had a moral dilemma about whether I should bury him in or out of the coffin, something about it bothered me. I think it had to do with the fact that it was less of a coffin and more of a display case. Almost like the poor guy had been the vampire equivalent of a collectible trading card in a plastic sheath. I wanted him to be at rest and this just didn't seem like rest. There were three large padlocks on one side of the coffin where the lid met the body. They were old and had started to rust. I thought about trying to pick them but I had only picked modern locks. I could probably run an internet search on how to do it but I wanted to be done with this and I was tired of standing in the rain so I decided to just snip them. I went to my garage real quick and grabbed my bolt cutters. I went back to my backyard and snipped all three locks. I don't know if the metal was extremely soft or if the rust had weakened them or if I was just stronger now with the tonalli running through me. 'Tonalli,' that word is growing on me. Either way, the locks popped off easily.

I opened the lid, reached in and snagged that sweet Thompson Submachine Gun, or the slang term for it the 'Tommy Gun.' I thought about taking the man's sword because it looked nice, but he should have it, a weapon to take with him to heaven. Something was telling me the sword was his and that I shouldn't take it, I tried to follow my instincts. I carried the tommy gun over to the glass topped table I kept in my backyard. It was under a shade so that would keep the rain off of it. I grabbed the shovel from my shed and started digging a nice hole along the border of my fence next to my flower bed. Tomorrow I would go buy some nice flowers from Home Depot and a non-obvious grave marker of some kind so I could mark this spot. If he hunted vampires, he was a good guy in my book and he deserved a place of respect. I had only been digging for a few minutes when I swear I got that weird feeling like tingling in my shoulder right under where my pauldron lies, I felt a presence behind me. I was wondering if it was Lydia but she wouldn't have come out here to get all wet again, she just told me she was going to get into dry clothes.

Now I was really paranoid. I knew Lydia was inside yet someone was behind me. I had left my WASR inside but I still had my Glock on my hip. I didn't want to drop the shovel and grab for my Glock though if the person behind me had a gun, they would open fire if they saw me do that. I really only had one move, spin and try to hit them with the shovel. I spun as fast as I could and put on the tonalli juice. BINGGGGGGGG. My shovel's steel head smacked into the sword my attacker was carrying and bounced back at me, the attacker had parried my hit. I gained control of it and swung it again but this time my attacker hit the wooden handle of my shovel and chopped off the steel shovelhead. I threw the handle at him which he expertly cut out of the air, but by then I had already drawn my Glock and had it pointed at his heart "If you move, you die. Slowly lower the sword!"

It was dark outside and I had left my back porch light off for obvious reasons, like you don't want your neighbors to see you burying a corpse, and visibility was still shit because of the rain. I burned more tonalli to see my attacker. My vision cleared and the shadows and darkness receded somewhat, my attacker was none other than Otto Richter. What the hell is going on?

"Otto?" I asked. He still had his sword in his hands but he wasn't actively trying to attack me. I still had my Glock aimed at his heart.

"Who are you and where am I?" he asked with a slightly German accent.

"My name is Bearengar and we are in my backyard, I live here. Are you a vampire?" I asked.

"No, are you?" he asked.

"Nope," I stated.

"Well, I am sorry for the altercation Herr Bearengar. I am a bit out of sorts and not sure how I have come to arrive here," said Otto.

"I'm a little confused about that myself, a second ago you were dead in that coffin," I said and pointed at the coffin lying in the mud behind him. He glanced at it quickly, I never lowered my Glock.

"How about you sheath that sword, I'll lower this gun and then we can drink some beers on that porch over there," I said and nodded at my dry porch.

Otto sheathed his sword and walked slowly under the overhang of my porch and out of the rain. I thought I saw something move in one of my windows. I pushed the tonalli even further at my vision and the distorted image came into play. It was Lydia aiming my WASR at Otto, she had had my back the whole time. I walked over right behind him, we both got to the table but neither of us sat down. I holstered my Glock and showed him both of my open hands.

I looked down at the Tommy Gun on the glass table between us "I'm going to hang this up right here," I said as I lifted the Tommy Gun slowly, keeping the muzzle aimed downward and then hung it over my back porch light via its sling. Then I sat down at the table and Otto followed suit.

"Lydia, two beers please," I said in a slightly elevated voice, sure that Lydia could hear me through the back door.

"Who is Lydia?" Otto asked.

"A friend of mine," I said.

"Where are we exactly and what kind of pistol is that?" Otto asked.

"I have a feeling that the *when* will be more important than the *where* for you, but we are in Phoenix, Arizona. The gun on my hip is called a Glock 19, it's more powerful than what you are used to, well more efficient at least," I said.

"Why would you say the *when* is more important?" asked Otto with that same slightly German accent. At that moment Lydia walked out with three beers. Otto tensed for a second and then relaxed. Lydia stopped by him and stood still for a second, she put the beers on the table then she quickly ran out into the rain. She grabbed Otto's coffin and pulled it under the porch overhang so it would be out of the rain. She studied the coffin for a while.

"These runes here, they were under where he was laying so we couldn't see them. They are runes of spell longevity and spell maintenance, drenched in live blood as a power source. I smelled him and listened to his heart, he is a human... It looks like he was cursed with some kind of stasis spell. This box maintained it and kept him frozen," said Lydia.

"How did you hear my heart?" Otto asked.

"I'm a vampire of course," replied Lydia.

Otto jumped up from the table and drew his sword. The second he had moved I had jumped up as well and I already had my Glock pointed at his heart.

"If you move one more inch I'm going to shoot you to death and put you back in that box," I said.

"Bear, this vampire has you enthralled. Can't you see that?" Otto asked.

"She doesn't have me enthralled, I have her enthralled... technically I'm her supervisor and her team leader," I said.

"You found out how to control the undead?" Otto asked.

"Well Lydia is easy, I just give her lots of money and pizza," I said.

"HEY!" Lydia shouted.

"Oh don't deny it, you know it's true," I said. Otto looked between us like we were crazy. "Otto sheath that sword, we are all friends here, no one is trying to hurt you. If we wanted you dead you would be dead," I said. Otto once again calmed down and sheathed his sword.

"Why does she seem sane?" he asked me.

"That's a very long story, but the short version is that she has a magical ring that stops her from going insane and she was a really good person before she became a vampire, she is one of a kind," I said.

"I can tell I am making you uneasy so I'll go inside. If you hurt Bear, I will kill you," Lydia said before going inside.

"Otto, what is the last thing you remember?" I asked.

"I remember kicking down the door of my nemesis' home. A particularly nasty vampire named William. As soon as I entered the home I saw a flash of light and then I was here waking up in your backyard," said Otto.

"Well, that would explain why you were so combative. What year was that?" I asked him.

"That was 1927.... I'm afraid to ask, but what year is it now?" Otto replied.

"It's 2017 bud, you have been asleep for ninety years," I said calmly.

"MEIN GOTT! That can't be right!" he shouted.

"Can you keep it down my neighbors are sleeping?" I asked.

"How do I know you aren't lying, how do I know you aren't working for William?" asked Otto.

"Well I don't know William, but if I did I could have killed you twice now, also check this out..." I said and pulled out my cell phone. I spent about ten minutes with Otto showing him the phone, taking pictures with it, showing him a few videos I had recorded, he was very overwhelmed. "Do you trust me now, or at least believe we are in the future?" I asked.

"I won't trust you until I see you kill a vampire," Otto replied.

"I would love to... we have been wanting to do just that but we don't know how to find them," I said.

"I can find you one, but this close to your pet vampire it won't work. I have a vampire detector but she will throw off the findings," Otto said.

"You have a vampire radar?" it was my turn to be surprised.

"What's a radar?" asked Otto.

"Doesn't matter, so if we get far enough away from Lydia it will work?" I asked.

"Hypothetically, yes..." replied Otto.

"Well let's go!" I shouted.

We started heading towards my garage with Otto following closely behind, he had grabbed his Tommy Gun off of my light. He was in awe of the interior of my house.

"You live in a castle of opulence Herr Bearengar," Otto said.

"This? This is an average home for a medium income family. America is the land of opportunities, if you work hard you can have all of this and more. Wasn't it that way before?" I asked.

"Somewhat, things were starting to get bad before I... before I was frozen," he replied. I saw Lydia in my living room,

"I heard it all Bear, you better be careful out there," said Lydia.

343

"I'll be fine, I have Otto here for backup. Besides, you don't have to be the best fighter to survive a vampire attack, just the fastest runner if you know what I mean," I said jokingly and Lydia laughed, but I don't think Otto found it funny. We headed into my garage where again Otto was struck with wonder.

"These are your automobiles?" he asked with wonder in his voice.

"Yeah, they are a little better than the Ford Model T aren't they?" I asked rhetorically.

I grabbed my WASR and a crossbow that had a quiver full of bolts mounted below it off of the wall of my garage for Otto. Then I hopped in the Dodge Charger and he followed suit. Once he was in, I handed him the crossbow.

"You can't use the Tommy Gun inside the city. You will wake up dozens of people and the police will arrest us. Do you know how to use the crossbow?" I asked.

"I am familiar with its use," Otto replied.

I drove us over to Maryvale, one of the worst parts of the greater Phoenix area. The place was rife with illegal immigrants and drug dealers. This is the exact kind of place where a vampire could murder and eat people and no one would come looking.

"This is the area where I think there might be vampires, you got anything?" I asked him.

He reached into his overcoat and pulled out a large iron key and gripped it tightly in his fist. He closed his eyes and pointed in a general direction forwards and to the right of our current position. I drove the car towards where he was pointing and he moved his finger slightly towards a neighborhood.

I had to giggle a little to myself at the situation I was in, sitting in a car with what was essentially a time traveler using a magical key as a vampire radar and on my way to kill said vampires; *and people said I wasn't going anywhere in life, pffft!* Otto didn't seem to mind my giggling, he was so focused on using his magical key thingamabobber. I just kept heading towards the direction of his pointing.

Finally, he said, "STOP!" I slowly depressed the breaks of the car not wanting the tires to lock up and make noise, this wasn't my first rodeo. "They are in that house, at least three..." Otto said while pointing at a home close by.

"How can you tell?" I asked,

"The strength of the pull, this isn't the first time I've done this, Herr Bearengar," he said.

"Okay I trust you, but just call me Bear for now please," I said. He nodded and unfolded himself from the car, he loaded the crossbow

345

and then lifted his sword about an inch out of its sheath and let it fall back down. He straightened his fedora and cracked all of his knuckles, I guess he was ready for some serious shit.

I was ready as well, giddy almost, my body had developed a love for potential mayhem. All of the best times in my life were when I was in danger. Growing up poor as dirt, the only way I could get my adrenaline fix was breaking the law, which I now regretted. Then as an adult, I sought adventure in the military. In Afghanistan, if you weren't being shot at, you were bored as hell. My body craved this, and I had an edge I had never had before; my enchanted arsenal and my tonalli.

"You know, I'm wondering why you aren't asking me why I'm using a gun and I have asked you not to," I told Otto.

"I recognized your Maxim, Herr Bear," Otto replied tersely.

"Please don't call me Herr Bear, it sounds too much like Care Bear, just Bear, please. Also, what is a Maxim?" I asked.

"The device on the end of your weapon," said Otto.

"Oh, we just call those silencers now," I said.

"Bear why are these crossbow bolts not silver tipped?" Otto asked.

"Do they need to be?" I asked.

"Ideally yes, vampires spend more time healing after being hit with silver," said Otto.

"I had no idea, we have just been shooting the crap out of them or burning them in the sun," I said.

"That will work, but silver works better, let's go. I'll take the back you take the front. Make some noise when you enter and when I hear your signal I will enter the back," said Otto.

Chapter 22

I walked up to the front door and saw Otto head around the side of the house, he jumped the wall to the backyard and I saw his overcoat slink over the block wall behind him. I waited a minute for him to get into position, then I kicked the front door. It didn't budge and I didn't balance my weight correctly so I fell over, *that's embarrassing*. I stood back up and pushed a little tonalli into my muscles and kicked the door right on the handle as hard as I could. The door cracked and broke inward, I was still pushing my tonalli so I swept into the house quickly and slammed the front door shut behind me. I had three people sitting on a couch in front of me watching television with a dead woman between them, the dead woman's head was on one of their laps. There was fresh and dried blood everywhere. I was aiming the WASR right at them but they were just all smiling at me and not moving.

"Now yous can't leave," I said to the room in a mock Italian/mobster accent.

I wasn't sure if all three of the guys on the couch were vampires or what but the one on the far right with the dead girl across his lap starting laughing "*A Bronx Tale*, I love that movie! Good joke kid, but you broke my door so now you have to die," he said.

"Wait a minute, so all three of you are vampires?" I asked. All three of them split their disgusting mouths open and their faces started contorting into different visages of horror as their teeth elongated and sharpened.

"Cool, just checking," I said and then I started double tapping each of them in the chest, starting with Mr. Loud Mouth. I had only got to the second one when they were on me, these suckers were fast. These guys made the vampires at Dante's house look like pussies.

The one who had laughed at my joke was so fast he was in front of me in a second and he grabbed me by the jacket and threw me across the room. As I was flying across the room one of the other vampires sped across the room in front of my trajectory, then threw his arm out like a clothesline. I was still being carried forward from the throw so the vampire's arm hit me right in the neck and I fell to the floor hard on my back.

They all started laughing which really pissed me off... I pushed my tonalli hard focusing on healing and strength, then I did a kip up. As I was flying upwards I still had my WASR in my hands thanks to the one point sling. The one who had clotheslined me was the closest so I turned my WASR sideways and hit him in the face with the buttstock. Then I threw a savage kick which he caught and he refused to let go of my foot. That was fine, I had so much tonalli running through me I felt like a superman. I simply pushed off with my opposing foot and flew up into the air, unleashing a kick to his head with the foot I had pushed off with. Once my foot connected he let go of me.

His friends must have known I meant business now because the leader used vampire speed and ripped the WASR right off of me as I was landing, he even broke my sling. Then he threw the WASR like a dart at the wall, where it lodged itself right into the drywall.

"Hey fucker, that's expensive!" I yelled at him.

Then a crossbow bolt landed in his temple. Otto was around here somewhere but I didn't have time to worry about that, I still had a supercharged vampire somewhere. I turned my head and saw him heading towards me. I threw my dagger at him and it landed squarely in his neck and sank in up to the hilt. He grabbed at the dagger to try to pull it out but I pushed tonalli at the link between myself and the dagger. Instead of trying to pull it towards me, I pushed it away from myself. The vampire's hands were coated in his own blood and the dagger was trying to drive itself all of the way through his neck. He was trying desperately to stop it, but he just couldn't hold on to it with his bloody slippery hands and so it drove itself all the way through and out the back of his neck, then into the wall behind him.

I turned back to the one who had been hit with the bolt in the head. He had yanked the bolt out and was climbing to his feet. The one I had kicked in the head was also climbing to his feet behind me, oh farts. A crossbow bolt flew into the chest of the one behind me but the one in front of me, the leader, used vampire speed and picked me up by my armor. I grabbed his forearms and tried to pry his hands off, but they were like iron bars and they refused to move. He slowly started lifting me off of the ground with a devious smile on his face, then he started pulling me towards him and his mouth started opening wider, homie don't play that shit. I pushed my tonalli hard into my muscles and started pulling on his arms and screaming right into his face. I pulled and pulled while pushing my power ever harder. I could see the vampires concern but I couldn't overpower him completely and he soon knew it. So he continued pulling me towards him. I had a knee in his chest and I was trying to push myself away still. The vampire was completely distracted with me so he didn't see Otto sneak up beside us.

Otto let out a mighty roar and yelled "FOR GOD!" and he swung his sword in a two-handed grip over his head right at the vampire's arms. OH SHIT! The sword was flying right next to me so I tried to make like a piece of paper and get skinny. I closed my eyes and felt the air displace as the sword flew inches from my face. Then my feet hit the floor, I opened my eyes and looked up. The vampire was staring at me pissed with two bloody stumps where his forearms and hands had once been. I looked down and saw his disconnected hands and forearms were still gripping my jacket, *EW gross*! I knocked the hands off but then was grabbed from behind by one of the vampires in a bear hug. We struggled back and forth. I flexed my tonalli and the vampire almost lost his grip but again, I couldn't out power him. I had an idea!

I started turning the vampire by shuffling my feet until his back was aimed in the same direction I had thrown my dagger. Then I pushed my tonalli again into the link between myself and the dagger but I used the normal pulling magic. The dagger flew right at us trying to return itself to me but since he was the closest and standing between me and my dagger, it flew right into his back. He let go of me to face the attacker he thought was behind him stabbing him. I was now presented with the vampire's back with my dagger embedded in it, *don't mind if I do*. I grabbed my dagger and yanked it out and then drove it into the top of the vampires head with a tonalli powered thrust. Otto was behind me stabbing the de-armed vampire to death with his sword. I didn't see the last super powered vamp had gotten up and before I noticed him he delivered a nasty side kick to my ribs, I felt one crack and fell over. The vampire that had kicked me pulled my throwing knife out of his buddies head and threw it at Otto. It hit Otto in the chest so hard he spun around, his overcoat spinning behind him and he hit the ground.

"NOOO!!!" I shouted, I harnessed all the tonalli I could and felt my ribs pop back into place and heal. I rushed the vampire then, jumped through the air and landed on him. He fell backward and hit the floor with me on top of him. I was seeing red and pushing my tonalli so hard that my whole body was flaring with pain. I bounced the vampire's head off of the ground a few times and then I don't know what possessed me to do this but I bent down and bit his nose off. Hot blood squirted into my mouth which I spit back out into the vampire's eyes to blind him. Then I started punching and punching, the vampire below me was fighting back. He was punching me as well and breaking or cracking my ribs, but I just kept healing them. I'm not sure for how long I was face punching but the vampire's head had started coming apart in my hands. Then I noticed the vampire next to me, the one who had taken the dagger to the brain, he was rising. Otto jumped on him and drove his sword through the vampire's heart. He then pulled the sword out and chopped the vampire's head off. The vampire turned into soup.

"Otto, how are you alive man?" I asked. Otto pulled his overcoat and suit open and showed me the inside of his vest, it was lined with chainmail.

"Otto, MY MAN! That is awesome brother!" I yelled.

"Move," Otto said dispassionately. I got off of the downed vampire and Otto cut his head off. I got up and did an inventory check. My WASR was still stuck in the wall and my dagger was somewhere... I recalled my dagger using tonalli and it flew through the air into my hand.

"Will you teach me that magic?" Otto asked.

"The magic is in the dagger, not me, well mostly. It's not really something you can teach, it has to be given, it's called tonalli. Keep showing me vampires to kill and I will get you some. Otto do you have any idea why these suckers were so strong? The last ones we fought weren't as strong as them," I said.

"They may have been older than they appeared which I doubt, or they had an extremely strong maker." Otto replied.

"Okay Otto, in the grand year of 2017, you can't leave crime scenes everywhere you go. In the late 1980's we had massive leaps in forensic science technology which can't really be explained in a single night. Needless to say, we can not leave this place looking like this. Also, we need money to continue our vampire hunting endeavor so we need to plunder this house for valuables. I'll call in some back up to help us," I said.

I thought about calling Lydia but it was about six a.m. now according to my cell phone clock and the sun would be up soon so I called Rook and Griffin and told them to meet with Lydia at my house. I apologized for the early hour but this was Striker's business. I texted Lydia and told her to expect Rook and Griff and to give them the cargo van.

I had finally calmed down enough to look over at the T.V. which had surprisingly survived the chaos, the vampires had been watching *The Addams Family*, weird. Otto was looking at it now too, "You guys didn't have this in the twenties right?" I asked.

"No we did not. We had films, but not like this in the home. That clarity is wunderbar!" said Otto.

"Well after tonight is over you can watch as much as you want back at my place. I'll even help you pick which shows to watch," I said.

Otto and I picked through the house looking for valuables but this place actually seemed pretty run down, and I mentioned as much to Otto. He got an inquisitive look on his face and disappeared into a side bedroom.

I heard him yell, "Bear, come in here!"

When I walked in, he was in the closet of the room. He had pulled up the carpet and underneath there was a hatch. We went down the hatch, this was the real treasure trove. It was just a very short hallway with three bedrooms branching off of it. Each bedroom had a reinforced metal door which were all currently opened, but could be locked from the inside. These were the real living quarters, the house above was just a decoy. This was where the vampires could hole up in case of emergency and during the day to make sure if their house ever burnt down or some other emergency they would be sequestered down here below safely. Each room had its own set of unique valuables based on the personality of the vampire that resided in them. One room was just covered in shelves that housed records from every era. I wasn't really a music guy but I bet those would sell for a ton of money. One room had a coin collection that even amazed me, along with other small collectibles. The last room was the most opulent and it was absolutely covered in Nazi artifacts.

I looked over at Otto thinking he would be pissed but he just looked confused,

"Oh yeah, this is slightly after your time, you aren't going to be happy when you find out what this stuff is," I said.

"It is not. I recognize this symbol, it is the unit patch for the American 45th Infantry Division and the Buddhist symbol for peace," said Otto.

Okay now I was confused so I pulled out my phone and did a search on the military unit Otto mentioned. Sure enough, their unit insignia until the 1930's was the swastika.

"I'm sorry to be the one to tell you this Otto, but a madman took over Germany in 1933. He did terrible things and the world rallied together against Germany and stopped him," I said.

"Don't be sorry Bear, I am American, I was born in Illinois. I fought against the Germans in the Great War," said Otto.

"Why do you have a German accent then?" I asked.

"In my time it was not uncommon to only speak German in the small farming communities of America. I myself didn't learn English until I was eight years old. When I left the small town I grew up in, they were still printing the newspaper in the German language," said Otto.

"Wow, I had no idea. We have a lot to talk about," I said.

Griffin and Rook made good time making it over. I didn't call Zach because I knew he would be getting his kids ready for school, then heading to work. I made introductions between Otto and them. It was a little awkward since they had all seen him when he was in the coffin.

"Otto, Griffin and Rook here are also both veterans, they served in the Army. Otto here is a veteran as well, of World War One. Army, right Otto?" I said.

"Yes, I was an Army Intelligence officer. I spoke German well so that helped me in that position," said Otto.

"This is too fucking cool," said Rook.

"Well we will have lots of time to discuss all of this, but we should really get out of here soon. Let's load all these valuables into the van, clean this place up and then skedaddle," I said.

We loaded the van bottom to the top with stuff. Anything we thought was even remotely valuable, we took. We even took the coffee table since it was in good shape and we had room. We took all of the Nazi artifacts as well, not something I wanted to keep around my house but I'm sure someone would pay big bucks for them. There wasn't much we could do to clean the house up since it was covered in blood new, and old. So we just misted bleach everywhere from a couple of spray bottles. By the time we were done the sun had just come up. I seriously considered just burning the whole place down but I didn't want the fire to spread to any neighboring homes.

"Check it out Otto, technically this is the first sunrise you have seen in ninety years," I said.

"I'm having a hard time believing it," he replied.

"So am I," I said.

Otto and I jumped in the Charger and started heading back to my house. We took the I-17 north back to my place and now that the sun was up, there was a lot more to see. I live in North Phoenix so we passed our local amusement park Castles and Coasters and you could see their largest roller coaster sticking into the skyline. It had been a quiet drive up to that point I had been trying to give Otto a chance to take in the sights.

"I am not sure if I should be happy or sad about being here. I had no family in my time, no wife, no kids, but I did have some work friends. The world is doing well though now, at least that is how it looks. Everything I have seen so far is amazing, and you seem to be happy about living here," said Otto.

"Otto, this is an amazing time to be alive. I'm sorry for what happened to you but you should look on the bright side of things. You can make a life here, I will help you. Hey, you said 'work friends' what did you do for work?" I asked him.

He didn't say anything for a minute and then he said "I killed vampires, no more questions for now please."

We beat the van back to my house for obvious reasons. My neighbor was leaving for work and he waved at me from his car before pulling out of the cul-de-sac.

"Your neighbor is a negro?" Otto asked.

"We don't call them Negroes anymore, Otto, they are just people like you and me," I said casually. I wasn't mad at him, he comes from a different culture.

"In my time the coloreds were separated from the whites," Otto said.

"There is no segregation anymore, everyone lives with each other. My neighbor, the one you just saw, I'm proud to live next to him. He served in the U.S. Air Force for over twenty years, he is a veteran just like you and I," I said.

"What is the 'Air Force'?" asked Otto.

"It's a branch of the military that focuses on air superiority. They fly fighter planes. I'll show you some today on my computer. Computer... that's hard to explain too, it's basically a machine that can give me any photograph I want. I'll teach you all about it," I said.

"That sounds... interesting, and I am glad your negro neighbor is a good person. I harbor no ill will towards the colored people, in fact, I once helped destroy over one hundred members of the Ku Klux Klan!" Otto said excitedly. *Okay, now that is a story I have to hear.*

360

We stood in my driveway just letting the early morning sun hit us as we waited for the van to arrive. When they showed up I asked Rook and Griffin if they wanted to come inside and have some coffee, but Rook was going to the gym and Griffin wanted to get home and eat breakfast with his wife. They asked me if I needed help unloading the van or with anything else, but I told them no. I would just drive the whole thing over to the Lawyer's law firm later so he could give the stuff to the auction houses. When we went inside, Lydia had started breakfast. I could tell Otto was on edge around her.

"If you trust me then you trust Lydia, she has saved my life before and has helped me become more powerful as well as kill vampires," I told him, he just nodded at me and stayed silent.

Lydia served us both big heaping plates of hash browns, bacon and eggs. Then she went back and got herself a plate of the same. Otto and I started eating but Lydia poured a gracious amount of blood all over her meal. Otto's face was that of shock and he started reaching for his sword.

I spoke up before he touched it, "It's animal blood Otto, relax," I said not knowing if that was true. It might have been human blood from Dante's house or the half and half mix Lydia and I had discussed. I hadn't been monitoring Lydia's eating habits out of respect for her, I trusted her. For now it was best to let Otto think it was animal blood. Otto slowly put his hands back on the table.

"My apologies new friends. This world is still new to me and in my time all vampires were psychotic maniacs."

"They very much still are, Lydia is one of a kind," I said. Lydia stayed quiet but she smiled at both of us. "Otto, did you want to get some sleep or did you want to stay awake and learn about 2017?" I asked.

"I would like to try and rest," he replied. When we were done eating I showed him my man cave, the only empty room in my house since Lydia was in the guest room and I was in the master bedroom. The man cave had a fold out futon in it so I pulled it out for him and laid out some sheets and blankets. I put a few bottles of water and granola bars in his room in case he got hungry or thirsty. I also showed him how the shower and bathroom worked. Maybe he already knew but I wanted him to feel like a welcomed guest.

"Alright Otto, I am going to take a shower and get some sleep myself, it was nice to meet you. I really like you Otto and you are welcome in my home, but if you try to hurt Lydia while I am sleeping I will be extremely displeased," I said with a little menace in my voice, to which he nodded.

Mia hadn't really been too curious about Otto, I took that for a good sign. I told Lydia thanks for everything and if she needed help that she should wake me, then I went to my room. Mia followed me in, she probably wanted to sleep too. I peeled all of my nasty armor, weapons and clothes off and went into my bathroom to shower. Once I was done showering I looked in the mirror, HOLY SHIT! I was absolutely ripped. Every muscle in my body stood out rock hard. They hadn't gotten that much bigger but they were massively defined. Had the tonalli done this to me or was this something to do with how I was using it? It made sense in a way. The tonalli sped up healing and building muscles is just a form of healing, you rip your muscles and then they heal stronger. I wonder what would happen if I did some serious workouts while slightly pushing my tonalli?

Chapter 23

I woke up around noon feeling completely refreshed. I had only slept about five hours but I still felt great. I ran right to the mirror, I was in my boxers and I just stood there staring at myself. I had been working out since I was fourteen with my friends in their garages. After that, I went to open gym every day of high school. Then I immediately joined the military and pushed my body to whole new levels of fitness that I didn't even know were possible before that point and I had never had a great body. No matter how hard I tried, my body just never seemed to get that stereotypical 'muscular physique.' Sure, I was in great shape before, but I never really liked the way my body looked, but now... I was so ripped that my muscles had muscles. I bet I could go apply to be a shirtless model anywhere in town now and get the job ahead of anyone else. I was absolutely giddy with excitement. This was something that genetics and childhood undernourishment had robbed me of, something I had worked for my whole life for and never been able to reach, but now I had it!

I had always been confident and cocky, but now I was in real trouble. I had to show someone, maybe I could show Lydia! No, that would only confuse her and send her a mixed message. I couldn't show

Emily either, not without her wondering how I went from having a slightly better than average body to looking like an underwear model overnight. I guess this would just have to be my little secret... That's okay, it was so worth it. I checked the time on my phone, it was just about noon. I called Zach, he was at work on his lunch break so I gave him a very rough summary of what had happened last night and told him that he was on call the second he could get away. I needed him to take the van and its contents to the lawyer's office, get an itemized receipt for everything and then take the van in for repairs and upgrades of his choosing. He said he would get it done, it was only fair since Rook and Griffin had helped this morning.

Mia was sitting by my bedroom door with her tail wagging. She probably needed to go outside or get a drink. I opened the door and she darted right to my kitchen and started drinking her water. Her water bowl was by my back door so I walked over and opened the door so she could go pee if she had to, I was too paranoid to have an actual dog door. The house was pretty quiet, the others must have been sleeping still. Lydia was up all night too I realized when I thought about it. I heard Otto's door open and his footsteps slowly come into my kitchen. He was fully dressed in that three-piece suit still.

"You want some coffee?" I asked him.

"I would like that very much," Otto replied.

"We have to get you some clothes today. Your clothes are nice, but a little out of date. For now, I can give you a pair of my jeans and a t-shirt, they should fit you," I told him.

"Very kind of you Bear. I saw your awards in the room I am staying in, you are quite an accomplished man," said Otto.

He was talking about the unit awards and certificates of completion I had gotten while in the military. When I got out, I didn't know what to do with them so I bought a bunch of cheap frames and hung them up in my man cave. They may have seemed important to him but all of those awards and certificates didn't even qualify me for a job flipping burgers, it's funny how that works.

"Where is your pet vampire?" Otto asked.

"Please don't call her that, she is actually a good person if you give her a chance," I said. Otto ignored me and moved the conversation on.

"Will you teach me of your world today?" he asked.

"Of course! I would love to, let's start now. I think the easiest way would be for me and you to watch a few episodes of my favorite shows on the television and then I can pause them from time to time and explain things," I said.

"What about books and newspapers, are those still popular?" Otto asked.

"Yes those things very much still exist, they are just rare. We can go to a bookstore today and get you a few books and newspapers on the way back here. People actually still read a lot, they just do it electronically now. That's a whole other topic though, I'll show you my E-Reader today as well."

A few hours went by while Otto and I sipped coffee in my living room and watched my favorite shows. We had to pause it often so I could explain modern technology or modern slang, but for the most part, he seemed to be loving it and comprehending the bulk of it. Zach stopped by and met Otto, but he was in a rush. He had to take the van to the lawyers and then to the repair shop and try to get home in time for dinner. He told us that eventually he was going to have to tell his wife the truth if he kept disappearing like this. That's his problem, his relationship, if he wants to make a ton of money and destroy evil he would have to figure that problem out on his own. I was always in favor of having non-believers throw knives at Lydia though!

Lydia woke up and joined us in binge watching television. Otto was uncomfortable at first but he was so excited about learning about my time and watching the shows, he quickly forgot to be uncomfortable around her. Everyone was getting hungry and I felt bad that Lydia had been making all of the food lately so I told her to stay seated and relax, and I got up and made us a snack. I tried to think what would amaze a man from the 1920's the most so I just heated up some Pizza Rolls in my microwave. He was thoroughly impressed with my quick culinary skills, if he only knew. The sun was going down so we could all leave soon. I had an idea.

"Lydia, I know we shouldn't, but let's show him video games," I said.

"Don't you think that will be a little overwhelming?" she asked.

"He has to learn sometime," I replied.

We loaded up a few different games and just showed Otto what we were doing at first and then we handed him the controller. He was terrible when we began but he picked it up quickly and was soon openly laughing with joy as we destroyed aliens together on my big screen. The sun went down and Lydia mentioned we should all go. Otto snapped out of his blissful gaming trance and regretfully set the controller down. I went to my bedroom and grabbed a pair of jeans, a Magpul t-shirt and a pair of my nicer tennis shoes. I gave the clothes and shoes to Otto and asked him politely to change into them.

"Bear, I can't wear these I will have nowhere to conceal my sword or chainmail," he said.

"You don't need a sword or chainmail where we are going, but I understand the need to be armed," I said.

"No, you don't understand. A Knight of my Order must always be ready to face the forces of evil," he said.

"A knight of your what?" I asked.

"It's a long story Bear, one I am not ready to share. The point is I can not leave your home unless I am properly armed and armored," said Otto.

"Wait here Otto, let me see what I can do," I said.

I went and got a briefcase I used to have to use at one of my old jobs and I put the silenced 1911 handgun we had plundered from Robert inside, and I slid a few full magazines into the internal pouches that were meant for pens. I also grabbed my old light tan windbreaker. I brought them back into the living room and I opened the briefcase in front of Otto.

"Can we do this? You can carry this case tonight with this weapon inside of it. I am sure you recognize the platform, correct?" I asked.

"Yes I carried one during the Great War," said Otto.

"So you carry this, then you put this jacket over the clothes I have given you and you wear your chainmail under the t-shirt, the jacket will hide its bulk. Oh, one more thing!" I said, then I ran back to my man cave and opened a small locker I had in there with odds and ends. I grabbed an extendable baton in a nylon belt sheath and went back out to my living room. "Check this out!" I said. I opened the sheath and slang out the extendable baton. *SHING*. That iconic noise filled the room "You can also wear this on your belt under the jacket!" I said.

Otto looked at me approvingly and said, "This will work very well." I handed him the baton and he took a few practice swings with it. "How do you collapse it?" he asked.

"Just bang the tip straight down onto the carpet. Don't do it on my tile though, it will fuck it up," I said.

He slammed the baton down onto the carpet and it collapsed down into its handle. He practiced extending it and closing it a few times.

"Please keep that forever Otto, consider that a gift. Mia will stay here while we are out and guard the house," at hearing her name Mia loudly barked. "Trust me, she is much more than meets the eye," I said. I pitied the fool who attacks Mia right now. I don't know what the tonalli is doing inside of her body, but I had a feeling the next person she got mad at was going to seriously regret whatever they had done to piss her off.

Everyone got ready and we headed out, we took my Mitsubishi since it comfortably sat four. We went straight to Scottsdale Gun Club first. There were better gun stores out there, but this was the only place I knew that carried bulletproof vests. I told Otto to not say anything around the store employees because they could cancel a sale for any reason. I bought a bunch of hollow point ammo in different calibers, I had an idea about that. Basically, I wanted to put a few drops of silver into each hollow tip. I figured if I kept it really light it wouldn't screw up the ballistics. I bought a few more collapsible batons, some more Pepper Blasters and a few more soft armors. I also picked up two Glock 19's with hybrid holsters. I would give one to Lydia and one to Otto at our next Sunday dinner. We really needed the business to open soon. I was tired of keeping all of this surplus at my house, a proper armory would be nice. I also really needed those checks from the lawyer. I was maxing my credit cards out like crazy. According to the lawyer though, the first check should be rolling in, in just a few days.

The whole time we were at Scottsdale Gun Club, Otto's face was alight with wonder and happiness. I could tell he wanted to say a million things and ask a million questions, but he stayed quiet like I had asked him to. The employees wouldn't sell guns to people they thought were crazy so I needed Otto to look like he belonged. Once we were done there I drove us all over to a really beautiful outdoor mall here we have called Desert Ridge, It's right off the 101 and Tatum. This place was really nice, they had those little speakers hidden in fake rocks in the landscaping so no matter where you went you heard beautiful music. There were giant pillars with stone bowls on the top of them filled with roaring fires. They had AstroTurf everywhere so it gave the illusion of lustrous green grass. All of the concrete there was stained Arizona red and had some kind of clear gloss rolled over it. It really was a nice place. Otto couldn't stay quiet any longer once we were walking up to it.

"BEAR THIS IS AMAZING!" he shouted. He was right, this place even impressed me.

"This is an outdoor mall. They have everything here, food, books, clothing, etc. Try to act normal, please. Ask as many questions as you want," I said.

We walked around for an hour just so Otto could take it all in and ask questions before we went shopping. We went clothes shopping first. We got Otto a few pairs of shoes and boots once we got him sized, Lydia is an expert shopper so that went fast. Then we bought him five pairs of jeans and a bundle of different colored t-shirts and polo shirts. Lydia grabbed him undies and socks. We headed over to the bookstore located in this mall and bought a couple history books that went from 1900 until now. We also bought a few books on World War Two and some books on modern technology for kids. Seems a little demeaning, but I couldn't find anything else better for a time traveler from the past.

"Well, did we work up an appetite? Everyone want to eat?" I asked.

Lydia and Otto both agreed they were hungry. We all went and got some Chinese food and sat near a fountain that was shooting colored water into the air. There were lights below the water which added the color. There was a live band playing nearby. Lydia pulled out a little travel sized vial of blood and poured it over her food. Otto noticed but didn't say anything.

"Bear, thank you for showing me one of the best nights of my life. It's still hard to believe I am here. Part of me thinks I have died and gone to heaven," said Otto.

"You aren't dead yet buddy, and we have some hard times ahead and vampires to kill, but we work hard so we play hard. Keep up the good vampire killing work, and you will earn some money and be able to do this whenever you want. Or if you want, you could retire and do your own thing, no one said you have to hunt vampires, your life is yours," I said.

"I had not thought of that... I don't know if I could imagine myself not hunting evil," he said. Then he didn't speak again for a while. "I think there is a vampire nearby," said Otto unexpectedly and harshly.

"Yes, hello my name is Lydia, we have met," said Lydia.

"Nein, another one. My device has been throwing mixed signals the whole time we have been here." He pulled out his iron key and held it tightly in his palm. Then he stood up and walked a few feet away from the table and closed his eyes. "There is another nearby, I'm feeling two pulls. One is from Lydia but the other is different, unique..." said Otto.

"Follow it, Otto," I said and Otto took off at a trot. Lydia and I grabbed our many bags and followed him. We walked for about five minutes until Otto pointed at a man. The man noticed him pointing and he took off down a service corridor between businesses.

We went down the corridor after him, he was at the end looking for somewhere to go. It was a dead end, there were only some dumpsters and a set of iron doors that went somewhere but I was sure they were locked. The vampire started heading towards the doors, locks don't mean much to a vampire. A round landed at the vampire's feet kicking concrete shards at the wall near him. I turned and looked where the shot had come from. The briefcase I had loaned Otto was laying on the ground open, Otto was standing next to it in a classic Weaver stance. Otto had fired the silenced 1911 at the vampire, a warning shot. The vampire knew he wasn't going to be able to pull on the doors, not without Otto shooting his back full of lead so he turned and faced us.

"He comes for you! He knows you killed his son!" the random vampire shouted.

"Who's coming and whose son did I kill?" I asked.

"You will see soon enough!" he shouted.

"Well you won't, you will be dead, let's go faggot!" I yelled back. Don't get me wrong I'm not a homophobe. In fact one of my best friends that I served with is gay, but I grew up in the nineties and that is just what people called each other back then, old habits die hard.

I threw my hands out to my sides and flexed them opened and closed, finally leaving them open. Something was telling me to lean forward and flex my shoulders in the vampire's direction, an open sign of hostility. I kept my hands open, palms forward showing the vampire that I was unarmed. I flexed every muscle in my body and started heading towards him. I had my Kershaw Blur pocket knife and my Glock 19 in a concealed carry holster, but I had all but forgotten about them at this point. I had tonalli flowing through me heavily and I was only focusing on the challenge in front of me. I didn't even care that my friends were there, *this vampire was mine.*

I came straight at him and he threw a heavy blow at my face which I dodged. I sent a return uppercut at him which connected with his chin. He flew back a few feet and then spit some blood on the ground and looked up at me with a toothy bloody smile. Then he came at me with vampire speed, he hit me like a train and I went flying. I rolled on the concrete a few times and hopped to my feet. I keep forgetting that I am not as strong as vampires, damn it! This tonalli is dangerous. I need to rely on my weapons and training first before I go all He-Man retard.

"Are you done yet, Incredible Hulk? Can we fight him seriously now, as a team?" asked Lydia.

"Yeah, I'm sorry," I said.

I had embarrassed myself. That was no way for the leader of The Strikers to act. Otto, Lydia and I fanned out. Otto was in the middle, I was to his left and Lydia was to his right. I flipped out my extendable baton. Lydia walked over to Otto and pulled his off of his belt which she then flipped out herself.

"Cover us, Lydia and I are going to get some stick time!" I shouted.

She and I converged and started pounding on the vamp. He was trying to parry the hits, but there were too many and they were coming in too fast. He was stronger than Lydia and I, and when his hits connected with us they hurt... *bad*. Finally, he got a lucky kick into Lydia's stomach which threw her back a few feet. She lost her footing and landed on her back. I took the opening and went on the offensive against him as soon as he was focused on Lydia. I smashed my baton into his temple rapid fire style a few times. He staggered back dazed so I did it again as hard as I could which only further dazed him.

I grabbed him by his shirt and jacket, then dragged him over to the dumpster and started lifting him to throw him in, but he kicked my upper leg and pain shot outwards from the impact point through my body. He might have cracked my femur. I was trying to maintain my hold on him, but he was fighting back now. Lydia must have gotten up because she was next to me all of a sudden hitting his head with the baton. Then she also got a grip on him and together we hoisted him up and into the dumpster.

"Move!" Otto said, he then got between Lydia and I and put the 1911 over the edge of the dumpster and dumped the magazine into the vampire. He was still squirming around trying to get out, so Lydia and I started smacking the shit out of him with the batons again.

"GO GET A MAGAZINE, RELOAD!" I told Otto.

Otto went and grabbed a few more magazines for the 1911, then reloaded and kept shooting over the edge of the dumpster into the vampires face. Otto's scattershot tactic wasn't working so he dumped an entire magazine into the vampire's head.

"This is fucking ridiculous, we need real weapons!" I said.

"You need silver ammunition!" said Otto.

The vampire was still for a second after being severely beaten by Lydia and I and having over 30 rounds of .38 Super dumped into him.

"Well someone has to cut his head off," I flipped out my little Kershaw Blur.

"That's all you Bear," said Lydia,

"Technically I am your elder, have some respect for your elders young Bear," said Otto.

"You guys are assholes," I said, before jumping into the dumpster and starting to cut around the vampire's neck. I had one foot on his forehead and one on his chest. He started thrashing around wildly below me "HELP!" I yelped out as I tried to maintain my balance.

Otto put the 1911 flush with the vampire's temple under my foot and pulled the trigger a few times. JEEZ, this guy was strong, and he was regenerating like crazy. If there were three vampires at his power level we would have gotten our asses kicked, luckily there was only this one. I kept cutting at the flesh around his neck after Otto had given him a few more lead lobotomies. I had basically cut all of the flesh away but I couldn't separate his spine with my tiny pocket knife.

"Otto shoot this spine please," I said.

Otto reached into the dumpster and put the silencer against the spine and pulled the trigger a few times. Then I jumped on the vampire's head and heard a really disgusting snap as his head was cleanly broke off his body. The body turned to soup around me once the head was removed... The bottoms of my jeans were absolutely soaked in blood and viscera. There was a spigot on a wall nearby so I cleaned my hands under it but the bottom of my jeans were still wrecked. Luckily I had black shoes on so you couldn't tell with them. I took my little auto-knife and just cut the bottoms of my pants off. I had turned them into ugly shorts but at least it didn't look like I had gone traipsing through a blood pond. I put the cut off pieces of my pants into one of the shopping bags against a box of shoes.

"Let's get the fuck out of here... I want to go home and shower," I said.

We all got to the car and were driving home. Otto was up front with me mostly because I don't think Lydia felt safe having her back exposed to him.

Otto turned around in his seat and offered his hand to Lydia "Lydia, I owe you an apology. You fought admirably this evening and I have been unfair to you. I am truly sorry," said Otto.

Lydia took his hand and shook it, saying "It's water under the bridge Otto, I accept your apology." We were all silent for a minute.

"I have an apology to make as well, I shouldn't have rushed the vampire. I should have waited for my team, I won't make that mistake again. Something about the Tonalli made my brain turn off, or something. Either way, no excuses, I'm very sorry," I said.

"Dude, that was so funny though when he threw you!" Lydia said before laughing. Otto joined her in laughter and then I did as well.

Chapter 24

The rest of the week was spent mainly trying to get Otto acclimated to modern times, which is way harder than it sounds. We bought him a burner phone with some standard apps on it, and it basically blew him away with complexity, and we had gotten him the most basic model we could find... Our first check from the lawyer's office came in. They had sold a few of Dante's oldest valuables at the auction houses, the check was just a hair over $350,000. The lawyer told us he had sat in on one of the auctions and quite a bidding war had broken out, apparently, Dante had good taste in antiquities.

I was nervous as hell to deposit that check and this would probably be the last time I could do something like that. I might be able to explain this check away as selling family heirlooms to the IRS but I could never deposit this much again, at least not until we got the business off of the ground, then I would have a way to launder it. I would have to look into getting some overseas accounts. I can't believe I'm even thinking that. A couple of months ago I was basically killing bugs for a living and now I'm so rich I need an overseas account, this is nice. I begrudgingly deposited the check and pulled out $18,000 cash. I would be giving $4,000 each to Lydia, Rook, Griffin and Zach for the work they had contributed. I would give $2,000 dollars to Otto since he was the low man on the totem pole and was not even technically a part of the team yet. I would be paying myself $7,000, but I could just leave that in the account and access it with my debit card. The 7000 was my part of The Strikers pay, and enough money to start paying down my credit cards since I had been maxing them out constantly with Striker's related expenses.

Once I got paid, I went out and bought Otto a cheap laptop and loaded it to the brim with anti-virus software. I know how old people are with computers... I know Otto technically isn't old but compared to him, the average nursing home grandma is a computer expert. I set the laptop up in my man cave where Otto was staying for now and explained to him how to use it and how to search for things on the internet. Later that night I took Emily to the nicest restaurant in town. I had to wear a long sleeve t-shirt to cover up my new defined muscular physique. She wanted me to stay the night but I didn't want to end up taking my shirt off and then have to explain why I was so ripped. She did know I had been seeing a personal trainer and working out a lot so maybe in a week or two I might be able to explain it; she would probably think I was on steroids, but that is better than telling her the truth... that I had been trading the souls of the wicked with a Demigod and fighting vampires. Which in turn strains my muscles so hard that they rip and then the Demigod provided magic heals them better than they ever were before.

At Otto's insistence, we did a bunch of research together on my computer on how to make silver bullets which yielded zilch. So we switched our research over to how to mold silver which yielded amazing results and it looked like it would be easier than we thought. You basically only needed a few things. For one, of course, you needed a crap ton of silver, which you could buy anywhere. You needed a blacksmith's crucible which is a little bowl that doesn't melt under extreme heat. That is what you melt the silver in. Lastly, you need a small torch which can also be purchased almost anywhere. At this point, we could have molded actual entire bullets made of silver, but silver is too light and the bullet's trajectories would be fucked which is why everyone shoots lead. So instead we would be putting just a little bit of silver into the tips of the lead hollow points.

The first run I did we threw a bunch of shitty old silver jewelry into the crucible and I heated it all up with the torch until it was molten. The old jewelry had a lot of foreign material in it, that crap all floats to the top of the crucible, it is called "slag." At that point I stirred the molten silver and skimmed the slag off of the top with a long carbon rod, this accomplishes two things. You don't want to pour that slag into any mold you have, our mold, of course, being hollow point bullets themselves, and the stirring ensures that the silver is fully melted. Neither of us were metal smiths so we were just hoping for a few drops of silver per bullet which is easier said than done. It's hard as fuck to pour molten silver and the tip of a hollow point is a tiny target. We failed more then we succeeded but we did end up with about twenty usable rounds.

We had loaded .38 Super first because It went to the only silenced handgun that we had at the moment, the 1911. We took all of the cars out of my garage and filled a bunch of sandbags up and then lined them against one wall. Technically, this wall was already bulletproof but I didn't want to fuck my wall up. I shot ten rounds at a paper bullseye target we had pinned to the sandbags using the silver ammo and Otto shout ten rounds at a separate target also with silver ammunition, our groups looked great.

As a further test, we also shot ten normal rounds each and compared the groupings. At this short range, the groupings from the lead rounds compared to the silver round groupings were about exactly the same. Who knows how they would do at a distance, we would have to test that as well but for now, we had some shitty silver ammunition that works! Silver actually shrinks a little bit as it cools which was making some weird things happen inside of the hollow points and we were afraid that the silver might actually fall out of them if we moved them around too much so once all of the silver had completely dried we also poured a little bit of glue into the top of each hollow point. The entire process took a long time and it was extremely expensive so, for now, we would just be making sure every third round in every magazine a Striker was using had some silver in it.

Rook and Griffin had stopped by on Friday during that week and eaten dinner with Lydia, Otto, and I. Zach didn't want to spend too much time with us and make his wife suspicious and he was planning on coming over for the Sunday dinner meeting anyway. They questioned Otto all about World War One and the role he played in it, he was very excited to answer. However, he strayed away from almost any question that had to do with his vampire hunting. Finally, he just told us that he wasn't ready to share that side of his life yet, my friends didn't push the subject. Otto had been kind to us and was in a very strange situation where he had little to no control over his fate. I had a lot of empathy for the guy, I can't even imagine how I would deal with being randomly thrown ninety years into the future. I'm sure none of this was easy for him.

I asked Otto if he liked cigars and he said he did. So I brought enough cigars out for everyone. Even Lydia tried one for her first time.

Something she had avoided while she was human but now that she was a vampire she didn't have to worry about lung cancer. I had been hesitant to smoke too many before but now with my tonalli induced healing, I could just erase any damage the cigars were doing to my body instantly. We stayed up late that night smoking cigars and drinking as we told Otto and Lydia about a lot of the terrible stuff we had done as kids. Most of which was kind of funny and we had been drinking a long time so we were laughing at almost everything regardless. I noticed I kept losing my buzz so I had to focus to stop the tonalli from clearing the effects of the alcohol out of my body. I figured it out quickly though, I was mastering the basic aspects of tonalli usage. I was still afraid to tell my friends about it, but I was going to have to at this upcoming Sunday dinner. They deserved to know and they needed the same combat edge that I had.

Griffin and Rook ended up crashing on my couch because they were so drunk. Luckily I have a huge sectional with more than enough room for two people to sleep separately, so they didn't have to go nuts to butts. The next morning we all had coffee and donuts together before Griffin and Rook left. When they left, Otto thanked me again for an amazing night and he told me how lucky I was to have such good friends, he didn't have to tell me that though, I knew it. We spent most of that day bumming around. I got in some much needed gaming and relaxing. I drank way too many sodas since I wasn't worried about my health like I once was and I got to catch up with a lot of my online friends. Lydia was in her room doing something, I don't know what. Otto was reading the books and newspapers we had bought him and taking occasional breaks to watch me game.

Around four in the evening that day (Saturday), I went out to my backyard to train. I once only had a work out bench back here and a few free weights, but now my backyard was basically a giant home gym. I had tripled the amount of throwing knife targets, they were everywhere. I had a giant punching bag on a weighted iron stand in the middle of my yard. I had laid a bunch of wrestling mats over my lawn, and I had added a few more exercise machines. Normally you couldn't do any of this since the Arizona sun would destroy the leather on the equipment within a year but now that I had constant money flowing in I didn't really care. I would just replace it if it got ruined. Besides once we got the business up we could put a gym inside of it and I could move all of this equipment there.

I did a light jog around my yard and stretched. Then I worked my punching bag for a while with some assorted kicks and punches that I had picked up in my mixed martial arts training over the years. I turned on a little bit of tonalli speed and power but kept it low enough that I wouldn't break the bag. I was a machine, sweat started pouring down my face as my standard psychosomatic body systems kicked in but I wasn't feeling tired, in fact, it was the opposite. I was watching my legs and arms connect with the bag so hard and fast that the iron frame was rocking despite the combined weight of it and the bag weighing upwards of three hundred pounds and being bottom heavy, I was filled with childlike joy and wonder at the sight. Other kids grew up wanting to be firemen, dinosaurs, jet pilots, etc. No, I wanted to be a T-800 Terminator like Arnold. I wanted to be a relentless killing machine in the name of good, and now I was close to that.

I dropped the power level and increased my speed. My arms and legs turned into blurs. I wasn't vampire fast but I was absolutely professional fighter fast, probably faster, and my stamina wasn't even close to running out. The backdoor behind me opened and Otto came out carrying two training swords built out of wood and coated in a thin layer of foam.

"How about some real training? I found these in the room I am staying in!" he shouted and threw a sword at me, I caught it out of the air with a smile on my face.

"Sounds great!"

I didn't know shit about swords so this would be interesting. You are probably wondering why I have random training swords laying around. The answer is simple, when old curmudgeons sit around and order glass cats off of the television, I sit around and order weapons and ammo from the internet. *Don't judge me, at least I admit my issues!*

I turned my tonalli almost all of the way off and let the passive side of it take over.

"I'm ready when you are, old man," I said to Otto, my comment made him laugh.

He came at me with a very choreographed overhead strike. I understood the basic concepts of sword fighting so I turned my training sword sideways to parry the hit. He let his training blade glance off of mine and he went into a roll right past my knees. He came up quickly and pulled my legs out from under me with his sword.

"Don't take the obvious bait," said Otto as I did a kip up and nodded in his direction. I turned on a little bit of tonalli speed and sent a flurry of wild sword strikes at Otto, he carefully parried each one. I jumped back before he could retaliate.

"Otto! You secret sword badass! I am thoroughly impressed!" I said.

"All of the warriors of my Order must be proficient in sword use. Tomorrow at your 'friend dinner' I will tell you about it, a little. For now though, let's train!" he said.

Then he came at me fast, I still had my speed on and I was barely able to keep up with his strikes, he was beyond good. We continued

388

whacking the shit out of each other for about twenty minutes until we were both completely drenched in sweat.

"That was awesome Otto, we should do that again soon. You will have to teach me some of your moves and tell me the best way to become a better sword fighter," I said.

"That is the best way, what we just did, exposure to it. Of course, you can train movements and go over technique, but what works for some might not work for you. The best way to become better is to practice with a skilled opponent," said Otto.

That made sense, learning what works best for you, experimenting and thousands of hours of practice always trumps casual instruction. We rested and drank a bunch of water and then we got back to working out. I showed Otto all of my modern exercise equipment but it didn't need much instruction. Working out is basically pushing or lifting heavy things a lot so it doesn't take a rocket scientist to figure it out, in fact, I find it kind of boring. We spotted each other on the bench for awhile and then switched over to barbells. I showed Otto how to isolate a few different muscle groups with the barbells, he was really interested in this part of our exercise session. I still felt pity for Otto when I looked at him, all I saw was a man stuck in a strange place relying on the kindness of strangers to survive.

The next day, Sunday, was the day of our family and friends dinner and I was nervous as hell. I figured the best way to drop this information onto my friends was with copious amounts of alcohol. I rented a slushie machine filled with margarita, *yes you can do that*. It surprised me as well and it was way cheaper than I thought it would be. It arrived at noon but they told me the machine would keep the frozen margarita cold. I had it filled with some top shelf shit, no expense spared, my friends deserved it. I was still nervous so I started drinking as soon as it arrived and pacing around my house. Lydia must have noticed my nervous energy because she came up behind me and started massaging the knots out of my shoulders. I knew it wasn't right and I should tell her to stop but I couldn't. It just felt too nice and I was too stressed out.

"You are nervous about telling them?" she asked as she rubbed my shoulders.

"Of course, what if they think I'm a monster?" I asked.

"You aren't a monster Bear, you kill monsters," replied Lydia.

"Well I hope my friends feel the same way," I said.

I regretfully pulled away from Lydia's soothing hands and thanked her. Then I did what I always do when I am stressed to all hell. I read a little bit and played some video games! I had been playing video games with the same group of people online for almost a decade now and they were very curious as to why I hadn't been gaming lately. I didn't really know what lie to tell them and I was sick and tired of juggling lies so I kept it vague and truthful.

I told them that I had started a new job and I was busy as hell getting acclimated to the schedule and duties that it required. About halfway through my gaming session Emily called me and asked if she could come over to my place tonight. That created a real problem for me because I couldn't explain the power of the tonalli to my friends if Emily was around. I toyed around with the idea of telling her the truth, but I didn't want to lose her and I was pretty sure she would think I was batshit crazy if I told her I was a vampire slayer. So again I had to feed her some obviously bullshit excuse about why she couldn't come over, she was not happy with me and I wasn't happy with me either. I had to tell her something soon.

I had told the team to show up around five in the evening so they all started rolling in around then and were pleasantly surprised about the margarita machine. Especially Zach who told me word for word that his kids had been little shit heads that day, that made me laugh. I knew no matter how much Zach complained, he loved his little curtain climbers. I had the guys from Pizza By Napoli catering, they had stopped by about ten minutes before everyone had shown up and set out a bunch of pizza, wings and garlic knots. The sun was still up so we were having the meeting around my dining room table, so Lydia wouldn't have to experiment with extreme tanning. Mia was beyond excited to see everyone and she was running person to person and shoving her head into their hands expecting them all to pet her which they graciously did, everyone loves Mrs. Mia. I waited to speak until all of my friends were efficiently plied with alcohol and pizza.

I stood up from the table and smacked my silverware against my plastic cup full of margarita trying to get everyone's attention, that of course made no noise at all and I felt like a jackass. So I raised my voice and said "Can I have everyone's attention please!"

All of the side conversations died off and realized I was more scared about this than I ever had been fighting a vampire. "I've got a big announcement to make!" I shouted once I had found my confidence.

Rook interrupted me, "Let me guess, you and Lydia are getting married," he said jokingly and everyone giggled and Lydia blushed profusely.

"Ha, no! Lydia is awesome though and any guy she marries will be a lucky son of a bitch. I really don't know how to tell you all this so I'm just going to spit it out. I have been trading a Demigod for powers that enhance my body and I would like it if you all would do the same," I finished and stared at all of my friends who were dumbfounded at my insane proclamation.

Rook spoke up and asked, "I'm assuming you are talking about the same Demigod that granted that rat Percival his strength and longevity?"

Everyone was quiet now, listening intently. Even Otto was filled in on this situation, we had told him about our raid of Dante's house and how we had captured Percival and ultimately what I had done to him and learned from him. I think Otto had suspicions about how and why I had been so fast and strong during our vampire encounters but he had been a polite guest and not pushed the subject with me.

"Yes, they are one in the same. Don't confuse or associate Percival's character with Mick's. Mick is the Demigod's name. He isn't really good or evil, not in the sense of how we define those terms. He is on some kind of cosmic conquest in another dimension with rival Demigods. I'm not really sure what his exact endgame is but I assume it is to become a full god in a different plane of existence that has nothing to do with earth or us. Either way, he doesn't live in our dimension or even want to live in our dimension. He is a business and numbers man at his core. We bring him a product that he can process and he refines it and gives it back to us after his surcharge. He gets his piece of the pie and we get ours, it's actually a great deal for both parties," I paused there to see what was on their mind.

"You are being really casual about stealing people's souls. I think that is what we are talking about, isn't it?" asked Griffin.

"You are being too vague about the definition of 'people'. You were all party to plenty of murders. We murdered vampires indiscriminately. Living, thinking, sentient beings... we didn't check if they were good or evil first. We assumed they were evil because we knew their type and we murdered them. I'm suggesting we do the same, but with humans instead of vampires. For example, the other night Lydia and I traded the souls of three would-be rapists to Mick and a few other malcontents.

My point is, would the world really be a better place with those who are willing to rape out prowling the streets at night? Or should people like us, people who have the power to stop them, do something about it and become more powerful in the process?" I asked.

Chapter 25

I could tell that my last comment had them thinking.

"Explain the process in greater detail please," said Zach.

"Basically you find a piece of shit out there somewhere. What I am personally suggesting is that we use child molesters. The sex offender list is public record in the state of Arizona. My proposition is that we find a few of them in out of the way places, abduct them, and take them out to Mick. You sacrifice them in front of Mick after a small ritual and Mick renders all of the energy that powers them into something called 'tonalli.' He splits the energy fifty-fifty, you get half and he gets half. The tonalli has two sides to it, a passive side and an active side. The passive side of it makes you a little healthier, a little stronger and you live longer based on how much tonalli you have inside of you, I think. Percival only aged five or six months in about a span of thirty years, due to the passive side of tonalli. It's almost like he was burning tonalli in lieu of aging, but I'm not exactly sure how it works honestly. I do have many theories though."

I paused for a second because I could tell Griffin wanted to say or ask something.

"You said this tonalli makes you healthier? As in, it can heal you?" Griffin asked.

"It is still new to me as well, but from what I can tell the answer is a resounding yes. All of the little aches and pains I had racked up from Afghanistan and my years of service were gone almost instantly once I had the tonalli inside of me, but it was painful, very painful. I doubt it could heal something like cancer passively but old injuries, small wounds, etcetera, heal very quickly. The tonalli is finite though. Imagine it as a large gas tank with a tiny hole in it. The fuel is always slowly dripping out, that's the passive side. The active side would be the equivalent of putting the pedal to the floor with the same gas tank, the vehicle is doing a more strenuous activity so more fuel is used," I said.

"I think I understand the not aging principal then," said Griffin. I nodded at him and he continued, "Ageing is still a relatively new medical sector to study, but basically it's when your cells die or become damaged and then never return to a healthy state or just never return at all. If the tonalli is healing you constantly, maybe it is healing those damaged cells or replacing the missing ones which would normally never happen. It gives the appearance of immortality but that isn't what it is. It's simple cell replacement and repair," said Griffin.

"That is just fucking cool," said Zach.

"I wish I would have known about that before I became a vampire," said Lydia.

"This might not have helped you. Muscular Dystrophy is a gene mutation. It has nothing to do with cells, tonalli might do nothing to someone with it," said Griffin.

"So what's the active side of this tonalli stuff?" asked Rook.

"The active side is unexplored by humans, or at least any that are alive today. We could ask Mick if there are any other humans using tonalli but I doubt he would answer. He didn't specifically mention it but I got the feeling he hasn't really been to earth very often since the time of the Aztecs and if someone else is feeding him power, he probably wouldn't want to rat them out to us. Which is a good thing, because that means he won't be ratting us out to them or anyone else either.

Speaking of the Aztecs, I didn't pull that word 'tonalli' out of my ass, that's the actual Aztec word for what Mick imbues you with after the trade, but that is just part of it. Mick was telling me that the human body isn't meant to use or harness this much energy so he has to give you a small part of himself as well. I think we told you guys about the purple flash we saw leave Percival's body after I killed him, that was Mick's essence being reclaimed by him. Anyway, back to the subject at hand, the active side of tonalli. I haven't actively explored it fully yet but I've been able to isolate increased speed, increased strength, and this," I said, then I pulled my dagger and threw it across the room. I was going to try something new though this time, before the dagger landed in my wall I pushed my tonalli into the magical link between myself and the dagger and then the dagger flew back at me and I grabbed it out of the air.

"FUCKING AWESOME! I need to get me some of that tonalli!" Zach shouted.

"Don't be confused by that display. So far as I can tell tonalli doesn't work outside of the body. You can only alter, enhance, or manipulate yourself, but what I just did there was push tonalli at something that was already a part of me, the dagger's magic link. I'm still experimenting and I hope to learn more tricks like that soon. I've also purposely healed a small wound on command as well," I said.

Griffin looked pensive, Otto had said nothing, but Rook and Zach looked excited about the prospect. Griffin's opinion was the one I wanted to hear the most, he seemed to be the one who was having a moral problem with what I had been doing.

No one said anything for a moment, then Griffin spoke up,

"I am morally okay with killing child abusers but I won't be party to casual murder. If this ever gets out of control I'm out and I will report you to the authorities," he said it with not a hint of humor in his voice.

"I would expect no less," I replied.

The tension in the room died off and we all refilled our margaritas and discussed the prospects and possible things we could do with the tonalli. I went to my safe and pulled out everyone's cash and the Glocks I had bought for Otto and Lydia. I came back out and set their share of the cash in front of each of them. When I got to Otto and Lydia I gave each of them a Glock in a holster on top of their piles of cash.

"A present for each of you," I said and both of their faces lit up. Before they could properly thank me, I raised my voice one more time.

"One more order of business, please everyone!" The room quieted down once more.

"As you all know the vampire hunter known as Otto Richter is officially stranded in our time and stuck with this lousy group of misfits. I say we have a vote to officially invite him to join The Strikers, the premier vampire killing outfit in the world as far as I know," everyone was laughing after that.

"I vote in favor of letting Otto in, he has helped me kill four vampires now and he is an amazing swordsman. I think he would be an invaluable asset to our team. Everyone else in favor say AYE," I said, and then the whole table shouted, "AYE!"

"Well Otto, what do you think, you have been approved by the group, the position is yours if you want it. Will you join The Strikers?"

Otto was smiling largely but his eyes were betraying him, they were sad, maybe thoughtful.

"That is a very kind offer, my new friends. I feel it is only fair that I tell you a little about myself and my motivations before I accept it. If you will still have me at that point I will gladly accept the position.

I was once a member of a Holy Order associated with the church. We were a branch or maybe the evolution of what was once the Templars. I was in an isolated cell, all of the cells were separated from each other in case we were captured by the enemy; we would have no way to betray our brothers. My cell was murdered one by one by the vampire William and his sycophants. We chased him across the states as his dark cabal left bodies and crime scenes in their wake. I was the leader of my cell and my mad desire to find and stop him led to the demise of every member of my team. I never lost that dogged determination and once I have the funds and knowledge, I intend to go after William again, I will do anything to stop him."

"What was the name of your Order, have you tried to find them since you have been back here?" I asked.

"We didn't have a formal name we were just holy knights of the church, men that were loyal to god and willing to fight the supernatural in his name. It was safer that way you see, for the vampires knew of our existence and searched for us vehemently, but without even a name to use for us their search efforts had no real way to gain traction. The church funded and organized our expeditions.

I used the internet search engine to look up the exact church that we used as a point of contact. It was burnt to the ground in the 1930's and never rebuilt. I also looked up the exact priest who would give my cell our missions, he was murdered shortly after my disappearance and he had no heirs. I don't know if my order still exists, and if they do exist, I don't know how to contact them. I don't plan on stopping my hunt for William either; if he is still alive, I will kill him. I also never plan to lead men again, I did that before and they all died. I would be happy to be a part of your team in any non-leadership capacity, as long as you help me hunt William."

"That sounds fine to me, this William murders good people and he killed your friends. He sounds like he needs to get real dead, real soon. Once we get our business up and running and are able to launder more money, we should have the financial means to hunt William appropriately. One thing you conveniently left out, Otto, is what you think about dealing with Mick and gaining the power of the tonalli?" I said.

"You are the team leader, I am a member of the team. If you think it is for the best then I will follow," said Otto. *Vague, but at least he was on board.*

"Okay, I propose we get you guys your first dose of tonalli tonight. Lydia and I have already picked out four high level child abusers off of the sex offender registry. They live alone in quiet neighborhoods mostly full of old people who go to sleep early. Basically, they are the perfect targets. If you need any more motivation, here is a list of their crimes and mugshot photos," I said and reached into my pocket.

I pulled out a stack of folded paperwork and threw it on the table. It was the dossier of each sex offender. I had only picked the worst of the worst, mostly people who had raped kids... My friends wouldn't be feeling any compassion tonight. Rook reached out first and took the stack. I stood silently, arms crossed and watched him read. I've never really seen Rook angry but his face was made of stone and fire after glancing through the paperwork.

"These fuckers are going to die," he said.

Good, I needed them angry and motivated to work. Everyone slowly looked at the paperwork, even Otto. After Otto was done, he slid the paperwork back into the middle of the table and said "Monsters," under his breath.

"So finish your drinks and armor up, we got some fuckin work to do!" I shouted.

Everyone headed out to their individual cars to grab their armor and weapons. I saw Lydia disappear behind me into her room. When everyone came back in from their cars with handfuls of gear, before they could start armoring up Lydia asked them to follow her. She had us all go into my living room, she had five garment bags laid out on my coffee table. Each garment bag had a piece of scotch tape with a name on it. There was one for Otto, Rook, Griffin, Zach, and Lydia.

"Please take the one with your name on it and try it on," said Lydia.

Everyone opened their garment bags and pulled out very modern cut obviously expensive leather jackets. There was a lot of appreciative whistles and whispers of "whoa," these jackets were well crafted. Everyone tried them on and they fit like gloves.

"Good. I am glad they fit, I had to do my best to guess your sizes. Each one should be a little baggy, they are meant to be worn over your bulletproof vests to conceal them. I've lined them heavily with layers of kevlar. I also added a piece of kevlar lined polymer over the heart in each jacket, you should be able to feel it if you press down on it."

Everyone touched the areas above their hearts and felt a lightweight piece of sturdy material under the leather.

"I also placed some small pieces like that over the spine up to the collar and down to the tailbone. There are so many that they should bend as you bend and not cause any stiffness. Polymer won't stop bullets but it might stop people who try to stab you in your hearts or spine. Bear I will have to retrofit your jacket if you want the same protection added," Lydia finished.

Everyone in the room was staring at her, I think I saw Rook wipe a tear out of his eye. Rook, Griffin and Zach dog piled Lydia in a ginormous hug. Otto waited patiently until they were done and then walked up to her and grasped her right hand with both of his.

"I will never forget this kindness, fraulein," he said, then he let her hand drop and stepped back.

"Lydia, those jackets must have cost you a fortune!" I said.

"Yeah they did, basically all of the money I had," she replied.

"Get me an invoice for them, you aren't allowed to pay for the cost of them, that's an order. I'll pay you back with the company cash fund as soon as possible," I said.

"Okay Bear, but you don't have to," she said.

"It's not up for debate. Alright everyone, enough standing around! Get geared up and let's head out to the cargo van. We've got some monsters to hunt!"

As everyone was heading out to the van I pulled Lydia to the side and wrapped her in a big hug. "Thank you for protecting my friends," I whispered into her ear. When I pulled back her cheeks were flushed.

"So what's in the garment bag with your name on it?" I asked.

"Oh this old thing?" she said while holding the bag up. She unzipped the front of the bag and pulled out a female cut ultra dark brown leather jacket. I thought it was black at first until the light hit it. Lydia threw it on and it looked great on her, it mixed well with her light brown hair and showed off all of the right curves.

I had to put my tongue in my mouth and get out of there, "Looks great Lydia, good job!" I said and then headed out to the van myself.

***

Capturing the pedophiles had been beyond easy. They lived alone or with their extremely old parents. Everyone else in their lives had already most likely abandoned them due to their heinous crimes. That was one aspect of criminal justice that always bothered me: the parent's ability to overlook and forgive the crimes of their children...

Between Lydia's vampire prowess, my tonalli enhanced muscles, and the teams enchanted items, we were in and out of every house in minutes with not a soul noticing. We wore all black bulletproof face masks that I had found online. We had also covered the license plate with painters tape just in case. Everyone was wearing Lydia's new leather jackets over their bulletproof vests which really helped us with blending in during city operations. People don't respond well to private citizens running around in bulletproof vests. The jackets were a nice touch that I didn't realize we needed. They were way too hot to wear during the day, but they weren't too bad at night.

We were on our way out to the desert now and the van was filled with nervous energy and tied up pedos. Griffin slid his bulletproof mask up and let it rest on top of his head.

"I don't know about you guys but I'm nervous as hell," said Griffin.

I slid my bulletproof face mask back in a similar fashion and replied to him, "Don't be, Mick is actually a really respectful guy... Well, it's best to not think of him as a guy, he is a very respectful Demigod. I've been polite with him and he has been polite to me, he's old school like that."

Everyone else slid their masks up.

"I wish we would have had these masks in my time, I had a friend who died from a bullet to the face," said Otto.

"I wouldn't want to get shot in the face while wearing one, even if the bullet was stopped I bet it would break face bones," I said.

"Yea, fuck that noise," said Rook.

The van was riding like a dream now that Zach had tuned it up. He ended up taking it to the shop he worked at and he got us a huge discount. I really wanted to add some kevlar panels inside of it eventually, at least enough to stop handgun rounds for now, plus it would double as insulation. Zach was currently up front driving, with Lydia riding co-pilot. Mia was in the empty spot between Zach and Lydia's seats, facing towards the back of the van and occasionally growling at the pedophiles. I didn't want her to come but she had insisted. Rook, Griffin, Otto, and I were in the back with the four prisoners. Zach's shop had bolted in a crappy little bench against one wall of the van which was what we were all sitting on. Otto had his feet up on the back of one of the pedophiles. They were all lying on the ground crying. I think they knew what was coming, *fuck'em*. If you don't want to get sacrificed to an alien Demigod then don't diddle kids!

Once we got off of the highway, Lydia guided Zach on to the least bumpy desert trail and got us far away from civilization. We needed to start using new spots to bury the shitheads from now on. I would hate for some hiker to find one and then end up finding ALL of them. That would bring down all kinds of federal law enforcement onto our heads. Lydia found us a relatively clear spot in between a bunch of desert brush and a large boulder. We put the boulder between ourselves and the highway, we were so far away that we couldn't even see the lights of the highway, but it's better to play it safe. We lit a small fire on the side of the boulder farthest away from the highway, then pulled all of the pedophiles out of the van and threw them on the ground belly first in a line. I threw a handful of salt on each of them and started saying the invocation to summon Mick.

The large purple flame erupted from the desert soil about ten feet in front of all of the pedophiles. Out of the flame stepped Mick in that iconic purple suit with a smile on his face, the flame died off behind him.

"Ah, my good friend Bearengar! Welcome back!" said Mick.

"It's good to see you, Mick, welcome back to you as well. These are some of my best friends and I'm hoping they can become your friends as well," I said.

Then I went down the line one by one and introduced each one of my buds to Mick. I had instructed them beforehand to be polite. I think Mick liked it and it couldn't hurt to have a Demigod on our side.

"Well, should we get started, Mick?" I asked.

"Please do, also ensure your friends know that the first time hurts the worst. I'm assuming you want the power from these sacrifices split evenly among you?" Mick asked.

"Yes please, split the power evenly between all of us except for Lydia of course." I was sure that Mick wouldn't have 'accidentally' sent

Lydia power but I wanted to make sure he knew that I was above board and not trying to pull a fast one on him.

I looked over at my friends to check if they were all still ready to go through with this, they stayed silent, some nodded to me stoically, Mia just wagged her tail.

Welp, there is no time like the present. I went down the line of the pedophiles and slowly slit their throats one by one. The pain was pretty mild for me with the power infusion being split this many ways, but Griffin, Zach, Rook, and Otto were all rigid and their faces had gone white. They were clenching their teeth so tight I thought they were going to break. Then they all passed out one by one. Otto was the last one standing but even he succumbed to that inhuman amount of pain. I remembered that experience well, that sucked. I was still morbidly interested seeing it from this side of the table. All of my friends had a faint purple glow for a moment and then it faded. Lydia, Mia and I were the only ones standing. Mia went from person to person smelling them and making sure they were okay, then she sat down facing away from them. A standard guard position for canines, *good girl*.

"Well, I feel bad just leaving them in the dirt. I guess we should have thought of this and brought some lawn chairs or something. Help me carry them to the van?" I asked.

"Let's do it," she said.

We carefully carried them into the van and laid them gently on their backs. Probably a good move, we have lots of native snakes and scorpions here. Without saying anything I grabbed one of the shovels from the van and started digging some holes to put the pedophiles in. I pushed my tonalli hard and it was easy. Just having a fresh infusion of the stuff made me feel... well *godly* for lack of a better word. I completely understood I was basically the equivalent of a really strong and fast human but I was deadly before I had this upgrade. *Now I'm something far beyond that*. Lydia grabbed a shovel and helped me dig.

We pulled all of their wallets and jewelry off of them and then unceremoniously dumped them in the holes. We doused them all in bleach and then started pushing the dirt back over them. Once we were done I looked up at Lydia with a smile, intending on telling her a joke or singing a goofy song about burying people but her face was sad.

"What's up, Lydia?" I asked.

"What's up! That's all you have to say to me!" Lydia said and then she stormed off with her back to me.

I walked over to her, "Why am I in trouble?" I asked.

"Because you are fucking clueless, I have all of these emotions and thoughts swirling around and you don't notice any of them!" she shouted.

"You know what you should do is take all those emotions and thoughts and bury them deep down inside of yourself and never talk about them again, that's what everyone else does," I said.

"That's not funny Bear," she said.

I stood there for a minute awkwardly, not knowing what to say but she spoke first.

"The truth is Bear, I love you, I don't know when I came to love you but I do. It's not just that though... I am in love with you. I love the way you smell, I love your voice, I love your sense of humor, I love everything about you. I know you are with Emily and I am not asking you to leave her. In fact, I like Emily, I tried to hate her and I just can't. She is a good person and a great fit for you... Me and you are going to live a long time. Enjoy your life with Emily. When she is gone, I'll be here waiting."

Holy shit, talk about dropping a bomb on me. I did like Lydia as a friend, a great and amazing friend. I thought she was beautiful sure, but I was with Emily and Emily made me really happy.

I was about tell Lydia something, but she told me to shut up. What the fuck did I do now? I opened my mouth to speak again but she said "Seriously shut up, I hear something."

She stood still for a minute and then she bent down and put her palm to the earth.

"We have a lot of heavy vehicles coming at us. I thought I heard a small sedan coming at us as well earlier but we were driving and it was hard to differentiate the sound from our own vehicle. The sedan went quiet but the heavy vehicles are still heading right at us," she said.

"Is it the cops? I'm not fighting cops, I'm not hurting the good guys," I said.

"I don't think so, no sirens and there is no helicopter following them," she said.

I pushed my tonalli and thought of my hearing, I stayed stone still and listened. I could hear it now too. Something was coming, a lot of somethings.

Chapter 26

It sounded strange... mix matched vehicles and muted demonic sounding shouts. "Should we run?" asked Lydia, good question.

"I don't think we can, we are in an unarmored van with low clearance off-road. If they have an off-road vehicle and guns they could catch up to us easily and cut us to swiss cheese and then the vultures would descend. If we push the van too hard out here we could also break down or get stuck in the sand, there are too many variables. This boulder at least provides some layer of cover. Get in the van and back it up to this boulder, literally touch the bumper to it, it will extend our cover. We can't let them get an offensive foothold if they have superior numbers. We have to hit them hard before they can even get out of their vehicles. We have to make them think we have more numbers with a heavy volume of fire. If they are coming to hurt my friends, they are going to regret it," I said.

Lydia looked at me resolutely and started heading towards the van. She backed it all the way up to the boulder until the bumper touched just like I had asked her. Meanwhile, I scanned the desert for the incoming vehicles with my WASR. We needed to keep some long range ordinance in our mission vehicle in the future. Not having an optic sucked. I pushed tonalli at my eyes and sharpened my vision. There on the horizon, it looked like I could just barely see a dust cloud in the night. I climbed on top of the boulder, it was jagged and about six feet tall. I laid prone on the top of it the best I could to keep watch which was hard because it was craggy and sharp as hell. Lydia cleanly jumped on top next to me.

"The van is parked," she said.

"Get the boys out, the van isn't bulletproof and it's a big target. Put them behind this rock," I told her. She nodded and did a backflip off of the rock, *holy shit Lydia!* I don't know when she had spent time practicing but she must have been putting in some serious training hours.

The first of the vehicles came over a small hill about three hundred meters out from us. I had an extreme moment of hesitation where I thought maybe it was just some good people doing some late night off-roading, but why would they be heading straight towards us then?

No, it's too much of a coincidence... the strange noises, their heading. They were coming to do us harm. When I was in the Army, the qualification range we shot at went out to three hundred meters and I had fired expert level on that course repeatedly with a beat-to-shit M-16 that had been abused by thousands of fresh recruits. These fools coming at me now were only at two hundred and fifty meters or less and I was pushing tonalli into my vision and muscles. I was also wearing a magical pauldron that helped me hit the target more often than not, *these guys were toast*. They were lined up in a generally straight column trying to avoid cacti and desert brush by following one another through one of the only usable vehicle paths in this area, *thanks for lining up boys.*

I centered the old Romanian sights on the driver of the front vehicle, an all black van. I ripped off ten rounds with my sights centered where I thought the driver's chest was. It was too dark and he was too far away for me to see if I had hit but the vehicle veered heavily. I started peppering the whole vehicle after that, especially the cargo area until my magazine was empty. The van was losing speed and the vehicles behind it were at such close intervals they weren't ready for the sudden deceleration. The second vehicle in the convoy rear-ended the van, the other ones behind the first two swerved out of the path of the vehicles that were now blocking the route but that only caused them to drive through desert brush and untested ground. Which is not something you want to do in the middle of the night. The Arizona desert is littered with small boulders, small cacti, soft patched of sand that tires sink into, not stuff you want to be driving over.

The vehicle that had rear-ended the van was backing up and getting out of the way. A very large lifted truck was pulling up behind the downed van and was pushing it out of the way with its front bumper. I sprayed the windshield of the truck but the impacts looked strange. I used tonalli to try and push my eyes even farther but my eyes rebelled and pain shot out of the back of my eye sockets into my brain. I guess I had tried to push too much. Before the pain had caused me to close my eyes I had seen my rounds weren't fully penetrating the windshield, was that thing armored? Lydia jumped back up on the rock carrying Griffin's old SKS.

An SKS is a Soviet Semi-Automatic Carbine, it's a hell of a rifle. At one point they were very cheap so Griffin had grabbed one up. The SKS takes ten round stripper clips which I could see Lydia had a handful of. I could also see every third round of the stripper clips had been misted with some silver spray paint to let us know it was one of our special bullets.

We hadn't had time to get uniform weapons yet and Otto and I had only mainly been making silver filled bullets in 9mm and 7.62x39 which is why Griffin had brought his SKS. He didn't own an AK variant so this was his only rifle in 7.62x39.

"Wait don't fire yet!" I shouted at Lydia.

I pulled some special Surefire earplugs out of my vest and stuck them in my ears. They let low decibel noises in and stopped high decibel noises. They would make conversation easier to hear but protect me from the gunshots. If we survived tonight I didn't want to have fucked up ears, but maybe the tonalli would fix that? Oh well, better to be safe. I also unscrewed the silencer from the end of my WASR. You can actually fire so fast that a silencer will catch fire and burn up. I stuck the silencer into one of the pockets on my vest.

"Okay fire two clips, target random vehicles," I told Lydia. She had followed my example and put in her own Surefire earplugs.

She started popping rounds off at random vehicles in the enemy convoy so I followed suit. It was a mishmash of vans, cars and lifted trucks with seemingly no order between them. We were popping tires, cracking windshields, and killing indiscriminately. People were jumping out of downed vehicles and trying to take cover behind the other vehicles that were slowly moving forwards in our direction. Some of them were making it to cover but a lot of them were getting picked off by Lydia and I. Each vehicle could only go as fast as the vehicle in front of them, and the vehicles in front of them were getting shot to shit by us. Well, I guess that rules out casual off-roaders if they are still heading our direction. I saw a flash from the passenger window of the large lifted truck that had been pushing downed vehicles out of the

417

path. I focused my tonalli enhanced eyes on the area. It was a fireball, and it was getting bigger. *No, it was getting closer!*

"GET DOWN!" I shouted at Lydia, but I was already standing. I grabbed the collar of her leather jacket and jumped off of the rock pulling her with me.

I hit the ground feet first and Lydia twisted in the air like a cat and did the same. The second we landed the boulder behind us shook as it was coated in sticky flames. So it wasn't an explosion, it was more like some kind of, well I don't rightly know, some kind of magical Molotov cocktail. I assumed magical because I couldn't think of any kind of conventional weapon that could do that.

"Do you want me to go around them on foot? Maybe I can pick some of them off," Lydia asked.

"That's called flanking Lydia, and no I want you here where I can see you and keep you safe. Wait a minute, if we thought of flanking they probably did too..." I said right as I heard the footsteps coming at us.

Something supernatural tackled Lydia. She was tackled so hard and fast that the momentum of the hit carried her and her attacker off into the desert and over a small berm out of my sight. From the opposite side where Lydia had disappeared at, two rounds were fired, they both hit me in the back. I spun around and instinctively ripped off most of a magazine in that direction while moving towards cover. I stopped moving and firing when I got behind the first saguaro I could find.

I reached back behind myself and felt my lower back where the rounds had hit. They hadn't even penetrated the kevlar of my leather jacket. I paused and listened, I heard labored breathing from where the shots had come from. I took a quick peek around the cactus. There was a man there doubled over with a pistol in his hand and wearing tactical gear. I must have landed a round on his vest for him to be bent over like that.

He was trying to scan the desert to find me but it looked like he was having trouble breathing. I rushed him, I needed intel. I was running straight at him with tonalli enhanced speed. He heard me coming and raised his pistol. I veered to the right as he fired his first round it whizzed right by me. He tried to compensate by swinging his pistol back at my new position and snapping off a quick round but I veered left this time and his shot missed me again. I was on him now and I open hand smacked him so hard on the side of his head I think I blew his eardrum out. That made him involuntarily fire his pistol into the dirt. Then I smacked the pistol out of his hands.

I grabbed the straps of his vest and lifted him into the air. "Who are you!" I shouted at him. The man's face registered primal fear after seeing how easily I could man-handle him.

"I'm a mercenary, I was hired for a job, please don't kill me," the man begged. What the hell kind of mercenary whines like a small child in the face of danger?

"Are you human?" I asked.

"What! Of course I'm human. Listen, man, I didn't sign up for this bullshit, they said this would be easy! I've got kids, I..." he started rambling so I smacked him again.

"Lay down right fucking here and don't move, and I will consider not killing you!" I yelled into his face.

I bent over and picked up his pistol, the only weapon I could see on him and stuck it into my waistband. Then I started looking for Lydia. I saw her about two hundred feet away exchanging amazingly fast blows with what had to be another vampire. It was hard to tell but it looked like she was getting her ass kicked. I shouldered my WASR and aimed it in their direction. They were moving so fast I was afraid to fire and hit Lydia. I aimed slightly behind the vampire attacking her and let off a couple of shots. He stopping fighting Lydia for a second to look at me. Lydia took that opportunity to draw the Glock 19 I had bought her and dump a magazine into his face, *good girl.*

Once he was down she jumped on his head with both of her feet and then jumped up and down a few times for good measure until the vamps head was flat. I used a hand signal and pointed at the van, and I started running that way myself. Otto was getting up as I was running over. He climbed on top of the hood of the van and then ripped off a magazine at some unseen target with his tommy gun. The van started taking return fire and a few tracers flew over his head so he jumped back down and got behind the boulder.

I ran over to him, "Bear, there are many vampires here!" Otto told me.

"Yeah, welcome to the party pal," I replied. Lydia ran up beside us, "Lydia, get in Griffin's medical bag and get some smelling salts. Wake up the sleeping beauties here. Otto, I need you to put ear plugs in, then I need you to make sure the others get their earplugs in as well," I said, they both hopped to their tasks.

I crept along the side of the boulder until I could get a view of what was happening. The enemy vehicles were making a barricade about ninety meters away from my position. They were blocking the only easy route out of here and making a nice line of cover for themselves. Some of the vehicles were disabled back where I had attacked them at the original choke point, but at least fifteen had made it this far and were lining up. Some of the vehicles had people riding on the hoods and roofs and in the beds of trucks. Those must be some of the stranded passengers from the vehicles I had disabled.

Well, better keep them honest. I picked three easy targets, people on the hoods or roofs of vehicles that were joining the barricade of vehicles. I tried to remember everything I had learned about competition speed shooting, every technique I had learned over the years. It was a complete zen moment for me, I was calm. I came around the boulder and in less than a second I snapped off three shots at the chest of each target. They were all clean hits. No one had responded yet so I opened fire at random on the rest of the vehicles and then ducked back behind the boulder.

As soon as I was safely behind the boulder again a thousand round staccato of return fire hit the front of the boulder in the position I had been firing from. I went to the van and grabbed a duffel bag I had brought. I had smoke and CS grenades in there, also a couple of nasties Otto and I had whipped up. We had used some of my black powder from reloading bullets to make pipe bombs. We had loaded the pipe bombs with old silver jewelry and silver excess from our smelting activities. Wait a minute, where the fuck is Mia! I looked all around our area and couldn't find her anywhere. Lydia was waking up each of the guys with smelling salts still.

"Lydia, where the fuck is Mia?" I asked her.

"She ran off when you climbed on top of the boulder and I haven't seen her since then," Lydia replied.

"And you didn't think to tell me!" I screamed back at her,

"We have been busy Bear!" she yelled back.

I didn't have time to worry about that, I had to keep my friends alive. I reached into my duffel bag and pulled out some smoke grenades. I didn't want to return to my position on the side of the boulder where the enemies had seen me so I snuck around the side of the van dragging my duffel bag with me. I threw the smoke grenades into the enemy barricade. Then I threw a few CS grenades. If you aren't familiar with CS grenades just imagine a smoke grenade but instead of smoke, the grenades let off a noxious chemical that makes you choke and activates your mucus membranes. Snot flies everywhere and the urge to close your eyes is overwhelming. My drill sergeants used to throw them at me and the other recruits during basic training, *good times.* One of the drill sergeants had even nailed me with one when I was in a port-a-potty dropping a deuce.

If you haven't tried to wipe your butt and make a hasty egress while being choked by chemicals, you haven't lived.

I high tailed it out of there before the enemy could fire on my position. I grabbed some of my homemade pipe bombs. I lit two and threw them both over the boulder in the general direction of the enemy barricade with tonalli enhanced throws not even sure if I would get close to the enemies. I waited until I heard them both explode and then peeked around the side of the boulder again and started firing at random into the barricade and the people trying to take cover. The enemy was in disarray, some were choking on gas, some were putting on gas masks, some were laying in pools of their own blood from the explosions. I must have stayed too long because the dirt at my feet started exploding as enemy rounds hit it. A round smacked me in the stomach and hit the plate in my vest. Then a round tore through my forearm and one ripped through my knee.

I fell over not being able to support my own weight. Someone grabbed me and dragged me behind the boulder as more rounds landed on my position. I looked up, it was Lydia. I focused and pushed tonalli into my wounds. Pain flared in them and I almost passed out. Purple light fired out of the wound in my forearm and knee and then the pain was gone. I looked down at my forearm, the skin was complete underneath the blood that had been spilled, it must have been a fast round to have been able to pierce my jacket.

"Thanks for the assist Lydia," I said. I heard an electronic-enhanced voice come from the enemy barricade.

"Cease fire, cease fire. Come out from behind that boulder, let's parley," someone was shouting from a megaphone. All of my friends were struggling to get to their feet after being rudely awaken with the smelling salts.

"Otto fill these guys in on our situation, get them ready. I'm going to parley, get these guys into position to cover me ASAP," I said.

I slapped a fresh magazine into the WASR and then walked around the boulder trying to look confident. I don't know how many men and or vampires they had started with but I saw at least twenty men leaning over car hoods with guns aimed at me. They were in sorry shape from my bullet and gas barrages and explosives though. Some of them were still actively choking on CS and smoke. I also saw six people standing on the tops of vehicles unarmed or with swords staring at me with brazen confidence on their faces. I would bet any amount of money that those were the vampires and the ones with guns were the humans. There were two men standing on the roof of the lifted black truck with the bulletproof windshield, these must be the leaders of this operation. They were both wearing exquisite slim fitting Italian suits.

The one with the megaphone lifted it to his mouth and started talking, "You are outnumbered, you think you have hurt us but you haven't. You took out some of the fodder, the pawns in this game of chess. I know one of you killed my son and I want to know which one. Surrender the one who killed Dante and the rest of you can go free."

I didn't believe that sucker for a minute. He was going to kill everyone here regardless. If I thought he really would have let my friends go, I would have happily traded myself for them but I knew he was lying. I could tell now looking at him that he was clearly Dante's father. He had the same features and the same broad shoulders. I pushed tonalli into my voice and throat not knowing if this would work or not and I also picked up a rock that was about the size of my fist. I tossed it in the air a couple of times and checked the weight.

I tested my tonalli enhanced voice, "HI THERE," I said to the man on the megaphone, my voice came out supernaturally loud, *awesome*. I was sure all of the mercenaries and vampires could hear me so I continued. "First of all, no one is surrendering anything. I'm the one who killed your son, me and me alone. So if you have hatred for someone, have it for me. So you know you outnumber us, that's fine. We welcome the challenge, we aren't the weak prey you are used to though I'm afraid. We have abilities, let me show you." I threw the rock as hard as I could pushing my speed and strength as far as I had ever pushed them with tonalli. It was an extreme flare of my magic. It was just a second, right at the time of my throw.

Even though the tonalli flare had only been for a second, my body exploded in pain once the rock left my hand. The human body had limits and when I pushed them too far, I paid for it in pain. The rock flew straight at the megaphone man with striking speed. It bounced off of the air in front of him and a blue force field appeared for a second visible in the air before disappearing again.

The noise from the impact was like thunder. I had really thrown that thing hard. The man behind Dante's father had his hands facing me palms forward and he had visibly rocked back when my rock hit the force field, he was pale and sweating now. That must have been who was making the force fields.

The man put the megaphone to his mouth again "Interesting, I've never seen a human do that before, but as you can see I have brought someone with abilities as well," he pointed his thumb over his shoulder at the warlock next to him.

"It's you, YOU SON OF A BITCH!" shouted Otto. I turned behind me, Otto was standing on the roof of the van aiming his Thompson at the warlock. My friends were arranged in various positions of cover around him aiming their weapons at the barricade. They had all donned their black bulletproof face masks, they looked like demons. Otto had his face mask pulled up and resting on the top of his head.

"You know this guy Otto?" I asked.

"This arschgesicht is who put me in the box, I remember now! He works for William, I need him alive!" Otto said with his accent so strong I could barely understand him.

427

So Dante's father was shielded, but were his men? Maybe I could get him out from behind that shield.

"How about you and me settle this like men? One on one, or are you afraid I will kill you like I killed your son?" I was goading him into an uncontrollable anger and I could tell it was working well.

I whispered into my palm hoping Lydia was listening, "Tell the guys to focus fire on the shooters. We can't fight the vampires if we are pinned down." I heard movement behind me, Lydia was passing the message on, good.

"You will die tonight!" Dante's father shouted. Then he jumped impossibly far through the sky heading straight towards me, *I always liked skeet shooting.*

I aimed up into the sky and started firing on his descending body. You can't dodge in midair and even though it was a hard target most of my bullets were smacking him. Every other one bounced off of a force field but some were landing. I glanced at the warlock and his face looked more strained than ever now that he was trying to maintain the force field with Dante's father on the move.

Then all hell broke loose, my team used the distraction I was providing as the center of the show to open fire on the gunmen. Four tonalli enhanced veterans versus twenty mercenaries. I didn't get to watch it but I would assume it was a pretty one-sided fight honestly.

Dante's father landed in front of me, OH FARTS. He came at me fast so I put on the speed as well. He started slashing the air in front of me with his hands. I focused on his fingers and noticed they had somehow elongated into talons. As he threw wild blows at me I tried my hardest to dodge them. I saw his face start to stretch, his human features were falling away. His eyes took on a dull red glow and his fangs stretched out of his mouth. His whole figure was getting bigger, his suit was breaking in places, and his skin was going from pale to grey. What the fuck was this guy? He got in a hit on my face because I just couldn't keep up with his insane speed. He raked his talons across my cheek. Blood sprayed from my face and I felt wind come into my mouth from the gaping hole he had put in my cheek. Then he punched me in the stomach so hard that the plate in my vest dented inwards and I flew backward.

I was rolling now from the momentum of his hit. I was hitting rocks, small cacti, Joshua Tree saplings, and all kinds of things you generally didn't want to roll over. My leather jacket took most of the beating but my exposed face and eyes were taking a lot of damage. I think I felt one of my eyes burst at one point as something sharp punctured it but I was pushing tonalli into all of my wounds even as I was rolling and I felt the eye reform in the socket, *that was super not fun*. I tried to get to my feet but Dante's father was already on me. He hit me on the top of my spine and I felt something crack. He flipped me over and started raining blows on me. I felt my bones breaking in my face and upper chest. I tried to throw him off of me but he just casually snapped the arm I tried to get leverage with, luckily it was just my left arm. I'm right handed.

Mia jumped out of the darkness with enhanced speed thanks to her own tonalli. She hit him with her full body weight and latched onto his neck. Where had she been this whole time? His blood sprayed me and sprayed into Mia's clenched mouth. He fell backward into the dirt and Mia shook her head back and forth trying to rip the flesh from his neck, she was doing a good job. He stiffed armed her and she went flying with a loud yelp into the night. Something snapped inside of me, no one hurts my Mia.

I started forcing the healing processes of my body even faster than before but it looked like Dante's dad was going to beat me to full recovery. He started unsteadily pulling himself to his feet and holding his neck together with his hand. I could see the flesh of his neck beneath his hand stitching itself back together. As soon as he got to his feet a large round smacked him in his hip, blood and bone sprayed out the opposite side of his body.

What the fuck was that? We both looked in the direction it had come from but I couldn't see anything, just empty desert. I took a chance and glanced over at my friends, they were fighting the six vampires and the warlock, and it looked like they were losing. I had to finish off this asshole quickly. I was still trying to put myself back together, pushing tonalli so hard into my injuries that most of my skin was glowing purple. The pain was... exquisite, my body was trying to pass out but the tonalli healing wouldn't let me. Dante's father could see me glowing and probably decided he didn't want a part of whatever I was doing so he started heading towards me with murder in his eyes. I started getting up to face him but another large round smacked him right in the temple and blew his brains all over the desert, again I looked in the direction I thought it had come from but I didn't see anything. Who's out there?

I looked back to Dante's father, his skin had gone an even deeper shade of grey, and the wound on the side of his head was starting to heal. This bastard is tough, I drew my cutlass and chopped off Dante's fathers head while he was still recovering, good riddance. I ran to where he had thrown Mia but she was already getting up "Let's go, Mia, we need to help our friends!" she barked when she heard her name and started running behind me.

Chapter 27

The scene in front of me was pure insanity. Rook was running around the battle like a demon from hell, so fast I could barely track him. He must have figured out how to push tonalli into the greave, like I could with my dagger. He was cutting people with his enchanted flame dagger in one hand and firing his Glock in the other and I swear he was leaving a slight purple blur behind him. Zach was choking a vampire to death in his hand with the God Gauntlet on it, and firing his Glock with his opposite hand. Griffin was supporting everyone with suppression fire from his SKS. Otto was in a heated sword fight with two different vampires and losing badly, he had blood and gashes all over himself and his wounds were all glowing with purple energy as they knitted themselves back together. Lydia had the Remington 870 shotgun I had given her and she was trying to take out the warlock but he was maintaining a force field around himself and supporting the occasional vampire with one as well which was giving our opponents the edge.

Otto needed help the most, "Mia go help the boys!" she took off to join the fray. I saw her leap onto the nearest vampire and start eating his neck. I still had my cutlass in my hand from when I had cut off Dante's fathers head and I thought about rushing in to join the sword battle, but that would be the honorable thing to do, fuck that. I sheathed the cutlass and shouldered my WASR. I ripped off an entire magazine at the two vampires attacking Otto. A bunch of my rounds got through but some pinged off of temporary force fields that the warlock was throwing up. I kept alternating my fire between the two vampires so the warlock would have to shift focus with his temporary force fields. That asshole warlock needed to be taken out of the game.

My mission was accomplished, I had drawn the vampires attention enough for Otto to get the opportunity he needed. Otto shoved his sword into one of the vampire's mouths and pushed, the sword erupted out of the back of the vampires head. The vampire's friend lifted his sword to strike Otto down but a purple blur flew past and ran an enchanted fire dagger across the back of the vampire's neck, it was Rook. Rook was burning too much tonalli, he needed to conserve more. The cut on the vampire's neck exploded open and bloody, steam flew out of the wound. I wanted to watch the rest of Otto's fight but I had to do my part now that he was safe.

I reloaded my WASR and turned it towards the warlock and let him have it. I was trying to overwhelm his shield so I wasn't aiming much, just pulling the trigger as fast as I could. The faster I fired the more he had to work to keep the shield up. My WASR ran dry, I was out of magazines for it so I drew my Glock and the pistol I had liberated from the mercenary earlier. It was some kind of H&K that I wasn't familiar with. I aimed it at the warlock and pulled the trigger to test fire it, it worked. The warlock looked confused since I had only fired one round. So I answered his unasked question by raising both pistols in unison and firing them both as fast as I could until their magazines ran dry. He was barely holding the shield up now. I drew my cutlass and rushed him. I started pounding on his shield with the cutlass. Lydia appeared on the other side of him and started firing her shotgun at his shield.

Zach stepped up next to me with the God's Gauntlet and started punching the shield with it. Every time he hit it with the enchanted gauntlet visible cracks would form before slowly healing. Otto came next and started slashing his own sword across the shield, having finished off the vampires he was fighting. Rook started doing strafing runs with his dagger, blurring past the shield back and forth with amazing speed, and slashing it with his fire dagger. Every time he hit the shield with his dagger a tiny explosion would happen. Then Griffin stepped up to the shield with his dagger of pestilence and started slashing it, the shield was picking up a dark hue and cracking where he was hitting it. Mia tried to jump over the force field but the warlock changed the field's shape from a circular wall into a half sphere, Mia ended up landing on top of it. Mia reared her head back and her teeth all began to glow purple and elongate then she sank her fangs into the shield and started throwing her head back and forth like it was a giant chew toy. The warlock couldn't hold it any longer under our combined attacks, so he changed tactics and he went on the offensive. He let out a mighty shout and a shock wave rushed out from his body and bowled us all over. Since Mia was on top she flew off into the night.

Rook had been the farthest away at the time because he was lining up for another strafing run so he was still on his feet. While we were all trying to get up he rushed in for another strafing run while the warlock's shield was down. The warlock spun and shot sticky fire at him. It fully engulfed Rook and he fell down into the dirt burning, NO! Lydia tried to rush him but the warlock had somehow telepathically lifted a boulder in the air. He saw Lydia's rush so he threw the boulder at her. It hit her right in the chest and carried her away. I ran over to Rook while the rest of my friends attacked the warlock. He was still burning I picked up a bunch of dirt and smothered the flames. I felt along his neck and arms for a pulse, he had one. Good, the tonalli would heal him eventually, if he had any left...

I pulled Rook away from the battle. Once I had him about twenty feet away, I raised my sword and rushed the warlock as well. He was busy fighting Zach, Griffin, and Otto. He let out another shock wave and it knocked the three of them down. Then he raised his hands, they were engulfed in some kind of black swirling mass. He was about to throw it at my friends so I shouted to get his attention.

I was still running at him and he turned towards me instead. I threw my sword at him and he threw the black shadowy mass. My sword flew end over end before it landed point first in his shoulder. The black foggy mass hit me and pain exploded all over my body. I pushed healing tonalli into my body and tried to block the pain but not much happened. The pain kept up and crippled me. I fell over just trying to breathe and I could only watch for a minute as my friends continued to fight.

Lydia was still gone somewhere crushed beneath a boulder, and Mia had flown so far away I wasn't even sure if she was alive. So it was just Otto, Griffin and Zach fighting the warlock. He would have trouble now though that I had impaled him. He threw more sticky fire at my friends but Zach extended his God's Gauntlet in front of it. I saw a translucent kite shield form for a second directly in front of his gauntlet. The fire hit the ghostly shield and washed over it before dissipating, nice move Zach!

That really pissed the warlock off so he telepathically threw Zach away from the battle. Zach flew through the air and landed back first on a saguaro, that had to have hurt. I fought my way to my feet and I tried to push tonalli strength into my legs but nothing happened. I tried to imagine my 'fuel tank' to check how much tonalli I had left but nothing was working. I think I had ran my power well dry. It didn't matter, my friends needed my help.

I fought against the pain and reloaded my Glock. I remembered Otto wanted the warlock alive so I shot him in the foot. Blood sprayed out of his fancy Italian shoe. He threw up a force field on his back and turned towards me. He telekinetically pulled my sword from his shoulder. A sick sucking sound came out of the wound as the sword was removed from it. I started firing on him more but my bullets were pinging off of small mini force fields he was creating. He had my sword floating in the air now aimed right at me, he threw it at me with his power. It flew faster than a bullet and went right through my vest and the plate protecting my stomach. I flopped onto my back, the warlock stood above me with his hand extended. Some kind of invisible energy was coming from his hand and pushing the sword further into my stomach. The sword was coming out of my back now and going into the dirt below me, pinning me to the earth. I was learning that there were all new levels of pain I had yet to experience.

The warlock started chanting something unearthly and his hands began to glow green, "I have something very special for you" he told me. Whatever that meant it wasn't good. Behind him, Otto was wailing on his force field. Griffin had actually penetrated the warlocks force field with his pestilence dagger and was cutting open a door. The warlock's strained face told me he could feel that. He spun on Griffin and yelled, "FINE, YOU CAN HAVE IT THEN!"

He dropped the force field on that side of himself and threw the green energy onto Griffin. Griffin's whole body started drifting into the air and began spinning. Griffin started screaming and screaming as he floated higher and spun faster. All of my friends were screaming now as we watched one of our loved ones slowly dying in front of us, being consumed by the green energy.

Griffin rose higher, spinning faster and faster, screaming louder and louder. His skin flashed invisible off and on as the green energy consumed him. I could see his skeleton every few seconds, almost like an x-ray. The warlock was smiling up at his handy work enjoying the show with his hands still raised in the air seemingly controlling the green magic. So Otto took the initiative and swung his sword overhead, cleanly chopping off both of the warlock's hands. The green energy Griffin was being held in just stopped and disappeared, with Griffin still inside of it. Griffin was just gone...

I felt tears slide down my face, I had failed my friend. I was bleeding out with the sword in my stomach. I couldn't even move, it had me pinned to the ground. I had no tonalli left to heal the wound.

That's fine I deserved to die, I had let Griffin die, maybe even Mia and Rook. I closed my eyes and willed myself to die but I felt soft lips gently on mine.

I cracked my eyes open and there was Emily, she was kissing me and crying, "Oh Bear, what have they done to you," she said.

"Emily, what are you doing here?" I croaked out and then coughed up some blood.

"I'm trying to save your life you lovable asshole, like I've been doing all night. Who did you think shot that guy you were fighting earlier?" I noticed now she had an old Mosin Nagant on a sling over one shoulder.

"You didn't think I was just going to let my baby daddy die did you?" she blubbered out in between tears.

"Baby daddy? You are pregnant? You shot a vampire with a Mosin? Why are you so awesome?" I tried to keep talking but a lot of blood was coming out of my mouth.

"Stop talking I am going to get you help" said Emily.

"He doesn't need help, he needs to summon Mick," Lydia said as she stepped up behind us.

She had the mercenary I had let go of earlier by the back of the neck. He was struggling to get free but he couldn't overpower Lydia's superior strength. Lydia threw a handful of salt on him. There were

439

fires everywhere so that requirement of the ritual wouldn't be an issue.

"Say the words, Bear," said Lydia with her own tears in her eyes. I didn't know if she was crying because Emily was pregnant or because I was dying. Either way, I had a reason to live now, I was going to be a father. I wouldn't abandon my child like my parents had abandoned me. I gurgled out the summoning ritual with blood sputtering out of my mouth the whole time, I didn't care... I had a renewed strength, a purpose. This is what dying feels like... I finished the ritual after coughing up what felt like a gallon of blood and the purple flame erupted from the ground. Emily's eyes were alight with wonder and fear.

Out of the flame stepped Mick, "Wow Bear, you really look like shit," said Mick.

I gave him a big toothy smile with teeth full of blood and flashed him the 'A-OK' symbol with my pointer finger and thumb. Even while dying I still have my sense of humor. Lydia spoke up since I wouldn't be talking.

"Hi Mick, I'm sacrificing this guy and I want the tonalli to go 90% to Bear and 10% to Rook, Is that okay?" Lydia asked.

"I can do that, commence the sacrifice please," said Mick. Lydia took my dagger out of my sheath and then slit the mercenaries throat.

I felt the tonalli come back to me like an old friend. I felt my body healing, then I spit up a bunch more blood. That must have been what was left in my stomach.

"Hey Lydia, pull this sword out please," I asked.

"Oh gross," said Lydia, but she complied. She stepped over me with a foot on either side and cranked on the sword until it slid out of me, I felt every inch of the dirty blade as it was dragged through my body and gasped with the pain. Emily's face went pale but she didn't pass out.

I honestly wanted to crawl up into a ball and cry with the warring emotions inside of me. I was torn up inside about losing Griffin, but I had gained a child. I couldn't let my team see me break, it was time to lead. I looked over at Otto and Zach, they had applied tourniquets to the warlocks arms so he wouldn't bleed out and they were tying him to a camping chair with military grade 550 cord.

"Where is William!" Otto was shouting into the warlocks face. He was doing it all wrong, interrogation is all about false hope.

"Stand back," I said to Lydia and Emily. Once they were out of the way I did a kip up, my loose blood flew everywhere.

"Show off," said Lydia, I looked over at Emily but she was still in shock from seeing Mick arrive.

I heard a few barks to my side so I turned and looked into the desert. Mia came running out of the darkness absolutely soaked in blood. I bent down and scratched behind her ear and whispered to her, "I am so glad to see you, Mia, I love you so much, I can't lose you."

I started walking towards the interrogation. Lydia, Mia, and Emily followed me. I picked up one of the warlock's hands out of the dirt. I gently guided Otto out of my way with a hand on his shoulder.

I stood in front of the warlock, "Listen man, If you tell us where William is, I'll give you this hand back and drop you off at the nearest hospital. You don't get the other hand back because you killed my friend. This is the best deal you are going to get. Walk away from this with one hand and your life. Tell me where William is," I said. I set the hand on his lap for good measure and then walked away a few feet and feigned disinterest.

I waited forty seconds or so so my words could sink in and he could understand the deal and the levity of the situation. I walked back over to him and made a big show of putting a fresh magazine in my Glock and chambering a round.

"Okay, times up bub, are you going to tell us where William is or are you going to die in this barren desert. I'll leave your corpse right here and let the coyotes eat you. Your choice." I meant what I had said. I really would kill this sucker with no hesitation. He could tell I wasn't lying... about that part.

"Okay I want to live, don't kill me, I'll take the hospital deal. I last saw William in the 1950's in Detroit, Michigan. He was, and is the King of Michigan," the warlock said. Mick was still standing in the desert where we had summoned him.

He casually walked over to us all, "Are you going to sacrifice this one?" he asked while pointing at the warlock.

"I hadn't thought of it, why do you ask?" I said.

"Well he has lots of life force, many 'souls' I think you would call them. They reside inside of him. I don't know or really care how, but he has been trapping souls inside of his shell to live longer. If you were to sacrifice him the payout would be beneficial to the both of us."

I looked around at everyone, eventually, my eyes landed on Emily. If she was pregnant I didn't want her to go through this ritual. I didn't know what tonalli would do to a baby.

The warlock could tell I was considering it, "WAIT, I TOLD YOU WHERE WILLIAM WAS. YOU SAID YOU WOULD LET ME GO!" screamed the warlock. I casually walked over to my duffel bag and grabbed my container of salt. I poured a handful into my palm and walked back over to the warlock and threw it at him.

"Mick, make sure none of this energy goes to Emily," I said and pointed at Emily. "Otto, would you do the honors?" I asked,

"Gladly" Otto replied. Otto screamed and swung his sword, he cleanly chopped off the warlock's head. Lydia threw a handful of salt on the corpse.

The power infusion was the most painful yet. I gritted my teeth and let the pain wash through me. As the tonalli was coming in I tried to direct some of it to shut off my pain nerves as even more power flowed in. Rook was still on the ground unconscious but he woke up screaming from his own infusion. Otto fell down to one knee and pinched his eyes closed. Zach fell onto his back and let out a scream. The pain stopped, and we all shakily got to our feet, even Rook. Mick stepped backward into a roaring purple flame he had summoned and waved goodbye before disappearing. Then I noticed something, all of Rook's hair had been burnt off, even his eyebrows. His skin was fully healed from the warlock's flames but he was completely bald now.

"Check out this Mr. Clean looking mother fucker," I said, which elicited a few giggles. Rook reached up and touched his head and felt bare skin.

"SHIT!" he shouted.

Rook looked around and then asked, "Why is Emily here and where is Griffin?" I tried to answer but my voice didn't want to work. I felt my eyes moisten and I tried to fight back tears but I let one slip. I had to be the leader now, I don't get to be weak...

"Emily provided cover fire for us during the fight and Griffin, he... he died a hero and a warrior fighting the forces of evil." I was having a hard time controlling myself. Emily came up beside me and put her arm around my shoulder.

"He was a good man, I didn't know him long but he fought with the strength of ten," said Otto. Zach and Rook had started crying now as well. It was getting harder for me to hold myself together once I saw them crying.

"He was always really nice to me," said Lydia, she was also openly crying.

We stood there for a minute thinking about our fallen friend but we had to get out of here before the sun came up. I was about to tell my team to pack up, but a brilliant green circle made of light opened up in the sky above us and the sound of screaming was coming out of it. We all backed up, not sure what kind of evil trap the warlock had left for us. Once we were all about ten feet back I pushed Emily behind me and I aimed my Glock at the portal. The rest of my team followed my cue and aimed their weapons at the portal. A man fell out of the portal face first into the desert, he landed hard and let out an "OOMPH!"

He jumped up wild-eyed. He had a strange looking spear in one hand. His hair was long and in wild disarray. He had a beard down to his nipples and a quiver and bow over one shoulder. He was wearing something that looked like a snakeskin loincloth around his waist, and he had two pauldrons made of tree branches, leaves, moss, and vines. I noticed he also had shin and forearm guards of the same materials, just loose branches tied together with vines. Then I saw that one of his forearm guards was made of metal... and it had a red cross on it... NO WAY, that's the vitality bracer!

"Those fucking assholes didn't tell me the portal was going to come out sideways, and in the sky! I walked through standing up! You know what, I don't fucking care. I AM HOME!" the forest man shouted.

"Griffin?" I asked, it must have clicked with all of my friends.

"Yeah, it's me. Oh yeah the beard and hair, you guys probably don't recognize me. How did you all know I was coming back today?" he asked.

"Bro look at us, it's the same day. We just saw you die like ten minutes ago. How are you here?" I asked him.

"I didn't die, that asshole warlock banished me to a different planet or dimension or something. I've been fighting for eight months to get back here. Holy shit it is good to see you guys!" he shouted. He ran over and gave us all hugs one by one. He stunk pretty bad but I'm sure

446

we all did too. My clothes were literally wet with my blood still so I wasn't going to judge him.

"We really don't have time for this, when the sun comes up and people find the evidence from this firefight there are going to be authorities all over this place. Everyone grab everything that is ours, or that looks incriminating. Pack it into the van and let's get the fuck out of here!" I said.

We all started working, there really wasn't much we could do. There were burning and disabled vehicles everywhere. We just picked up stuff that belonged to us and put it in the van. I wasn't worried about fingerprints, we were all wearing gloves during the fight.

"Will you ride with me?" Emily asked me. I told my friends I was riding back to my place with Emily. We started walking back towards her sniping position, Mia followed us. When we got to Emily's car I told her we needed to pick up all of her Mosin Nagant brass so there would be no evidence of her involvement. We did it quickly then we all jumped in her car. "You know your dog Mia really saved me tonight," she said.

"Tell me about it and get to my house quickly, I'm starving. I lost so much blood tonight I think my body needs calories to replace it," I said. She slowly drove us back to the highway, careful not to bottom the car out or damage her tires on the desert terrain. We got on the highway and she started to tell me her story.

She had found out she was pregnant that day after taking a half-dozen pregnancy tests and she had wanted to come to my house and tell me about it but I had told her she wasn't allowed over. She was emotional and upset about that and she didn't understand why I wouldn't let her come over. She drove over to my house anyway against my wishes and saw all of my friend's vehicles parked out front. That just made her angrier that they were allowed over and she wasn't.

She wanted to see what we were up to so she parked down the road from my house and waited until we had left, then followed us out to the desert. She stayed very far behind us with her head lights off and when she saw us stop the van, she took a different route to the nearest high ground so she could watch whatever it was we were doing. When she pulled up and got out of her car, Mia was there waiting, she said Mia scared the shit out of her because she wasn't expecting her. She didn't understand how Mia had found her or why she was there and she tried to shoo her away but Mia wouldn't leave her side. I had a sneaking suspicion it was because Mia knew she was pregnant with my child.

Then she saw the enemy vehicles roll in and the firefight begin. A few weeks prior she had been throwing around the idea of her and I going shooting. I had been really happy about the idea of it. She wanted to surprise me so she had asked her dad for a rare gun to impress me. He had given her a 'scouterized' Mosin Nagant. So when the firefight began, she grabbed the Mosin Nagant out of her car and tried to remember how her dad had taught her to use it. Because the Mosin was 'scouterized' it had a small magnification scope on it that she wasn't familiar with in the slightest, but she had just put the "cross" (her words) on the bad guy that was attacking me and shot him a few times. I stopped her story there.

"Wait a minute, you shot near me with an untested scope that you didn't zero yourself?" I asked.

"What does zeroed mean? I just put the cross thingy on the bad guy and shot him."

I facepalmed hard.... She could have easily killed me. "What, you are upset with me? I saved you!" she shouted.

"You did, thank you, just what you did was really dangerous. I'll teach you about zeroing scopes later. Finish your story please," I said.

"Well, like I was saying I was trying to shoot all the bad guys by putting the cross thingy on them. It was hard to see a lot of them because it was so dark but my dad's scope had an illuminated cross thingy in it."

I had to interrupt her, "Just call it a reticle please, it's been a long night," I said.

"Alright, Mr. Picky. I was shooting them all when two of the bad guys came up that hill at me. Before I could even shoot them, Mia fought them both and killed them. She saved my life. Now It's time for me to ask the questions. I don't even know where to start. Everything back there was so confusing. I think you have some explaining to do Bear, but before you say anything else I need to know if you are ready to be a father." She looked very worried. Hell, I was worried just hearing that question but I already knew the answer.

"Of course I'm ready, nothing would make me happier," I said and then I took one of Emily's hands and held it all the way back to my house.

Epilogue

A few weeks later, Bear and Emily were at one of the nicer restaurants in town enjoying a nice dinner, the sun had just gone down. Across the street, the vampire assassin watched them from the roof of a business with a good vantage point. He opened his military grade hard case and slowly constructed his custom sniper rifle. Once he snapped the scope into place he popped open the bipod and got into a nice prone position with the rifle hanging just barely over the roof of the business he was on top of. He viewed his two targets through his top of the line scope. He had been told the male target was extremely dangerous and wily. He checked behind himself one last time and made sure his area of egress was clear and then he sighted down on the male one more time. If he truly was dangerous, he wanted him dead first. He hadn't been such a successful assassin by taking unnecessary risks.

He had waited for a night like this for a long time, it was dribbling rain and especially cloudy and dark for this time of the evening. He had been briefed that his target had uncanny eyesight, so the limited visibility this weather was providing was ideal. He slowly moved his finger from the receiver to the trigger, but before he could pull the trigger he heard a strange noise to his left. He shifted his face a few inches towards the noise and he saw a female figure clad in tight, all black cotton clothing running straight at him with a katana raised over her head. He tried to lift and swing the heavy rifle in her direction but she was much faster than him. She slashed downwards with a diagonal cut and hit the corner of his head at his eyebrow.

The sword flew cleanly threw his face and exited out near his chin. Brains splattered the roof and the assassin slumped over as the top half of his head slid off. Lydia pulled down her black cloth face mask and pulled her cell phone out of her bra. She texted Bear, "Tango down, enjoy your meal. L out." Before she sent the text she added a silly kissing emoji face, Bear would like that. She pulled the scope off of the man's rifle and aimed it at Bear. He opened his phone at the dinner table and read her text. Then he turned and looked right at her and gave her a thumbs up before going back to his dinner. Lydia wondered if Bear could really see her from there. Bear was tricky and always getting better with that tonalli power of his, she wouldn't put it past him.

She didn't know why but she said this out loud "No one will ever hurt Bear or his family while I am alive." It felt good to say it, she needed to say it. The rain started coming down harder. She knew she should leave the area and go do something productive, maybe even find romance for herself but instead she picked up the scope and watched Bear for just a few more minutes. She was glad Bear was happy but it still broke her heart thinking about him with another woman. She had to put that behind her now though. Bear loved Emily, so she would protect Emily. Lydia boxed up the assassin's expensive rifle and wondered what it would sell for.

"Mama is going to get a new pair of shoes!" she said to the night. She pulled her cloth face mask back up and started jumping from building to building to get back to her vehicle.

End of Book 1

If you want to keep reading in the Striker's universe, pick up the next book, it's out now!

Look for it on Amazon or the Kindle store, it's called.

I'll Be Back: Griffin's Tale

It explains where Griffin went those missing 8 months, and I really think you will like it!
Check the next page in this book please!

A note from the author:

Hi all, thank you so much for reading my book, it means so much to me! If you want to talk to me about the book, please do! Join my facebook group at the link below and we can discuss your likes and dislikes about it, or things you would like to see happen in the series.

https://www.facebook.com/groups/CoryGaffnerBooks

If you noticed a typo or something that needed to be grammatically fixed in this book PLEASE post about it in my facebook group OR shoot me an email at CoryGaffner@yahoo.com

Please Please Please leave me a written review on Amazon, it would really help me out! I can't stress how very important that is. Until a book gets 50 "mostly positive" or "positive" reviews (meaning 4 and 5 stars), Amazon basically hides it from most searches. Literally writing something as simple as "Fun read," or "Great book," could have positive and lasting effects on my career for years to come.

Also if you have the time, head over to my author page on Amazon.com and Press the little "+Follow" button below my picture. If you don't press the Follow button then Amazon won't tell you when my next books are coming out.

If you enjoyed this book at all, I highly recommend you check out my other books as well.

About the Author

Cory Gaffner spends most of his days working with foster kids in a few different roles. He has been and sometimes is a full-time foster father. He is an honorably discharged combat veteran of the U.S. Army. His hobbies include throwing knives at stuff, competition shooting, and playing video games late into the night.

He currently lives in Arizona with his wife, sons, and two guard dogs. Cory is an independent author meaning he writes, edits, produces, pays for, and publishes his own books. That means he needs your help! The best way to help him is by leaving a constructive review that will help potential readers find his books!

Cory is a very laid back dude, so if you would like to get a hold of him join his facebook group "The Literary Works of Cory Gaffner."

www.ingramcontent.com/pod-product-compliance
Lightning Source LLC
Chambersburg PA
CBHW060136260626
47160CB00001B/4